Remember Ruben

MONGO BETI

Translated from the French by Gerald Moore

Published in the United States of America 1980
by Three Continents Press
4301 Cathedral Ave., N.W.
Washington D.C.

ISBN 0-89410-241-9 (paper)

HEINEMANN
LONDON · NAIROBI

843
B457r

Heinemann Educational Books Ltd
22 Bedford Square, London WC1B 3HH
PO Box 45314, Nairobi

EDINBURGH MELBOURNE AUCKLAND
SINGAPORE KUALA LUMPUR NEW DELHI KINGSTON

ISBN 0 435 90214 8

British Library Cataloguing in Publication Data

Beti, Mongo
   Remember Ruben. – (African writers series).
   I. Title   II. Series
   843'.9'1F   PO3989.2.B45R/

   ISBN 0–435–90214–8

Published
by
HEINEMANN EDUCATIONAL BOOKS, INC.
70 Court Street
Portsmouth, New Hampshire 03801

Printed and bound in Great Britain by
Richard Clay Ltd, Bungay, Suffolk

To Diop Blondin, proud son of Africa, my young brother, murdered in the foul prisons of an African ruler. Africa, harsh mother, forever fertile in mercenary tyrants!

First Part

EVERYTHING FOR A WIFE NOTHING FOR A GUN

The least I can say is that we can't fairly impute to Mor-Zamba's arrival all that has since exasperated us. To tell the truth, Mor-Zamba asked nothing of us; Mor-Zamba went his own way.

There was a time, soon after Abena's disappearance, when, simply to escape remorse and to keep the truth about events crouched in the darkest corner of our memories, we took delight in uttering diatribes. It started with the late Engamba, whose enraged accents proclaimed the atrocious ingratitude of which our guest had always been guilty, in contrast with our own boundless generosity, so worthy of record. Then we took turns to add details of all the good we had done him, how loyal were our intentions, how sincere our desire to do well in all circumstances, how admirable our innate and refined sense of hospitality. We kept inventing disasters for him, each more sweet than the last, to prevent our hatred and anger from wearing thin.

But looking back, how much we are revolted nowadays by the bad faith of Engamba's twisted speeches, uttered so soon before his own death; speeches in which, struggling to rehabilitate himself, he would compare Van den Rietter, that model of an upright stranger who, seeking a place in the city, occupies it with a grateful modesty; with Mor-Zamba, always so lofty and never friendly. After all, he would say, to beg is to beg.

Mor-Zamba begged us, beyond any doubt, by quitting the pathway to leap over the gully which borders it, and which separates it from the territory of our city; two worlds strange, even hostile to one another. Having climbed up the slope, did he not proceed to pluck our oranges, thereby despising our hospitality in every way? What town of Essazam could tolerate such an affront without dishonouring itself for ever? As if it were not the custom among our people for any traveller pinched by hunger or by thirst to pick a fruit along the path, to harvest a sugarcane, or even an ear of maize from a nearby field which he could roast at the next house he found, and so continue his way without exposing himself to the noisy curiosity of a crowd which hadn't even the excuse of being unvisited. For Engamba, a mature man and one who gave himself out for a sage, stirred up the women and children till they were beyond themselves, then presided over the uproar, which prefigured so many to come.

It was we who, having obliged the wandering child to accept our hospitality, forced him to make a stop, then a longer stay, and finally to fix his abode with us.

True, the young traveller did help himself at an orange-tree growing on the clan lands; but, according to tradition, such a tree doesn't belong any more to the occupants than to the passers-by who, as necessity demands, may enjoy it as liberally as the water of the stream, the freshness of the forest shade, or any other blessing furnished by Providence. No one had planted that orange-tree, so far as we could remember; no one claimed to be the owner.

Undoubtedly it was an early hour, with regard to our own eating habits, to endure quietly the sight of a man, of a child, of a young person, eating a whole heap of oranges by the first glimmers of dawn, so fresh and misty after that night of rain. And Engamba all at once came clumsily up the path, dragging his foot, to accost and reprimand the child as if he had been an escaped animal.

'Listen, child, is this the hour to stuff yourself with oranges whose juice, in this cold, will freeze your stomach without filling it? At this hour of the morning, child, no fruit is food for a human being; the beasts themselves wait a while, till the first rays of the sun, before they think of eating them. Whoever you are, young fellow, look at me well. I've just got up, I too, and I've had nothing to eat yet. I'm hungry too; I feel pangs in my stomach which demand instant tribute. But am I therefore going to gorge myself with oranges at dawn? No, I wait serenely till my wife lights the fire and heats up the burning fodder which will slide down my blessed throat and give life to my benumbed and ancient carcass. Whoever you are, stranger, why don't you enter confidently into our city to ask for food

4

from the first of our incomparable women you meet; women renowned through all Essazam, because their generosity has made it a tradition to fill the hunger and quench the thirst of wanderers, man or beast, with no other motive than to cultivate ancestral virtues? Who are you, anyway, if the fame of our prodigality has not reached your ears? Eating oranges at the gate of our city, in the fog of a wet morning? Won't this affront dishonour us for ever? Happily, young traveller, when the offence is daughter of ignorance rather than malice it merits, not hatred, but sympathy.'

At this point Engamba broke off, pulled his arm free of his cloth, and pointed his finger at Ekoumdoum, whose triumphal way, just gleaming in the daylight and dashing off from the pathway, climbed a gentle slope, stretched itself vaguely, and ran off into the mist, beyond which, one guessed, it crossed various more modest streets, became a humble track, then a path, to bury itself finally in the forest like a river swallowed by the sand. From this direction, one saw close lines of mud-walled and thatched houses along both sides of the street; some of them long and low in shape, pierced with numerous doors along the façade; others high and thick with only a single doorway, whose identical, repeated shape gave to the view an impression of order and discipline, augmented as the rising sun enabled the eye to pierce further into this décor, so banal and definitive for the child, this experienced traveller.

'Whoever you are,' repeated Engamba, pointing his finger to Ekoumdoum, 'enter our city, walk confidently up this welcoming avenue and knock on the door of that house down there, you see it? That one there, where I'm pointing; yes, the one with a plume of white steam promising succulent dishes within. Yes, as I say, go and knock at that door. I'll say no more. Just knock and you'll see. Whoever you are, stranger, you'll long remember the welcome you get down there, it's my own house. . . .'

Even allowing that the generous man took such excessive pride in this most admirable of virtues, Mor-Zamba was still astonished that he draped himself in it like a robe, to strut before an unknown traveller who had asked nothing of him.

How often since we have striven, each one in turn or all

together, to recapture that moment when the wandering child appeared among us for the first time; have striven to recapture his gestures, the disturbing serenity of his face, though not his words, because, even when he had finally consented to be tamed he still remained for a long while walled in silence. But then, quickly leaping back into the pathway, he resumed his plundering of oranges with the same fervour as before, disdaining to reply to the invectives of the orator. Some of us, looking back, suspect that he regarded Engamba with a sort of suspicious curiosity, wounding him at first into offering the most eloquent speeches, but later into revealing himself as the most implacable foe Mor-Zamba possessed; others, however, seem to remember that the young stranger didn't even glance at Engamba, but stood motionless beside him, as if his speeches had inspired an obscure interest, elusive even to his own mind.

If it is true that the first man we meet in an unknown city gives us, for better or worse, a definitive image of its real character, what sort of effect was produced in the soul of our young wanderer, meeting, at the gate of Ekoumdoum, the apparition of Engamba, with his great stature already slightly hooped by age and malignity, those sly familiars; with his long spindle-shanks thrust into feet like pedestals, swollen by elephantiasis; with the jointure of his lips flecked with a light foam; with, above all, those eyes which rolled ceaselessly in their sockets?

The one thing we all remember is that Engamba, vexed no doubt by the total indifference of the child to all his appeals, and uttering his usual untimely remarks in an ever higher tone, approached the child as if to seize him by the hand like an imp whom one has decided to lead by force.

But, apart from that, we have the greatest difficulty now to agree on anything. Engamba, for example, always insisted that Mor-Zamba showed his fundamental irreverence at that moment by a rude gesture, whereas decorum throughout the world forbids youth to behave badly before an elder, on pain of incurring his wrath, since age is always ready to administer to inexperience the rough lesson it deserves. That's what Engamba kept repeating endlessly.

However it was, the row finished by waking up the inhabitants at that end of the city who, hearing these altercations and recognizing Engamba's voice, thought it was something serious and feared that their brother might be in danger. They came running out, therefore, ready to lend him a hand. When we were gathered around the two contestants, of whom one remained obstinately silent, the unknown face of the young traveller, his naked and amazingly powerful torso, his hips draped with a rag, his placidity in the face of the one who abused him and even attempted to seize his hand, his persistent appetite at that ungodly hour, all these things amounted to an intolerable affront and inflamed us to such a degree that there was no feature of this living nightmare which didn't invite our intervention.

And when, for the fifth or sixth time, the one who was to call himself Mor-Zamba made that quick flick of the arm which always freed his hand from Engamba's grasp, the latter's son, rushing to his father's rescue, entered into concert with Engamba to beat the wandering child, who hadn't hesitated to inflict this humiliation on the venerable father of a family. All this happened very quickly – or is that only an impression caused by the fog of memory? Almost at the same instant that Engamba's son leapt into the path and threw himself at Mor-Zamba, a whole flood of men, women and even children, all of them still half-asleep, broke over and submerged the combatants. We ran, we chased and jostled each other, we crashed together, we shouted little and spoke even less. It was a fit of collective madness which it pains us to remember now.

When the tumult had subsided a bit, an old man, to protect Mor-Zamba, who was now overcome with fright or, more probably perhaps, with rage, threw his skinny arms about him with a feverish gesture and blew upon his horn. All around them, the women offered cruel remarks and giggled; the children, led by young Engamba, performed a half-grotesque, half-menacing ring-dance, refusing to obey the injunctions of their helpless elders, who called them from afar and ordered them not to torment a stranger upon the road, this being a place sacred in tradition; the men, who had arrived rather slowly on the scene, began in an embarrassed and troubled way, to ask about the

7

events and the new personage, trying both to understand and at the same time to calm the disturbance. And, in the midst of all this crowd, Engamba continued stolidly abusing the young stranger, the wandering child who had repaid with insult and injury the most shining offer of hospitality in the memory of man – the most magnanimous, the most disinterested.

A moment later, the old man of the fevered, protective gestures, taking Mor-Zamba's willing hand in his, led the young traveller into the city, which they entered quietly side by side, while the glowing sky breathed off the last wreaths of mist with one puff and everything suddenly burst into life throughout Ekoumdoum.

Even though he had found refuge in the old man's house, Mor-Zamba was to get no peace that day. Very soon, a woman whom he had heard bustling about in the adjoining room brought them a meal, steaming in broad wooden platters. Much to the old man's relief, the boy scarcely waited to be invited and fell to with the same appetite he had shown on the pathway at the moment when he was assaulted. The elder judged that Mor-Zamba was tasting hot food for the first time in a long while; but he refrained from asking the question, and it seemed to him that his reticence was appreciated.

But Mor-Zamba had not even finished eating before his torments began again. The urchins of Ekoumdoum, eager to return to their favourite sport, gathered before the old man's honoured threshold and began to jeer at the boy, teasing him for his supposed greediness. They even began to throw pebbles at him and to heap him with insults. Then, as if the whole of Engamba's family had been commissioned to persecute him, who should come but the old rascal's wife, boldly pushing into the house of the respected elder and rudely interrogating the young traveller:

'Ah, little man,' she began in a soothing voice, 'where do you come from? What is your country? What is the name of your clan?'

But soon, getting into her stride, she began to yell intemperately:

'I'm asking you who your mother and father are, what is your clan, and where you think you're going? And you have nothing to say? What kind of a kid are you, who can't even respond to the questions of his betters? Hasn't anyone ever taught you to respect age? Why did you leave your people? Why did you abandon your town? And where the devil are you going? Now will you answer me?'

But no, Mor-Zamba had no intention of replying; he just kept on munching peacefully. He was starving, that's all one could positively say about him, who seemed pledged to keep his own secret buried forever.

However, at the entreaties of the white-haired elder, who was saddened and amazed by the row, the urchins ran off and Ma Engamba reluctantly crossed the threshold, not without casting at Mor-Zamba a glance of bitter hatred which she seemed to have matured before even setting eyes on him.

Left alone with his guest, the old man waited till the latter had finished his meal and then said:

'Now my child, you shall do exactly as you wish. When you've had a good rest, you can continue your journey, if that's what you want to do. But perhaps you'll choose to try the love of an old man, of a father to whom Providence never offered the gift of a son. In that case, my house is yours, and everything within it.'

Glancing furtively at the still silent child, the old man felt a vast sorrow rising in his breast, in the presence of this being who certainly hadn't sprouted from the earth like a plant; who must, like everyone else, have grown at a mother's breast; who must have known, beforehand, other communities; lived, perhaps successively, in divers clans without ever feeling at home in one of them, before quitting them and going inexorably on his way. What peculiarity of nature fed this urge for flight like a devouring flame? What infirmity had closed him off, perhaps for ever, from the joys and sorrows of common mortals, and shut him into the night of his solitude?

The old man saw Mor-Zamba, who had made no reply, stretch himself deliberately along the bamboo bed on which he was sitting, with confidence and a sort of determination, like a restive animal which has decided to entrust its wild youth to the care of an unknown old man.

All day long the old man walked through our city, declaring

everywhere he went that the boy, whom he had decided to call Mor-Zamba, was the victim of a mysterious sickness: he was undoubtedly either deaf or dumb; or both at the same time. Heaven itself had directed him to stop at Ekoumdoum, just as bush animals sometimes approach the abode of men, when the pain and misery of their sickness makes them search for care. But he met with nothing save scorn and sceptical laughter; the city was certainly full of excited speculation about the new-comer, but in a spirit far removed from the old man's compassion.

The children imitated Mor-Zamba's serene looks; they aped his gluttony; they turned to derision every attribute which separated him from themselves. Suspecting already that he would stay long among them, they looked forward to all the refined tortures they would certainly inflict on him, miming the hunts, the harassments, the beatings punctuated with harrowing groans, the scenes of ostracism. The young wenches waxed indignant over the rags about his loins; over his filthy, savage-looking mane of hair which smoked like a hot spring; over his legs, grey with the dust of the open air. Engamba's wife declaimed solemnly to her neighbours:

'The mothers who abandon their children in that manner, leaving them to wander the roads alone, my God, how I long to thrash them!'

'Has he even got a mother?' another asked herself sadly.

'He certainly isn't a wild animal,' declared a third. 'Of course he has a mother, or something of the kind.'

'But really, what sort of a monster is it?' demanded a fourth, 'a child? a man? To me, he doesn't look like a child, but a real man.'

'You're quite right there,' cried Engamba's wife, raising the stakes, 'that's quite true: he's very short, but nevertheless, I'd say, a real man. Have you noticed how strong he is? Have you seen his feet? A child so badly nourished ought to be thinner, perhaps even puny.'

'Do you know what?' began a young mother, silent up to then, 'this child was perhaps abandoned as soon as he was born: he's never, so to say, had a mother, or known any tenderness. He's grown up in the wild, like a little animal. Look, what does a little antelope live on? The same sort of things this child was eating when we first saw him. But a young antelope is certainly not skinny.'

'You amaze me!' Ma Engamba replied censoriously, 'as usual, you amaze me. I'm quite ready to agree that this ... man has been abandoned at birth by his mother, but all the same, that mother had a clan and a tribe; she must have lived in some town or other. Even here, don't we have many children whose mothers have disappeared, for one reason or another, leaving them at the most tender age? But no one has ever seen such children running on the roads all alone. We feed them and dress them; we bring them up just like our own kids; a stranger wouldn't even know the orphans from the others. Which family hasn't, at some time, brought up an orphan with its other children? No, you'd have been nearer the mark to say that the stranger is not a child, but a malicious man who, taking advantage of his small stature, tries to pass for a child. But what for? I'd give my hand on it; he's nourishing some evil plan. Ah, my dears, look well after your goods! From now on, this stranger may rob our homes and then vanish. What else can you expect from a man who has neither a country nor a destination?'

For their part, the men also concerned themselves with the young stranger, who was peacefully sleeping in the house of his kind protector.

'They come in all colours as time goes on,' declared Engamba, still puffing with an anger which he was just beginning to control, and speaking in a broken voice which was almost a sob. 'To think that a mere brat, a mosquito one might say, should spit on you, just because you offer him shelter! All the same he was hungry, that imp. He has the appetite of a wild beast.'

'It's all the fault of that damned road,' his neighbour serenely offered; 'it's a route that would exhaust even the most mature. How could it fail to make this unlucky child lose his head? It's no more mysterious than that; the child had sworn to seek out all the fabulous countries along the way. If he'd gone on much longer, he could have said good-bye to the world.'

'We too,' began another, 'we too, in our day, used to follow the waters of the river, walking along the banks, fascinated by

11

the flow of the current. But we never got lost. That was before they cut their wretched road.'

'That's because we couldn't have got lost,' argued the one with the quiet manner. 'One can't get lost on a river bank; one always knows how to retrace one's steps; by going upstream or continuing down; but the road has neither downstream nor up; it's a monster without head or tail, that's what it is.'

The news of the event, which at first had affected only those parts of the city nearest to the road, now spread into the remotest quarters, and even into the bush beyond. Like pilgrims flocking to adore an image, they came in long processions, at once fervent, happy and sacrilegious, to tramp through the old man's house or, once it was full, to gather all around it, eager to catch a glimpse of this new marvel, a wandering and solitary child.

Waking from his short sleep, Mor-Zamba was stared at, spied upon, touched, sniffed at, examined, listened to, interrogated, mauled, cajoled and wheedled as perhaps no one had ever been before. To all these assaults, the supposed monster presented a silent serenity, or rather a frozen air of absence, which overwhelmed us and convinced us we were seeing a unique spectacle. The old man had to receive visitors late into the night; something he hadn't done for a long time. But the next morning the crowd once again invaded his modest dwelling. This continued for several days, without the child ever revealing anything human in his gestures, or showing the slightest desire to speak to anyone. His venerable, white-haired host remained more than ever convinced that he had to do with a deaf-mute who, as a result of unusual circumstances, which were in no way unnatural and ought to be identifiable, had found himself wandering on the track and, tempted always to go a little further, had ended by losing touch with his country and his own folk.

If one succeeded in keeping him here, some city or other, whether near or far, would surely send people to enquire whether Ekoumdoum had seen a child passing on the road, whether they had sheltered him, and in which direction he had gone.

The wanderer was neither deaf nor dumb, as we realized long after his arrival at Ekoumdoum; nor was he suffering from any other sickness. On the other hand, no one ever came searching for this fine child, to the great surprise of the one who had taken him in, and who congratulated himself more warmly every day for having named him Mor-Zamba.

These two were tied together from the first by a strange relationship, which had its pleasant aspect to those who observed it closely. The old man not only showed himself a father to Mor-Zamba but also, one might say, a master almost irritatingly vigilant, though always discreet. He treated his charge like an insufficiently tamed and capricious animal, which one doesn't take out without first getting a firm grip of its halter. He had heard it said that lonely vagabonds often took secretly to the road again, after the first meal of the day, when the sun's rays were just beginning to shine. This was the hour when, the cities being emptied by the general movement to the farms, these eternal wanderers found themselves struggling with their demon, and were seized with a sudden vertigo which they scarcely ever resisted. Mor-Zamba's host became accustomed to stay nearby during the mornings, even if he had to give up those little duties which compose the rhythm of existence for sedentary old men.

But as soon as the sun entered the second part of its daily course, the host, smiling and carefree, abandoned himself to his usual activities: he was safe for that day, at least; his young voyager wouldn't disappear now.

Did Mor-Zamba really think of slipping away? Nothing seemed more improbable to us at this time; to those of us, that is, who were less passionately attached to Mor-Zamba than the man who wished himself his father. And this was, truth to tell, yet another mystery surrounding this young boy who already hid so many.

He kept himself hidden in the house of his protector; when he did come out, he never ventured farther than the back veranda, seating himself on the edge of it, leaning against a post, with his legs stretched out in the dust, his eye at first wandering vaguely, but soon frowning; for, in truth, it seemed to him that furtive shadows were gliding among the banana palms which seemed to form a debonair and fruitful vanguard to the forest, beginning a few metres behind the line of the houses; but perhaps his dread of Ekoumdoum's urchins made him see everywhere the shadows of his terrible persecutors. Then he would suddenly spring up, thoroughly disturbed, and rush precipitately into the house where, if the old man was not present, he would even barricade himself in.

When was it that Mor-Zamba finally emerged from this torpid fright? It was a scarcely credible event which made us suddenly take note of the change which was going on in the unknown child, whom it committed irrevocably, without possibility of return. No doubt it was towards the end of the year, in the harvest season, that the child chose the latter part of a torrid day to make his first exploration of the countryside, which until then had seemed to him as hostile as the darkest jungle. Perhaps he hadn't formed any definite plan when he found himself following the path which led to the river. He was probably confident that no one had seen him, since, at that hour, the inhabitants of Ekoumdoum were all dispersed in the fields. But in reality it took only a few moments for Engamba's son, always idle as he was, to assemble other louts of his own type, give them their allotted tasks and, avoiding the attention of any adults who might still be in town, lead the gang in pursuit of Mor-Zamba, as if they had been hunting a leopard.

Reaching a turn of the path and emerging from a patch of bush, the boy stopped in his tracks at the sight of a vast expanse of black, shining waves which broke against the very feet of the trees. It was a poignant and astounding spectacle, like a dramatized tale surging up abruptly from an immemorial past, and satisfying a long-cherished desire, as if the only thing that mattered had always been to find oneself thus, upright upon the bank and gazing out over the flowing tide of the river.

He was drawing near to the first haven which presented itself to his astonishment; sandy, spacious and free, it seemed rather the work of time than of deliberation; two canoes were beached there and two others were moored at the downstream end. On the opposite bank he saw another haven of the same aspect, but lined with small boats, surely awaiting the hour when the inhabitants of Ekoumdoum, having finished their labour in the fields, would come flocking back to cross the stream. Without hesitation, he drew away; his untamed animal instinct had made him take the upstream path through the undergrowth, and after he had continued thus for some time and thought he had put enough distance behind him, he had flicked off the loin cloth which his ancient protector had given him in place of his original rag and had begun to bathe himself. For a long while he crouched on the bank, sheltered hereabouts by the last line of trees and, finding the water much too cold, had lightly sprinkled himself; then he pushed cautiously into the stream, as if groping in the dark, doubtless trying the bottom before throwing himself headlong, and striking out; but he would have no time to do so that day.

Mor-Zamba had not heard the arrival of young Engamba's little mob, which was ranged on the bank above him, and, when he finally saw them and began to stiffen with fear, guessing their intentions from their threatening looks, young Engamba was already stripped. Fixing his eyes on those of the young bather, to whom he should have been bound in friendship as one of his age-grade, he advanced step by step into the waves and struck Mor-Zamba brutally with his fist, plunging him into the water. Mor-Zamba refrained from any retaliation, fearing the vengeance of those who were watching on the bank; he hoped that it was no more than a harsh trial, and that they sought only a momentary humiliation. He kept himself under the water until, at the last gasp of his lungs, a great heave of his body, propelled by his refusal to die, freed him from the other's iron grip, which he never failed to display for the admiration of all Ekoumdoum. Young Engamba had no intention of letting slip this providential victim, this stranger on whom he could safely vent all his lust for sacrilege, violence and even murder; he tore after him through the water, which exploded and boiled around them. The other oafs, who witnessed everything, said

15

afterwards that Mor-Zamba owed his escape only to his skill as a swimmer. No other vengeance was left to young Engamba and his companions than to carry off Mor-Zamba's loin cloth, abandoned on the bank and, later, to set fire to it.

Meanwhile Mor-Zamba, wild with terror and now convinced that they sought his life, swam effortlessly to the other shore. He sought hiding in the bush and remained there all night, numb and sleepless, watching in expectation of his pursuers, whom he felt certain would cross the river in their turn, doubtless by canoe, in order to lay hold of him.

They, however, had returned surreptitiously to the city, where the old man, seeing the night fall without bringing home his protégé, became anxious and raised the alarm. They questioned the urchins severely, and separately, but they replied with effrontery that they knew nothing of Mor-Zamba's whereabouts. They had simply gone to bathe in the river, as usual; no, they had seen nothing of the young stranger who, in any case, was not in the habit of venturing so far from home. Taking her son's place and replying for him with indignation, Mrs Engamba even tried to turn the tables to her advantage; hadn't she always said that the stranger, who was a slave by nature like all strangers, was sure to run off one day? If anyone had ever expected anything better of Mor-Zamba than ingratitude and flight, well, he had only his own folly to blame for it.

'You'd do better to go and search your own house, to make sure everything is in place,' she concluded, addressing the old man. 'Perhaps there's a nasty surprise waiting for you.'

'Flight? Why should he fly?' the old man stammered, gravely troubled despite himself. 'No one was keeping him here.'

'Go and inspect your house then!' Mrs Engamba cut in.

At the old man's request, the worthy men of Ekoumdoum spent that night in long, vain searches through the woods and bushes, beating all the parts which lay between Ekoumdoum and the river.

It was already the case then that our farms lay exclusively on the other bank, and so it happened that the following day, as we crossed over in the usual way to visit our farms, Mor-Zamba appeared to us, all dressed in leaves, shivering in the most pitiful manner, his eyes rolling with terror and his body bearing the stigmata of his white night in the forest. But, most miraculous of all, Mor-Zamba now spoke, and his speech seemed to us extraordinarily coherent and harmonious, leaving aside a few stumbles inevitable in the circumstances, as he recounted to us his misadventure.

We were struck with shame on hearing that our own sons, born and brought up amongst us, for whom we had unhesitatingly vouched only the night before, had carried their prank almost to the point of murder against a young stranger of their own age, who had done nothing to them of which they could complain. Seeing our discomfiture, the old man, who had meanwhile resumed his charge of the boy, deemed it the right moment to force matters by a striking action. He waited till nightfall, when the fathers of the town were gathered to their hearths from the various tasks which often took them out of Ekoumdoum; then he posted himself in the middle of the street adjoining the roadway, blew a long blast on his horn to draw attention, and announced in a voice all the more impressive in that it came from the darkness and bore the accent of Justice on the heels of Crime:

'I want to talk this evening to the fathers and mothers of those for whom the name "monsters" is scarcely adequate. It is to those fathers and those mothers that I want to say a word or two. I will ask them just these few questions: have you done everything in your power to stamp out this terrible hatred in the souls of your children? Have you always explained to them that a wandering and inoffensive child is a sacred being? Are these new modes of conduct? If so, who has introduced them among us? In my youth, we always sought to win the friendship of strangers; we strove to set them at ease, loving them like brothers and if they happened to be of our own age, with what joy would we receive them! Nowadays, we try to kill them. I'm talking to you, progenitors of these beasts in whom nothing is human but the wrapping! Ah, you'd better pray to Heaven that no son of yours ever finds himself wandering unarmed and alone amid a strange people. Just pray that here on earth, where anything can happen, your sons stay forever within reach of your protection and your blessing. But truly, who can promise that? . . .'

17

As soon as we heard these imprecations, which seemed to menace the future of our own children, we burned to submit them to the ritual of purification, and, in order to establish right away the guilt of each one, we interrogated them all so cruelly that each of them had to reveal whether he had taken part in the criminal attempt, what were his grievances against Mor-Zamba, who had thought up the whole thing, by what means and under whose leadership they had been enlisted.

It soon became clear to us that young Engamba had been the guiding spirit of the whole adventure, and that the other adolescents had only been lured by the promise of an amusing escapade.

What jewels of eloquence, of solicitude and vigilance, must the old man have displayed, in order to retain his guest after this dreadful affair? This was something we could never discover. The purification of the guilty took place on a day of rejoicing whose gaiety led one to think that Mor-Zamba had been finally adopted by our city, having paid such a price of entry, and that henceforward he could consider himself one of us.

Anyway, it turned out that the precautions and suspicions of the two sides disappeared as if by magic, and from now on Mor-Zamba was able to explore the city that he knew so little, traverse the forests of the clan and bathe in the river, without running the slightest danger.

The initiative of a kind-hearted woman was decisive here. This mother, convinced that the lonely child had been reared at a mother's breast, as she often argued, had from the very first taken Mor-Zamba's part. After young Engamba's exploit, she came more into the open; she instructed her eldest son, who was about Mor-Zamba's age, to undertake a delicate mission towards him; he must persuade the youngster to pass a few hours in their house. Times had really changed, for now, with the old man's encouragement, Mor-Zamba easily consented and, for the very first time, the people of Ekoumdoum could see him laughing and playing with a native youth. But the spectacle still troubled them, because they wrongly reflected that nothing in the previous behaviour of the wanderer had prepared them for it. In the following days, other young people of Ekoumdoum came forward and, after loitering as if they wanted to be begged to join in, finally ended by taking part in all their gambols and pastimes. The last to come was young Engamba, seeming sulky and irritable, as if jealous of the warmth and comradeship now shown by his brothers towards the stranger; they in reply showing him a certain coldness, almost as though they were putting him in quarantine. At last, every one of them wanted to take the young stranger home and offer him a fraternal welcome there. Only young Engamba still held out.

In this way, the memory of the fracas which had accompanied Mor-Zamba's arrival in Ekoumdoum gradually faded from our minds; we became accustomed to his presence among us and any visitor would have been astonished to learn that he was not really one of our own. Happily, we seldom spoke of it and one might almost have thought we ourselves had forgotten the fact. But does one ever really forget things of that kind?

Engamba was right to say that the stranger was like a drop of oil suspended in water, forever indissoluble. But whose fault was that?

So, life had resumed its normal course, flowing smoothly and secretively, falling like the sound of a trickle of water in the shadow of an ancient tree. Mor-Zamba grew almost visibly, and this made us realize that he had truly been a young boy when he arrived among us. His long existence in the open air and in the forest had left him with the gifts which one observes among wild animals, to such an extent that, without wishing to do so, he excelled all our own sons, not only in sports, but in all other activities. He ran faster, threw the spear more accurately, swam more powerfully and danced more supply. Having at first been inexpert in hunting, owing to his long vagabondage and lack of training, as we learnt long afterwards, he let himself patiently learn this savage art from his old host, showing a modesty which would soon win its reward; for it became a common sight to watch him cross the city and gain the house of the now envied old man, his young shoulder bent under the disproportionate load of a wild beast.

We all felt a resentment and humiliation which we vainly

tried to hide. We would say, for instance: 'Of all the sons of our city, Mor-Zamba excluded of course, it's young Engamba who is the most virile and the bravest wrestler....'

Why did we set Mor-Zamba apart in this fashion? We found no lack of arguments to make this attitude appear legitimate, and even natural. If anyone chanced to ask us the reason, we would reply that we didn't know Mor-Zamba's exact age, and had perhaps put him into the wrong group; so long as there was any doubt on this point, Mor-Zamba couldn't be fairly compared with the others in the matter of his skills. Wasn't the real truth that the mystery of his origins, a stain more odious than leprosy itself, divided Mor-Zamba forever from the other boys?

During this same period, his character seemed to change in a way which couldn't fail to trouble the old man who had received him, and who was often tempted to tackle him about it. It seemed that Mor-Zamba had to trample on his pride in order to force the last defences of the Ekoumdoums and to see himself finally accepted. This was the time when he could be seen displaying a kind of complacency towards everyone which seemed to have no limits. Playful, amiable and eager, ready to give away everything he possessed even without being asked, he developed the habit of accepting every task thrust upon him, just to show his goodwill. Exactly as the old man feared, this led to a situation where the inhabitants heaped him with such limitless demands that Akomo himself wouldn't have been able to look them in the face. Fortunately, the old man was able to help Mor-Zamba, at least in sharing out the claims, in soothing wounded expectations and in disarming, whenever possible, the revenges born of frustration. It was as if we rivalled each other in heaping upon Mor-Zamba the heaviest burdens and the most degrading tasks, even when there was no need whatever, perhaps not even any reason, unless it was just for the pleasure of hearing him groan.

Did we even feel any gratitude towards him?

An unfortunate event exposed all our habitual reservations towards the one who had been a vagabond child.

After the death of her long-absent husband, and when her children had grown up, our sister Mbolo had returned to live among us in the city founded by one of her ancestors, honoured by many succeeding generations. Mbolo was one of those women who are forever regretting that they don't belong to the stronger sex. So it was that our sister came to live among her brothers, as a man might do, rather than with the clan of her vanished husband. It was we who had to help her in all the necessities of life, on pain of hearing the widow bewail the absence of all the support formerly rendered by her man.

But among ourselves we justly complained:

'What about those children whom our sister Mbolo left to embellish the clan of her late husband; have they forgotten all about her? How could they abandon their mother to the extent of never paying her a visit, or lending a hand with her heavy labour in the fields?'

This ingratitude of her children was a permanent subject of astonishment for us, amounting sometimes to indignation and even scandal. She, however, remained obstinately silent about her offspring, refusing to judge them in any way.

One morning old Mbolo easily obtained Mor-Zamba's help to clear her field, in the heart of the forest, in that part of our lands left fallow, so that creepers, bushes and enormous trunks formed an inextricable tangle. But, vigorous though he was, Mor-Zamba was not exempt from the frailties which attend our nature; not to mention the exertions of the preceding days, which must have taken him to the limits of endurance. When the day was scarcely half-spent, he felt a shooting pain which forced him to hurry back to the city, without informing Mbolo, and to take to his bed.

The day was ending when Mbolo also returned to the city; she'd had plenty of time in which to mature her rage, which made up in frenzy what it lacked in justice; her rolling eyes, her wild, sawing gestures and the vehemence of her tirade gathered a crowd around her, before anyone even realized that Mor-Zamba was the target of all her insults and invectives.

'What's he done to you, then?' she was asked on all sides.

What had Mor-Zamba done? His crime was that he failed to dedicate the second half of the day to Mbolo, even if he died of it. Upon the stranger doomed to suffering, upon this brute, mothers, flouted and neglected through the decadence of the

21

clan, could vent all their bitterness, fed by years of humiliation and annoyance.

But it was worse than that. The following night old Mbolo deprived herself of sleep in order to make the rounds of all the elders whose counsel governed the life of the city, holding forth to every one of them in these terms:

'This man, this Mor-Zamba, what a filthy creature it is! He eats and eats, yet refuses to work. What has become of our city, founded by our great ancestor for the happiness and glory of his descendants? A dumping ground for feeble, greedy and insolent strangers? Ah, let me tell you, this can't go on! I'd rather die than witness this decadence a moment longer. I want you to chase this man out of Ekoumdoum, and the sooner the better!'

Let us admire the sages of our clan who, on this occasion, judged her attitude severely, affirming without prevarication that her case was thoroughly bad. But they failed to point out, as they should have done, that Mor-Zamba was as free as any man in the city, so that no one in the future should be tempted to dispose of him like a war-captive; or that to be born outside our clan, or even to be born God-knows-where, could not be considered as making him a blemish upon us, as lots of people seemed to imagine. It's surprising to relate how far the sages of the clan fell short of the role which might be expected of them in this affair. Perhaps they were left behind by the novelty of the whole situation. It's true that in those days our clans were not yet accustomed to the constant presence of strangers among us, as later became the case. We failed to protect Mor-Zamba with courage and firmness; otherwise our clan would not have known all this tumult since. One might think that we didn't know how to act in the matter, despite our inherited traditions of hospitality, stretching back through all the generations between us and the founders of our city.

The bards with their sweet instruments, those experts in all the exploits of Akomo, offered us different versions about the origins of the hero who had founded our ancient race. Some said he came from a tree; others from the snake of the great river which divides the shores of life and death; others declared they didn't know where he sprang from, having suddenly appeared

22

among us, a young man huge, strong and beautiful, with a voice of thunder, a martial and noble stride, a brow furrowed with lightning, an open heart. Yet who would take refuge in Akomo's doubtful origin, in order to refuse him his homage?

Expel Mor-Zamba? It had become as bad as that. The following day, just as the night was falling, the good old man, who had spent most of the day in conference with his fellow elders, opened his heart to his young guest, by the flickering glare of the log fire.

'My dear child, I can see only one sure way to end this fever of distrust; what's more, far from making any innovation, we would be conforming to an ancient custom. I'll give you a piece of land to which the whole clan recognizes my right of ownership, for good reasons. There you will put up a house, and in that way you will establish yourself among us, so that no one henceforth will challenge your right to be an Ekoumdoum man, no matter where you were born. This is the custom, as I said. And, after all, you're quite big enough now. Indeed, you're already a man, in point of strength and stature. But, my dear son, building a house is no easy matter; that's how an adolescent wins for himself the soul and judgement of a true man. No doubt you've noticed that one of the near-by houses is in ruins; it belonged to my late wife. That's the piece of land I will give you. Pull down the ruin and put up your own house in its place. The vigour of your arm has assisted so many Ekoumdoum families! It's high time their sons lent you a hand in return. Apart from that, my advice will help you, day and night.'

So once again Mor-Zamba had to struggle with the forest to wrest from it all the materials he needed; a task which was cruel and demanding not only for a barely-grown youth, but even for an adult long hardened by heavy toil. Never, however, was a hardy enterprise undertaken with a better spirit or a deeper inner joy. It seemed to Mor-Zamba then that nothing was insurmountable, if its accomplishment would finally win him a place amongst us. This was a fabulous, new Mor-Zamba, such as we had never seen, and such as we can scarcely imagine nowadays, with his boundless enthusiasm, abnegation, and tolerance for our malicious pranks. Was he even hurt by that first rebuff, when he quite naturally asked for the aid of those who had grown up with him, and whom he had so often helped?

'Ah, Mor-Zamba, my dear brother, you come at a most inconvenient time!' cried one. 'Why didn't you come a few months ago, or a few months hence? How gladly I would have welcomed you then, and how eagerly I would have assisted you!'

'Alas, my poor friend, Mor-Zamba,' said the second, 'alas, I feel so feeble these days, my poor brother. You know, since I was ill, I don't seem to have ever regained my proper health, apart from an occasional brief respite. Alas, my dear, dear brother!'

'I can't possibly come with you right away,' declared the third, 'but rest assured I'll do my utmost to get free, and then I'll join you in the forest. So, Mor-Zamba, just go ahead, in confidence that I'm doing my utmost....'

So they went on, one after the other, with the sole exception of Abena, the son of that family which had shown him so much friendship from the very first. What's more, we knew that our sons exchanged the most revolting remarks behind his back, remarks whose infamy time has done nothing to soften. Wasn't young Engamba greeted with sniggers, rather than reproof, when he had the skin to say:

'No, but did you hear that vagabond? It isn't enough that he should be allowed to establish himself here; we have to go and build his house for him! And we have to praise him to the skies! It's always the same with these strangers: the more you give, the more they grab.'

During their long months of isolation in the forest, the two friends chafed over this defection, making it their sole subject of conversation. Felling the trees, cleaving them into posts for the skeleton of the future building, or tressing the thatch for the roof, Abena and Mor-Zamba frequently broke off to exchange remarks in which their mutual tenderness conflicted with their

24

common pitying contempt for their companions, left behind in Ekoumdoum.

'My young brother,' Mor-Zamba would exclaim, 'has the creative zeal of your youth always been so conspicuous in Ekoumdoum? And what a sense of solidarity! That's a theme on which I'd like to hear a speech by that old fool Engamba!'

'Mor-Zamba, my beloved brother,' Abena might reply, between two grunts, balancing his axe in his hands, 'don't talk to me any more about that lot. I've nothing to do with them; I no longer know them.'

'You're wrong, old chap. Don't feel like that about them. What would life be without its disappointments?'

'Something wonderful! A lovely dream!'

'Or rather an illusion, you mean.'

And, towards nightfall, while they were catching fish or grilling them over the fire, before lying down to sleep in their hut of branches, the same subject cropped up again and invaded their discourse, like the flavour of a bitter herb in a tasty dish:

'You know,' Abena began, 'if I hadn't been born in Ekoumdoum, I don't think I could endure its people a single day.'

'You must be wondering how I chose to settle among you,' said Mor-Zamba. 'One day, perhaps you'll understand.'

'You are a marvel of patience and tolerance, Mor-Zamba. But tell me, don't you sometimes yearn to take the road again, to go a bit further, and see what the people are like over there?'

'One day you'll know, perhaps.'

'As for me, yes, I often long to push off.'

'You? You must be mad!'

'Yes, yes.'

Mor-Zamba guffawed uncontrollably at this, and ended by saying:

'You always exaggerate the sadness of life; you are wrong.'

On the last night, when his companion had just repeated the same reproach, Abena replied in a way which left him baffled:

'You console yourself, Mor-Zamba, by thinking of the good old man who took you in. You say to yourself: "As long as there are people like this old man in Ekoumdoum, and others who resemble him, all is not lost." Only, I'd just like to say this: your host is no longer a man, he's already a corpse, one might say. There aren't many left of that generation, and soon there won't be any. Then we'll have nothing but a bunch of degenerates like Engamba.'

'And then?'

'And then, will you still be able to live in Ekoumdoum?'

It took them several days to carry all the materials they had gathered or prepared in the forest to a dump, about half-way to Ekoumdoum and an equal number of days to carry them on by head-load into the city. When we saw again these two men whose existence we'd forgotten, thin and even haggard with toil, we were convinced that there had been some modification, not only in each one of them, but also in the love which bound them.

After every one of their trips, we saw the stock of their materials swell, witness of an effort which seemed more like that of fabulous beings than ordinary mortals. And several times a day the people of Ekoumdoum would gather in a circle to admire, with cries of amazement and passionate admiration, the fruits of their titanic labour. The two friends became symbols at once of energy, friendship and determination, so that the city adopted the saying: 'When Abena and Mor-Zamba are leagued together, what mountains can they not move?'

As for our young people, they didn't quite know where to put themselves; the fame of what the two friends had accomplished pushed them into obscurity and confusion. Hesitating between spite and a plea for forgiveness, one saw them sometimes beginning to sketch out gestures of approach; then, failing any sign of encouragement from the two stalwarts, they would draw back into little muttering conclaves. Mor-Zamba, whose generosity then amounted almost to a passion, was inclined to make it easier for them to purchase a reconciliation; it would have been enough for him if a modest feast had been organized to celebrate the return of the two friends to Ekoumdoum, in which all the youth of the place would take part. The old man was in favour of the idea; it's dangerous to leave our neighbours to stew in the recollection of their wrongs towards us. And what better way than a feast, to throw open the doors of oblivion? But Abena was against it; as if he wanted finally to burn all his bridges, he said that those people were not worth the outlay of so much delicacy.

So, the two friends resumed their labours alone, under the eyes of those who secretly longed only for a sign. They dug holes as deep as their arms and planted the posts which outlined the four walls of the house; then they prepared a framework of bamboo and, with the aid of the old man, fastened the wicker mats to it, one by one. Now they had to adjust the double trellis of bamboo to the close wall of posts, in such a way that the uprights were wedged into the pisé. It was a long job, but one demanding more patience and skill than physical strength.

While they worked at this relatively relaxing task, the old man busied himself in Ekoumdoum with a scheme which would not only relieve the two friends of a heavy task, but would also reconcile them, a little despite themselves, with the community, from which a moral difference was gradually estranging them more and more. The women of the city, especially the young ones, were the instruments of this plot. The good old man had discovered a treasure there, in running to the natural guardians of peace in the clan. Their zeal was astounding on this occasion, for not a whisper was heard of the many intrigues made necessary by the planning of the event.

Fascinated by the progress of their work and drunk with their own pride, the two friends had lost all notion of reality; they were oblivious both to the custom which makes the building of mud walls a day of festivity and solemn ritual, and to the impossibility of the task for two men alone, whatever their strength and endurance.

That year the rainy season was late in coming. But, as soon as the first shower had fallen, although it was already evening, the people of Ekoumdoum saw the two friends making preparations which left no doubt that they intended to profit by the next one to prepare the mud and apply it to the wickerwork of the walls. Questioned by an agent of the old man, Abena's mother, who was now the only person really in the counsel of the two young men, confirmed the evidence of these signs.

Now it happened that, the second night after the first shower, as if nature wanted to make up for lost time, a long storm shook our city right up till daybreak, and even returned intermittently thereafter.

The two friends, who had been on the look-out every night, were not taken by surprise. They rose instantly and each of them began to dig a trench, to trample the loose soil and then to knead it patiently before carrying it to the house. Here they began to fill, working from top to bottom, all the empty spaces presented by the trellis of bamboos and the upright posts.

This was the moment chosen by the good old man to unveil a plot prepared with so much care. Suddenly a horde of women descended on the two friends, shouting, shoving, roaring with laughter, singing, gesticulating, seizing the pounded clay and carrying the balls of it to the feet of their companions, posted all along the walls, who were applying the mud with great speed and dexterity; these maenads were digging, pouring water, kneading the clay, running, stripping the two friends of their tools and threatening to overwhelm them.

The spectacle was so pleasing to Mor-Zamba and the old man that their eyes filled with tears; but Abena, whose resistance had been fairly roughly put down by the intruders, kept gazing around him with perplexity and this despite his mother, who had arrived with the first wave, and who took him aside to argue the good sense of accepting assistance without which the two friends would never finish their task. For the covering of the walls is considered difficult and exacting, even amongst experienced men.

'You ought to be rejoicing,' this admirable woman told her son.

'I am rejoicing, Mother,' he replied, in a most unconvincing voice.

'Really, no one would think it,' she reproached him.

'Mother, do you really want me to caper about and play the fool?'

But the following hours of the day revealed all the ramifications of the plot. At dinner time, the young girls of Ekoumdoum, to whom the occasion offered the first opportunity to display their cooking skills, came to lay out rows of dishes whose succulence and abundance equalled the voracity of the benevolent mothers. And, at the end of the day, the same girls exceeded themselves in offering to their elders a positive banquet. But in the meantime, when the pace of work had slackened somewhat with fatigue and the afternoon was wearing on, the good old man produced a band of singers recruited from the far end of Ekoumdoum, lying towards the distant palace of the chief; performers who had been waiting hidden but fully prepared all day.

They sang without the orchestra of xylophones which would normally accompany them when they danced in the chief's palace, because the old man did not wish any men to be involved in this affair. But when we saw them thus deprived we, the men of Ekoumdoum's main street, spontaneously supported them with our drums, instruments which may be less melodious but are certainly more joyful and compelling. This was also the opportunity for the majority of our young men to redeem themselves; displaying on the drums a miraculous skill which drew from Mor-Zamba more than one passionate accolade; for he was anxious to reward their tardy zeal by showing them that he had decided to forget the past.

So our city had finally helped the two friends, thanks to our womenfolk, it's true; but they were none the less women of the clan and they worked to such effect that in a single day they managed to cover all four external walls of the house. Mor-Zamba knew well enough that he still had to build the internal walls, to fix doors and windows and to complete the whole job with a coat of rough-cast, which was the work of an artist. But, according to the Ekoumdoum tradition taught him by the good old man, he had effectively built himself a house by carrying the enterprise thus far. Even if he could not yet live in it, he was entitled to celebrate his brand-new home.

We were all invited to the fête and we trooped along, in all good conscience and in a perfect satisfaction with ourselves, which let us dance and feast, rejoice and congratulate each other on the happy issue of an affair from which we had often thought of dissuading Mor-Zamba, and which we had certainly been far from wishing well. Revolted to the heart by our cowardly frivolity, Abena, who had to find some way of venting his

29

bitterness, waited for that stage of drunkenness which favours eloquence without dousing truth; then he strode into the midst of the joyful throng, blew with burlesque clumsiness on the old man's horn to command attention, and began:

'How you disgust me! Oh, how I despise you all! Yes, I must tell you, that business of your wives was nothing but a snare. You were disappointed to see us pursuing our fantastic enterprise to a successful conclusion. Admit it! You hoped all along that we'd get discouraged and give up. You sent along your wives so that one day you could make an issue of the clan's support, in order to take away our credit. I'm certain we could have done it without you; we could, we could....'

He could say no more, strangled with sobs and suffocated by his own rage. He had come to the point of hating his own people so much that he couldn't restrain it, but we were still far from guessing the depth of a feeling which only time would reveal. In the midst of the stupefaction which greeted Abena, we could hear his mother crying in a low voice:

'My God, what have I done to you? Who has given me such a son? Who has thrown such a fate upon me? What have I done? ...'

Now the madness seemed to fan itself: instead of trying to pacify the raging youth, as everyone expected, the good old man advanced into the middle of the crowd and, profiting by the general emotion, added:

'Any other time, I'd no doubt have knocked the block off this young whippersnapper; but tonight, don't look for any such thing. On the contrary, I'm much more inclined to applaud his diatribe. For after all, what would any decent man call you if this story was told to him? Did you ever consider how you would be judged, or in what light you would be seen in other cities? You like to claim for yourselves that you are the best-looking, the bravest, the most hospitable, wise and generous; in short, the best and most privileged of human beings – the favourites of Fortune. Imagine for a moment what other peoples and other cities think of themselves. Don't you suppose that they have just as flattering an opinion about themselves as you have? Won't you agree with me that it's only by the light of their strict observance of their own rules of conduct

30

that we should judge the worth of other clans? Very well, let's go on to consider how we compare with them in this respect.

'Now, if we go to enquire among the clan or city nearest to ourselves about their treatment of those – if there are any – whom they adopted, and promised to show the same justice and affection as to their own sons, do you suppose we'd ever find anything more odious over there than your conduct towards Mor-Zamba? If it is not in our everyday conduct, can you tell me in what you base this conceit of yourselves? When we contemplate the glory of our ancestors, we are convinced that good blood can never be false to itself; that we'll never see a leopard bring forth a hyena. But haven't we often heard of giants who beget dwarfs? Do you need me to remind you of that familiar episode in the life of Akomo, the founder of our race? For a long time he tried, without success, to lead his people to war in a country reputed to nourish giants. When they finally made up their minds to go and invade this formidable land, Akomo and his brothers encountered nothing but dwarfs, whom they crushed without even striking a blow. These former titans had shrunk, having proved unworthy of their fathers in violating the noble traditions which these had established and, generation after generation, pursued. . . .'

These words were probably uttered more in desperation than in the hope that they could any longer touch the hearts of those who heard them. What is certain is that they announced the final rupture between the two friends and the city of Ekoumdoum, and that no ensuing event, be it the warmest of embraces or the most passionate vow of brotherhood, could join again the ends of a knot cut for ever.

We are all agreed that from this moment the tempo of our lives and the pace of events seemed to lurch forward abruptly, like a man who has been idling along and is suddenly given a push in the back or a blow with a cudgel. We must admit the fact, even if we don't understand it or wish it – whatever Engamba may say – that Mor-Zamba marked for our city the beginning of a curse, after which everything seemed stranger, or should I say sadder, more disquieting, more hostile perhaps; in any case, more bitter, as if some malevolent pressure had squeezed all the juice of life towards the future, condemning us henceforth to an uncertain and exasperating expectation. As for this future, it looked very far off to us, like a country in which we could only arrive, if we ever did, by crossing many perilous rivers and fighting with enemies of every sort; or rather, it threatened to reveal itself momentarily, like an equivocal dream; one of those visions which mingle intuitions of horror with splendours of ineffable beauty.

First of all Father Van den Rietter, who up till then had appeared only occasionally in our city, as if to show off his fine red beard, now came to install himself in Ekoumdoum. But he went right to the other end, to a real bush place where nobody ever went, where they went rarely even after his arrival, so that for a long time it seemed as if he had not really come at all, and that he was still refraining from interfering with our all-night dances. He brought three servants who were not of our people, but who, doubtless finding that time hung heavy in that remote spot, came and lingered in our houses whenever they could. It was from them that we learnt, for the first time, of another impending war among the whites, starting over there in their own country; but this war would prove so destructive that no people on earth would really escape it. It was as if someone had told us a frightful folk-tale; we were able to believe it in the night, but the nightmare fled with the approach of dawn.

Apart from this, traffic on our little road became more frequent, both of men and still more of vehicles. But the road was a world apart from ours, and it was chance alone which had made it brush against our city; it was certainly not by any wish of ours. It had been built not long before, under the direction of three helmeted whites, by men who came from other parts and did not speak our language. We were greatly agitated by the echoes of their muffled blows in the forest, coming at first from far away, then gradually approaching, and finally penetrating right into our territory. Then our chief was summoned to Tamara, where he was ordered to shelter and feed this army of labourers. That's how it came about that we were obliged to welcome these unexpected guests in our homes, but they proved, thank God, very gentle, sober and sympathetic. However, the pace of their work soon drew them away from our city, where they were no doubt taken in charge by another chief and his helpers, so that we heard no more talk of them. The road, however, remained, and we were instructed by the chief to maintain it, and even to clear it of the noxious weeds which invaded its margins; but this was just like paying tribute in fear to a detested monster.

No true Ekoumdoum man would climb into one of those deafening, roaring elephants which ran over its surface and one of which, every five or six days, or perhaps more often, would pass round the edge of our city, raising a cyclone of red dust which continued swirling long after its disappearance. Before Mor-Zamba came, our intercourse with the road was limited to those rare, unknown passers-by who chose to climb the ravine separating it from our domain, in order to approach the first houses of Ekoumdoum to ask for food or drink. For our own journeys, we still preferred to turn our backs to the road and follow our old tracks, even though we had to scale mountains, follow precipices, brave the rush of torrents, or part the broad breasts, sometimes placid but often treacherous, of great rivers winding along in silence.

As for salt, matchets, spades, hoes, iron axes, cotton cloths, tin bowls, metal cooking-pots and ear-rings – in short, all the things we didn't make in the city – we received them all from the Milandawas, without even quitting Ekoumdoum. This supply went on from the end of the first European war and was only interrupted when the guerrillas took control of the town. These Milandawas came soon after the harvest-season, in sampans covered with a hooped roof of thatch, so that they resembled little floating tunnels. They pushed and manoeuvred these boats by means of long poles, thrusting them to the river-bottom and leaning against them. Coming and going over the bridge of these broad boats, they passed all their lives on the water; eating, sleeping and receiving their customers there; for it was their custom to install an impromptu market on board. In the gloom of the hold, we could guess at a disordered heap of merchandise, which they exchanged for money or, failing that, for groundnuts, yams, smoked meat, dried fish and other products of our labour, which they were able to resell very profitably, as Father Van den Rietter one day explained to us, in an area where the poor soil prevented the people from gaining a decent living.

They used to moor in a bay some way above Ekoumdoum, where their boats were ranged in dozens side-by-side, and for almost a month there would be an incessant stream of people moving between them and Ekoumdoum, like the uproar of an interminable festival. It was no doubt because of these excellent Milandawas that we for so long despised the road and its virtues; by the time Mor-Zamba came, they were already very able traders, proverbially honest, practising less and less barter, to our delight, and paying such good prices that it wasn't worth our while to form caravans and march to a distant trading-post some three days off, as many other cities did.

Only the chief made frequent use of the road, either because he was summoned to Tamara by car, which happened several times a year; or because he was carried along it in his hammock, supported on the shoulders of four men of his household or, yet again, on his bicycle, which would be followed by a strapping fellow running on foot watching for the moment when his master tired of pedalling; for then the chief would dismount and let his retainer push the bicycle up the hill, where he could begin riding again.

Setting off in this way for Tamara, capital of the province, the chief Mor-Bita – so named because of his valour, which had won him the favour of the French in recognition of the stiff battles they had fought in conquering this area – found himself serving among the new masters of the colony. He would return after an absence of a fortnight or so, bearing instructions which he revealed to no one except his two clerks.

To tell the truth, the chief, his wives, his clerks and even his servants were not really of our people. But it was a forbidden topic to speculate about the origins of this man, or about how he came to be placed over our city. So it came about that the younger people, born since his arrival and having always known that he was thus confined in his residence, very far from the road and the main street, right in the high part of Ekoum-doum which he scarcely ever quitted, came to the conclusion that it had always been so and never dreamt of questioning his legitimacy. Only the mature men knew that formerly things had been different, and altogether different before the advent of any white man among us.

Just as the road was content to brush against our city, so the chief was evidently resolved to keep himself morally aloof from Ekoumdoum, floating above our clan like a heavy vessel upon the river, into whose bitter gulfs he could not plunge without coming to grief. There was no doubt that he feared any attempt to strike root in our clan, which never furnished a single one of his wives, who amounted to some thirty at the time of his final disaster, although there were only five of them at this juncture. Having become a Christian while he was a soldier, the chief had for a long time observed the tenets of his religion even in Ekoumdoum, but when it became clear that his first wife could not give him a son, he most regretfully took refuge in polygamy as his only protection against the injustice of fate. How amusing we find it, looking back, to think that Father Van den Rietter, who lived so long among us, remained a dupe up to the last, never suspecting the true relationship between the chief and our clan. Perhaps we deserve credit for having kept up appearances to perfection.

It was at this time, too, that Mor-Zamba began a painful affair with a woman whom he'd have done better to avoid like the plague. The two friends now kept themselves ostensibly aloof from us, and so, deprived of the distractions of our youths, which were all linked with their incorrigible laziness, they were obliged to spend their time in profitable activity, though often in a manner most unusual for men of their age in our city.

When they had finished Mor-Zamba's house, they turned their attention to fishing, after reconditioning the boat and nets of an old man who was no longer able to practise the trade.

One morning, while sitting on the bank hidden by thick undergrowth, Mor-Zamba, who felt himself completely alone, was called by a voice which filled him with surprise. He turned and saw standing, some distance away, a tall, slender woman. It took him some time to recognize her, for she lived in an old

35

part of the town far from the centre; furthermore, she had a very bad reputation, though she'd borne two young children and was provided with a frisky husband. The woman advanced step by step, smiling broadly. Suddenly, she addressed Mor-Zamba thus:

'Young man,' she called, 'how are you getting on?'

Instead of keeping an obstinate silence, as he should have done with a woman like that, Mor-Zamba instantly replied:

'Woman, I'm as well as can be expected of a sturdy fellow like me. And you, woman, how do you feel?'

'Young man, I'm very far from being as sturdy as you, but being equally young, why should I feel any less well?'

'I wonder if you are really as young as you claim? But I'm sure you'd do better to go on your way, woman. Think of your husband's rage if he learns that you have approached a solitary man!'

'All right, young man, all right, I will go on my way. However, seeing your height and your muscles, how could I suspect that you fear the blows of an angry husband?'

Then she did go off, but not without casting over her shoulder plenty of ravishing smiles and winks at the baffled Mor-Zamba.

In Mor-Zamba's mind, the memory of this woman lasted no longer than her presence. But soon afterwards he heard a ripple of laughter right behind him: she was back. She had balanced a sugarcane on either shoulder and was trying to walk without losing them, with her arms outstretched.

'You want to know what makes me laugh, not so? You remind me of my elder brother; yes, yes, truly, it's my elder brother I'm speaking of; the younger one is nothing but a child. Yes, my elder is big and strong, just as you are. He attacks any job with the same fiery spirit as you do. Yes, I've had my eye on you for some time; does that surprise you? Only I'm not sure, you know, that my elder brother is really a man. I think I've heard his wife whispering that he's only a man in appearance.'

'In appearance? What does that mean?' asked Mor-Zamba, more amused than surprised.

'Not a man! Not a man! Isn't that clear and simple enough!

No! Don't try to make me think you don't understand. In that case, you're even thicker than I thought you were. Exactly like my brother, so there!'

After this came a whole flood of cajoleries, quite superfluous now, however, as Mor-Zamba had already decided to walk into the trap offered by this shameless creature. Within a few days, their passion amounted to a frenzy. Abena, who had missed nothing of this from the start, let things be, with the disdainful indifference of a man who has no interest in women, because his life is filled with an altogether different dream.

Mor-Zamba and this notorious trollop always met in a cave, deep in the forest on the other side of the river, rain or shine. But instead of soothing her husband with shows of tenderness and submission, as any wife would who wanted to avoid suspicion, this woman inflamed him with refusals and insulting provocations. It seemed as if she wanted to exasperate him. And when, unable to stand any more, he finally blew up, she cried out as if to give him a death-blow:

'Call yourself a man! Oh, you poor little squirt! Do you want me to tell you what a man is, eh? All right, since you want to know, just remember the name Mor-Zamba. That one, you poor thing, is a real man, and not a pitiable sparrow like you, who knows nothing except how to beat his wife, as if that were a great achievement. But Mor-Zamba – there's real virility. And, believe me, I know what I'm talking about.'

'So you've been sleeping around again, you poor fool,' replied he. 'Is that anything to boast about?'

'Certainly I have!' she yelled, 'yes, I've been with Mor-Zamba. And if it depended only on me, I'd go on with it.'

'Look what you've sunk to, you poor little fool,' he rallied, trying to save his face. 'Look what you've sunk to! Giving yourself to people whom nobody knows, to any wandering dog, as it were.'

'A wandering dog? Perhaps, but a male one, little fellow. A male, not a female in disguise. Ah, you wretch, if only you could imagine what you lack, not only would you keep your trap shut, but you'd go and hide your miserable equipment in the depths of the forest. Ah, if only you could imagine. . . .'

The scandal of this woman's conduct, however common the

37

event might be, seemed intolerable to the young men of the city, who met in a sort of council of war presided over by young Engamba. Abena, who had been invited to participate, declared right away that he wouldn't stay unless Mor-Zamba was also accepted. The proposal was rejected, but only after exchanges which so revolted Abena that, blind with rage and indignation, he decided to tell a few home truths to his comrades: they were just looking for a quarrel with Mor-Zamba and this affair was nothing but a pretext. After all, every one of these louts had lost his virginity to this woman, whose willingness was notorious, and the impotence of whose husband was public knowledge. So, how could they reproach Mor-Zamba for a liaison with the one person who would still welcome him?

Young Engamba replied by threatening to flatten such insolence with his hammer of a fist. The quarrel which followed didn't take long in coming to blows and, naturally, young Engamba was the victor. But Mor-Zamba knew nothing of it till nightfall, when Abena's mother burst into his house crying:

'My son is getting himself killed on your account. What are you waiting for? Get up, stranger. Run and defend him!'

Which is just what Mor-Zamba did, confronting Engamba right in his father's house. This fellow threw himself on Mor-Zamba like a young lion; they rolled over and over, across the threshold and out into the yard; but the spectators, although armed with bamboo torches, couldn't easily distinguish them in the darkness; they heard only the crunch of heavy blows, followed by grunts which indicated the ferocity of the struggle. The two men were again on the ground and suddenly the rhythm of the blows indicated that only one of the combatants was still striking while the other lay paralysed. This phase seemed interminable to the spectators. When the elders could at last separate the two, they discovered what might have been guessed from the start. Mor-Zamba had a score to settle with young Engamba and had given him such a terrible lesson that the victim howled with anguish, weeping more copiously than any young wife thrashed by her husband. We couldn't recall ever seeing the like. Such humiliations are never forgiven, and we knew that from now onwards an immortal hatred was fixed between Mor-Zamba and the Engamba family and that no one would ever find a way of reconciling them.

Very early the next morning the young men of Ekoumdoum, who had been harangued all night by a large group of adults presided over by old Engamba, armed themselves with spears, pikes and pruning-hooks; they surrounded the house where Mor-Zamba and Abena were sleeping, as if to take it by assault. But Abena's mother, that extraordinary woman whose generosity had so faded in her son that she herself could scarcely recognize him later on, after watching their manoeuvres for some time, suddenly came up to the young fanatics and addressed them in this way:

'Go on, then! Why don't you go in and massacre them? One of the two, my son Abena, is your own brother. His blood will spurt over you and stain your hands. Let's see who will be prepared to cleanse you from such an abomination. Go on, then; go and wallow in sacrilege and ill-fortune.'

At this moment the good old man, who had guessed their route and had followed events by intently listening to all the signs, took station in front of his door and addressed the enraged young avengers:

'Mor-Zamba and Abena didn't sleep there last night; they are with me. You'll have to come and get them here, but first you'll have to trample over my body. As that great woman has just told you, the curse of parricide will pursue you all the rest of your lives. Anyway, I come to make you a proposal, in the name of my son Mor-Zamba. Yes, my son Mor-Zamba has charged me to speak to you thus: "If you are men, come against Mor-Zamba one by one, and Mor-Zamba, as if in play, will lick you one after the other. For Mor-Zamba doesn't believe you are real men, but only dressed-up women!" That's what Mor-Zamba charged me tell you. So will you please get into line, without further ado? What are you waiting for?'

But neither the amazement of their fathers and mothers, who formed a demanding crowd, nor the sarcasms of their sisters, nor, for those who were married, their wives crying:

'But he's quite right to call you little girls all dressed up! Are you so degenerate that you can no longer explain yourselves man to man and fist to fist with a lad of your own age? What's all this noise about, then?'

None of these taunts could move the attackers to put their courage to the proof.

So, at the insistence of all those who had disgustedly watched this scene, they dispersed to their respective houses, with heads lowered, tasting the bitterness of their own timidity. But Mor-Zamba had to swear on oath before the old man to see the slut no more; he couldn't stand permanently under the weight of these reproaches.

There were other events about this time, whose meaning and importance we were incapable of seizing. One day, the chief, who had gone as usual to receive his instructions, returned precipitately. He seemed preoccupied, so that one might think he'd been ordered to number the whole clan and offer all the effective male adults to the service of Tamara. In fact, such a task could not have pleased him, as he had always failed in his efforts to achieve the like. Whenever we were called to make a census, we always pretended to be dead. What would the chief do this time, if he wanted to succeed? It was just at this time that the clan was all enthusiastic about a wrestling match with our neighbours, the big city of the Zolos; this was a traditional contest, but one which had gradually fallen into abeyance since the arrival of the whites, except for an occasional twitch of animation, like the spasms of the dying. We have learnt since that our chief, Mor-Bita, was the real inspirer of this competition, having suggested the idea to his colleague, the chief of the Zolos who, being a violent man and a lover of martial spectacles, was nevertheless the beloved and chosen son of his people, and one who had no desire to count them.

We never really understood how our chief utilized the preparations for this match as a means of taking his census. Be that as it may, we discovered later that he estimated us at six thousand men, women and children – an estimate, it must be added, far above the reality, even if one included the scattered villages around Ekoumdoum.

The Zolos were said to be very warlike and we were hopelessly out of training; what's more, we knew it and were appalled by it, so it was no problem to persuade our squad to include

Mor-Zamba, the only man whose strength, if not his skill, could save the honour of Ekoumdoum. The daily practice of grips and parries, as well as the elimination bouts, were all conducted in the chief's house and under his supervision. It was here that Mor-Zamba discovered the strange hideout of Mor-Bita; a little bamboo enclosure outside the great 'palace' of brick and glass windows which the chief had not even had the trouble to construct; the equivalent of fifty ordinary dwellings, to contain his wives, relations and servants.

The first time that Mor-Bita appeared, the wandering child saw in him, not a mortal enemy, but a man perhaps once tall enough, but now bloated with fat, with a dull eye, a debonair manner, the gestures of a humble, conciliating person, even a feeble and uneasy one, concealing an insidious but persistent reputation for cunning and ferocity.

On the last day of training, the eve of departure of our team and its very numerous escort for the Zolo country, the representatives of our clan, who included Mor-Zamba on this occasion, had the privilege of hearing this flat speech by their chief, who had never condescended formerly to open his mouth before them:

'So, my friends, you are the ones on whose shoulders our reputation rests; it's a responsibility whose weight you must feel. Well, you must know by now how matters will be arranged, and my friend the chief of the Zolos will tell you again. You are going to fight against an equal number of Zolo representatives. Well, then, it's simple enough; each beaten wrestler is immediately eliminated; which means that the winning clan will be the one which has an unbeaten champion at the end or – why not? – several unbeaten champions. So, as you see, it's quite simple. So, my children, be of good heart!'

The encounter took place in a large clearing of the Zolos' city, filled every day with spectators, shaken with the thunder of drums, washed over by the cries and comments of the crowd. We were the first to show off our champions, choosing the finest and those most apt to strike terror; but we soon retreated when we saw those of the Zolos, so supple, aggressively muscular and well put together. Had we walked into a trap? We already felt the dark eye of defeat fixed upon us. Our women supporters, instead of assuming a blatant gaiety, shouting songs of defiance and dancing provocative insults, were already sinking into a humiliating silence, even avoiding the glances of the others; instead of praising the glory of our heroes, they were already muttering against the fate which made them daughters of Ekoumdoum.

And these were no vain fears; the first few days saw most of our champions tumbled in the dust, one after the other. On the third day, young Engamba, who'd made a good impression till then, was overthrown by an obscure opponent. We knew that our fighters had been decimated; that whereas we had only one champion still on his feet, the Zolos had four. This news astonished us the more when we learnt that the providential champion, the lone hero still carrying our reputation on his shoulders, was Mor-Zamba. We even took consolation from the news, as if he had first seen the light of day at Ekoumdoum, as if we had never reproached him as a stranger. Suddenly, he was one of us; no one objected to that; no one was even surprised. All night long we acclaimed and fêted him, like a spear snatched up in the pathway by a man pursued by a lion. Our women enveloped him with burning looks of tenderness and gratitude.

We were no less incredulous of our hero's chances. And, what's more, the first phases of Mor-Zamba's encounter with the four Zolos filled us with despair. They had clearly conspired among themselves to wear Mor-Zamba out, and his first opponent did nothing but break every grip as soon as it was taken. But Providence saw that Mor-Zamba instinctively refused to be put out of countenance by these crooked manoeuvres; he even displayed an amusement which put the crowd on his side, taunting his opponent to take courage and make more use of his arms than his legs, calling on the public to witness the cowardice of his antagonist. In any event, much of the day went by without a result, and when finally Mor-Zamba threw down this over-cunning Zolo champion, we regarded it as a gift offered only to make us the more ridiculous; certain among us even wanted to concede defeat right away. What shame is there in openly acknowledging that one is beaten?

Thank God, we did nothing as decisive as that. If the first Zolo had no other tactic than to break off combat, the second, equally without imagination, relied simply on his strength to break Mor-Zamba, who quickly got wind of his intentions. The Zolo, urged on by his supporters, threw himself on Mor-Zamba like lightning and gripped him so hard that his forearms were trapped in a flash; then, moving always with the same diabolical swiftness which gave his adversary no time to recover, he contorted his torso and butted Mor-Zamba in the side like a ram, throwing him off balance. Now he lifted our champion off the ground and held him an instant above his back, before throwing him over his head by a quick twist; but, each time, Mor-Zamba was just able to turn himself in the air so that he fell, not on his back, but on his belly, letting out a brief cry of pain which was both a grunt and a groan. The young Zolos invaded the arena and began dancing victoriously around the two duellists, who were fighting to recover their breath; the elders approached without haste, wagging their heads in denial and, after a brief consultation, declared that there was no result as yet, and the struggle began again.

The Zolo was almost fully-grown and, for that very reason, quicker to lose breath; towards midday he seemed also to lose some of his pungency and fierceness. His vigour, up to now incomparable, began to wane, despite all the frantic encouragement of his supporters.

Now we began to realize that Mor-Zamba would perhaps triumph over this devil of a man, whose fiery assault had so long filled us with despair; now the frenzy changed camps, and it was we who were swept along by it: roaring, shouting and leaping high in the air, we kept ceaselessly circling the arena. We rolled in the dust; we kept slapping Mor-Zamba's legs with fly-whisks, which stung his flesh cruelly. We didn't notice exactly how our champion finally overthrew his doughty opponent; they had just stumbled over again, partly locked by the arms, half lying and half crouching, leg to leg and shoulder to shoulder; a position which should have indicated the end of the bout; however, they suddenly grappled again, their sweating bodies were once more knotted together, and this time it was the Zolo who, at his last gasp, collapsed like a burst wineskin. Almost without effort, as if with a flip of the finger, Mor-Zamba rolled him over on his back, poised briefly above him, teeth and muscles clenched anew, and held him stretched on the ground, his face exposed to the blinding glare of the sun, his shoulders bathed in the dust, and his clan in ignominy.

The despair of the Zolos, even though they still had two champions to bring on, made us suspect that, contrary to what we feared, they had bungled their strategy and brought on their best fighters first. After these were overthrown, one might say that the match was over so far as our hosts were concerned, and that the remaining bouts would be nothing but a cruel ritual.

But we still feared a trap and our anxiety was boundless when, next morning, Mor-Zamba threw himself at his third opponent under the angry stare, this time, of the chief of the Zolos. While the whole arena shook with cries of encouragement and volleys of drumming, the two men advanced on each other; arrived at the right distance, near enough to touch, they opened the combat in the customary manner, each opening his left armpit so that the right arm of his adversary fitted into it as if into a sheath. Our breasts tightened and we didn't even dare to breathe. Was it possible that we'd win? Mor-Zamba, the wandering boy, the clanless one, the reprobate, could he be the architect of our victory?

Bent forward and locked together cheek to cheek, the two men danced a strange ballet, with their torsos poised obliquely above legs parted and thrust backward, luring each other into holds which were either quickly abandoned or redoubled in strength. Suddenly Mor-Zamba contorted his whole belly, like a python thrown into a furnace; he slipped out of the Zolo's grip and seized his whole body in the vice of his embrace; the other wriggled furiously, making vain little stabs with his feet, the only part of him which remained free. Mor-Zamba swept him briskly off the ground, held him at arm's length while the Zolo furiously tried to hook one of his legs and suddenly it was all over. Mor-Zamba threw himself violently forward and flattened his opponent to the ground with a loud thud, holding him flat on his back at full-length, his face also exposed to the pitiless gaze of the sun.

44

Recovering quickly from our stupor, while our Zolo neighbour wept tears of humiliation, we rushed into the arena and seized Mor-Zamba, bearing him off in triumph. Our delight was indescribable. The Zolos, who were decent and loyal people, came during the day to share our joy and made no secret of their envy for the possession of one whom the whole world now called, without reflection, our 'phenomenon'. According to them, he was invincible, and it certainly wouldn't be their fourth champion, a mere boy, who could keep him long in suspense.

During the evening a delegation of Zolo elders came to tell us that their fourth fighter had withdrawn and Mor-Zamba was declared outright victor.

To have seen how we carried him in triumph that night and the several ensuing nights, how we snatched him from one another to heap him with praises and adoration, who could have doubted that Mor-Zamba was at last, definitively, one of us? Our journey home was a solemn, grand and memorable experience, passing through the forest by night in the glare of our bamboo torches; or lighting it again with our fires when, after a long march, we made camp to sleep the sleep of champions.

As victors always do, we kept dancing our triumph on the banks of every river we crossed, rocking the hills and forests in the cradle of our melodious songs, or romping joyously with the many Zolo girls who had agreed to accompany us part of the way, some of whom finally entered Ekoumdoum with us and have remained there ever since.

The elders went before us, burning with impatience to recite our triumphs to those who hadn't the privilege of witnessing them. But we young ones lingered on the way, never failing to pillage the fields we passed, to hunt venison or to grill fresh-caught fishes over our fires, to haunt the edges of the villages so as to steal their palm wine and soak ourselves in it; ever celebrating in Mor-Zamba, not the cursed stranger, but the conqueror.

But the passage of events soon recalled us from these dreams to the realities of life. Every old man conceives of some folly sooner or later, and that's just what happened to the good elder who had welcomed Mor-Zamba and who, perhaps exalted by our delirious triumph among the Zolos, planned to marry the person he had long considered his son to one of Engamba's daughters. It was a mad idea and one which seemed not only an affront to common sense, but also to harmony within our city, which it divided into numerous hostile factions; some steadfastly supporting the old man, whom they'd always considered a model of wisdom, dignity and reserve; others, who lacked his generosity, inflaming themselves at his presumption and taking ranks, perhaps unwillingly, behind Engamba, who represented for the time being a bulwark of the tradition which opposed any union with a totally unknown stranger.

The good old man, with the consent of his protégé, called the clan into council and regaled them with a joyful feast, before telling his guests that Mor-Zamba had lost his heart to the eldest daughter of Engamba, and that he was charged by his son to ask her hand of her father.

As the old man had expected, his declaration was followed by exclamations full of surprise, stupefaction and scandalized alarm; but, after a few moments, one of his peers took over the discourse to ask solemnly that the daughter concerned be consulted. This redoubled the indignation of the greater part of the assembly, who abominated strange customs which could only cause the disintegration of families and the flouting of fathers. Despite this uproar, the advice to consult the young girl was finally adopted, no one quite knew how. Between her sobs, the child, who was profoundly embarrassed and dumbfounded, managed to stammer out, distinctly enough, that she agreed to Mor-Zamba's proposal.

We thought for a moment that Engamba was trapped and that he had no alternative but to accept the good old man's proposition. This shows how little we knew him. First of all he objected to what he called incest: Mor-Zamba had been adopted by a member of the clan, he had become effectively one of its children and couldn't therefore marry a daughter of the clan without committing a sacrilege. It was easy enough to show him his error, that there was no question of incest here, that many famous precedents had established the sanctity of such unions.

46

Engamba had so far kept his real thought well hidden, but it flashed out suddenly:

'Matters of this gravity demand reflection; why don't you give me time to consider? Are all these people called together to force my hand this evening? After all, I am the child's father. Well, am I not her father? Who among you would like to claim that he took my place in my wife's womb? Marriage, just like that! And with whom, I ask you? With a man of whom no one can tell me where he comes from or whither he's going. An odd sort of son-in-law! I need time to think it over, so please leave me in peace....'

This speech made a great impression on the gathering, and, in the end, Engamba won the first round, for the good old man, who was not disheartened by Engamba's ill-will or his proverbial obstinacy, didn't bother to fight it out, because he was still convinced that the storm of sympathy aroused by Mor-Zamba in the Zolo expedition must finish by pushing a majority of the assembly to the young man's side.

Now some of the inhabitants of Ekoumdoum, counting on Mor-Zamba's chagrin at seeing himself refused Engamba's daughter, tried to humiliate him in every possible way. Some of the older men even approached him in order to say:

'There are plenty of girls here, Mor-Zamba. Why fret yourself by running after Engamba's only daughter? Why her in particular? Listen, why don't you go and look for a wife in your own country. Girls around here are very difficult to get, you know. Just put yourself in our place.'

Or else:

'Poor Mor-Zamba! Engamba's girl is not for you. Do you really want her so much, you rascal? You'd really like to do it with her, eh? You can speak quite freely to me, you young devil. I see by the light in your eye that you've already been there, you rogue.'

Or again:

'Listen old chap, I know a widow in a little village not far from here. She's still not bad to look at. A little bit wrinkled, I know, but still just what you need. And not at all difficult to get. She's not exactly free, of course; she's living with someone already, a kind of cripple; but in any case, she'd certainly prefer you, I believe. I hope you're not going to be fussy about it?'

One of us even told him one day:

'Since you're so keen on Engamba's daughter, Mor-Zamba, why don't you go home to your own people for a while? You can come back with your father and mother, and I'll bet that Engamba will change his tone in the presence of such venerable people.'

Abena was furious at Mor-Zamba's complacency and wanted him to thrash the audacious fellows who treated him so contemptuously, but he didn't know that in reality his friend was little attached to the girl, and thus indifferent to all these insults.

'Heaven has given you all that strength,' Abena would say, 'to make goodness triumph and to punish evil-doers. Such people should always be punished; they destroy all the happiness of life. You are wrong to let yourself be so humiliated.'

Always full of joviality and high spirits, Mor-Zamba would reply that he'd swallowed so many insults in his time that he'd become insensible to them.

'I don't really understand why,' he explained, 'but somehow I know that all the hatred of these people hasn't the least importance.'

'No, tell me the truth: you reckon that you owe them something because we have received you among us. You kid yourself that the clan has been very generous towards you. Just listen to me. At the start it was just a caprice, and now it's nothing but a game. And what a game! So you see, you owe nothing to us, really. Rightly speaking, my poor friend, it's we who still owe a debt of gratitude to you.'

Abena didn't need to make a long proof of this last truth; it was enough for him to support Mor-Zamba by being always at his side during the second phase of the struggle which the old man, feeling the approach of death, now opened against Engamba. Following his advice, Mor-Zamba made separate visits to all the most influential members of the clan council; these were old men, all afflicted by one infirmity or another, but all equally interested in the affair. It was the first of these sages who filled the two friends with the deepest perplexity, giving them the sense of a leprosy or an incurable poison working within the flesh of the clan. It was from that night onwards that Mor-Zamba, filled with unease, pledged himself to the cult of the obscure dream which would never cease to fascinate his friend.

Like all well brought-up young men, they didn't come empty-handed to visit an elder, but offered him a keg of palm wine. The dry, sad old man, who was lying on a bamboo couch beside the fire, sat up and poured himself several calabashes before offering some to his wife, an old woman whom the two friends noticed for the first time when she came up. As if fearing that he would lose it, the old man kept pouring calabash after calabash, which he either drank himself or offered to his companion; a sight which softened Mor-Zamba but infuriated Abena, who had expected it and had counted every second of it in advance. Between two bumpers, the elder, who now looked less aged to Mor-Zamba than he had thought at first, yawned, moaned, sighed and cracked all his joints.

'He's going to speak, and I know just what he's going to say,' whispered Abena in his friend's ear.

And in fact the old man began a long speech, delivered in a monotone:

'Mor-Zamba, my son, you can't imagine how grateful I am that you should imagine I can be of assistance to you. Your confidence honours me and rejoices me. Ah, my little one, you see how old I've become! The burden of innumerable seasons of labour, of incalculable misfortunes, of daily griefs will soon bear down the friend who speaks to you. Yes, my poor Mor-Zamba, you have in me an unhappy father, a man so reduced that he's nothing but a rag, a shadow, at the very moment when so many trials assail him. Look, if you'd just seen me struggling today, if you'd just seen the struggle of daily tasks for this corpse who scarcely has the strength to talk to you, if you'd seen me slicing, cutting, panting, knocking myself up, you'd have taken pity on me, my son; you'd have cried out: "Stop this moment, my dear old father, stop! You break my heart. Go back home, sit down near the fire and don't bother about anything any more; I'll finish this job for you. I'm young and strong enough. It's nothing but a morsel to me, so to speak!" That's what you would have said to me. For you know, my dear son, when the elders of a clan have to clear the land and build the houses themselves, well, it means the whole clan is profoundly sick. I don't know how it goes with other clans on this earth, but I know that things are pretty bad here....

'Let alone that I have to clear my own farm; just look at the roof of my house, my child; what a sieve! No problem about counting the stars through that. Is that a roof? I don't ask Heaven to give me your limbs or your strength; that would be too much. I could manage with far less, just enough to cut and truss a bit of thatch. Ah yes, my dear child, a clan like this is very sick indeed....'

At this moment he was interrupted by Abena, who had been vainly digging his neighbour in the ribs, in the darkness of the hut.

'Dear father,' he began, 'don't worry yourself any more; we'll tackle that job for you tomorrow. Within twelve days your house will have a completely new roof.'

The old man now went into a long, excited rigmarole, going so far as to promise the two friends that their first children by their future wives would both be sons. Then, as if restored to health and even vivacity by a miracle, he voluntarily opened the subject which had brought them. He reassured them, between gulps of wine, that his experience and knowledge would easily get the better of Engamba's ill-will.

Nothing that the two friends told him, in accounting for their visit, seemed to surprise the old man.

'In any case, this man has children, and big children too!' cried Mor-Zamba.

'And so?' asked Abena ironically.

'What?' Mor-Zamba persisted, 'do you approve here of children deserting their aged parents?'

'You've seen nothing yet,' declared Abena sententiously, but none the less mysteriously.

'I've spent my whole life,' the old man intervened, 'vainly imploring the Heavens to send me at least one true son. This old man you've just spoken to had several, naturally enough. And yet, before you came, we two tasted the same bitter and solitary old age. Yes, this old man before you had children; the children grew up and now they are men. You've seen them yourself, Mor-Zamba: they were the companions of your childhood, short though it was; you know what kind of men these are. Have you ever seen them show, by the least word or gesture, any veneration for their begetters? Such children are nothing but a curse. When we were young, we others, we held our parents sacred; we hadn't the heart to see them suffer. But times are sadly changed.'

'What exactly has happened since then?' Abena enquired.

'Plenty of things, my poor child. The whole night would not be too long to tell them.'

'Try to tell us briefly.'

'To my mind,' said the elder in a lowered key, 'everything began to go wrong when they imposed the new chief on us.'

'Yes, you're right,' Mor-Zamba exclaimed, 'tell us about that, then.'

'He doesn't do us any harm, it's true, stuck up there by himself. All the same, he's there, and we are powerless to get rid of him. We are powerless, that's our plight; for our wives and children are witnesses of that powerlessness.'

'But who is he and where does he come from?' insisted Mor-Zamba.

'Before the war, we had a chief who was one of us. But then, well, the French came and took over. They arrested the chief and all his family, declaring that they had been allies of the enemy. We never heard of any of them again. Don't repeat this to anyone; the children must never learn these terrible secrets. And they brought in this other man, declaring: "Here is your new chief."'

'But why don't you go further back?' asked Abena. 'For, after all, before the first whites came you didn't have any chief at all.'

'What! You know that, my son? You are wrong; and yet, you are also right. In the old days, we didn't have a chief. We discussed our affairs among ourselves and no one had power over us.'

'And they insisted that you choose a chief among yourselves!' exclaimed Abena.

'Yes, to be at our head on every occasion, and for everything.'

'And you agreed to violate your traditions?'

'It wasn't a question of traditions! We were fighting for our survival, my child. We had no firearms among us. And against a good gun, a spear is as useless as empty hands.'

'I see your point, but don't you think, considering it carefully, that all this degeneration we see began at that time? How could your children not see your powerlessness when you feebly abandoned your traditions in accepting a chief, no matter who he was?'

'Because, at that time, we were not really at fault. One doesn't resist a gun, when one is empty-handed.'

'Yes, but not having a gun indicates a failure of some kind; perhaps of proper pride, or of vigilance. Your impotence dates from far back, when, on the pretext that they might turn their guns on you, you gave in, dishonoured your ancestors and betrayed your traditions of vigilance and valour.'

'Be silent, you poor child! What experience do you have of such things?'

In saying this, the old man was chuckling. He was in the habit of teasing Abena, as one does a small boy; he pretended to be amused at the young man's diatribes, whereas in reality they disturbed him.

'Try instead to follow my advice,' he continued, with the same false gaiety. 'Believe your old father, my poor Mor-Zamba, a wife is worth all these affronts. I didn't know it until I lost one of my own. In the course of your other visits, behave exactly as you did here; offer yourselves to complete all the necessary jobs. For the rest, I place confidence in Abena's high spirits.'

'I'm beginning to wonder,' began Abena in a sombre tone, 'yes, I'm beginning to ask myself whether the possession of a wife is worth so much palaver. Wouldn't it be better to struggle for the possession of a gun? If, instead of wasting time chasing after wives, each of you had taken the trouble of arming himself with a gun, would the chief who was imposed on you still be in his palace? Everything for a wife, nothing for a gun! Oh how, my noble and venerable father, can such extravagance be called wisdom?

'I won't give up my point, though I revere you as my elder; a chief, one man alone, ruling for life, in defiance of ancestral traditions; isn't that misfortune enough? But an imposed chief, this beast, this orang-utan who has built his home in the forest near-by; one might think at first that he's an obliging neighbour, one who doesn't intend any harm, one indeed who spreads everywhere the balm of his amity and the harmony of his protection. But time, which strips off the mask, brings more self-assurance to this abusive guest. Already he grows fat, less on the plunder of our crops than on the honey of our quarrels. All around him, the land has become his resource, his uncontested property; soon no one will dare to cross this ever-expanding estate. Then, his progeny is ever growing and multiplying, like a young baobab which presumption has allowed to grow inside a house, whose branches soon break the roof and whose buttresses burst the walls. Bit by bit the clan falls apart, crumbles into ruins which are trampled and, finally, flattened by the feet of the conquerors. The orang-utan has triumphed, the monster has gobbled everything. An imposed chief; that's what it means, my noble elder. How could you agree to live with an orang-utan, you and your fathers? The stench breathed out by the monster has long been choking our clan, and see how it's now nothing but a corpse in the process of slow decomposition. We have become nothing but a heap of rottenness, hated and despised by ourselves, like a leper who contemplates his own perishing limbs. So, my wise father, what is a wife worth, in comparison with a gun?'

Never had Abena spoken his mind so fully in a single burst. Nevertheless, the two young men did as they had been advised by the good old man and, by the end of the season, the clan council was unanimously on Mor-Zamba's side; it was also agreed to exercise all necessary pressure on Engamba to induce him to consent to his daughter's union with Mor-Zamba. But, during the course of a pathetic session, Engamba was still reluctant to change his former stance and, as usual, managed to extract a further delay from his fellow-elders, which he utilized to ply them with gifts and so gain in his turn the support of the clan, to such an extent that, when called together again expressly to resolve the affair, this assembly, reputed to be a rampart of judgement and a rock of correctitude, was almost swept away by the tide. The decision could not be made one way or the other, because the leaders of the clan, even when pushed into a tight corner, always managed to extricate themselves without being compromised.

It slowly became apparent that these sages, so especially solicited, took delight in being courted by both parties and, rather than cut off such an abundant source of favours, were inclined to prolong the situation indefinitely. On their own part, however, having quickly got wind of the elders' malicious strategy, the two opposing camps, though acting independently of each other, slackened off their warlike enthusiasm and, in consequence, their munificent zeal. The affair no longer attracted passionate interest in Ekoumdoum and was gradually forgotten, even though it hung always in the air, like a thunderstorm which, having fired its volleys overhead, retreats slowly and grumblingly into the distance.

Engamba took advantage of this unlooked-for interval to realize a project which, having long obscurely haunted him, now suddenly and dazzlingly illuminated his spirit. In secrecy and silence he embarked on a journey of several weeks which took him to a man revered for his great age and enjoying the credit brought him by the possession of many goods. Like an old criminal conspiracy, a long-standing friendship tied Engamba to this man, as well as a debt, incalculable according to some Ekoumdoums, and amounting to several dozen heads of cattle according to others. This debt had been contracted at a critical moment in Engamba's life when, as a young man, provided with an orphaned cousin, a girl brought up in his name, he decided to marry her to a man who was unanimously held to be of very good family, but a member of a clan so distant as to be almost inaccessible to the spirits of that age.

In return for this little cousin, and that is the main point, Engamba extracted a sum of money which set every daughter's father dreaming, and which he had put away in hope of himself taking a bride very soon. But, on the other hand, knowing that such a deal leaves the girl virtually the slave of her husband, and wishing to avoid this blame, he resolved to invite the family of the young man, summoned from so far off, to a sumptuous feast which would so impress them that it would confer an aura on the young bride and oblige her husband to treat her with respect. For this purpose he took care not to touch the sum with which he had just furnished his money bags, and took recourse to the obliging but none the less calculating generosity of the patriarch. Now he dreamt of obliterating that debt by a complicated system of alliances, of which this first step would rid him of that thorn-in-the-flesh Mor-Zamba, whilst involving him with partners too distant to be aware of his evil reputation, as his tortuous spirit preferred.

When he arrived at his destination he received such a flattering welcome that it swelled his ambition and his sluggish spirit. At the outset his host, who was not given to sweet talk, addressed him in this biting manner:

'What's happened, Engamba? I don't see behind you a procession of men and women driving the cattle you owe me, or weighed down under baskets of presents to rejoice my old eyes. Have you come to tell me of some disaster which has ravaged your country and ruined you yourself?'

'My dear, good friend,' replied Engamba in a stifled voice, 'just bring me a keg of wine before I open the business of my visit. As you have guessed, it's a real disaster which is threatening me.'

'A keg of wine! That much is your due!' exclaimed the patriarch, getting up painfully and hobbling out onto the veranda to shout his orders.

Scarcely had he returned, when he was followed by one of his big sons, who deposited a keg of wine beside the lonely and pitiable traveller. Engamba himself poured the wine into his cup and drank greedily; after six draughts he couldn't continue, but gave a long sigh of contentment and laid the cup on the floor. He maintained his silence, however; he kept running his tongue round his mouth and seemed afraid to begin. But the patriarch aroused him roughly with an imperious demand:

'Well, haven't you quenched that thirst now, Engamba! I'm dying to hear your news and I don't like to be kept waiting.'

'Many years ago,' began Engamba, 'a child arrived in our city. Whence did he come? Whither was he going? Who had fathered him? No one knew the answer, and the child himself least of all. The little vagabond was adopted by one of our people, an old man full of fancies who'd never had a child of his own.'

'And so,' the patriarch interrupted, 'what became of this child? Is he dead?'

'Far from being dead, he's grown up into a man, a real strapping one; he's thrust himself into the breast of our clan and now dreams of taking a wife. You can't imagine on what girl this orphan has fixed his choice.'

'Yours, I suppose!'

'My old friend, your wisdom never ceases to amaze me and fill me with admiration. You've guessed it. It's my own daughter he is seeking.'

'Isn't that quite natural?'

'Quite natural! Quite natural!' fumed Engamba, 'never will I give my daughter to a vagabond of no lineage. Never!'

'And who's talking of you giving him your daughter, my poor friend?'

'Do you really understand?' cried Engamba, hugging his host distractedly. 'You at least can imagine the anguish and the agony of a true father!'

'But why come all this way to tell me this? Just to hear my advice, I suppose? But haven't you a surfeit of sages in your own clan?'

'I'm coming to that. Our sages want me to give my daughter to the vagabond; they are influenced by his adoptive father, a man highly reputed for virtue and who loves this boy as if he were his own child.'

'But he is his child, Engamba! He has fathered him by adopting him.'

The patriarch seemed to reflect for a moment.

'My dear friend,' he resumed, 'if your clan is united in deploring your attitude, you would be quite wrong to turn away from the event which makes you so angry. It's a most embarrassing business.'

'I've come to ask you for your help. Your name alone would be a providential security for me. What's more, I've always wanted to ally myself to a man like you, so wise, so rich in goods and with so many descendants. In you I would acquire a second family, in whose breast I could take refuge from all the

56

vexations and insults of this life; that's how our forefathers allied themselves and they never regretted it. Your household is overflowing with boys and girls. For my own part, I ask no more, in all modesty, than one boy and one girl near to puberty. I offer you my daughter for whichever of your sons you choose; that's the purpose of my visit.'

His visitor fell silent, but the patriarch, suspecting that this was a mere interruption rather than the end of the matter, asked:

'And what do you want in immediate exchange?'

'Your wisdom still fills me with admiration.'

A crude, irrepressible bellow of satisfaction shook the traveller. But the patriarch glanced at him furtively and askance, as at a man with whom one measures one's confidences because, truth to tell, he lacks dignity.

'I like your plans,' he said at last. 'As for the cattle, I agree to say no more about them. But don't ever forget this; one doesn't normally give that many head of cattle for just one girl.'

Engamba stayed many days with the patriarch, to enjoy the liberal hospitality of the man with whom he was now allied. When he returned to Ekoumdoum, he failed to rejoin the clan council in order to give an account of his mission, and this gave rise to all sorts of rumours and conjectures. The momentous arrival of the patriarch himself in Ekoumdoum, in a palanquin carried by his sons, confirmed Engamba's intrigue to circumvent the decision of our elders that he should give his daughter to Mor-Zamba. The patriarch deluged the city with presents, summoned the clan council to a copious feast in the clan house, and addressed them as follows:

'By the way I have just entertained you in your own city, entirely at my own expense and with the assistance only of my own retinue, have you at last begun to comprehend the immensity of my fortune, you who usurp the venerable title of sage, yet show so little sense? How can you expect to force your brother to give his daughter to a vagabond? Old men whitened only in futility and blindness, has Engamba told me the truth of it? If so, you've all gone mad. Since this girl is available, I'll tell you the motive of my visit to your city; I will take her as bride for my son, this one whom you see right now beside me. Have you any objection? I'm ready to hear you.'

The patriarch's presents, the big feast he had offered the elders and his confident effrontery had so intimidated the council that not one of its members was ready to oppose this frightful old man. The young were strictly forbidden to enter the communal house, where the council always assembled, so that Abena was not able to give the patriarch the answer he deserved. The good old man himself, taken aback by the turn of events, couldn't immediately think what course of action to take. Would Engamba triumph at last?

'What a bunch of clowns!' groaned Abena that night, in bitterness and defeat, when the two friends joined the old man at his house as usual, sitting around the glowing hearth which scarcely penetrated the shadows of the room. 'They're so good at making crooked and nasty deals. As for getting themselves a gun, not a chance! Bunch of clowns!'

After sitting a long while in silence, and doubtless in deep thought, though the two friends could hardly distinguish him in that nest of shadows – the good old man declared abruptly that there was still one recourse open, though one he wouldn't like to adopt, were he not obliged by his distress to do so. Then, getting up briskly and approaching the fire, he turned to them:

'Come close to me, my children. I'm going to tell you a terrible secret.'

The two friends hastened to lean over the now crouching worthy.

'Do you know what this is?' he asked, holding out a herb which, though withered, the two lads instantly identified and named.

He asked them the same question in showing them some nuts, also well dried, which they were equally ready to name. The good old man, closely watched by his protégés, plied each ingredient on a grinding stone, mixed together the powders thus obtained and sprinkled them over the glowing embers. A strange, heady colour filled the house and he pronounced many times this seemingly magic formula:

'If there is no evil, let Providence remain silent; but if, on the contrary, Justice is injured, oh Providence, let us know it this very night!'

Very soon, at an hour which Mor-Zamba now believes was between eleven and twelve, a vast horde of owls assembled, as if they had come from every corner of the world to make rendezvous over Ekoumdoum, and kept up their sinister, hideous serenade until the first hours of dawn.

'Exactly as I thought,' said the old man, who kept vigil all that night with his two disciples. 'Yes, that's it. Justice has well and truly been injured, and Providence, consulted by us, announces a coming misfortune through the voices of these birds. The clan has violated a sacred law and will be well punished for it; I shall rejoin them tomorrow and tell them: "Your cowardice, together with the pride and egotism of Engamba, have unloosed the bonds of disaster; it glides even now over our heads; it will swoop at any moment...." That's what I shall tell them tomorrow. There, my children, you know everything now, your education is completed, for I have nothing more to tell you. After the wisdom of the living, I have just exposed to you the wisdom of the dead.'

There was no need to summon the council next day. The nocturnal song of the gathered owls was a language so powerful that, at first light, one saw the extraordinary spectacle of the patriarch and his train fleeing from our city as if the whole place were in flames.

The cause was not heard so soon, for all that. Some days later, the good old man collapsed in his house while performing a simple task, and died.

Things remained for a long time in the same state, no one daring to give them a decisive push, fearing goodness knows what sacrilege.

However, it wasn't long before we realized that only the protection of the old man had maintained the position of Mor-Zamba in our city. As soon as he disappeared, we perceived that Mor-Zamba was now like an edifice without foundation. For when, after an interval of hesitation following the death of the good old man, Engamba opened a campaign of calumnies against Mor-Zamba, not one of the six thousand supposed members of the Ekoumdoum clan really opposed him, except the eight people in Abena's own family. One could scarcely imagine how the death of a man, a single man, could so change the complexion of things. Mor-Zamba was pursued by a malevolence which, it seemed, must soon explode into violence. Despite Abena's insistence, he refused to yield to fear, coming and going, bathing in the river, fishing or weeding, without taking the least precaution. One might even have thought he defied his enemies, now seasoning his conduct with an ostentatious arrogance. Perhaps this was merely the expression of his despair.

Abena was right to fear a plot against his friend but, contrary to his fears, it wasn't an ordinary ambush which awaited Mor-Zamba. Engamba was plotting with the chief Mor-Bita, a man to whom no one in our clan ever resorted, preparing a trap which we only learnt about long afterwards, when the chief, falling into the hands of the guerrillas, confessed his crimes and named his accomplices.

First of all we saw a detachment of soldiers arrive by the road, penetrating our city by its street and mounting towards the chief's palace, rifles at the shoulder, cartridges in their belts, puttees tightly fixed, fezzes straight; these men were huge and very black, with long perpendicular marks on their narrow faces. In fact, this was not the first intrusion they had made among us. Mor-Bita, having no real police, but only two harmless messengers who acted as scarecrows when the collection of head-tax was not going fast enough, would send to Tamara, in any grave situation, for the dispatch of several dozen armed and uniformed men. Sometimes they just seized upon a malefactor and carried him off; but at others, for reasons we couldn't understand, they stayed in Ekoumdoum for a whole season, camping in the grounds of the palace, but descending from there to commit various depradations, like seizing a young girl or even, more rarely, a married woman, without the chief ever showing the least concern about the sufferings imposed on his people.

But this time they had the look of men making a tour, going from city to city; they pushed before them a group of men all red from their march on dirt roads or stony paths, without ever having the chance to bathe. Who were these men, each tied to each successively by the same long rope? What crime had they committed? To what punishment were they led? It wasn't long before we discovered, because that very same night a skirmish broke out at Mor-Zamba's house, where the two friends were now sleeping, between a party of soldiers coming from the palace and Mor-Zamba, assisted by Abena. When we arrived, the soldiers had overwhelmed Mor-Zamba and tied his arms behind his back; he had the bloody mouth and swollen face of a man who had received countless blows. Abena too, with his face unrecognizably swollen and spitting blood, was held by his mother as one holds a man determined to kill himself by plunging in a river above a whirlpool. She kept crying tearfully to him:

'I beg you, I beg you, calm yourself! What good will it do? I implore you, have pity on your old mother.'

Abena struggled manfully, but his mother wouldn't let go and was aided by his father, a man normally self-effacing, timid and enfeebled, so that at last the two of them managed to render him powerless.

While three men held Mor-Zamba in the light of a hurricane-lamp, and the latter sniffled, either with tears or, more likely, with the blood which ran into his mouth and nostrils, the soldier who seemed to be in charge advanced upon our surrounding horde without showing any fear of our numbers, doubtless putting trust in his well-armed men and their full cartridge-belts, and declared:

'You would be unpardonable not to realize that, even in your remote and savage country, the authority of the white man must be respected. Well, the whites don't like vagabonds, these people who leave their own country and come to live in the bosom of a clan not their own. This kind of person disturbs the natural order and troubles the souls of others, understand? Anyway, what are they fleeing from? For they must be fleeing from something, if they quit their own people like that, not so? What crimes may they have committed in their country? Do you understand that?'

'But of course we understand,' we feebly chanted in chorus.

'All right,' cried the soldier, 'we've already got hold of this one, that's fine. Are there any more strangers among you?'

'No, no others.'

'Are you sure?'

'We'll offer our heads on it.'

Father Van den Rietter had, for the first time, mingled with the rest of our crowd; we thought for a moment that he might be true to his precepts and order the soldiers to release Mor-Zamba and clear off. Mor-Zamba looked so piteous that anyone who wasn't, like we Ekoumdoums, rigid with terror, must have been so revolted as to throw himself on the soldiers, and beat them for their cruelty. But the Father never said a word and they took Mor-Zamba away. Next day we saw him descend the main street amidst the other captives, enter the high road and disappear from sight.

Abena now cultivated Father Van den Rietter, whom he had always despised, without revealing that what attracted him was neither his religion, nor his hero Jesus Christ, of whom he spoke so often and so passionately in his sermons, but the opportunity of inspecting his gun more closely. The missionary took him hunting, Abena having a remarkable gift for starting marmosets, which Van den Rietter was particularly fond of shooting. He was a young man, very cunning and mistrustful, with a magnificent red beard which was the admiration of Ekoumdoum.

One day, their conversation turned on Mor-Zamba and Van den Rietter confided to the young black that, in his own opinion, the prisoner had been taken to the town of Oyolo.

'What makes you think that?' asked Abena.

'There's a big labour camp at Oyolo; they are building a great military base there because at any moment war will break out in Europe, and it must spread at once to here. It's only a matter of weeks now.'

Abena was often tempted to ask Van den Rietter why he had done nothing to defend Mor-Zamba; but he feared that if he opened the subject he would be unable to restrain some violent action and, as the missionary seemed to him a dangerous and unpredictable animal, he confined himself to Van den Rietter's gun, which he took between his hands and gazed at admiringly, turning it this way and that.

'It's a fine gun, eh? A Winchester 303 carbine, with seven shots. You can kill anything with that, a hippopotamus, even an elephant.'

'And how many men?'

'What a dope!' cried the missionary in his own language, which Abena didn't understand. 'One doesn't use a hunting gun for that.'

'Suppose all the same that you had to use it for killing men, how many could you get with it?'

'What a fool! What a fool! What a fool!'

Van den Rietter could speak these words freely enough when he was dealing with the people of Ekoumdoum; it was enough that they tickled him, surprised or sometimes annoyed him. Abena never got the information he wanted. Most often they parted coldly.

'Are you coming to Mass tomorrow morning?' demanded Van den Rietter of the young black who had seemed to him at first an easy prey for Jesus Christ, doubtless his first conquest in Ekoumdoum, apart from a few old women who had flocked to him at once, and the children whose parents had soon sent them, not to be initiated into his religion, but to learn the alphabet and other secrets of the whites.

'I don't know, I don't think so,' Abena replied.

'Remember, if you don't do something about it, Hell awaits you,' threatened Van den Rietter.

'That couldn't be worse than what I experience now.'

Van den Rietter fell silent then, as if he didn't understand. And perhaps he really didn't? But he'd seen him so often with his friend, his lost brother who, it seemed to Abena sometimes, was calling for his help. This man, who called himself a messenger of the God of goodness and mercy, must have suspected his martyrdom in being separated from Mor-Zamba. Once again, Abena longed to ask him the reason for his indifference to Mor-Zamba's suffering on the evening he was captured.

By tenacity and quick-wittedness Abena gradually got from the missionary the information he needed: this concerned the distances, the routes, the means of life and the manners which existed in the country and city of Oyolo. Finally, he confided his plans to his parents, and his mother demanded a few days to prepare him some provisions, but really to turn him by all means from his plan, by setting before him all sorts of diversions; even including Father Van den Rietter and the friendship which, she insisted, the missionary felt towards him, and which he must exploit for the sake of his future.

'Look, Mother,' replied Abena, 'he only wants small boys around him. Whoever approaches him is immediately put in the position of a servant, one way or another. I'm too old to serve another man. When I've gone, send him Mor-Bile; he's only just been circumcised and at that age one can still learn to serve others.'

In fact, on the eve of his departure, he told Van den Rietter that his young brother, Mor-Bile, would come henceforth to guide him in hunting and generally help him in the ways he had previously demanded of Abena. The missionary asked him nothing about his journey, nor the reasons of it.

So as not to say farewell to the whole city, he faded away one night, slightly embracing his own family and saying to his weeping mother:

'Listen, Mother, a child is not all that important when one has six others, not counting those still to be born.'

'Have you gone mad!' she yelled, unable to stop crying.

Thus it was that in the space of a season, unless we no longer remember the matter exactly, our city lost its two greatest hearts; its soul, one might say. We didn't realize it at once, but this was a wound which would never really close again. For the next twenty years we were to be sapped by all kinds of vexations, like those experienced, perhaps, by the newly-born, thrust suddenly from the warm and palpitating womb which shadows them, crucified by the harsh light of day, deafened by the cacophony of life, shaken by the freezing vibrations of the air.

We had to wait these same twenty years to learn, little by

little, of the Odyssey, worthy of Akomo himself, lived by the two most admirable sons of Ekoumdoum.

Under the pitiless eye of the scarfaced men, Mor-Zamba and his companions of misfortune marched for many long months, their numbers steadily growing as they traversed new cities and countries, or visited new clans. Even the clans which had not got strangers among them were nevertheless required to produce a hostage, and later two or three hostages, as if the demands of the soldiers increased with the length of the expedition, or perhaps with the proximity of their destination? At last the caravan was so long one couldn't see the end of it; then, as if they had filled the measure to overflowing, the scarfaced ones ceased their human levies and forced their prisoners to march faster; so that, after a few days, they entered the immense camp near Oyolo, a camp called Gouverneur Leclerc, named apparently after the white chief who commanded the whole country and lived in Fort-Nègre, the capital. The new arrivals were dispersed over several quarters, each bearing a particular name. Having been sent to the Samba quarter, Mor-Zamba was stranded in a long, low barracks already inhabited by a hundred or so men, the rhythm of whose savage existence must immediately become his.

Woken very early by the whistle, the workers shaved in a trice, all together in a tub which stood in the yard before the entrance of the barracks. A few seconds later, all the Sambas, assembled in this big courtyard, formed ranks and moved off in the direction indicated by a scarface, armed with the eternal musket. When the work was far away, they might be forced to run there, singing all the way. They dug roads all around Oyolo, cleared land with the axe or the machet, or even helped to build houses in the European quarter. But the most dreaded labour was that of building bridges by diverting the course of rivers. Fortunately this was done by rotation, and the same teams never stayed more than a month at a time, or they'd have been condemned to a hideous death.

Sometimes they were set to lighter but more humiliating tasks, like carrying night-soil or clearing refuse from the streets; burying the dead from the hospital, if they had no family to do it; or, occasionally, digging them up for an autopsy or a police enquiry. They were even required to dig pit-latrines for the native quarter, or to clear them when they were blocked up.

When the siren went for midday, the prisoners stopped work to eat cassava, which they dipped in a groundnut soup served by women all dressed in black, who poured two ladles in the bowl of each prisoner before moving off, their iron pots on their heads. Without giving them time to relax, the scarfaces instantly drove them back to work, which continued ceaselessly till six in the evening, when they were driven back to camp, haggard and limping.

On Sundays, they were allowed to leave the camp and stroll in groups, surrounded by the scarfaces, through the streets of the native quarter. With the complicity of their guards, who became a bit more human at the sight of the happy crowds, they could sometimes visit relatives or friends, if they had any in Oyolo, which was rare enough; or enter some squalid bar to spend some of their meagre pay on maize beer, 'Holy Joseph'[1] being still little known there; always under the eye of the scarfaces, who were ready enough to join in the toasts.

Mor-Zamba owed to his extraordinary constitution his escape from pneumonia, malaria and amoebic dysentery, three scourges which decimated the captive workers at the very outset of their stay; they being, like him, from the peaceful and carefree tribes inhabiting the equatorial jungle.

Although he had found lodging easily in the village closest to the camp, though over a kilometre away and within the noise of the town, Abena was dogged by ill-luck all through the week. Having arrived in Oyolo on a Monday, he couldn't hope to find and embrace Mor-Zamba before the following Sunday. He loitered everywhere that he thought his friend might pass; he tried to spy him among the flock of workers, so driven, emaciated, grey, ragged and woebegone. But it was a gamble to guess the work allotted to a particular gang, for then men were seldom sent several times to the same place, and were never told their destination till the morning, just before leaving the camp Gouverneur Leclerc.

[1] The name of this locally-brewed gin in Cameroon is 'le Bienheureux Joseph'.

66

One day towards the end of the week, however, so far as we can now make out, he was suddenly staggered, as if struck by lightning; his heart stopped still, his gaze riveted in the midst of that hastening crowd of labourers, on one man, Mor-Zamba! It was his brother! He called, he ran near enough for Mor-Zamba to see and long to make him some sign, smile at him or return his greeting; but all this was forbidden during the week. Whilst in ranks, the workers were denied any communication with civilians. Mor-Zamba had just infringed a strict order. A Saringala gave him a pair of butt-blows on the head which nearly killed him. The wretched fellow lowered his head and put his hands to the injury, without for a moment slackening his pace, and without a glance of compassion from the other faces amid that torrent of forced labourers. Abena was rooted to the spot with anger and astonishment, just as if he'd been nailed there, and with unwitting tears coursing down his cheeks.

He began to move again, following the procession at a good distance until he reached the site where the men of Sambatown would work all day. It seemed that their job was to replace a wooden footbridge across the river with a slab of concrete resting on cement piers, so that the road could be widened. Their gang was replacing another, which had already diverted the road and the river, and had even begun to dig the trench destined to receive the piers. But, the night before, a torrential rain had burst the frail embankment carrying the diverted river, and the flood was threatening to carry away the temporary footbridge, made only from crudely-squared trunks. The water had filled all the lower part of the area and, in order to work, the men had to flounder constantly amid the boiling waves, which carried tonnes of bright red mud. Many times Abena saw Mor-Zamba forced to swim, or even to plunge right into the water, in order to carry tools or materials; he stayed under for several seconds and emerged more hideous than a spectre, spitting crimson liquid from his jaws. Abena stood there all day long, insensible to hunger or thirst, fascinated by a spectacle which looked to him like a horrible nightmare, so stupefied that he seemed stuck there for life.

On the following day, his heart misgave him at the thought of following Mor-Zamba to this or any other site, for he feared above anything to be witness of some other brutality inflicted on his chosen brother. The son of Ekoumdoum, offspring of a noble clan, almost unrecognizable in his hunger, lean and fearful in his cast-off clothes which were rapidly turning into rags, wandered through the native quarter and finally risked plunging into the European town, a ghost of the proud young man so full of virile assurance that he had been, as it seemed to him, long, long ago. He was seized with panic at the idea of finding himself face to face with an Ekoumdoum man, by some miracle; he distinctly saw the other draw back in horror, open his mouth, roll his eyes and begin yelling with fright.

The only consolation which had soothed him was suddenly withdrawn when on Sunday morning, following another tornado which had shaken the whole city throughout Saturday night, he heard word that the Sambatown workers would not get leave, because the frail roofs of the hospital workers' quarters had been torn off and must at least be patched up that very day. Nevertheless, he stood all morning in front of the barred gateway of the camp Gouverneur Leclerc; at about eleven o'clock he saw a missionary coming out. His black soutane and long knotted cord wound several times around the waist reminded Abena of Father Van den Rietter; there must be some Christians among the workers and the missionary had doubtless been saying Mass for them; or rather, profiting by their misery, perhaps he was trying to draw them to his religion as the sole consolation left them. This was a favourite tactic of the missionaries.

He was an old man with a long white beard, frowning to see above his spectacles; he moved with a rapid, confident and ringing step, but sometimes with an unequal, hurried stride as he tripped on the cobbles of the pathway. Abena began following him at a distance, without really knowing what attracted him to this fantastic personage; then he gradually drew nearer but, as he seemed a harmless booby, the two little choirboys trotting behind the Father, anxious as puppies, paid him no attention. On reaching the mission, the old man disappeared into a long, storeyed house, surrounded by arcaded verandas, while the two boys plunged into a common shed, doubtless their habitual lodging.

Abena was in the fix of a man who has lost his friends and doesn't know how to retrieve them. He was wandering without a goal, and so decided to explore the mission. It was a vast establishment, and he was much astonished that he was able to traverse its lawns and brick pathways, to cross great squares bordered with coconut palms and paved with gravel, without anyone paying the least attention, or making any enquiry about him. Around the church and the school he encountered other strollers who seemed as admiring as himself. His explorations soon led him to the cemetery, an avenue closely packed with mounds, each topped with a wooden cross, and divided by a very wide alley, almost an avenue, which was filled with other strollers. Abena, who was walking abreast of two talkative youths, suddenly took note of their strange conversation:

'That old fool Dietrich!' exclaimed one of them with a guffaw, 'he can run as fast as he likes, he'll never get me. If I go to his school, it's only, as my grandmother says, to extract a bit of learning. She says that if you see a crumb fall, you must quickly pick it up like a sparrow. As for going to gather up the cows' dung in a bucket and carrying it to old Dietrich, as for that, he can just keep running after me.'

'Cow-dung? What an idea!' the other burst out with a chuckle.

'Oh yes! Didn't you know? At first he demanded a school-fee. To begin with, one needed money, and nobody had any, or scarcely anyone. Then he thought up the cow-dung. If any schoolboy is broke, he says to him: "If you want to stay in my school, you must fill up two buckets with dung every week. Otherwise, I can't keep you here." '

'And they want to do it?'

'They want to do it? And how! They examine the roadway amid the hoots of the onlookers; they scour the alleys of the Muslim quarters, where the animals are kept before going to the slaughterhouse, and every time they stumble on a heap of dung, see them stoop down and hop! into the bucket with it!'

'Incredible! But how do they manage it?'

'Oh, it's not too difficult, you know. If I've sworn never to do it myself, it's really because I could never tell anyone about it. Can you imagine it? A fine figure I'd make, eh! Yes, with a piece of corrugated iron or anything else which is flat, strong and flexible, you can work just as with a shovel, even a bit better perhaps.'

Without ceasing his roars of laughter, the first speaker, the more boastful one, continued to brag of studying at the school without either paying fees or humiliating himself by filling a bucket with cow-shit amid the sarcasms of all the witnesses. He had found a much better way, he had; he'd made a pact with his schoolmaster by modestly greasing his palm. And on certain weeks he didn't even pay up, on one excuse or another, always a new one. In any case, now that he was compromised, his teacher wasn't going to give himself away by denouncing his pupil.

By now, Abena had grasped the gist of the situation and saw how he might turn it to his advantage. Dietrich, the old missionary of the white beard and spectacles whom he'd seen this morning leaving the camp and had followed to the mission, was a fanatical vine-grower and was striving to cultivate here the very vines which grew in his native village. For this he needed a particularly active manure; this was how he'd struck on the idea of the cow-dung and of using the poorer students to collect it for him.

From Monday morning onwards he was on the job, equipped with an old bucket; without enduring more than one wounding pleasantry, he had soon filled it to the brim with the precious material. Between the Muslim quarter and the Catholic mission it seemed to him that the stench, which at first had barely troubled him, grew steadily stronger with every step taken and threatened to asphyxiate him altogether. Several times he had to set down the bucket, turn away and hold his nose, to give time for the mounting waves of nausea to subside, and to keep down the grilled groundnuts which he'd eaten one by one that morning, to give himself the illusion of a long repast. Fortunately, as the week wore on, he perceived that he was gradually getting used to the fetid odour; his astonishment at this left him perplexed, like many other discoveries made at this stage of his adventures, which were to mark him so profoundly that he came to accommodate himself to experiences so disagreeable that the very thought of them had made him tremble at first.

When he arrived at the mission, he posted himself at the foot of a coconut palm and waited till he could see the old whitebeard; sure enough, he came out of his office at about half past ten and went towards the church, always with the same assured but hurried and uneven step. Perhaps he was going to make his devotions, or to confess one of the faithful. Without hesitation, the son of Ekoumdoum approached and greeted him.

'Father, Father,' he cried, 'see what I have brought you.'

At first, the old man seemed dumbfounded, scrutinizing for a long while this big boy who had far outgrown his own students, but fascinated by the bucket of manure, at which he kept casting concupiscent glances. Then he suddenly burst out at Abena, like a man relieving an irritation too long suppressed:

'Why did you do that? Who are you? What's your name? What do you want here?'

Abena explained that the scarfaced soldiers, those who were called Saringalas, had raided his country, Ekoumdoum, and had captured his brother for forced labour at Oyolo, and that he was shut up in the camp from which the young man had seen the missionary coming one morning.

'I can't do anything for him,' Father Dietrich protested. 'No, I'm afraid I can't intervene; there's nothing I can do. We must bear with patience the trials which God has sent us, my son. Wait till your brother has finished his sentence, that's all I can tell you.'

The old man was about to go away when Abena, on the verge of despair, almost grabbed him by the sleeve, surprised at himself for such audacity. He explained to him with the volubility of a man who ventures his all, that having seen him the day before when he came from the camp where he had presumably just said Mass, he had thought of striking a bargain with him.

'Two little boys accompanied you yesterday. Why don't I come with you as well, even if I'm no longer a child? You can

71

surely find something for me to do there? In that way, my presence in the camp will be explained. I can talk for a moment to my brother, touch him, perhaps embrace him. If you accept my offer, I'll fetch every morning from now to Sunday a bucket of manure like this one.'

In the face of such a tempting bargain, Father Dietrich showed only a flicker of hesitation:

'You won't help your brother to escape? Promise me? You won't try anything against the authorities?'

'It's only so as to embrace my brother, I assure you.'

'All right, it's agreed; bring me two buckets of cow-dung every day, as you've just promised. And on Sunday you shall come with me to the camp Gouverneur Leclerc.'

The ease and amplitude of his victory rejoiced Abena, and lent new truth to the adage current in Ekoumdoum: 'Provided you don't go to him with empty hands, the white man will always give you satisfaction. With those people,' they would say, 'you must always bring something to exchange. It's not like among ourselves, where relationship is an open sesame in all circumstances. Common blood, what rubbish! Those people will rule over us for a long time yet. Giving, giving, there's real life for you, there's wisdom! What mountain can one not remove with such a maxim!'

In a truly amazing fashion, Abena forgot the memory of the rest of that week: the hunger, the loneliness, the humiliation of his foul and lowly task, the exhaustion at the end of the day, were all erased by his excited expectation of finding Mor-Zamba again.

As he had already been told, the camp was like a secret city on the edge of Oyolo, an impressive agglomeration which old Dietrich and his unusual escort traversed in depth, under the eyes of inhabitants mostly glued to their doorsteps, to whom the rare spectacle of these exotic visitors gave occasion for laconic but cheerful comments, which Father Dietrich certainly hadn't enough finesse in the local language to understand.

The workers manifested a gaiety, a spirit and a *joie de vivre* that amazed Abena, who had seized from their daily appearance the painful memory of brutally tyrannized animals. Now there was no trace of that haggard and frightened haste which marked them at the work-sites, where they laboured as if hallucinated; nothing of that headlong swarming of their long naked limbs along the streets of Oyolo. Real townsmen, they had donned clothes which looked dazzling to Abena, who asked himself, from their manner of scrutinizing him, if they were not amused at his outlandish village garb.

With all the abnegation of a martyr to the only real and true fraternity, the son of Ekoumdoum was just beginning to taste the bitterness of his shabby state when he suddenly heard his name distinctly called out. He turned and saw Mor-Zamba's face, whose ecstatic expression alarmed him as he was ignorant of the manners of the place. Within the camp, hedged in by barbed wire and bristling with watchtowers, the men had complete freedom of movement, especially in daylight; their guards having no fear either of escapes, which had never taken place, or of mutinies, still inconceivable to prisoners who were reduced to begging dogs at the mere sight of a musket. Abena therefore continued his way amid cries, appeals, and perhaps hoots of merriment, walking in Father Dietrich's footsteps with the dignified, upright and imperturbable gait of the pious assistant to a saintly man. He hoped secretly that Mor-Zamba, if misery had not already thrown him at the feet of the white man's god, would still follow him to the chapel, and that once there they would find the chance to exchange a few words during Mass.

But Mor-Zamba leapt upon him, seized him by the shoulders and, with his greater strength, spun him round:

'You're mad,' he yelled joyfully, 'why don't you stop? Why don't you answer me?'

Abena tried to break free, rolling his eyes and throwing terrified glances around him, astonished at not instantly seeing a scarface brandishing a musket-butt like a cudgel.

'Poor fellow!' he whispered to Mor-Zamba, 'you're going to get yourself knocked down again on my account. Better follow me to the chapel and make as if you don't know me.'

Before he could finish, Mor-Zamba burst out laughing, mouth hanging open and head flung back.

'Is that what you're afraid of?' he managed to say, when he'd calmed down a bit. 'You know, I really was afraid that you'd gone mad, seeing you behind this white-bearded old chap, between those two weasel-faced boys. Nothing to fear here, comrade; inside the camp they leave us in peace, the moment we are by ourselves.'

Although he understood very little of the language, Father Dietrich had finally guessed that his strange companion had found his long-lost brother. He had already reached the chapel and now retraced his steps to Abena:

'Now that you are here in the camp, you have no more need of me today. If you need my help again, you will be welcome at the mission.'

As soon as he'd gone off again, Mor-Zamba inundated his friend with a flood of speech which affected him like a strong wine, whose injection into the bloodstream makes us dizzy.

'Are you really a friend of this old man? You, old chap, I don't know you after all. How did you manage it? Tell me everything. I bet you had to hide from your mother that you were leaving! Otherwise you wouldn't be here. Where are you sleeping, brother? Do you get enough to eat? With whom do you spend your days?...'

Suddenly seeing the tears on Abena's cheeks, Mor-Zamba became aware that he was playing the sad role of a dying man who consoles a healthy one.

'You know,' he said, becoming grave again and leading his friend into a barracks full of men, 'you know, what happened to me, after all, was nothing but a bad moment which will pass. It seems we shall be liberated as soon as the war's over.'

'Perhaps never, then,' teased Abena. 'You know there's always a war among the whites. So, you'll be liberated at the end of which war?'

Exhausted by two weeks of emotion which had brought him to the verge of a breakdown, dulled as if by a festival coming after too long an anxious waiting, the son of Ekoumdoum sank down on the bench which Mor-Zamba showed him, while the latter addressed the crowd which surrounded him:

'This is my brother, yes, my young brother. You wouldn't believe how far he's come to rejoin me, if I told you. Yes, yes, he's my true brother.'

Abena listened as if in a dream and gazed at the unusual activities going on around him. Mor-Zamba was now wearing a sort of white robe and was wielding a bright steel instrument with two arms, like a fine pair of scissors. He was busy above a long, low and hollow table, covered with a thin metal sheet, whilst near-by stood another table, much higher and narrower, filled with bottles of many different heights.

Amid the uproar, each one came up in his turn to Mor-Zamba; sometimes placing his exposed leg on the table so that the man in white could dress his wound with water and a red or blue liquid, applied with a little piece of cotton at the end of the scissors; sometimes, after a brief conversation, swallowing two or three white tablets which Mor-Zamba took from a bottle; sometimes lowering his trousers and turning his backside to Mor-Zamba who, as though he'd been doing it all his life, would confidently insert a needle and empty the syringe with a long, slow pressure of his finger.

To thank him for his care, the sick would greet him with spasmodic hugs, with swoonings worthy of the act of love, or, more frequently, with hammerings on the back accompanied by hoots of laughter. Abena couldn't trust the evidence of his eyes. Mor-Zamba, plunged into this unmerited hell, was exactly the same Mor-Zamba as he'd known in Ekoumdoum, consoling others, caring for their needs, overflowing with advice, always ready to offer service or to rush to the aid of the unfortunate and the weak. He had come to lament the sad fate of a slave, but what he found was a lion, barely hampered by his chains.

For the rest of the day, whilst showing him around the whole camp, Mor-Zamba described their life, without anger or indignation, as a condition quite acceptable and normal. He was acting as a kindly, if untrained nurse to his companions. At first, a real nurse had come every Sunday to take care of the worst sufferers; then they had decided that Mor-Zamba, who was assisting him, might just as well take on the job in the evenings after work, or all day long on Sundays. Of course, his work was not paid, at least not officially. The high authorities, those one never saw in the camp, apparently did not wish that families should rediscover their sons; but if by chance they did, they were allowed to pay them a visit, but they could let them know that they would await them somewhere in Oyolo, and that on Sunday they must direct the steps of their group that way, even if they had to bribe the Saringala guards. For these scarfaced men were extremely corrupt; so much so that they could be tempted with a very small sum. They would disguise a father or a brother as a worker making some repair to a barracks in the camp, so that he could talk with the prisoner for a few minutes. It was enough to have some official business there, to be authorized to come and go as one wished, all day long. Abena, for example, was from now on always Father Dietrich's man; if, by any ill-chance, someone should try to check him, he had only to say that he was assistant to old Dietrich and everything would be settled.

'And in spite of that, no escapes?'

'Never, old chap. No one ever thinks of that here. In the first place, it's better not to incur the enmity of the scarfaces; nothing can protect you from their revenge. We have no rights to claim, no regulations to quote. Once, they spent an entire evening roughing up some poor bugger. I don't even know what they had against him. Perhaps it was just a drunken caprice. Next day, the poor fellow couldn't get up. The hospital was alerted but, as usual in urgent cases, they didn't send two men with a stretcher till afternoon. No doubt he was already dead before he left the camp.'

'And on hearing that he was dead, you did nothing? You said nothing?'

Mor-Zamba made no response and, after a silence, said:

'Now that you've seen me and spoken to me, you'll go back to Ekoumdoum, not so? Don't trouble about me. You can't stay here, you'll die of hunger. And then there's the loneliness. You know, life in a town is a horrible affair. You want to prove your affection to me, eh? All right, then, I beg you, go back to Ekoumdoum.'

'No question of that!' Abena cut in, 'I'll stay in these parts until your release.'

'Don't be so obstinate; perhaps I'll never get out, as you just said yourself. What good will it do you to wither away standing at the gate of the camp, watching me come out at dawn and return at dusk, knocked-up and all covered with mud, perhaps for another dozen years or so?'

'There must be something I can do here.'

'Nothing. I've thought of everything since I've been here. I've listened to the conversations around me. I've watched everyone. Well, there's nothing to be done about it. Go back to Ekoumdoum.'

'Never!'

He left the camp at nightfall, carrying a little of Mor-Zamba's money, whose tiny salary was all saved up. From the following morning, he returned to the task which had now become a habit; he collected two buckets of cow-dung during the day and carried them to Father Dietrich at the Catholic mission.

'You're a very brave lad,' the old man told him. 'I'm afraid that difficulties may overwhelm you, so far from your country, while you think only of consoling your brother by the comfort of your presence. So come and live at the mission. I'll feed you, and you'll at least be sure of passing every night under a roof. But I can't pay you anything, having to struggle enough as it is. A bucket of manure a day will do, my son.'

So Abena came to sleep on a straw bed, concealed in the fine orchard of the mission, right off near the presbytery common-room where lived the choirboys, the old man's servants, always dressed up to the nines and seeming to look down their noses at the newcomer.

Abena then thought of speaking to Father Dietrich, which pleased the latter enormously. He tried many times to get a more exact idea of the location of Abena's country, but was left baffled by the imprecision of the young man's replies. Dietrich took him in front of a map, but Abena had never seen one before. He stood gazing at the big coloured sheet, mouth open, eyes starting and arms hanging loose. Finally, by means of questions about Abena's itinerary in coming to Oyolo, the tribes he'd encountered, the rivers he'd crossed, the administrative stations he'd passed by, the old man managed to situate Ekoumdoum in the extreme south-east corner of the colony. To discover the position of his country with regard to the rest of the colony, and even in some degree to the rest of the world – for the old man showed him how it was bordered, not far from

Ekoumdoum, by British territory; by Spanish right on the opposite side, and by French colonies at the top and down both flanks – really stirred up his imagination.

'Well I never!' exclaimed the good old man, 'so that's your country. And that's where Van den Rietter is now? So far away? What an amazing man! Does Van den Rietter get on with your people there?'

'He's had a house built outside our city.'

'That's the first element for his future mission. Does he go often to see the people in their homes, talk to them, live amongst them?'

'No, he stays in his house, with his servants; he doesn't come out except to visit the chief.'

'What a marvellous boy!' Dietrich resumed, with rather more hesitation in pronouncing this luminous truth. 'What a splendid apostle, all the same!'

Thus was established a sort of alliance between the old man of the long white beard and the proud son of Ekoumdoum, until then a vagabond exposed to the buffets of fortune. He became a handyman for Father Dietrich, though his main task remained, by tacit agreement, the collection of cow-dung, in which his expertise, zeal and dispatch acted as a model for the needy students and helped them to overcome their squeamishness. Every Sunday, he followed the missionary into the camp, where he passed the day in company with Mor-Zamba, the voluntary nurse. This was one of those sops which life offers sometimes to wanderers, in compensation, one might think, for their deprivation of all normal sentiments; the happy illusion of a short rest in their tormented journey.

Soon enough two events occurred, doubtless in correlation with one another, as Mor-Zamba surmised. Abena disappeared and, at the same time, the good old man Dietrich was replaced at the camp Gouverneur Leclerc by another priest; much younger, this one; with an almost adolescent air, loud speech, a confident and martial stride and a square black beard. His style immediately displeased the converted prisoners, who deserted the Mass in a body on his first appearance; then gradually ceased to go there at all. This was the strange circumstance which lay at the root of the affair. In the interval between the

Mass and the sermon, during which old Dietrich had always busied himself in arranging his ornaments, his candlestick and the rest of his accessories in a small box, young Father Desmaisons, his replacement, had the habit of smoking, taking long drags at his cigarette with an avidity which hollowed his cheeks, and leaving the young choirboys to look after his things. On that first day, he plunged his arms up to the elbows in the deep pockets of his soutane, couldn't fish anything out, gaped at first with surprise, then turned suddenly indignant, fuming and red with rage, turning round and round in circles. Rather than tell himself that he had doubtless forgotten his cigarettes at the mission, the obligation of fasting before the Mass having hitherto prevented him from indulging his vice, and hence from thinking of his tobacco, he conceived the idiotic idea that he'd been robbed, and tried right away to frisk all the witnesses of the scene which, taking place outside the chapel, soon drew a crowd of non-Christians who were both profoundly and justifiably astounded at this humiliation. Father Desmaisons' application, his determination and manifest conviction, made this search an interminable ordeal for dozens of poor buggers, unfolding itself right in the heart of the camp. Needless to say, his fury was in vain. Father Desmaisons then went cursing out of the camp, without delivering his sermon, while his bewildered acolytes rushed after him.

It became clear that Desmaisons did virtually everything in the opposite manner to the good old Dietrich, and people said that he'd been in the war and was soon returning to the front. Next Sunday he came back, but on a motor-cycle this time, the little choirboys having preceded him on foot. He had become a sort of curiosity in the prisoners' eyes and, like an insufficiently tamed beast, he drew a crowd of idlers who always kept at a good distance, as if they feared being mauled or charged. It was only on the third Sunday after the searching incident that Mor-Zamba, who had hitherto been ranged among the thin ranks of the converted to hear the Mass, took his courage in both hands and tackled the young missionary as he left the ceremony, to ask news of the one he called brother. As usual, the young missionary replied distractedly, as if to someone in the wings, saying he was far too busy to bother himself about what had happened to the man in question. Couldn't he be ill and in bed, perhaps? The following Sunday, Desmaisons was struck both by the systematic boycott of which his Mass was now the object, and by Mor-Zamba's insistence and pathetic air of a man gripped by profound moral suffering; he agreed to speak to Dietrich, who was better qualified than a newcomer like himself to say what had become of Abena. But on the ensuing Sunday he confessed with a resigned air that he'd forgotten to ask the old missionary about his vanished employee. He admitted it was strange that an exemplary worker like Abena should suddenly take to his heels. The fifth Sunday after Mor-Zamba's original request, in his desire to keep at least an illusory connection with the camp, he went straight up to Mor-Zamba and spoke to him in an almost friendly way; he had spoken to Father Dietrich, but the old man himself knew nothing about Abena's disappearance, which was now almost two months old.

It was not until some months before the end of the war, just after the closure of the camp Gourerneur Leclerc and the liberation of its denizens, that Mor-Zamba finally learnt the fate of his friend, and the cruelty of a destiny which had once again robbed him of the only comfort he had known in so long a time. Even this knowledge did not come all at once, as if Providence, with rare compassion, would only let him enter step by step, into the night of his deprivation.

At the Catholic mission, where old Father Dietrich was said to be dying, the African employees, as quick with rumours as the people always are, set him on the way; his brother had joined the army in 1941 and God only knew to what distant land he'd been sent to fight; but the war was drawing to an end and the combatants would soon return to their homes, if they'd survived. His brother probably had survived; for hadn't the Germans often refused to fight against black regiments, objecting to the disloyalty of involving Africans in the quarrels of whites, with which they had nothing to do? At least, this was what the people of Oyolo said, and they were always so well informed about everything.

So he should go and enquire, they urged, in a suburb of Oyolo called Toussaint-Louverture, where he might perhaps meet Abena's fiancée and so get a message from his brother, who certainly wouldn't have failed to tell him of his departure unless prevented by some military marching order.

Toussaint-Louverture, the principal African quarter of Oyolo, had only received this name, in a spirit of derision, with the arrival of the first wounded black survivors from the desert battles, mainly from Kufra and Bir-Hakeim. The colonial administration suspected them of exerting a certain moral influence on their compatriots by repeating distorted and embittered tales about their life alongside the white troops, often with deliberate exaggeration, and so saw in them the revolutionary mob of some future black terror.

At night in Toussaint-Louverture the rats drew blood from the foot-soles of the sleeping inhabitants. On rainy days, one sank up to the ankles in the red mud, nicknamed *poto-poto*, which filled the streets of the town. Here, the people had no need to force their natural generosity in order to welcome newcomers. Thus Mor-Zamba found lodging in a shanty filled with young bachelors, all unemployed except for one who worked for a family in the European quarter, and who came and went so late and early that he was scarcely ever seen, although his companions depended on him for their meagre subsistence. Like a second pillar in a community tottering under the weight of misery, Mor-Zamba brought the cement of his savings, which exceeded the hopes of their brightest days; a dependable manna which he doled out with a prudence, a firmness, and even a natural avarice which instilled such respect and admiration in the little band that, without having wished it, and as so often happened to him later, he quickly found himself unanimously chosen as leader.

After a stagnation corresponding with the length of the war, the town was beginning to pick up, and the visible acceleration of its economic life bred insensate hopes among the blacks. It was said that the whites, discouraged at seeing their own continent perpetually at war, were going to arrive en *masse* and flood the country with capital; that everyone could flatter himself with a future of work and felicity.

Apart from two or three little riots in a few weeks and the distribution of leaflets written, so the administration thought, by the ex-servicemen and the wounded of the first units recruited by Leclerc, but in reality by the Frères Africains, the general exaltation of Toussaint-Louverture found an additional spice in the real high life, the inexplicable relaxing of restraints, the intense feeling of liberty which then prevailed. Here at Ekoumdoum, we heard from everyone the same accounts of this marvellous epoch, now so distant; from visitors who stayed, on each occasion, no more than a few days or even a few hours in our city; as well as from Mor-Zamba himself since. As with all other towns in the colony, Oyolo really meant a trim European city, with tarred roads, rigorously separated from the African suburbs that surrounded it, of which the most important, attracting all the wanderers, the good-for-nothings, the scroungers and the forsaken, was Toussaint-Louverture, formerly called 'the City of Foreigners'; the administration hoped thereby to isolate this always tumultuous city from the other suburbs, which were no more than big villages almost exclusively populated by the clans of the local tribes.

The streets never emptied in the evening, either in good or bad weather. As soon as night fell, the people guided themselves through the abrupt darkness by hurricane-lamps, which hung from their fists like big will-o'-the-wisps. It wasn't like today, if we are to believe Mor-Kinda, who has recently gone to live incognito in Oyolo; in those days all the Africans suddenly felt themselves to be brothers and one saw them greet each other in the street, marching in compact groups, arm-in-arm and often singing; one could go into a little bar pompously lighted with a pressure-lamp, high and shining in its cylindrical glass with the big, dazzling mantle within; a plate of fish and a glass of beer didn't then cost a fortune, were not then reserved as the privilege of members of the sole political party, as the Juggler tells us they have since become. Or sometimes, at a crossroads, one could encircle a seller of meat grilled over the fire and then rolled in powdered pepper. In exchange for a small coin, one would seize a skewer; one pulled at the beef by squeezing the slender stick of bamboo between the incisors and puckering the lips, eyes closed a moment to exclude the fumes of pepper; one tore off a lump and chewed it while clicking the tongue and the fingers of one hand, so much did the pepper inflame the mouth and, soon after, the whole body.

On certain days in the fine season, between November and February, when at nightfall the fresh evening air gradually encroached upon the last pockets of the day's fierce conflagration, it seemed as if the whole quarter had poured into the street. As is inevitable in such situations, while the crowd pressed together, consolidated, flowed or swirled like the waters of an eddy, it sometimes happened that an ill-chosen word or an unsettled account over a girl would set one group to challenge another, perhaps even to the point of fisticuffs. But, as is the rule among brothers, such affrays never led to anything. As soon as the antagonists were called by the spectators to a reconciliation, they would gather around a glass in the nearest bar and profit by the chance to buy round after round for the fortunate witnesses of the tussle. Rows like this were then ordinary and inoffensive events, never lending themselves to denunciation by some envious or bribed sycophant, resulting in deportation, forced labour, or even in public execution, as happens nowadays under the reign of Massa Bouza.[1]

For perhaps two years, Africans could come and go quite freely, even in the European town; you'd have said that at the end of the war the world had been turned upside down by some strange magician; that for the first time in ages the high-ups had understood that the blacks, being here in their own country, could behave as they thought fit.

The unionists played no small part in modelling the features of Toussaint-Louverture, and in giving it that reputation which filled the European town with blind fear, and its press with sarcasms. They were called the 'Frères Africains' or 'Ruben's men' – Ruben being then only the head of all the black trade unions in the country. They had their own building here, a

[1] Pidgin for *Maître le Biture* (Master Boozer).

modest shed whose facade bore a notice reading 'Labour Centre', open from morning till evening, and sometimes into the night. Here one might see serious employees reading through a dossier, or examining the different papers in it, or flicking feverishly through some treaty or code concerning the labour laws. These men were friendly and approachable, unlike those working for the administration; always trying to render service to their fellows, and thus earning their nickname the 'Freres Africains'. Whoever was in dispute with his boss (and all bosses were white in those days, or the vast majority of them) could go into the Labour Centre assured of a friendly welcome and encouraging advice, or, if need be, vigorous support and even the taking over of his case.

During these two years of euphoria, Mor-Zamba remembers that Ruben himself made about three appearances, and that each of them led to a great celebration in the quarter, despite the fact that his arrival was never announced in advance and that most people didn't know where he was coming from or where he went after the demonstration, held in front of the Labour Centre, to which the whole population was invited, whether unionists or not. Ruben had no need to make long speeches in order to draw frantic applause. He was a tallish, or rather thinnish, man with a head disproportionately large; the expression of his eyes and his whole face being already sad, as if he were tormented by the presentiments of a father undermined inexorably by a hidden malady, who despaired of his children who must soon be abandoned to the whims of destiny.

According to Mor-Zamba, the people of Toussaint-Louverture must have been at least dimly conscious of this sort of premonition for, as soon as the closest of his entourage had hoisted him onto the platform and his lips started to move, even the farthest ranks of the crowd began to applaud him, without hearing a word he said; and their cries were, paradoxically, full of comfort and encouragement for the man who had come to advise them to resist the return of oppression and all forms of constraint. The people really adored him like a god, a sort of black Messiah, even those whose nature or egoism disinclined them from that sort of thing. Perhaps the magician who turned the colony upside down after the war was none

84

other than Ruben. People felt like children hatched by the protective gaze of their father, a fine warrior stooped over their cradle; their prattle was the cruel curses addressed to their masters; their self-confidence changed gradually to arrogance; no longer able to wriggle in the cradle, they began to swell their chests.

With the aid of his little group, at home in the quarter as a fish in the river, Mor-Zamba was not long in finding the girl referred to as Abena's fiancée. She lived on the fringe of Toussaint-Louverture, in a kind of hamlet which had remained an island of the local clans. Along with her elder brother, himself almost a child still, the young fiancée had also been seeking Mor-Zamba; she had recognized him only a few days after his exit from the camp, by his tall stature and other details furnished by Abena; but for a time she contented herself with observing him at a distance, not daring to approach him till she was certain of his identity. She and her brother had just settled on a plan for meeting Mor-Zamba when the latter entered their hut, identical with all the others in Toussaint-Louverture, and far different from the spacious houses built in Ekoumdoum, with its abundance of materials from the near-by forest, so easily obtained with a little courage and ability. A graceful and slender girl, very poorly clad, with a dreamy look but an ironic, almost sarcastic smile, Jeanne seemed already to be a real woman inside, carrying like an imaginative pregnancy, though without bitterness, the chagrin of a man's fallacious promises. In the midst of her silent but welcoming family, she recounted some of Abena's adventures to his brother; as for the rest, which she didn't know, it was described in a letter which she soon went to fetch from an adjoining room; a sheet of paper folded in sixteen, crumpled like a banknote which has yellowed from lying too long hidden in the crack of a doorpost. When Mor-Zamba admitted his inability, she asked her brother to read the letter, crouching on the floor of beaten earth beside an oil-lamp, turning the page towards the smoky flame.

In any event, it seemed that the stupid routine and uselessness of his existence had soon begun to weigh on Abena. After the arrival of Father Desmaisons, sent to supplant Father Dietrich, who was considered too old now to face up to his duties, the proud son of Ekoumdoum had soon divined that the passion and heedlessness of his new master were more those of a fanatic than a servant of God. Once again on his guard, anguished by his precarious position and his inability to do anything effective to soften Mor-Zamba's martyrdom, he began looking for a radical way of escaping this situation. He had struck up a friendship with a young schoolmaster at the mission who taught him to read; a sort of instinct guided him towards fierce application, coupled with infinite modesty, in his efforts to learn; he made astounding progress, without ever suspecting it himself.

His new friend, the young master, was a man like himself, restless and impatient before the ugliness and absurdities of life, waiting for the unexpected and ready for adventure. Now, suddenly, the small garrison of Oyolo was swollen by many new units mingling black and white troops, whom the inhabitants of the town, in fright and admiration, watched every day marching in disciplined ranks to the parade ground or the firing range. First girls were demanded for the service of the newcomers, then young boys. The schoolmaster informed Abena of this; they discussed it dreamingly, suspecting that the recruitment must continue, and would soon change its character. That is exactly what happened; they began now to ask for young men able to read and write. The two friends went to volunteer and were accepted after a brief examination. It only needed a few weeks' instruction to win for them the certificate for drivers of military vehicles, after which they were soon sent into action.

'Where's that? What action?' asked Mor-Zamba with a start.

'In Europe, for some of them,' replied Jeanne, the little fiancée, in a gentle voice; 'in the desert, for the best instructed. For others again, the desert first, then Europe.'

Throughout his classes at the Oyolo barracks, where the quarters were located, Abena went back every night to the mission to sleep. Dietrich, who was now very old and almost at his last gasp, no longer controlled the activities of the young man, in whom he nevertheless had complete confidence; nor did Desmaisons who, not yet having a firm grip of things at the mission, was at present uninterested in most of the employees;

86

so that neither of them noticed anything. On the other hand, Abena didn't dare to disclose his project or the reasons for it to Mor-Zamba, who would be certain to think it a madcap scheme. So it was that the departure of Ekoumdoum's child came like a mysterious disappearance.

'...However,' Abena concluded his letter, evidently addressing Mor-Zamba, 'however, even if not with the gun which I'm certain to bring back from the war, if I survive, I'm sure that I shall have the power to wrest you from those butchers at the prison-camp Gouverneur Leclerc. I'm convinced that my name alone will then be enough to terrify our enemies at Oyolo and Ekoumdoum. I'm convinced that the end of the war will bring changes of which we don't dream at present. Perhaps you are right to consider me slightly "touched". However, if I am correct.... Imagine for a moment what will then be the future of Ekoumdoum, of our Ekoumdoum, for my little finger tells me that we shall return to Ekoumdoum one day, not beaten and bowed, but triumphant; that's to say, as liberators of our people from a subtle, endemic terror which dooms them to abasement.'

But suddenly, in that Toussaint-Louverture so long ignored – only in appearance, no doubt – as if they had at last decided to take matters in hand and end a fête which had already, by their consent, lasted too long, the authorities of Oyolo installed a commissariat of police, adjoined by a prison to which they soon began dispatching very young people, sometimes real children, for the slightest offence, and often for no more than shouting 'Long live Ruben'. The Labour Centre was closed and its employees pitilessly dispersed, so that they could have no chance to establish a union headquarters anywhere else. Then exasperation, despair and dreams of vengeance began to torment the youngest inhabitants of Toussaint-Louverture. There were occasional little skirmishes, though of doubtful character, in the first shadows of the falling night, at the corner of one lane or another.

When the TLFC (Toussaint-Louverture Football Club) was thought by everyone to have a serious chance of carrying off the championship for the colony, the people of the quarter went in force to every match played at home, to cheer on their team; but

87

this was also, for the youngest, every time an occasion for settling scores with the forces of order: whether white gendarmes, African gendarme auxiliaries or Saringala reservists. These incidents bred panic, not only in the stadium, but also in the European quarter in the midst of which it lay, raising ever higher the tone of the local colonial press, two pages twice a month, which unfortunately found no reply in Toussaint-Louverture, now too poor, too worn out and, with the depression of the local union leaders, too disorganized, to give a fitting reply to its powerful neighbour.

However, hostilities continued on the sly and one Sunday, on the fringe of a football match, a large group of Toussaint-Louverture's youth, in the midst of which Mor-Zamba could be seen with his faithful little band, accosted a patrol of scarfaced Saringalas led by a white sergeant, who fled at the first signs of trouble. These Saringala reserves fought back with a mad courage which only a rekindled hatred of Toussaint-Louverture could inspire. Borne down by sheer numbers, they were wounded in many places; one of them was unable to recover from a particularly well-aimed stab.

All Toussaint-Louverture braced itself for reprisals, as swift as they would be violent; the police displayed a crafty indifference, and even a certain superficial friendliness; the young men of the quarter were foolish enough to relax their vigilance, imagining naïvely, and in their ignorance of the retaliatory spring which all police forces possess, that the affair was undoubtedly forgotten. It was just then that the counter-attack was openly launched; in two days a mass of very significant arrests were made; the youth of the quarter could no longer doubt that a great closely-woven net had been thrown over them and was perilously tightening. They made a pact; from now on they kept always together, side by side, determined to resist in a united body or meet death that very day. This strategy deserved the support of another, the ability to scent traps afar off and to avoid them. But no such thing. The rumour had spread that the police were actively seeking a certain Manengoumba, one of the most popular young men of the quarter, and that they'd put him in handcuffs the moment they saw him. At first, Manengoumba went to ground somewhere in the quarter, which was the sensible thing to do. Then one Sunday, throwing off precaution, he was determined at any price to attend a match at the town stadium; he went surrounded by a veritable ocean of young men, equally determined not to let the police arrest him, if they should dare to attempt it. They dared. Not on the way there, but on the way back through the European quarter, where the procession was cornered in hostile territory and had no hope of finding refuge, risking rather to be hunted and probably shot down like a bunch of rabbits, and where it was cut off from its natural realm by a barricade manned by a mixture of white gendarmes, African auxiliaries and Saringala reservists.

'Let's go forward en masse,' cried the young men to one another, 'don't break ranks!'

They advanced en masse, without breaking their ranks. Which is exactly what the police wanted, having put in position several light tanks, a battery of six heavy and one light machine-guns, not counting the individual weapons carried by each man; muskets or light automatics. Having little knowledge of French, and even less of the esoteric language of war, the young men didn't hear the orders and leapt through the first barrier, then the second; at the third it seemed, at least according to those who survived and could tell of it afterwards, as if amid the roar of an infernal thunderstorm, a thousand bolts fell upon them all at once. For more than a hundred lads who had scarcely yet tasted the sweet things of life, the stony road was the first bed of their fiery rest, before the deeper repose, the definitive quiet of a common grave, quickly sprinkled with lime, and burning hotter than a mother's breast.

It was certainly an unequal combat. Mor-Zamba understood then that he had a mission, to await Abena's return, for which he must keep himself alive and at liberty. Alive he certainly was, only God knew how fully. As for his liberty, it wasn't difficult to preserve it. After the good lesson they had just given to Toussaint-Louverture and which, lingering on, must deliver the fruits of wisdom for many more years, the forces of order and the two-sheet newspaper of Oyolo's European quarter forgot the wretched man whose death had been the origin of this paroxism, as well as the poor buggers, who, in the chain of consequence, might be his real assassins. Looking back on it clearly, was it really anything more than a blackman's palaver?

A bit of a rebel despite himself, Mor-Zamba could then easily quit Toussaint-Louverture and, after wandering for several months, a prey to the stupor bred by the nightmare of his friends' massacre, he arrived at Fort-Nègre, scarcely knowing how.

Fort-Nègre, capital of the colony; Fort-Nègre, great port with an inexhaustible reputation for hospitality; Fort-Nègre, metropolis with suburbs like tentacles, would be the vast jungle in which the little ant who thought himself trapped would perhaps find his safety by losing himself.

Second Part

FUGITIVE AND TORMENTED

Everything in Fort-Nègre resembled Oyolo; but at the same time everything made them different.

Fascinated by the extent of the capital, the length and breadth of the avenues, even in the African sections, the vitality, the glitter and the pomp of the white city-centre, the fearless tumult of the many-coloured crowd, the newcomer felt he was greeting a magnificent giant, leaving behind a dwarf swarming with lice.

However, just as at Oyolo, the white citadel of Fort-Nègre was besieged by a rampart of black suburbs; that to the east, a huge one called Kola-Kola, seeming to menace it, standing on tiptoe to size it up and boldly confronting it. In reality Kola-Kola, like Oyolo, played the tragic role of a naked vagabond pushed by the irony of destiny to jostle with a nabob, perpetually searching in anguish for a means to save his face. When the depths of his eyes implored, when his dreams stretched forth a hand, when his lips whispered of sympathy, his great height was an involuntary affront; the dazzle of his youth was an intolerable provocation, every one of his natural advantages betrayed him. If he was transpierced by a look of disdain, a stinging and blazing shaft, his hands fell to his sides in confusion, despite himself.

Like Toussaint-Louverture, Kola-Kola had long ago received its share of even crueller lessons. Several times put to rout, the African town had always recovered itself in time. Now more mature, more seasoned, more self-assured in its moment of welcoming Mor-Zamba, the oldest black city of the colony, admired by all its sisters, began step by step to master its independent destiny, whereas Oyolo's similar attempt had drowned in a bath of blood. Already Kola-Kola had its own code, laws unknown to the authorities in Fort-Nègre, opposed by the colonial forces, but current nevertheless. Kola-Kola was now trying to develop its own administration, and even to display an embryonic public life. Fort-Nègre had a governor

93

whose palace dominated the estuary; Kola-Kola had its prophet.

What curse, then, had always denied to the humble the felicity of overtaking the powerful? Like Toussaint-Louverture, Kola-Kola every morning dispatched thousands of its best children into Fort-Nègre to beg for the meanest livelihood. In exchange, and against all equity, Fort-Nègre offered the yoke; forced by necessity, the youth of Kola-Kola pretended to bow its head in the day-time; back in its own quarter at nightfall, once in contact with its mother-earth, it quickly proclaimed once more its inalienable liberty. Perpetual struggle, fool's market constantly reopened, constantly endured, constantly denounced on its own part, never finally consecrated, just like the one between Toussaint-Louverture and Oyolo, but a ladder so much the more fabulous!

The fugitive soon felt at home in Kola-Kola. The recommendation of Jeanne's family had won him adoption, as soon as he arrived, by some fine people related to the young fiancée, living in a long, low house of mud, similar to thousands of miserable structures thrown down at random, like the tents of a marching horde. All the same, the house of the Lobilas had an originality which might pass unobserved at first: little by little, over many months, perhaps years, a persevering and able hand had, at rare moments of leisure and as much to reinforce and protect it as to embellish or beautify it, covered its walls with cement, patch by patch.

This padded but very modest aspect echoed to perfection the determined will of the father to anchor his family in the tempestuous ocean of deprivation which was Kola-Kola, to shelter them from that wind of inconsequence which, too commonly in his view, shook the whole quarter. Like a man who might never have left his native clan, he thought himself a sage, a guide full of wise counsel, since his hair was already white. Having worked for more than twenty years as a labourer on the quays of the distant port, leaving at dawn and returning at early evening, he maintained that Fort-Nègre offered a chance to everyone; only the faint-hearted failed to find work, and the light-headed to make money or to put a little aside. This was the burden of the sermon which he never ceased rehearsing before his wife, who was a good deal younger than himself, and whom the sage had not gone to seek in his own country until the house was large enough to hold the two of them decently. She was a timorous, obstinate and unperceptive woman, who had got it into her head to follow the maxims of her husband, already become a byword in Kola-Kola. Every morning she took the train to Oyolo, got off at the first station, about fifteen kilometres from Kola-Kola, and worked on a little piece of land, striving to make every possible economy in the cost of feeding her husband. At the beginning of the afternoon, she started back on foot towards the town, carrying on her head a large basket, filled either with the products of her own labour or those she had bought very cheaply from the peasants near-by. All along the rough unmetalled road she sweated in great drops when the sun shone at white heat; or, if a shower caught her, she would shelter in the crude veranda of a riverside hut, standing bolt upright till the storm abated, unless the occupants chanced to invite her to come and rest on a bamboo bed, having set down her burden.

It was the chief hope of the family head to return one day to his homeland; he was accustomed to it, and only seemed to live in the expectation of that blessed event, unlike his eldest son, fully acclimatized to the city and nearly always absent from the family house until the night sprawled over the quarter, with a breast swollen with all the water of the evaporated Atlantic. The respect with which this very young man was regarded by his two sisters, by his still younger brothers and even by his parents, those incarnations of ancestral virtues, astonished Mor-Zamba, until it was explained to him in confidence by a kindly and engaging neighbour that Jean-Louis, a student at the Fort-Nègre college, studied there the same textbooks as the white children, sitting beside them at the same table. In a general way, neither the hard lives of the parents, their teaching ambitions nor, still less, their state of mind, exercised any attraction, so far as one could judge, on the younger generation. During the first month of his stay among them, there wasn't an utterance of these children or a single one of their attitudes which didn't secretly scandalize Mor-Zamba.

After tentatively trying out his talents for some while, always

95

for just a day at a time, on occupations as diverse as porterage, the selling of firewood by the piece, and even the hawking of cigarettes or groundnuts, Mor-Zamba established himself for the first time by entering the service of a Kola-Kola master. Unhappily, this was a wretched laundryman, without any equipment at all, who went with constantly changing but always sparse assistance to rub the customers' washing on a board in a near-by river, surrounded by rubbish and excrement. He was a sad and silent man, stingy to himself and pitiless to others but who, paradoxically, had not been brought out of extreme and many-sided mediocrity by these same defects. After nine weeks of hard labour, Mor-Zamba had still not touched a cent from his employer. The elder Lobila advised him to be steadfast, having long counselled patience. When the refugee from the camp Gouverneur Leclerc, after much beating about the bush, finally made an intransigent demand, he was paid scrupulously, but also given the sack. He swore to himself to never again enter the service of a black employer, the worst of all paymasters.

He had, however, some money in his pocket and Jean-Louis, the son of his host, having offered to show him the night-life of Kola-Kola, said to him as they passed through the soft shades of the gathering night:

'You're absolutely right. A black employer is never good for anything; I, for instance, would never waste my time with such people.'

'But you,' replied Mor-Zamba, 'are an educated man, you'd never need to do so. You'll soon have big diplomas, as I hear. Which one is it you've got coming already? Ah yes, the baccalauréate....'

'Don't deceive yourself, old chap. To make a big pile, education doesn't help at all, quite the reverse in fact. And as for me, it's only making a pile that interests me. What's more, you're wrong on another point; the old people think that I go every day to college, and I'll do nothing to rob them of that illusion, which is so useful as long as it lasts. But I'll tell you right away, I don't go near the college any more; I'd be wasting my time there. At my age, there are better things to do – one has to live! So, every morning I gather up my books and notes, but I go to the city centre and not to the Schools' Plateau. In Fort-Nègre, I nose about, I watch, I potter here and there, studying the airs and manners of those who've made good in life. I try to understand how they made it. Sometimes, I manage to get them to talk. I've already had a conversation with old Kristopoulos; all I had to do was offer him a girl. It was he who told me that school was a waste of time.'

'Do your brothers and sisters know that you don't go to school any more?'

'They have to know; so what? You're asking yourself why they don't show me up to the old folks? First of all, because they think, like me, that school is a bore. And as soon as they're too old to go to the Catholic Mission School, which is so far, you know, three kilometres there and three back again, well, as soon as they can stop going there, that's to say, as soon as each of them has grabbed a certificate, don't worry, they'll be delighted to have done with it. And anyway, they see that I'm right to do as I'm doing; I often give them presents which the old man could never give them. You've seen the checked skirt that my youngest sister has? Well, can you believe that it was I who gave it to her?'

They waited a moment at the side of an avenue while a lorry went roaring past, its headlights lighting up for a moment the swarming activity of the ghetto. Crossing the street in a few strides and plunging again into the shadows, they resumed their conversation:

'The old folks,' resumed Jean-Louis, 'haven't you seen already that they're completely blind? It's because they've had their time, that lot. Real life is no longer what they think it is. The important thing is not to kill yourself putting money aside, even if you're making heaps of it – and, to tell the truth, the old man doesn't make a thing, or almost nothing; so what's the use of economies? Just to go back there, to his old place, with a bit of jewellery, some bedding, a few pairs of boots, a sewing-machine, a bicycle, all the things that will impress the neighbours and make him a hero in that clan of yokels! Because, what's more, they are not really any more at home in Toussaint-Louverture, where you saw Jeanne and the others. No, it seems that we've been taken into the city boundaries; it was the chief of the Oyolo district who decided it, all by himself, like a big man. Do you get it? Our ancestors lived there; we didn't ask anyone to come and live with us; but the strangers came all the same, so many of them that now it's we who have to move off. And without any compensation, either! So now they're going to push us further off, always further off. That's the Paradise to which the old folks are yearning to return! Not for me, thank you! No, what I need is just to make one big deal; and then, overnight, I'll become another man, with wealth counted in millions. At one stroke, one will have enough for a whole lifetime.'

'Do you think it's possible?'

'Of course it is; why shouldn't it be possible? I'm in correspondence with a great Indian professor who, by means of the information I gave him, has worked out my horoscope. One day I'll explain it to you and you'll see. Do you want me to take you to a man with whom you'll have opportunities to make a real pile? One visit doesn't commit you, you know? O.K.? You'd like it? All right, then, follow me. Oh, perhaps you'll be a bit disappointed at first; perhaps you'll say to yourself: "Another black boss!" He's an amazing man, who doesn't anyway want to be a boss to you, but a real friend or, if you prefer it, a father. If you agree to have confidence in him, you won't regret it.'

Talking like this, they loitered wherever they came to a hurricane-lamp, the usual form of lighting in the African locations of Fort-Nègre. Before the windows of the still open shops, they scrutinized the faces, over which the oily light seemed to wash slowly; they dodged the street-hawkers, those maniacs who insist on selling damaged goods to an ever more difficult clientele; they sized up the girls who proposed the exchange of common bait for an unreasonable sum.

As on every Saturday night in Kola-Kola, the round of pleasures was conducted in specialized establishments, always violently illuminated, being the only ones with the money to afford electricity. Here, in a discreet bar set back from the street, a gramophone proffered the beguines of the Caribbean in intoxicating rhythm, and the still sparse couples on the big floor jigged about without really clasping each other, without any genuine excitement, like citizens who already see the dance as no more than a fashionable and perhaps boring ritual. Further on, the two men plunged into a jungle of packed houses, stretched out side by side, or jammed one against the other; they turned ceaselessly at the corners of little alleys, squeezed through gaps, slipped, jumped with both feet together over puddles, hugged the houses, to the extent of violating family privacy. Kola-Kola was a multitude of inseparable fragments, each set in its own square of a vast draughts-board. Crossing each other at right-angles, a dozen wide arteries demarcated several big rectangles which were occupied too hastily and savagely for the colonial administration to allot them according to its original plans, and across which little narrow or sinuous lanes wound at random, most of them impassable to cars, which were in any case almost non-existent then in Kola-Kola.

They soon arrived in front of a dance-hall whose entrance was blocked by the queue forming up at the ticket-office. The two men benefited from a private favour whose nature Mor-Zamba didn't grasp which exempted them not merely from queueing, but even from buying tickets. Quickly abandoned by Jean-Louis (who grabbed the girls one after another, pressing against them and spinning them round, his eyes gazing into those of his partner and his teeth fixed in a dazzling smile, or else pottered about chatting with different groups of his cronies), Mor-Zamba, towering over the crowd and recovered from the blaze of the electric lights, gazed out over a scene completely new to him. The agitation of the crowd and the contortions of the dancers, sometimes solitary, sometimes in mixed couples, sometimes paired with the same sex, seemed to him to fill this huge room to the very brim. Ecstatic girls surrounded the stage on which, right at the end of the room, the musicians swung away in their shirt-sleeves. A tall, thin mulatto, with his hair pomaded, seemed to saw at his violin with the bow, unfurling a ravishing melody, and at every pause stretching down his face and neck to be sponged with a wet towel by a big girl stationed below him. Beside him was a young man, all running with sweat but with no sponger to oblige him, beating with a disdainful air on a big drum, continuing to play even during the pauses of the orchestra, and being free then to change his tempo at will.

The majority of these night-hawks, too smartly dressed and too generous with the girls, doubtless came from Fort-Nègre or those other areas where the governor's ordinances, a dead letter in Kola-Kola, had all the force of law and forbade any noisy activity after midnight. To mention only the most important, these included the Government Presidential Area, the Police Quarters, the Teachers' Estate, the Schools' Plateau and the Race Course Area, where the population consisted almost entirely of descendants of the local clans. Here in Kola-Kola Ruben was master, and Ruben had decreed that on Saturday, to relax from a week of labour and constraint, the workers could perfectly well dance all night, being able to sleep all day Sunday if they wished.

In another night-spot were some very young men, each on his own as if left to himself by the indifference of his family, all dressed in a bizarre fashion, with scarves at their throats, round their arms or their waists, shorts or tight trousers, rustic straw hats tipped well to the right, dancing an unknown step, rhythmic and monotonous, striking poses and attitudes at once virile and lascivious, all to the jolting chords of a guitar.

'Those,' said Jean-Louis to Mor-Zamba as they came out, 'those are the sapaks[1] of Ruben.'

'Sapaks? What's that?'

'They are also called bandasalos; they are ready to die for Ruben right away, if necessary, and joyfully too.'

'Who? These boys?'

[1] Sapak is an approximate synonym for bandasalo, an orphaned adolescent integrated into a gang. These youths, unlike the classic gangs of rowdies, were quite politicized and sometimes composed of real militants. They acted as shock-troops for the revolutionary organizations of resistance when they wanted, at the time of Independence, to oppose the process of 'Bao-Daïsation'.* Fearless of firearms but inexperienced, badly armed and even worse trained, they were an easy prey for the modest expeditionary force sent by Paris to act as shield for the unpopularity of Baba Toura. (Author's note)

* Bao-Daïsation: Bao-Dai was the emperor of Vietnam installed by the French in an attempt to stave off genuine decolonization and liberation. (Translator's note)

'Boys if you like, but real toughs too.'

There was always talk of Ruben in this quarter, even in the most unexpected places.

Suddenly, just as they were passing through the brilliant halo of a little establishment lighted with electricity and built above a basement, which gave it an unusual elevation and necessitated a flight of steps, Jean-Louis took his companion by the arm and drew him irresistibly towards the bar.

Mor-Zamba was not a little flattered to find himself in a quite chic and modern room whose clientele, rather few because there was no dancing here, looked to him particularly select. Instead of the inevitable gramophone, here it was a radio which gave out a soft, indefinable music, whose meaning excited all sorts of questions in the breast of this old pensioner of the camp Gouverneur Leclerc. Not awaiting any orders from the two young men, a girl with a dragging foot plonked two bottles of beer on the table and demanded the price without ceremony; equally without ceremony, Jean-Louis slipped his hand into his companion's trouser-pocket and pulled out two notes to settle the bill for the beer. This procedure had no visible effect on the girl, who watched it with an impassive eye.

'And since you no longer go to college,' demanded Mor-Zamba as they began sipping, 'what do you do all day long?'

'I've already told you; my cronies and I try to think up ways of making a real fortune one day.'

'Can you give me a clear example of such a financial coup?'

'You'll see, old chap, you'll see.'

At a sign from Jean-Louis, the girl, who certainly knew her client very well, brought a tin plate covered with an assortment of grilled kebabs, well rolled in ground pepper.

The young man, who had a strong appetite after his passage through the dance-halls, took two of these, offering one to Mor-Zamba, and keeping the other. Then, to pay for the kebabs, he employed the same method as before, slipping his hand into Mor-Zamba's pocket to extract some more small notes and offering them to the waitress. In a few mouthfuls he had cleaned the kebab-stick, clicking his tongue the while, and in two deep draughts he drained the beer between his munchings.

At this moment, a young man came into the place whom Jean-Louis recognized and beckoned over to join them. Whilst fraternizing with the newcomer, Jean-Louis gave orders to the waitress for another beer and kebab for this acquaintance, which he paid for once again in the same manner.

'That'll do!' decreed this adolescent to Mor-Zamba; 'you've treated us enough. Let's go!'

Before bidding farewell to the newcomer, Jean-Louis questioned him closely about the news of a certain Georges Mor-Kinda, whom he referred to more often in their conversation as Joe the Juggler and whose recent misadventures, a real saga, seemed to exalt them beyond all reason.

'No doubt you'd like to meet the person we've just been evoking for you?' Jean-Louis demanded of Mor-Zamba when they were alone again. 'He's really smart, that one. He's already made two or three big deals, he has. But, with rotten luck, he's been caught each time. He's just got two years in jail for forgery, it seems, and for the use of forgery; that's to say, in the language of the nigger-slavers,[1] that he's drawn a cheque in the person of his master by imitating his signature to perfection. He was going to disappear from the house, when one day the master, quite by chance, began to suspect that someone had delved unduly into his treasury and called a *mameluke*.[2] Really, what a lousy fluke! Just to think that within two or three days, the Juggler could have cleared off. To have laid hands on him then, what a hope! You know what they say? You have to get up pretty early in the morning to catch a Negro in Fort-Nègre. And in Kola-Kola, I ask you!'

---

[1] Nigger-slaver: a spiteful and polemical synonym for a Nègrien or Fort-Nègrien (inhabitant of Fort-Nègre). The practice of so referring to the people of Fort-Nègre, wrongly considered as white, since its boundaries included two areas occupied by a total of two to three thousand African officials, has finally prevailed in Kola-Kola, to the exclusion of all other names. (*Author's note*)

(I have tried to preserve the pun in the original French on Nègrier (slaver or slave-master, and Nègrien (inhabitant of Fort-Nègre), but the effect is cruder in English. (*Translator's note*)

[2] *Mameluke*: Kola-Kola nickname for a policeman. In the end the term came to cover all zealous servants of the colonial order, down to the smallest of all African minions. (*Author's note*)

'And was it a big cheque?'

'I should say so. Two hundred thousand francs, old fellow. Enough to stay nicely submerged for a good while before surfacing again. Unless, that is, he'd decided to establish a fine little night club. Not in his own name of course; that would scarcely be prudent, with the *mamelukes* searching for one as they do. But there always comes a time when they get weary and give up. One simply has to wait for that moment. And you, what would you have done? Establish a nice little club or stay quietly submerged for a good long time, without stirring? Which would you have chosen, tell me?'

Mor-Zamba had never considered such a question; and, to tell the truth, it seemed to him a quite gratuitous and hence uninteresting one. How could a poor bugger like him suddenly find himself in command of a fortune of two hundred thousand francs?

In any case, he made himself unhappy for nothing in struggling to give Jean-Louis an answer at all costs, for the debate was never continued. They had arrived in front of a large house, very imposing for that wretched area; under the rough-cast of the bit of wall lighted by a brilliant ray from the front entrance, one could discern masonry, made of a mixture of brick and clay, a privilege reserved in Kola-Kola for traders who had already made their fortunes, or were on the way to it. The tin roof, in place of the usual thatch, was also an eloquent testimony. Through the big front door, left wide open in the usual fashion, poured a cacophony of record-music and shouts of happy conversation, all on top of a ground-base of infant cries in contest with hysterically exasperated mothers. Mor-Zamba sized up with an expert eye the excellent disposition of the various parts of the house. One entered by a sort of vestibule-cum-veranda, closed at either end by small rooms, doubtless reserved for servants, and leading to the double-doors of the front entrance. Through this last, one passed into a huge sitting-and-dining room, littered with cane armchairs, upright wooden ones and low tables, which suggested a junk shop rather than an interior with carefully selected contents. A narrow door served as passage from the big room to a rear courtyard, probably surrounded by a fence, as in the houses of all rich merchants, containing various common huts, low mud buildings without plaster and of poor appearance; these represented the realm of the wives and children and, in the half-light, here could be discerned all the tumult and confusion so characteristic of Kola-Kola.

A pressure-lamp shone on a sort of stand hung about with lace. Mor-Zamba, still dazzled by the light, did not at once see the man who wrung his hand insistently and whom Jean-Louis introduced as Robert. Did he merely greet the second man, Robert's companion, who was seated at table beside the host? He can no longer remember, so much was he stunned by all these discoveries.

'Sit down, sit down, then!' Robert kept tirelessly repeating. 'You've come just at the end of our meal.'

'No, no,' protested Jean-Louis, now sunk into a cane chair, giving himself a grand air and speaking as man to man with Robert, despite his own youth and the mature, almost elderly, status of his host. 'Don't put yourself out for us.'

Following Jean-Louis' example, Mor-Zamba seated himself in his turn, but chose an armchair several rows behind that taken by the precocious boy, who revealed his self-assurance and power at every new encounter. The meal was not really as far advanced as the master of the household had pretended, employing his well-known skill to avoid having to share with the new arrivals. A seductive odour spun up from the row of dishes ranged before the two men, no doubt containing dried fish cooked with spinach, beef in sauce and the yams of the back-country, which were famous for their fine flavour. Right in the middle sat a full bottle of wine, to which the two pals seemed resolved on doing honour by themselves.

Robert's manners, despite his ability to crack a joke, seemed to Mor-Zamba at first crude and rather casual, though cordial enough at the same time. One thing about this man, who would soon take him into his service, displeased him irrevocably right from the start; whatever he was doing, Robert would turn himself every few minutes to launch over his shoulder a little spit, imperceptible as a sigh. Another, slightly more pleasing singularity was the sudden switch from the mask of tortured hilarity worn by a drunk, to the frozen and stupid gravity of a

104

sensualist, or, suddenly again, to the crafty one of a sharp calculator, a swindler for petty stakes.

'Little Jean!' he suddenly cried in an authoritative tone, 'go and get two bottles of beer.'

A man then detached himself from a group seated at the far end of the room in a corner somewhat obscurely lighted, hidden as it was behind the mass of furniture. Until that moment, Mor-Zamba had scarcely noticed them; they were skinny young men seated around a low table scattered with empty plates, insufficiently filled formerly for sure, judging by the vague looks of those who had just cleaned them, for everything in their faces betrayed the atrocious hunger of empty bellies obliged to watch the master stuffing himself. This was the most lamentable category in Kola-Kola; properly speaking, the quarter had no real domestic servants. The few nobs of Kola-Kola filled these posts quite cunningly and economically by using distant cousins, torn very young from their clans by the desire for learning or the hope of mastering a trade, which drew them like a mirage; or else resorted to the brothers, sisters and cousins of their wives, despite the protestations of the latter. It was from these youths that the *bandasalos* of Ruben were most frequently recruited; for, quickly realizing that they had been duped, they would quit their masters and form themselves into a gang.

Whilst sipping his beer, Mor-Zamba now contemplated Robert's fellow diner, a man of the same age, but very discreet, almost self-effacing, with the narrow face often borne by those who are being undermined by a chronic illness. He forced himself to reply by little chuckles to the jokes of his host. Both of them seemed to be meeting on the eve of some important project, and Mor-Zamba could not refrain from thinking that they too were perhaps preparing a big deal. Did it mean that everyone in Kola-Kola, and perhaps in Fort-Nègre too, was contriving a big deal of some kind? This impression was confirmed when Robert, who had suddenly grown sombre, declared gravely to Jean-Louis:

'It's going to be necessary for you to write me another letter to the Director of Economic Affairs. That of yesterday won't do.'

'Why so? Is there something wrong with it?'

'But no, not at all!' protested Robert. 'To address a well-turned letter to a toubab,[1] there's no one to touch you, be sure of that. No, it's something else. . . .'

He launched into long explanations which Mor-Zamba had the more difficulty in following because they seemed to him made in the discreet tones of confidence. What is more, the beer which he had drunk all evening in such unaccustomed quantities was beginning to act on him like a soporific. He soon dozed off and was thus unable to follow the part of the conversation which concerned himself. It was then that Jean-Louis revealed to Robert, who was closely attentive, where Mor-Zamba came from, what kind of man he was, what trials he had been through, what fears he nursed, vainly of course, that the Oyolo police would come to look for him in Fort-Nègre.

'He's really a rare bird, a treasure,' Jean-Louis concluded. 'He's a man of incredible strength; I can vouch for that, having seen him several times confronting the Saringalas last month, when they made many assaults around Gallieni, looking for sellers of Holy Joseph. Well, all on his own, that man there put them to flight over and over again. And yet, in reality, he's an extremely quiet man, sober, cheerful and even complacent.'

Robert nodded his head understandingly.

'Educated?' he murmured.

'Nought for the question!' burst out Jean-Louis, with a chuckle. 'He can't even talk pidgin!'

'Still, there's one thing that surprises me about this man; he was a nurse, and yet he can't read? How did he manage to identify the phials and the pills? He must have deciphered the labels, not so?'

'Well, that's also a mystery to me,' Jean-Louis replied pensively. 'All I know for certain is that he can't read. That I can guarantee.'

'It's possible that he'll suit me, your man! I'll take him on trial. I'll give you a commission of five thousand; that suit you?'

'Only five thousand?' exclaimed Jean-Louis, with a sour face. 'You know, Robert, you'll never have anything but praise for my find.'

---

[1] Toubab: white man. (*Author's note*)

'I don't doubt it, my little chap. We'll talk about it again in a month, if you agree? Without any bitterness. You know me well by now, anyway, no one is more loyal in jobs of this kind than Robert. Isn't that so, Fulbert? You can witness for me in that.'

Fulbert woke up with a start and fluttered his eyelids several times, while Robert sneered:

'These people are certainly sleepy this evening. Fulbert, don't disturb yourself at all; you know you're at home here; you even know where your room is; your bed is ready. So, when you want to go to sleep, you know where to go. As for you, little Jean-Louis, take your friend off and explain our arrangement to him. I repeat: come back in a month and we'll discuss it again. Good-night.'

Robert knew right away how to win over his new employee, who was very reticent at first, by plying him with gifts which couldn't fail to turn the head of a raw Kolean; old clothes and shoes, but still in good condition, an iron bed, blankets, and even a mattress, which took the place of his mat laid on the ground and his one yellowish cloth. Mor-Zamba finally cut the figure of a man in his adopted family, gaining authority over the youngest children, whose appalling upbringing made them progressively more insupportable as they grew.

As for the duties of his new recruit, Robert took plenty of time about revealing them to him. When he had work for him in the house, he took good care to distinguish him from the servants, and had him eat at his own table, so that they held this upstart in quarantine and resented deeply that this illiterate and gauche yokel should be preferred to them.

But most often, Mor-Zamba simply accompanied Robert; in this way, he accompanied him into Fort-Nègre, to the offices of import–export firms, to the bank, where his new master made himself very small, much to Mor-Zamba's astonishment, and into the popular bazaars of the commercial centre, where Robert, like the other African merchants, was obliged to buy in bulk by his irregular footing with the administrative authorities.

It was above all during his selling trips through the interior that Robert took care never to be separated from Mor-Zamba. In the general way, all of the African merchants, needy enough people, together with some white merchants, the new arrivals, young hotheads, Lebanese and Syrians, or Europeans who were neither French nor British, such as the Greeks and a few rare Italians, lived heavily if not basically upon what they got from itinerant selling in the weekly or fortnightly markets, which were welcomed in turn by the small colonial towns of the interior, within a radius of almost two hundred kilometres of Fort-Nègre. Beyond that, the absence of roads, or the atrocious quality of the tracks which took their place, made all penetration risky or impossibly costly. On the eve of a market, the small African traders got together in groups of ten or fifteen to hire a lorry which would take them and their goods, so that they could be on the spot from dawn onwards. A rudimentary stall was erected in a flash, and there they awaited the first buyers. It was demanding and doubtfully worth while. The hoped-for customers were largely peasants who themselves, except in the cocoa season, made their livelihood by selling their ordinary produce which, in these petty urban centres, was also slow to find takers. It was a vicious circle. Between the two cocoa seasons, some peasants became so poor that they were forced to give up certain things which, elsewhere, were considered indispensable, such as soap, cotton cloths and even salt. Black Koleans and white slavers alike were reduced to finding compensation, of an entirely spiritual kind, in the thousand and one scenes of the eternal village comedy.

Particularly delightful to them was the permanent farce of Ginguene in contest with the peasants defending their ancestral lands. Ginguene, or Monsieur Albert, as the Africans called him, to avoid the perilous enunciation of his surname, was an official of the Department of Forestry, charged with creating a state forest by taking a large slice of land from the territory of several clans around Efoulane. No one at the top had noticed that the land chosen, no doubt by the throw of a dice, had a relatively dense population; that since every field was left fallow for many years after the harvest, the inhabitants needed for their survival such vast areas that they already felt themselves pinched, well before the honour which had just been done them.

As long as M. Albert and his two African assistants confined themselves to setting up marks, the inhabitants of the various towns, villages and hamlets observed him with amusement, merely making a few cracks at his expense from time to time, without risking anything, for M. Albert, to use his own expression, couldn't make head or tail of their dreadful patois. But one morning he arrived, accompanied this time by two unknown employees armed with picks and shovels, whose mission was evidently to mark out the places designed to carry concrete boundary-posts. Then the peasants suddenly realized, no one quite knows how, that once these posts were erected they would remain forever indestructible, like irrevocable symbols of their deprivation; the state forest would spread, little by little, and one fine day they would find themselves strangers on their own land; they would be driven out. They decided not to let M. Albert cut into the ground, like a man who marks his share in the flesh of a sow by driving his pegs into it.

As soon as Ginguene arrived in any hamlet, village or city and got out of his van, the peasants surged up, brandishing spears, matchets and lances. At once his two assistants ran split-arse from the scene and, without slackening their pace, turned a moment to shout with heroic loyalty to their boss:

'Look out, M. Albert! Those are real murderers, that lot, real head-shrinkers. Don't stay there, they want to finish you!'

Ginguene philosophically stooped down to gather up the tools scattered by the two fugitives, and began apparently preparing to perform the task himself; cutting a hole in the ground, setting into it a wooden post painted red, and straightening this by heaping the earth around it and stamping it down vigorously. But as soon as his back was turned the peasants, who hitherto had stood at a respectful distance, all ran forward together, plucked out the post and flung it far into the bush, scrabbled up the soil furiously with their feet and, to efface the last traces of Ginguene's labour, scattered some dead leaves over the fresh wound in the earth. When Ginguene returned, the black farmers retreated in a solid ring, the colonial official dug again, planted a post and made as if to depart. The peasants on the two flanks began a converging movement on the post, M. Albert spun round, the peasants froze in the magnificent pose of warriors launching a dashing attack; the two sides watched each other. A lorry drew up full of Koleans greedy for these moments of action. A man yelled from the lorry, in Bantu and in pidgin:

'You bunch of idlers, why don't you pitch into him, then?'

'Ah, get on!' the peasants yelled back in Bantu. 'As if it isn't well known that they all carry a pistol in their pockets. What do you take us for? We didn't fall from the clouds with the last rainstorm, you know.'

'Is that what you think?' cried the Kolean bravely, gripping the side of the lorry. 'A pistol in the pocket of *that* creature! But, you pack of idiots, haven't you *looked* at him?'

To think of it, had they really looked at him? So they looked at him, this little blond man, so broad-shouldered, with such blue eyes, with such a sly and fawning look, such starched and impeccable shirt and shorts, his skin so tanned on face, neck and arms, but still milky on the thighs, under the reddish down.

Sometimes, too, it was a fellow countryman of Ginguene who stopped his lorry full of off-cut timbers to shout at him, leaning from the doorway:

'Anything wrong here? Do you need a hand?'

'It's very kind of you. Don't put yourself out for me. But thanks, it's really nice of you. They're just big babies, you know, you only have to look them right in the eye.'

It must be admitted that this method was not uniformly successful; in certain very recalcitrant villages, M. Albert had to get an escort of Saringalas commanded by a sergeant of the colonial army. The presence of this last element introduced only a minor variation and, furthermore, scarcely added pepper to the sauce. A lorry packed with Koleans would draw up while, the first post being planted, the two camps observed one another with ferocious looks on their faces, with the exception of M. Albert's, which was as sly as always. This time, it was a philosophic Kolean who took over the task of suggesting to the peasants:

'What the fuck can they do to you? Wait till night falls and those savages push off, then pull up the post. They can't sleep here, after all!'

'We have to be on the look-out,' muttered the peasants, full of sententious superstition; 'we have to watch out; we'll have to pull out that cursed post while they're still here. Afterwards, it's too late.'

'What do you mean, too late?'

'We know what we mean,' cut in the peasants, sententiously as ever, but no less mysteriously.

If, on the other hand, it was a lorry full of white slavers, Ginguene's countryman would yell out, addressing both him and the old colonial sergeant:

'These boys are making a blunder, all the same. One day all this could end very badly indeed.'

'But, you know,' Ginguene would reassure his anxious and soft-hearted countryman, 'you know, they are just big babies....'

'Big cunts, yes!' observed the old sergeant, taking a swig of brandy from the neck of his flask.

An experienced merchant since he has given Ekoumdoum a system of popular distribution which offers current food crops at very low prices and which is an endless source of reflections on economics, Mor-Zamba often confides to us that the practice of his former master and the other Kolean merchants, pariahs of colonial business which offered them at best the role of crumb-gatherers, savoured at once of jack-of-all trades and of conjurer. Within the narrow sphere to which destiny had confined him, Robert, according to Mor-Zamba, often displayed a kind of genius; this truth grows dazzlingly bright every time he thinks about the acts carried out by Robert or the men who escorted him during the course of the first cocoa season he experienced with this singular man.

To start with, Robert made skilful use of his experience by getting Niarkos, a white merchant who was out of reach of even the biggest Kolean, to take him along as cocoa-buyer. Niarkos was an old skinflint who came to Africa late in life, invited by a relative already installed here who had told him that the colony was a land of milk-and-honey for a quick-witted trader. Knowing only a few words of pidgin, and none at all of Bantu or of French, trusting nobody, he was ceaselessly on the backs of his black employees, strictly controlling all their initiatives, operations and movements. Disliked by the Africans, who considered him too mean, he inspired in his countrymen the pity one reserves for presumption; wanting to make himself so difficult, how could this Harpagon[1] stay more than a few years in Africa? The fact was that, according to Mor-Zamba and contrary to what appeared at first, the chief desire of the traditional white slaver was not so much to pile up gold as to stay alive, to preserve himself for some years of happy retirement in Europe, just as a gourmet holds back a bit for the dessert at the end of a banquet.

Robert had long been tied up with Fulbert, who became driver to the Balkan as soon as he arrived, and had long heard with boredom his descriptions of the habits of this strange little man with the soft voice, before being struck one day on learning that behind his inoffensive mask of an olive-skinned Levantine, Niarkos had enough capital to buy, transport and even stock his cocoa, without borrowing a cent from his bank.

Following this, he also heard that this year, despite his age, Niarkos had decided to extend his exporting activities by buying a second lorry which, like the first, would be primarily devoted to the haulage of cocoa; and that, for the duration of the season, which is from November to January, the little Greek, who had finally given up trying to supervise everything, would install his headquarters at Efoulane, a hundred and fifty kilometres south of Fort-Nègre, from which he would branch out to scour the whole back-country of its cocoa. Gradually, perhaps without his being aware of it, the elements of a plot implanted themselves in his mind. Not only was Fulbert relieved of the perpetual presence of his master sitting beside him, forbidding him to follow the usual custom of rounding up his salary by illegally carrying passengers or freight, but also, as was inevitable during the unbalanced trade of the cocoa

[1] Harpagon: miser (a character in Molière's play The Miser). (Translator's note)

112

season, his lorry most often returned empty from Fort-Nègre; Robert would thus have a ready-made solution for the three months of the season to the permanent problem of the Kolean traders, that of transport for their goods. And so as to be quite certain of not losing this godsend, Robert took care, during the first three, less-active weeks of the season, to have his accomplice carry loads of merchandise which accumulated in a hastily contrived place at Efoulane, so that he soon had enough stock there to last for several months. Whatever happened to him, he was already assured that after the season the carriage of goods for the rest of the year would be in the bag, so to say.

And when he became the appointed acolyte of Niarkos, his audacity could only increase. To range out from Efoulane to the country towns, where the weekly and fortnightly markets were now swollen by the sales of cocoa, the Balkan sometimes mounted Fulbert's lorry, sometimes the other. When the little Greek took his place beside Fulbert, Robert always climbed without hesitation after him, and Niarkos was thus forced to push and shove himself against his driver, in order to make room for Robert and his associate. And even on these occasions Robert would imperturbably get his own men, who now included Mor-Zamba, to climb into the lorry with some of his goods. If Niarkos was so misguided as to query this, he would present these men and their loads, with condescending vagueness, as being indispensable to both his patron and himself. He played along with Niarkos, making him laugh like a child, turning him like a top, and even, for a lark, getting the Balkan to pay out ridiculous sums of money, just to prove his mastery over him.

As soon as they arrived in the town where the market was being held, he would vanish with his people and establish them before a stall, fixed up in a flash with packing-cases and embellished with goods at the wave of a magic wand, and in no time he'd be back beside Niarkos, like a man who'd just spent a few seconds drinking a glass with a childhood friend. And then, as if to excuse that innocent weakness, he took over control of operations with a zeal that filled Niarkos with an amazed, if silent, satisfaction.

'That's where,' Mor-Zamba often tells us, 'that's where

Robert really worked miracles. There was one cocoa sale, my baptism of fire, which I'll never forget. Yes, I know, I seem to be singing the praises of a rascal. But, after all, how can I evoke the Robert of those days without admiration? At least for the sheer number of his ideas, if not for their realization?

'This happened at Efoulane itself. Among the many regulations laid down by the colonial administration there was one, extraordinary and totally absurd, which has perhaps survived, who knows, into the no less absurd reign of Baba Toura the Drunkard; it forbade the sale of cocoa before eight in the morning within the perimeter of any locality having urban status, which was the case with Efoulane, even though the little town normally had scarcely any whites in it. The converse was that the peasants, often arriving from very distant areas, or wishing to regain their villages before the sun would shine from its zenith on their route, arrived very early in the town and were obliged to wait for hours on end, during which the buskers of the cocoa buyers unleashed upon them the eloquent floods of their most frenetic rhetoric.

'His amazing gab, his raucous voice, his tone both honeyed and imperious, made Robert a master of this game. On that particular day his exhortations held the peasants spellbound, massed as they were about the scales hanging above the concrete platform. At first they listened with a weary cynicism, like men who have heard plenty of this before; but soon their faces began to light up, their glances began to soften. Soon they laid down their burdens and made signs to their relatives or their friends to draw nearer. Robert began shouting his paeans for that extraordinary man, that boss of his dreams, Niarkos, instrument of Providence, white like no other white; only a few days in the country, he was free of that thieving mentality so well-known for drying up his brothers as soon as they arrived here, and which then consumed them like a gangrene until the blacks were obliged to turn away from them and stop their noses. No, Niarkos was generosity incarnate; his hand was as bounteous as the river which flowed perpetually from morning to evening, from night to morning, without interruption. He had brought thousands upon thousands of boxes crammed to bursting with the biggest banknotes in the world, with the sole purpose of showering them upon the blacks he loved, he also, to recompense the most zealous workers among them, and he had decided, oh how justly, to begin with the incomparable small cultivators of the interior, whom he knew well for their industry, their daily suffering, their anonymous energy, by offering them a price twenty francs above the official level, for their cocoa.'

Niarkos, having heard his name pronounced so often, and judging the purport of Robert's oratory by the harvest of beatific looks it drew, was smiling like an angel himself. All manner of people and of loads had now invaded the pavement, completely surrounding the concrete platform; it was now a real battle to move about, but nothing seemed to impede the coming-and-going of Robert, a prophet inspired by that unlooked-for Messiah named Niarkos. Suddenly, Robert held a whispered conference with one of his numerous assistants from Kola-Kola, one called Alou whom Mor-Zamba knew well from often seeing him at Robert's place, without ever imagining that he could play such an important role for the Kolean trader. Without interrupting his claptrap, Robert was ceaselessly surveying the surroundings with a rolling and somewhat anxious eye, or so it seemed to Mor-Zamba, who had been told that a big task was at hand. The mist dispersed and the sun, already scorching, unveiled the animation of a little town which was not merely busy with its normal occupations, but seemed to be celebrating some solemn festival in its calendar.

Niarkos' acolyte was now patrolling right in the midst of the peasants who were stuck all over the pavement and the platform, in front of the dais where his master was standing, with his left hand caressing the scales which balanced slowly, like some reluctant fetish. Nearby lay the Balkan's cash-box, crammed with banknotes ranged in their denominations. Robert declared to them with a rather formal camaraderie:

'At the beginning of this unique season, brothers, count the blessings of a Heaven which has sent this matchless man into your path. Brothers, this is the one you have been waiting for, the one whose coming has been announced to you for so many years! Isn't it true that you grew tired of waiting and began to think he would never come? Look carefully at him: have you ever seen him anywhere else? Admit that this face is quite unknown to you. Have I lied in telling you that your Messiah has just landed, that he is new, that he is clean, that he is good? How can a man who has given you the truth in one thing lie to you in others? Especially if this man is your own brother? The great day has arrived, my friends! Come, draw nearer! ...'

The siren sounded just then on the hill where stood the administrative headquarters of the district, announcing that it was eight o'clock, and the real business began. Men carrying sacks on their heads or shoulders, women bent double under the baskets strapped to their backs, the peasants rushed up and pressed around the scales, stretching their eyes to admire this marvel vaunted by a tireless orator. Each wave of arrivals sent a shock through the crowd; they shoved and even fought each other in the effort to be first at the scales, which were flanked by a little yellowish man silently smiling and a big voluble African with a tormented eye.

'Calm down, then, brothers, calm down!' shouted the orator. 'As I've just told you, we have in this very shop a multitude of boxes just like this one, look! All full with banknotes in just the same way. Everyone will get his share; it is only God alone who can recompense you like this. Ah, you down there! Yes, you, the chief! Come closer, come close to us. Let him through, then, you lot! Come up here to us, venerable one.'

Pushing his chest through the packed crowd, this man with the air of a noble patriarch bravely and arduously made a passage for himself, using his hands and elbows like a young man, exalted at having merited the notice of the talented acolyte of the new Messiah. Already very tall, he stood on tiptoe and puffed out his chest under the ready-made jacket cut from a thick and dirty piece of maroon cloth, embellished with blood-red epaulettes and brandenburg buttons, its flaps hanging low over matching trousers, which revealed themselves as terribly cork-screwed when he finally succeeded in hoisting himself onto the platform. Niarkos immediately granted him a vigorous handshake and, speaking to him with evident warmth, tried to tell him something amid the din of the mob, perhaps some kind of congratulation. But the patriarch, obviously not understanding his language, replied with an embar-

116

rassed and cautious laugh; at the same time, he was puffing to
regain his breath after the real triumph of getting through that
dense crowd, so excessively jealous and impatient of any
privilege.

'Venerable father,' Robert managed to say to him, dominating the hubbub, 'the master asks how many loads of cocoa you
are bringing him.'

'I have eleven people of my family.'

'Yes, you have people of your family,' Robert resumed, 'but is
each of them carrying a load?'

'The women are carrying from twenty-five to thirty kilos, the
men upwards of forty kilos.'

They were no further forward; Robert, on the verge of exasperation, said the only sensible thing in cases like these:

'Call your people, then, and tell them to come here. And, you
people, make way for the porters of this distinguished old man;
he's your elder, so let us deal with him first. We have respect for
age, we others, don't you know that? Come on then, the porters
of this noble old man; come on. . . .'

Instead of the dozen people expected, a whole tribe soon
surrounded the neighbourhood of the scales, drowning the two
assistants, the white man, still beatifically smiling, and Robert,
who seemed more disquieted and agitated than ever.

Mor-Zamba is nowadays convinced that Robert's motive was
to entice the crowd by treating the first-comers royally, as proof
of Niarkos' supposedly prodigious generosity, even at the risk
of overestimating their contribution. As they dispersed, they
would spread word everywhere that Robert and Niarkos were
buying above the official price. The peasants came flocking
and confusion spread everywhere. It was obvious that the successors of the patriarch with the brandenburg buttons would
have less cause than he to congratulate themselves on their
encounter with Niarkos and Robert.

Mor-Zamba, in any case, had no more time to see; work began
for him at that moment and he was constantly in the breech
until noon, so that it is only by means of disparate fragments, as
always, that he is able to reconstruct the events which unrolled
around the scales, which Robert manoeuvred and operated
with all the skill of a swindler; the scales danced, oscillated,

and swung back again. Displaying an outrageous virility and a juggler's dexterity, Robert, following the gyrations of the scales, tore open the baskets or the sacks which the peasants brought him, ripping the raffia or the jute, hung the weights on the arm of the scales with broad, flashing gestures and, without giving time for the balance to settle accurately, made signs to his men to take down the load and carry it off, throwing at the yokel a doubtless imaginary price, at the sound of which Niarkos bent feverishly over his cash box, pulled forth a large bundle of petty notes, and counted them interminably into the hands of the peasant, on which they formed an astounding heap. Finally, he would dispatch the buyer by shaking his hand and giving him little pats on the shoulder. But the latter was in haste to count and verify the marvel; he pushed his way impatiently out of the ever thicker mob surrounding the two partners and their numerous assistants; he rejoined the family that was awaiting him, gathered in a separate clump on the pavement, pushed ever further and further back by the invisible bailiffs of Robert, commanded by Mor-Zamba, to whom his master had carefully taught the lesson that the peasants newly returned from the scales must be thrust as far off as possible. For, most often, the family groups were now suddenly filled with lamentation, despair or threats of revolt, swollen by each fresh arrival. Certainly, they were quiet for a moment while they counted their gains, each one thinking that perhaps he himself had been luckier. They would count one by one all the little notes, setting them in the hands of a wife or a brother; having completed this operation, one saw the group recommence their sums by counting on the fingers of their left hand with the index of the right. Then indignant stupefaction was not long in wrinkling their brows; there was no doubt about it, they had been scandalously cheated, but what could they do? The lamentations broke out again, more piercing but more vain than ever.

'You're the one in charge, after all,' one wife told her husband; 'how can you let us be robbed like this? You should have demanded to know how much they would pay you for each load, when we divided the cocoa among the different porters. And if you weren't satisfied, you should have seized our cocoa back again. That's what we did only last year. Why did you let them rob us? Why?...'

'I'd like to see you do it,' whined the husband; 'if you think it's so easy with those two there! You don't have time to see anything, nor time to understand anything, you don't even know where you are, and already their men have grabbed the cocoa, carried it away and poured it into their own big sacks. It's like being stunned, and when you come to yourself at last, it's too late, everything has gone.'

'Move off, give room for others,' Mor-Zamba told them, though moved almost to tears by their cries of anguish.

Sunk in his own sombre thoughts, he suddenly heard himself severely addressed by Alou, who told him:

'That'll do, leave that to the little boys, they'll do just as well without you. An order from Robert: go quickly to that little hovel down there and put on the togs you'll find in the darkest corner, specially put there. Hurry up you slow-coach, how dull you are!'

Mor-Zamba complied and soon came back, though with some difficulty, and found Alou in the crowd, very bizarrely dressed, as it seemed to him.

'What!' whispered Alou, 'aren't you ready yet? But what a hat you've got there!'

'I found nothing but rags in the little corner.'

'So what, you big dope? When did you stop wearing rags? Look at that will you! Master has passed the stage of wearing rags, Master has risen in the world! Get off, then, and above all don't forget to put on the little hat.'

Mor-Zamba obeyed, overwhelmed by the hatred which Alou showed towards him. Here, at any rate, was someone who had a score to settle with him.

'Listen to me, dope,' cried Alou, with a thunderous look at Mor-Zamba, who had drawn near again, 'now you've got to play your part; up to now, everyone has done as best he can; there's no reason to have the shits, unless you're really what they say you are. You look fine like that, you know! You've no need to disguise yourself to look a real peasant, you haven't! O.K., go up to the platform and when you get there, as soon as Robert says to you, "Off you go, little fellow, there's some fine

119

cocoa," you go quickly to the scales, you unhook the load and go and lose yourself among the peasants. Then, with your load of cocoa, you go up again and give it to Robert to be weighed. In that way, Niarkos will count the price of the cocoa into your hand. Get it? Let me tell you, everyone who's done it up to now has done well. One of them managed to go up there three times with the same load. No, wait: don't do anything unless Robert says: "Off you go, little fellow, there's some fine cocoa." If not, leave the workers to it, those who unhook the loads and go to empty them in the big white sacks. As for you, that's not your business. Allez, go...'

'And if he recognizes me?' Mor-Zamba could not refrain from stammering.

'Who does? Robert? But haven't I just told you...'

'No, the white man.'

'You poor silly bugger, when have you ever seen a white recognize a black man, especially after so short an acquaintance? I've just told you that one bloke went up three times, didn't you hear? You'll do well to manage even once.'

It was, in fact, miraculously easy. Niarkos didn't even lift his eyes to this peasant, so similar to all the others, even when he thanked him with a warm handshake, followed by the ritual taps on Mor-Zamba's shoulder, which he could scarcely reach, even though he was perched on the platform.

But perhaps Robert had presumed too much upon his tactical intuition; or was he served with an excessive zeal by Alou, his chief of staff? In any event, the invisible army charged by Robert to guard the frontiers of the sanctuary against incursions by hostile hordes had been grossly overwhelmed, which could never have occurred if Mor-Zamba had kept his station. A howling band of men, women and children, doubtless a whole family, had managed to surround Robert and threatened to seize him by assault; for the moment, they showered him with curses as a kind of preliminary skirmish. Impassive, not even understanding exactly why they were after his blood, but troubled all the same by his bad conscience, Robert pretended for some time to ignore the whole matter, waiting for his men to take the initiative, but his men hesitated, taken by surprise, and the protestors grew more bold. Robert decided to resort to

120

diplomacy, always advisable when one is aware of losing control of events. Abandoning his juggling with the scales and the fruit of the people's labour, he faced the riot, not like a chief, but like an understanding father, and he was abundantly rewarded. Bit by bit, the reproaches changed to claims, and the claims to grievances; Robert then understood that at the root of all sedition there is a resentment; at the root of resentment a misunderstanding; at the birth of misunderstanding, a pillage! Yes, a neat little pillage of a peasant, cooked, tempered, tanned, patinaed by the smoke of a peasant's house, the pillar of the household, in a word. What adversity had not been able to do, jubilation would not achieve: at the spectacle of such buffoonery, the great man nearly rolled on the ground! What! It was like accusing a murderer of tickling!

No doubt one of his men had displayed excessive zeal in keeping a peasant's sack too long, without thinking of the consequences of such imprudence. Perhaps it was the champion in parading the same sack several times before Niarkos; he whose praises had been sung to Mor-Zamba by Alou. Usually, when they had emptied the cocoa into Niarkos' big sack, the workers dropped the sacks and baskets of the peasants in a sort of hall at the far end of the row of buildings, very distant from the platform; there the owners came to retrieve these objects which no one would dream of stealing, since they were utterly without any but sentimental value. Rather than presiding over a doubtless successful search for the sack of the protesting family, and thus lose precious time by interrupting and perhaps disorganizing a splendid session of chicanery, Robert managed to persuade the leader to accept a big, brand new sack, a sumptuous gift; but he still had to add a bribe of five hundred francs – enough to buy thirty sacks such as had been lost – before the peasant, having inspected his new sack for some time with unconcealed disdain, consented to move off, shaking his head in grief.

It had been a close shave, all the same. Robert drew from it the lesson that his system must function as a closed circuit in order to yield the best results, excluding at all times the slightest alien element, such as a peasant, or any object belonging to that absurd race. How could one be sure a muddy-arsed wretch would not notice, by chance, that the employee who had unhooked his sack had not gone to empty it where he should, but had gone to queue up with the other villagers? To guard against this risk, as soon as he saw in the crowd around the platform a man having the appearance of a family head or, better still, a grandfather such as he with whom Robert had opened operations an hour before, he would ask him if he was leading a group; if the man said yes, he was asked to gather all his people at once; they were asked to pour all their produce, which seldom amounted to more than two hundred kilos, into two big sacks. Then the family, or rather its strongest members, carried the sacks to the platform where Robert and Niarkos awaited them.

The little Greek had readily agreed to the systemization of this technique in order to save the time of his employees. Instead of dealing with the individual porters, they disposed of the whole family in a few seconds. Half an hour later, when Niarkos was so used to this system as to pay no more attention to it, Robert's agents resumed their thieving with more boldness and much less risk than before. Two or three of them would seize a big sack which had just been weighed, and which carried Niarkos' seal as well as the beans he had just bought; they brought it before Niarkos, to whom they looked like honest representatives of a modest and courageous peasant family. The scales would then register again the weight of his own cocoa, which Niarkos would joyfully proceed to buy once more, paying the money into the hands of someone who was, in reality, his own employee. In short, the whole thing was sewn up.

Everything was over by about eleven o'clock, it seemed to Mor-Zamba. Niarkos had nothing more to do than scrupulously check the stitching of the sacks of cocoa, their exact number, and the loading of them into his lorries, before disappearing into the little lodging prepared for him in the backyard of the shop.

Robert would not gather his forces together till the evening. By all the evidence, he must have been in league with Alou, who was in possession of the sums diverted from Niarkos' cash-box during the morning. Mor-Zamba suspected that the two men must have slipped off together while he and the others were straightening up the hall used by Niarkos to receive the peasants, and which they had to leave in the condition in which they had found it.

Whatever he might say, Robert never made a fair division of the spoils, which had doubtless already been split by Alou and himself; in fact, it was more a question of the two men deigning to make some reward to their minions. The sum which fell to him meant nothing either way to Mor-Zamba and seemed to him quite without significance.

'Three thousand francs!' cried Robert, teasing him. 'In one day, more than a Fort-Nègre worker makes in fifteen! What do you say to that, Mor-Zamba? And just wait! This is not all. Don't forget that at the end of the month Niarkos owes you a salary, because you are also working for him all the time! Don't tell me it was I who recruited you.'

That wasn't what really preoccupied Mor-Zamba. He was asking himself how he could twist the events of the day so as to present them to Abena when he came back, if indeed he ever came back.

Robert, who had noticed the disappointment of his men at the end of a day so rich in hope, descended for a moment to explanations: he had had to buy very dear, all the more so because they would be needed tomorrow in another town and in other places too, the silence of the ten workers attached to Niarkos' own establishment and who, despite themselves, had served as indispensable supports, but also as witnesses of the feats of trickery performed by the great man's helpers.

Then Robert carelessly felt in his pocket with his right hand, while his left hand lifted the cloth flap from his stiffened leg; he pulled out a crumpled packet of cigarettes, took one, hesitated before offering them successively to all the members of the gang who, in any case, included very few smokers.

'Now that you've got money, my children,' he told them, 'you might just as well buy your own tobacco, assuming that you really want to smoke. I can't supply you indefinitely. The job of your senior, which I am, is only to tell you about life; in short, to show you how to get along on your own from now on. The fact is I'm too kind, and that's a fault. It's always a fault to be too good. I can't continue for another two years surrounded by the same men, or much the same; we know each other too well. And when you know people too well, it's impossible to understand each other! So I warn you that next year I shall recruit only young men or novices. Now you know what you must do, except Mor-Zamba, of course. You must save as much money as possible this year, so that you won't need anyone next year and jump all alone into the water, every man for himself. I've told you so often: Why always count on me? I'm no phenomenon, for sure; it's not so long ago that I was a young lad like you. Only I didn't wait every day till someone came to offer me my share on a plate.'

He paused to take three long pulls and to strike a pose; then he began again, frequently turning his head in his usual fashion, to throw an invisible spit over his shoulder:

'So, Mor-Zamba, you certainly didn't dream of my little plot, not so? And there are plenty more like that, my boy; plenty that I will teach you, because I don't intend to let you go.'

'What luck he has!' muttered Alou.

'Ah, yes,' Robert resumed, getting more and more exalted, as if he were drunk, 'ah, yes, Mor-Zamba has good luck, I know. Look at him; just look at this splendid warrior. Since I had him with me, no one dares to come near me, my enemies have vanished as if by magic. By this stage of the last season, I had already suffered three or four attacks. You were already with me, Alou; but I can only think that you impressed no one; I've never been so often attacked. But, see for yourself, since Mor-Zamba came, a miracle! I'm left in peace. I shall make equally good deals, however; perhaps even better ones!'

'But, actually,' Mor-Zamba made bold to ask, 'what is that we have just done? Haven't we been stealing?'

'Exactly!' cried Robert, with a splutter. 'You've said it: we've been stealing. And the best of it is this; we shall go on stealing, for another two months at least. Listen, my boy, listen to me a bit: I shout the prices to the boss who never concerns himself with the scales, even supposing he can read them (for don't ever forget he's a Greek!); only, the prices I give him are always below the real ones; he knows it, because we are agreed beforehand. So he always gets back his own stake; don't worry about him, go on. But what he doesn't know is that I too am making a good thing out of it, by the methods which you know. Don't take on about it, young fellow; if there's a justice to punish the wicked, the whites should be the first to get it in the neck. And then, just remember this; there's this difference between a white man fleecing the peasants and me doing it; when he does it, he goes off to his own country with all his loot; as for me, what do I do? In effect, I give all the money back to the peasants, for their daughters. Or else, I go even to the remotest village to bring them salt, soap or cottons, and so spare them the risks of a journey of several days into the city. Just remember we've been to markets in places where no white would dare show himself. Weren't they glad to see us, those villagers, tell me?'

At the end of the season, that's to say at the beginning of February in the following year, Robert paid off his gang as usual, but didn't part with Alou until after a big feast held in his house at Kola-Kola, to which he especially invited Fulbert, whose role had been inconspicuous but highly fruitful; Mor-Zamba, more and more indispensable to the great man; and Alou himself. Robert took Alou aside when the meal was over and, after a few minutes, during which he must have given him the instructions which, he declared later, had become ritual, came back with an anxious and rather tired countenance.

'That Alou,' he confided to Mor-Zamba, 'is the youngest brother of my first wife. He must have made a hundred thousand francs during the long carnival we've lived through together. I've advised him to set up on his own account, but it's been the same thing all these years. He's an inveterate drunkard. In three weeks, he'll have drunk all his money, and we'll see him back here. His final aim is to live here with me, to be near his sister, as he puts it – and not to do a stroke; in other words he wants me to take charge of him completely. So he arrives; he installs himself. I can't chase him away, so I treat him like a servant. I tell him Alou, go and do such and such for me; or else: Alou set the table, it's time to eat. Above all, I make him eat with the servants. And that annoys him more than you can guess. However, I find that he's really a born servant, that one. When one is so stupid, one might just as well serve others without resentment. But look, I've married his sister, you see? I owe him everything, then, because he's my brother-in-law.'

Mor-Zamba asks himself today whether Robert himself was not a sort of Alou, everything considered; without caring to contradict himself, he begins to suspect that, just as this man he admires was inspired, full of go, absolutely mobilized towards a single goal, when he worked in the shadow of a white boss, so he became bungling, disorganized, futile, vain and totally inefficient when he had finally rejected the role of a subordinate, even an occasional one. This event came just at the close of the next season. This was really the big deal which Mor-Zamba was waiting for; or anyway, that's how it seemed to the refugee from the camp Gouverneur Leclerc, to that slightly slow-witted one who was nicknamed slyly, in Robert's entourage, the Bushman.

Robert and Fulbert bought a five ton Citroën, a T55 and, in the course of a solemn ceremony followed by a magnificent feast, entered into partnership, under the wise counsel of Jean-Louis, on a basis which must have been obscure enough, since it did not prevent the two friends from separating later in the most pathetic circumstances, which for long formed a theme for the historians of morals in Kola-Kola.

It was now the slack season, with its fortnightly markets in the interior where Robert and Fulbert, sole masters of their big lorry, penetrated with ever greater boldness, and where they had for their sole companion, at long intervals, a twenty wheeled log-carrier, a devilish looking mechanical monster.

For Mor-Zamba and for the other boys, black and white, who were employed or were taking their own chances, it meant long ordeals under the sunshine of empty markets, vainly awaiting the miracle of a solvent customer.

There were always the indescribable tableaux, perpetually renewed, of M. Albert's encounters with the brave people of Efoulane to which, as a courageous Kolean safely ensconced behind the railings of his lorry, Robert's acolyte contributed, in passing, his warlike exhortations.

Fulbert had two assistants to help him with the driving of the five tonner. One quickly abandoned this rough profession; the other, soon afterwards, broke both legs in falling from the running-board, where he had perched himself upright, regardless of the speed of the vehicle and his own half-drunken state.

'Why don't you take his place?' Robert advised Mor-Zamba. 'It wouldn't be a bad idea; you'd learn to drive, and by the time you get your licence I'll surely be ready to buy another lorry for you. In that way, we can stay together always.'

So Mor-Zamba became an apprentice driver. It was then an occupation full of dangers and outrageous events, so constantly trying and buffeting that this survivor of forced labour needed every bit of his physical and spiritual vitality to protect himself and to achieve the acrobatic skill which was the first requirement of that brotherhood.

The official driver, wholly absorbed in the tasks of his noble mission, depended on his assistant for all his most petty needs. Dubbed 'motor-boy' by the humble people whose symbolic incarnation he was, sometimes suffering and at others triumphant, the apprentice was required to perform at one and the same time as the comradely servant of his lorry, its nurse, its guardian angel, its administrator and the acrobat-rider of its platform, fugitive and tormented as life itself. One might have thought that Providence had invented the motor-boy solely for the entertainment of the mass of pedestrians who flocked the road joining Fort-Nègre to Efoulane, now freshly tarmacked. She sowed his path with opportunities to display his talents and to stare down these strangers so avid for spectacles.

Was the lorry about to move off? The motor-boy set himself on the watch, ear cocked for the precise moment when the roar of the engine would cease, transforming itself into a fleeting cry announcing that the cogs of the first gear had just engaged with those of the mainshaft; then, if the wheel began to shake after an imperceptible trembling, this was the signal for the motor-boy, an athletic veteran in the perilous feat.

He leapt suddenly forward, bent down briskly to pull out the wedge and straightened up to throw it over the side rail.

Adjusting his pace to the acceleration of the vehicle, he seized with his right hand the upright of the side rail and with his left the nearest bar; then a feline bound projected the hero on to the running-board. This whole manoeuvre was executed so swiftly that it was completed before the lorry had moved from first to second gear.

The hero then had a choice of two courses, one of which, elegant and full of scorn for danger, would force exclamations of amazement from the diverted onlookers, while the other, much better for his safety and repose, might draw hoots from the frustrated audience. One could either stay upright on the running-board, three-quarters turned towards the crowd and, smiling indulgently down at them, one hand on the hip and only the other still holding the rail, sink into a languid pose, then, seizing the half door, bend forward to exchange a few words with the distant occupants of the cabin. But this was an especially dangerous coquetry, above all when repeated too often. How many books have been filled with the evidence of witnesses to the tragic fall of motor-boys who showed an excessive inclination for this style!

Nothing is less secure than the mechanism for closing the cabin doors of a secondhand lorry, such as those invariably bought by the Kolean merchants, and the weight of a man is quite enough to make them open suddenly, throwing the unhappy apprentice on to the road where he lies stock-still, quite dead. A fine rain, falling a little earlier and then forgotten, has perhaps made the running-board slippery; absorbed in his sophisticated stunts, the hero lets himself go, entangling his naked feet on the muddy surface of the running-board, on which he is suddenly seen to bounce like a football, before rolling into the road and getting his head crushed as flat as a washing-board by the double rear wheels of the truck.

If the motor-boy was calm enough to avoid these perilous feats, he renounced at the same stroke the giddy excitement of popular acclaim. In that case, as soon as he reached the running-board, he would throw himself into the briefer but no less hazardous ascent of the side-rail, after which he found himself flat on his bottom on the hard planking of the platform, shut in by the railings like a monkey in a cage.

If the lorry were about to stop, the motor-boy had only to reverse the order of these acrobatics; one hand grasping the wedge, the other descending the rail by clutching convulsively, at each bar, the apprentice leapt into the road, ran beside the vehicle for a while and, at the very moment of its arrest, pushed the heavy wooden wedge under the double rear wheels to block them completely.

But all this was no more than the façade of the motor-boy's life and few people knew by what iron law, custom, more inflexible than any proper legal contract, bound the apprentice to his driver. In exchange for services of every kind which the motor-boy owed to his master, the latter engaged to teach him to drive within a time which was rarely fixed. The truth was that there were few drivers who did not consider their apprentice a kind of servant, or, even more, as a man of sorrows forever bound to their caprice.

One can imagine the sort of price which the corporation of titular drivers attached to their instruction and, in a general way, to their social position, as well as to the privilege that went with it, by learning that there were cases where the driver, against the promise of a long bondage in apprenticeship, exacted from his motor-boy a young sister still barely pubescent; in other words, a wife worth her weight in gold to a titular driver, a man usually well on in years at that epoch in the history of Fort-Nègre.

Now divided between service to Robert, his first employer, and to Fulbert, to whom he was newly bound as apprentice, Mor-Zamba got no enlightenment from these two friends concerning the precise distribution of his duties; it seemed as if they preferred to let him wrestle with this insoluble problem alone. He strove to be Robert's man no longer, save all day on Sundays, or holidays, and any time when they passed the day at Kola-Kola, rather than in a circuit of petty trading. And even during these tours, he often had to make himself double. During the journey, he was motor-boy to Fulbert and entirely submitted to his will. But as soon as they reached the town or village where the market was held, he was Robert's boy, carrying his stuff to the market-place, setting up his stall, enticing the customers, and even selling in the place of a man who was often tempted in the course of his journeys to go on the binge or to pass the time with his friends in a bar from which he would always return with his eye as clear, his step as serene, his little spit as mechanical, his laugh as abandoned and his voice as raucous as ever. When he considered the advantages and disadvantages of his ambiguous position, Mor-Zamba often doubted if he had gained by the change; but at other times he would congratulate himself on having embarked on a promising course, at the end of which he would enter the much envied caste of the titular drivers.

When Abena came back, having himself gone to war as a driver, he would certainly congratulate him also; he would say to him with that grave and thoughtful manner Mor-Zamba knew so well: You haven't wasted your time, have you? Well done!

He kept himself regularly informed about the arrival of ex-servicemen. More than four years after the war, they were still returning, though now only in groups of a few dozen. Whenever he saw a ship carrying some sons of the land in war uniform – khaki blouse and trousers, forage-cap perched on one ear, black half boots – old Lobila would tell his lodger, when he came home in the evening. Mor-Zamba, who was too exhausted at that hour to take any important initiative, would be content to sleep with one ear cocked for the return, often late enough, of Jean-Louis, and to charge him with a commission at the port for the following day. This youth would undertake nothing without recompense, pretending that he would lose some of the profit of his time by it. Nevertheless, some links had been forged between these two which, if they lacked warmth, were strengthened by necessity. Mor-Zamba learnt much from Jean-Louis, who, for his part, marvelled at the accumulation in the gigantic boy of a capital he had never anticipated.

Abena must still be somewhere outside the colony, probably in Europe, or elsewhere; the war had rolled over so many battlefields. If he had come back, he would have gone to Oyolo, where Jeanne would have told him that his brother had taken refuge in Fort-Nègre. Then Abena would have found him in Kola-Kola with little trouble, since nearly all the emigrants from Oyolo pitched up there.

Accordingly, Jean-Louis would go down to the port the following morning, where he sometimes found himself eyeball to eyeball with his father; but the young man was now so self-assured that he didn't bother to invent explanations for his absence from the college at that hour of the day. The ex-servicemen remained for several days, sometimes for weeks, in the town, haunting especially the port, where they supervised the unloading of their luggage. Although never announced on the local radio, which had just begun to broadcast for two hours per day, their arrival was none the less an event, and news of it spread rapidly through the city. Comrades who had returned before them put on their uniforms again, though these were now usually in rags; they went down to the port and paraded before the new arrivals, giving them the military salute by reciting their names, the ranks which they had won on the white man's battlefield – at the cost of such suffering as God only knew – their units, the campaigns in which they had taken part, sometimes the commander of that unit or, more rarely, for one had to be very well informed to possess such knowledge, the name of the commander-in-chief himself: Mundinga, Jean-Alfred, Lodgings Marshall; Damas; French Light Brigade, General Legentilhomme. Zogbekwe, Amoundale, Sergeant Major, Second Infantry Battalion, First Independent Mixed Brigade, Bir-Hakeim, Lieutenant-Colonel de Roux.

These swelling incantations, and all this ceremonial reveal-ing their access to mysteries formerly hidden, ravished the bystanders: dockworkers who had abandoned their work, despite the shrieks of their foremen; young students running from their deserted schools; whores scenting a good fortune. But as the war itself faded in the minds of the actors and the spectators of these scenes, so the atmosphere of blind rejoicing which had at first surrounded them gave way to resentment, and finally to anger. The newcomers, as they came ashore, let fall expressions full of disillusionment, bitterness and ven-geance. They had not been paid the demobilization bonus promised them, nor yet the enlistment bounty which, in breach of all good faith, had been deducted monthly from their miser-able salaries since the beginning of the war. The few things that they had bought with their savings had been seized aboard the boat; some had married in Europe and had children, but the authorities refused all appeals to let their families join them. They had not been given any formal pledge of priority in employment to reabsorb them into civilian life, nor of credit for the businesses they wanted to set up or the plantations they wanted to develop on their lands. They had simply been told: 'For all these privileges to which your heroic exploits give you incontestable right, you must first return to your respective colonies and make your application to the local authorities.' They could well have replied: 'The men to whom you refer us have nothing in common with us, they haven't fought in the war, with very few exceptions; they haven't shared with us the comradeship in arms which enables us to talk together, and even to understand each other, even though you are white and we are black,' but they had done nothing of the sort. As usual, they had been outwitted.

These protests flabbergasted the witnesses, who did not doubt the truth of the accusations. Furthermore, those of their comrades who had preceded them to the colony and had come to greet them at the port not only confirmed the complaints of the volunteers, they corroborated them by the ragged state of their boots and uniforms, the filthy condition of their hair, their incessant yawning, their starveling look; all proofs, according to them, of the ingratitude of those who left them in need, and not, as some malicious people would have it, the stigmata of vices which they might have displayed without shame in other circumstances, such as laziness, drunkenness or indifference.

First of all, they assembled in the bar of the port where the proprietor, a fat Marsellais with pomaded hair, tolerated their presence as long as they sat in the back room; the newcomers spick and span in their uniforms, trim as real warriors; their predecessors shabby and pitiful; all drinking beer under the condescending gaze of the owner who sometimes, like a man who has just received a consignment of goodwill, would felici-tate them, with an awkward smile, calling them 'our boys', on having returned home 'after the show'. Perhaps these were not quite the appropriate sentiments for the occasion, but it was better to put up with them than to be forced to gulp one's beer from the bottle, in the glare of the sun and amid the

132

compassionate looks of the idlers; leaning oneself aggressively and sloppily against the mercifully frequent balustrades of the port's colonial architecture, or against the bales of merchandise. For this became their fate when, their arrivals taking a more political turn, the Marsellais began refusing them entry to his establishment.

Finally, these warriors began to harangue the crowd of bystanders, who had grown somewhat pressing and noisy in their approbation:

'Brothers, between those people and us, nothing can be done. Perhaps you've been told that we led a fine life down there? I'll tell you, it was more like a dog's life, a life fit for dogs of niggers, yes! We were kept confined, in quarantine like the sick, never going out except to fight but always excluded from the victory parades. That was our fine life for you. . . .'

These revelations confounded the listeners, but anger did not let them shake their heads for long. However, the orator now broke off suddenly, judging his own clumsiness by the perplexed or frozen looks of his comrades; he had been wrong to open the painful chapter. Still wishing to form themselves into a caste and to preserve an ever-glorious aura about them, the ex-servicemen were long cautious about going too far in the story of the humiliations they had suffered during the war. The destruction of their prestige would have reduced them to the ranks, despite their odyssey. The first to reveal the truth without any false shame were the warriors who became militants of Rubenism.

But what did it matter? Towards midday, the idlers drifted off, both satisfied and frustrated; under their very eyes, a corner of the veil had been lifted on an epic more profoundly bitter than the depths of a ravine; it was for them now to imagine other precipices, other darknesses within it.

Jean-Louis mingled amongst the old soldiers; he induced them to talk, one here, one there, a third in a dive of the African quarter before a bowl of cheap maize beer or a glass of Holy Joseph. The old soldiers exceeded themselves on these occasions, putting into the hearts of their brothers who had never gone away a balm of pride hitherto unguessed at. We had been afraid at first that they would now despise our food, our

133

drinks and our women – in a word, the poverty of our everyday life – they of whom it had once been said that they had seen Paris and Paradise. The warriors quickly put paid to these apprehensions, showing that, quite on the contrary, exile and deprivation had sharpened their appetite for our native pleasures, which gloomy memory had invested with all the magic of a symbol for the real good life. Even Holy Joseph, which had not been invented, after many experiments, until near the end of the war, when their enlistments were ended, became the delight of our young heroes on their return, just as if they had sucked it in their cradles along with their mothers' milk. Under its influence they held their audience spellbound indefinitely, enlarging upon their battles, their sufferings, the exaltation of victory, the beauty of women. None of them had encountered Abena, neither in the desert, the Far East, Italy nor France. One old warrior who was particularly fond of Holy Joseph revealed to Jean-Louis, for the price of a glass of 'rotgut', that he knew how some of their comrades, while stationed at Frejus awaiting embarkation from Marseilles for Africa, had been solicited to re-engage, pocketing a handsome bonus which was paid to them on the spot, so that they would go and fight in Indo-China. Some had signed up, with their eyes closed. In any case, not all the survivors of the war against Germany were ready to return to Africa.

'Indo-China, what's that?' asked Jean-Louis in amazement. 'And why use our own boys to make war down there?'

'What!' snorted the old soldier, 'you go to school and you don't know?'

After glancing all around, his eyes twinkling first with goodwill and then with malice, he beckoned Jean-Louis to lean forward and whispered to him:

'You want to know what Indo-China is, young fellow? Don't try to imagine it, you'll never get near the reality. Better come to my place tomorrow; I'll tell you all about it and we can have a good laugh. Many strange things happen in this world, believe me. It's going to happen here too, sooner or later, don't you doubt it. But no one breathes a word about it, neither the two Fort-Nègre newspapers, nor the governor's radio, and for good reason! Anyway, everyone is struggling to guess what will

134

happen in future. Haven't you ever had that feeling yourself. Everyone wrinkles his brow to try and pierce the shadows, don't they? Come and see me and I'll tell you all about it. And, what's more, promise me to go down to the estuary and watch the waves which push, press, tumble forward and advance, always in the same direction. Well, those waves in the estuary, do you know what they are? They are us, yes, all of us; here, elsewhere, and over there in Indo-China; perhaps we may run against one another, overthrow and tread upon each other, and even fight each other, but we are all going in the same direction, do you understand?'

As Jean-Louis still seemed perplexed the old soldier, who was called Joseph, continued:

'It doesn't matter, my lad. Just buy me another glass; tomorrow, come and see me and I'll explain everything.'

After this Jean-Louis went of his own free will to the port or called spontaneously upon Joseph, so excited was he by the various phenomena revealed to him on these occasions, which seemed to him to enrich his own knowledge with every conversation, whether with Joseph or with one of the other ex-soldiers who disembarked, now in smaller and smaller numbers, like a trickle of water, drying up.

Jean-Louis' early accounts of his interviews with Joseph left Mor-Zamba first astounded, and then rather sceptical. Then, as if resigned to this new phase in his sufferings, he fell into the habit of tormenting himself with questions concerning Abena's motives in deciding to make war again in Indo-China, if indeed he had gone there. So it seemed as if he still hadn't managed to get a gun of his own? Was it really so difficult? Perhaps he had succeeded in getting one and, at the very moment of embarkation, the authorities had managed by a random check to discover it. They then would have confiscated the precious thing, at the very least.

It seemed to Mor-Zamba that Joseph had given the impression, in the course of his conversation with Jean-Louis, that he knew a great deal more than he cared to disclose. For example, he had discussed the natural suspicion that Abena might be dead. Why might not German planes have attacked a convoy in which the young man was moving, whether in

Cyrenaica, in Italy, in France or anywhere else? The lorry in which he was travelling, all alone in his cabin, would have taken a direct hit and nothing would be left of the driver. Or perhaps the plane, which was hedge-hopping, had contented itself with machine-gunning, which the old soldier himself had described as a frequent practice. The gravely injured driver would have died a few minutes, or a few hours later; he would have been hastily shovelled into a common grave, then quickly sprinkled with lime. Nothing would have been heard here, owing to the notorious inability of the colonial authorities to give serious news about African soldiers, even when they knew who their families were. Hadn't they often pronounced as dead soldiers who landed ignorantly at Fort-Nègre a few months later, bursting with health and happiness at seeing their native land again? Contrariwise, had they not assured families of the affectionate remembrance of their sons, when by the most elementary arithmetic it became obvious that these sons had been dead many months beforehand?

No, the old soldier Joseph had resolutely rejected all these hypotheses, declaring that a man like Abena, whom he had come to know by Jean-Louis' descriptions almost as if he had met the man, could not have died in such a fashion. But he could well imagine him, on the other hand, re-engaging to go and fight on the battlefields of Asia. Once one has sniffed gunpowder, he affirmed, it is difficult to resist its appeal. Abena had doubtless succumbed to the attractions, inconceivable to those who haven't felt them, of the lust for battle – the stutter of automatic arms, the surprise and confusion of the ranks, the explosion of shells spat out by the mortars or vomited by the guns with a lugubrious roar, the shouts of the officers, the brief fixation with the concept of unity, the breathless anticipation of an attack. He couldn't be sure that one fought in exactly that manner in Indo-China too; his information even made him doubt it. But if the methods of fighting down there were different, the old soldier was still convinced that the rest of the battle would be the same.

Now, whenever a new contingent of ex-soldiers arrived, Jean-Louis was sure to find his friend Joseph in the port, more and more abandoned to his vice of drunkenness, whose ever more repulsive and distressing appearance did not put off the newcomers, just as long as he preserved the relics of his ruined uniform. The drunkard dogged Jean-Louis' footsteps, over-heard his conversations with the new arrivals and ended his day with the young man in the den where they had so often met, at the far end of Kola-Kola.

'No,' he would observe, shaking his head, 'no, you're wasting your time; it's useless to go on searching. I'm just about certain now that your man's in Indo-China. Lucky bastard! If only he knew what's awaiting him here!'

'What's that?' Jean-Louis demanded.

'Oh, nothing,' replied Joseph dreamily, with a distant look. 'Perhaps he'll look after his pence better than I have. There have been days when I had plenty of them, believe me, and it wasn't bad at all. You see, my lad, it's the tragedy of the military man to lay out all his dibs.'

'Because of women?'

'Oh, you know how it is. The brothers like to boast that from time to time, for the sake of talking. Don't take them at their word. To begin with, what they say is not exactly gospel truth, is it? And as for women, there's no need to believe they've had as many as all that, in reality. People always get excited too quickly about women, and I ask myself why. Furthermore, as I've already told you, there weren't all that many of them, for the number of men that we were; and anyway we always came last, we others, as though it was fixed like that. No. that's nothing; one can always do without that. But I'll tell you what a real soldier can never do without. Eeech! Oooch!'

And the old soldier pointed his finger at the glass of Holy Joseph which sat in his left hand, whilst twisting his face in a hideous grin.

'Here's what a real soldier will never give up, as long as the earth is the earth. And if he's far from home, so much the worse. And if he's very far from home, a thousand times worse still. And if he's as far from home as we were from here, don't even try to understand, you'll never be able to.'

'But, about women,' Jean-Louis asked, on the first occasion when Mor-Zamba joined them, 'about women, you said there

137

were very few for such a large number of men. Were there really so many men as all that?'

'Ah, my dear! Ah, my poor lad! Don't even try to imagine how many!'

'Where did they all come from, then, these men?'

'Where from? But from everywhere, from every corner of the world, you know. The war made a rendezvous for all the races. There were the whites, obviously in the majority, because it was their continent. Yes, but when I say "whites" like that, it's as if I hadn't said anything, because these whites, if you really look into it, come in every possible sort. Every sort you can imagine! Big athletic blonds; little, malicious brown ones – really malicious! and nimble too, believe me!'

'Is it really like that?'

'Really, we had every possible sort. Anyway, you've only got to look at them down here; they don't resemble each other all that much. But over there....'

'And after the whites?'

'After the whites? After them, bless me, I really think it was the blacks.'

'How could it be the blacks? Are there really so many blacks as that on the earth? They've always told me that we are the race with the fewest numbers.'

'I don't know how many we are on the earth, my lad, but as for seeing blacks during the war, I'll bet you anything you like that I've seen them all right, and not a few of them, either. And there too, when we say "blacks", it's just a way of speaking, because we too, you know, are exactly like the whites; there's every possible kind of black man too. There are the American blacks for example; ah, those, my lad! Those are men, if you like!'

'There are blacks in America too?'

'Why not, young jackanapes! You go to their schools and you don't know that! And how is it that there are blacks in America? Where do they come from, or have they always been there, ah now, that would be too much to ask me. But one thing is sure, there are blacks over there. And more civilized than us too, if you want to know, with their own officers and all.'

'Black captains and lieutenants, you mean?'

138

'Even majors and colonels. Whole regiments having nothing but them, from second lieutenants to colonels. I've been told that they have generals, but those I've never seen myself. And look, I only tell you the things I've seen, isn't it so? Old Joseph doesn't like to tell tall stories, and when he hasn't seen something, he's not going to say he has. Among these American blacks I've seen everything, except generals. But then, you should see them on parade! What lords those boys are!'

'And what language do they speak?'

'Why, the language of their own country, to be sure – American. Anyone who can speak English can also make himself understood by them.'

'And are they really black? Black all over?'

'Oh, as I've said, they have all sorts among them: some very light skinned, like our mulattoes, and others as black as a Saringala.'

'Were there other kinds of blacks, apart from these Americans and our own boys, like you?'

'Well, there were the Saringalas, to be sure. But those, since they can't even read their own gibberish, are real animals, beasts of slaughter for the battlefield; you can do just as you like with them. I remember that when we left here to go up to the desert, we were all barefoot, the Saringalas and us. That's something I'll never forget, because the engines were still burning coal then and sparks flew into the trucks, burning our feet and legs. And I can assure you, I'll remember that a long while. Well, you can believe me or not, as you like, but we Oyolos managed to get hold of our boots. We all got together and wrote a letter of protest, all in French. As for the Saringalas, those people didn't get theirs until the eve of the first battles, I believe. But, watch out for them, eh! Swollen with pride, real animals, believe me! The guns can thunder away, the planes can roar and zoom at roof-top level with machine-guns blazing, the Saringalas won't bat an eyelid. For standing up to fire, they're champions, the Saringalas. Oh, the governor knows what he's doing in flooding us with them down here. Good soldiers who cost nothing are not found every day.'

'For standing up to fire,' Jean-Louis insisted, 'there were the Saringalas, then. Good, and what others were there over there?'

'Apart from the Saringalas? Oh well, there were the American blacks, for sure.'

'And apart from them?'

'Apart from the American blacks, well, there were ... gracious me, there was us, that's it.'

'How many blacks?'

'Many, many blacks, young lad, if you want to know the truth. There's no one more valiant under fire than a black man, so long as he has a gun, for sure.'

Then Jean-Louis and Mor-Zamba, disturbed by this truth, finally decided to reveal that Abena's main project at the time of his departure, was to get hold of his own gun and bring it back to their country; the drunkard's face froze, he threw a look all around, beckoned them towards him and whispered:

'Then it was for that he re-engaged boys! I understand it all now. He's hoping to find a crack in the wall of official vigilance one day. He'll never succeed; they'll take his gun off him every time, especially if it's an automatic, you know. So that was it! But they'll never let him do it, I'll bet you anything you like they won't.'

'And why not, exactly?' asked Jean-Louis.

'They're too scared, my lad; you must know that, you who go to school. Listen to me a bit; the trouble with a gun is that one's always tempted to use it. Tac, tac, tac, tac, tac, tac! Imagine a bit of that over here, that would be a laugh! The boy who has a gun here, well, he won't be idle; we certainly don't lack shits in the colony, beginning with the Saringalas. Tac, tac, tac, tac, tac! Boum, boum, boum! That would be a laugh! Listen now, you post yourself at the corner of an alley, with your gun loaded; you listen to them coming; there are three of them, and the bastards think themselves quite safe like that; they talk at the top of their voices, perhaps they even laugh aloud. Suddenly, there they are in front of you. You don't even have to take aim; before they know what's happened to them, tac, tac, tac, tac, tac! And you vanish, neither seen nor known I assure you. Imagine a bit of that here. What do you think would happen? Eh, tell me, what do you think would happen?'

'I don't know,' said Jean-Louis, hypocritically.

'In reality, I myself don't know either,' the drunkard

140

resumed. 'Perhaps the Saringalas would become more wicked, but they wouldn't swagger about any more. And that would be a mighty victory. To force one's enemy to stop swaggering, that's an achievement. And then you know what?'

'Well?'

'Nothing would be the same any more, my lad, you must know it yourself. The really terrible thing, enough to drive one mad, is when nothing ever changes. When you're coming back on the ship, you know, you have time to think; you say to yourself: It's impossible that things can still be the same, impossible. And what is terrible is to find that everything is exactly as before, lock, stock and barrel, pouah! Have you heard people talk about Ruben? Come closer; have you heard them talk about Ruben; the people of Kola-Kola, the petty workers of Fort-Nègre, the dock labourers? Say, my lad, have you ever heard talk of Ruben, you who are still in school?'

'One thing,' said Jean-Louis; 'I want to know one thing; is it true that they kept you isolated like men with the plague, and that they excluded you from the victory parades?'

'Just so!' cried the old soldier, after taking a deep swig of Holy Joseph. 'Absolutely true! Look, my boy, who was it who took Kufra? It's true that you don't even know what Kufra is; but what do they teach you in that wretched school? Well, I'll tell you who took Kufra, so open your ears wide. Just understand, then, that the victors of Kufra were none other than ourselves!'

'Who, exactly?'

'We, the people of this country, and the Saringalas too. Altogether, four or five battalions of blacks. So, Kufra, that's what it is, my dear.'

'And what about the others?'

'The others? Just look at them around here: do you often see them in front when something hot is happening? All right for shouting "Forward!" to other people, but that's about all. What's more, at that time, if you set apart the officers, they didn't have a single real combatant fit. They had nothing but us. And what happened then? We never had any of the honours of victory. When the Italians surrendered....'

'The Italians? Why the Italians? What were they doing down

there? I thought it was the Germans you were fighting in the desert?'

'Italians too! I'll explain it another time. But what the devil do they teach you at school? Anyway the honours of victory were to enter the citadel after the enemy's surrender. The citadel was called El Tadj; well, just guess what happened? We people, we were not permitted to enter El Tadj, so as not to humiliate the Italians: they had made that condition themselves before giving up.'

'And your leaders accepted it?'

'Just as I've said, my lad. And that was repeated many times in the course of the war. But as for me, I only tell you what I've seen myself. When he hasn't seen something with his own eyes, old Joseph is not going to say he saw it, right? We were left outside, we lot, in the sand and the blazing heat of the desert. But all that is history now. Now to the present: have you heard them talk about Ruben, my lad? Give me just one more glass of Holy Joseph! Have you ever heard them speak of Ruben?'

After many hours of conversation, Jean-Louis and Mor-Zamba left the old soldier without any illusions; there was no longer any doubt that the drunkard had never met Abena, for he could not have been ignorant of his obsession with obtaining a gun.

Jean-Louis, for his part, was above all intrigued by Joseph's political insights which, he believed, contained a mystery he could not be contented to obtain so cheaply. He was the more put out because he knew from experience that the ex-soldiers were too full of themselves to squander their praises, even if they were drunk, upon a person who had never surveyed a battlefield. Joseph was not mean in his praise of Ruben and Jean-Louis, whose family house was a few minutes' walk from the Labour Centre, still Ruben's residence at that time, knew the latter very well and knew equally that he had never been a soldier. Was Ruben, then, something other than he was thought to be by the majority of Koleans, even though they adored him — a hothead, brave as a lion, ready to say out loud what every

Kolean scarcely dared to whisper ... and doomed to be beaten flat sooner or later, like so many other giants who had gone before him? So he wasn't just a woolgatherer without any future, squeezing the clouds to draw from them a chimera at harvest which our youngest unborn children would not enjoy, worshipped by crowds in search of a myth, but secretly despised by the real sages, who persuaded themselves every night, while they lay awake, that when you got down to it there was only the belly and the abdomen? Was Ruben a guide carried along by the wave of his followers, in the midst of human billow glistening towards the future, as if towards a natural ocean? Was it true that, as the old soldier tirelessly repeated, not even God himself could halt the march of a colonized people towards freedom, always constrained by the tides of the estuary to pour its waters in the opposite direction?

That year the cocoa season was a poor one for Robert, according to all the witnesses, and especially Alou, who had of course returned to his brother-in-law's house, even though he was treated there like a servant. The trader might have bought cocoa in his own name, having amassed, by borrowing right and left, a modest capital which, though small, would have sufficed for the deliberately cautious scale of his enterprise. But, despite the flowery eloquence of Jean-Louis, the many appeals to the Director of Economic Affairs to give him the necessary permission remained vain, by reason, he was told, of the failure to offer the justifications long demanded for certain irregularities, which Robert himself had accepted as his responsibility. Sunk in the swamp of these obscure dealings with the administration and having, on the other hand, broken with Niarkos as a result of a quarrel about which Robert refused to speak to any of his people, the Kolean merchant was forced, like most of his fellows, to renounce the most lucrative trade in all the business of the colony. Without being able to realize his ambitious dreams, he consoled himself by redoubling his ardour and assiduity in the markets and cocoa fairs, an area in which the Kolean merchants had the field to themselves, because the controls there were very lax and even, in certain years, non-existent. Robert found other profits in transport, in association with his friend Fulbert, driver of the five ton Citroën who, doubtless for the first time in his life, became a personage sought out by men of influence, and who distinguished even himself by his zeal, now that he had become a master.

But Robert got his real revenge months after the cocoa-season, when his youngest wife, Dorothy, gave birth to a son at the Parant Maternity Hospital. Robert's twin passions were very young wives and male children. At the birth of the latter, he was beside himself with happiness; he ruined himself to the last cent with presents to mother and child and with celebrations which he offered one day to his friends, another day to his neighbours, another to his enemies with whom, it was said, he sought to make occasion for a reconciliation. After five years in the service of the Kolean trader, Mor-Zamba understood that this immoderate passion for male offspring was one of the things which condemned to the mediocrity of an always modest fortune, far below the emulation of the meanest Greek, this man who was otherwise so inventive, active and sometimes even well-advised. Father now of numerous sons, he had never considered the expense of celebrating the arrival in the world of each one of them; an expense which always reduced him to zero, or very near it.

All through that week, Robert's house was never empty and the party rolled on without pause. The trader had requisitioned a taxi to ensure an incessant stream of journeys, messages and visits by friends or relatives between Kola-Kola and the Parant hospital. In reality, this was used most of the time by Jean-Louis to parade through Fort-Nègre, taking care always to have at his side, Mor-Zamba, who was supposedly out and about in pursuit of the orders or the interests of his master. In this respect, the only constant mission of Mor-Zamba was to go every evening to the hospital and to keep company with Dorothy from seven o'clock, when the young mothers began their meal, until nine o'clock, when the bell announced the end of visiting hours. The taxi would carry Mor-Zamba and Jean-Louis to the door of this hospital; Mor-Zamba would get down and go to the maternity wing; Jean-Louis, who was repelled by that role, took the taxi back to Kola-Kola or, more often, to Fort-Nègre, to amaze his friends of both sexes. He would come back with the taxi a little before nine o'clock to collect Mor-Zamba. On the Friday evening, however, he consented to get out with Mor-Zamba, telling the driver to wait for them.

Mor-Zamba had confided to Jean-Louis that he was intrigued by the behaviour of young Dorothy, who seemed keen on starting an affair with him, and the young man had agreed to come and judge things for himself. There was no doubt that the girl was excessively pleased with her visitors; she poured out before them, as if to stun them, all the treasures of a carefree seduction. Kolean girls were proverbial for their looseness, as were their husbands for their complaisance, being too often elderly and so unable to give their young wives a fair ration of certain natural joys. Astonished by the coolness of her visitors, who were restrained by a mutual reserve common enough between two young men who have never before chased this kind of game in collaboration, she assumed that they were preoccupied by something and sought to help them dissipate their cares by recourse to a remedy whose virtue is never denied. Pointing to a big wicker basket beside her bed, she cried:

'But my God! What have I been thinking of? Just think that this is full of good things to drink! Yes, in there ... what are you waiting for? Go on, help yourselves; take some more, go on.'

Among the heap of presents which filled the basket there were in fact, scattered here and there, bottles of wine, flasks of spirits, boxes of sweets and phials of perfume. The young men went for the wine and spirits, whilst the fifteen fellow mothers in the ward, who had also been invited, displayed a taste for the more feminine wares. Led on by Jean-Louis, then, from that moment onwards Mor-Zamba, whose natural inclination was towards women of more modest station and capable of showing a bit of modesty, let his enthusiasm and interest in Dorothy grow step by step, and thus he let himself drink more than he was accustomed to. The two friends did not notice how time was passing, and it was not till an employee pointed out to them that visiting hours were long past and the clock was striking the hospital's 'lights-out' hour, that they decided to leave.

The taxi had abandoned them, no doubt unnerved by the late

hour. Unable to return to Kola-Kola through the centre of Fort-Nègre, forbidden to Africans at night since the bloody fusillades of October, 1945, they decided to make the detour by way of the Schools' Plateau, a quarter lying to the east of the town which was reached by climbing a steep escarpment. After the blazing heat of the day, and in their semi-tipsy state, it was a delight to them to walk through a night air beginning to grow crisp, to struggle and sweat on the slope and arrive at the summit, to slither voluptuously like men who believed with rapture, that thanks to Robert the next two days, like the five last, would be devoted to pleasure, if not to feasting. Jean-Louis vainly tried to conceal a bottle of rum under his shirt, the tails of which he let fall outside a very elegant pair of dacron trousers, whenever he passed the halo of the street-lamps, which grew proportionately sparser as they moved further from the European quarter. Jean-Louis intended to take advantage of this unforeseen detour to give the bottle to Georges Mor-Kinda, more commonly known as Joe the Juggler, to whom the young dandy found a peremptory reason for attaching himself because, in addition to all his vices, he was the brother of Alphonsine, a ravishing girl who passed every morning in front of his parents' horrible house on her way to school.

The Juggler's preference was for employment as a 'boy'; he liked to place himself, whenever he could, with white families in the centre of Fort-Nègre. When Europeans destined to install themselves in the colony came ashore, a whole flock of informers would alert Mor-Kinda and his friends, who, despising the officials, sought ardently after the businessmen, the traders and the professions where money is frequently, if not daily made. Many times relapsing into theft in all its forms, Mor-Kinda had not yet succeeded in hiring himself out and thus purging his last default; he was too well-known. During his detention he had often been lent to the Director of the Institute of 18 June, Sandrinelli; who reigned like a potentate over a school for boys, a school for girls, a school for apprentices and a whole settlement of abandoned white and mulatto children. When he presented himself in front of Sandrinelli, bearing in mind that when still a prisoner, he had often relieved madame,

146

though she was already surrounded by 'boys' devoted to the most tawdry household tasks, the director of the institute had immediately decided to invest the Juggler with the official function of watchman of the institution, although utilizing him half the time as a servant. Madame Sandrinelli thus had a supplementary 'boy' of proved competence and, which certainly didn't grate at all, paid for from the budget of the colony. For the Juggler, this post with an official was, for good measure, and for an old hand who knew all the ropes, no more than an initial step which must be of short duration. He would arrive at the institute towards four in the afternoon, address himself to the tasks indicated by Madame Sandrinelli; serve the evening meal to the family, rinse the dishes whilst ravenously gulping all the leftovers, wash the clothes dirtied by the children during the day and, by ten o'clock or ten thirty, go to a room in the school from which he was supposed to survey the cluster of little buildings which made up the Institute. In reality Mor-Kinda, who was rarely fasting by this time, slept immediately and didn't stir till four or five in the morning. In the twilight he would go and put his head under the tap in the courtyard, let a stream of cold water flow over it to refresh him, nibble some groundnuts whilst swigging a bottle of beer reserved for his breakfast, and wait, to consider his duty done, till M. Sandrinelli got up and dressed, an event which normally occurred at about six in the morning and of which the Juggler was informed by hearing the potentate calling in his watchdogs, released a moment earlier.

That evening, a little after eleven, Mor-Kinda had finished his work and had just reached the room where he slept when he heard his two visitors, who had climbed the wall of the school at a point known to Jean-Louis, scratching at his door according to the agreed signal. Although he did not yet know what a splendid present awaited him, he greeted the two men with delight.

'I've always wondered,' he said to Jean-Louis, 'how you manage to find me so easily in this maze of hovels. Hats off to you, old chap!'

Then turning to Mor-Zamba:

'And this one, I guess just by his size, is the famous thrasher

147

of Saringalas. You've made quite a name for yourself! How goes it Bushman? No, but just look at him! For a bloke as huge as that, what merit is there in taking a Saringala in each hand and banging their heads together? If I were him, I'd do the same too. Careful! let's talk quietly; the boss isn't in bed yet. In fact, far from it....'

Jean-Louis had just exposed the object of his visit and the Juggler, already in the grip of his delight, was holding his sides with laughter, but taking care that his guffaws, instead of exploding, came out as misbegotten coos. When he came to himself again, he opened the bottle and took a big swig before passing it to the others, who copied him; after which, leaning far backwards, he set the neck of the bottle to his lips and didn't straighten up till the rum had made several glug-glugs in his throat. All at once, he was seized with a sort of delirium of which his visitors, gasping with admiration at his prowess, did not catch the first words, but which, as the Juggler continued, froze them all the more with amazement.

'Ruben is in the hands of his enemies,' whispered Mor-Kinda, between two gusts of laughter (also whispered however), 'but yes, what did you expect? It was bound to happen, wasn't it? I don't know exactly how they caught him; but certainly they've got him at this moment, and no further off than in this very school. And under whose guard, do you think? I'll give you thousands if you guess. You don't believe me? O.K., follow me and see for yourselves. Shshs! quietly boys. We don't want to alert all those others who are assembled down there, in the boss's house: Deputy Langelot, Commissioner Maestraci, a commander of the colonial army, a young mameluke and lots of others. Stick to me like limpets, the night is really dark.'

In fact, not a single light was burning in the institute, a huddle of miscellaneous little brick buildings built in haste, some roofed with corrugated iron and some with tiles. The director, Sandrinelli, who was also called the Gaullist, was accustomed to say that electric light was an irresistible attraction to Negroes and that the darkness, on the contrary, frightened them so much that robbers and bad men fled of their own accord from his establishment, just so long as it was shrouded

148

in obscurity every night. Even among Africans, he was reputed to know Africa and what he chose to call the Negroes. He had arrived in the colony as a young hothead soon after the First World War, at a time when only pioneers would come to a country only just won by dire force from the hereditary enemy. Instead of imitating the other young colonial officials who, almost as soon as they arrived, swapped their official sun-helmets for a forestry concession or a trading post in the bush, he had obstinately remained a bachelor and a schoolmaster, not renouncing the first of these conditions until just before the recent war. Chief agent in rallying the colony to the cause of De Gaulle in exile in London, he had pleaded his frequent bouts of malaria as an excuse for not joining the forces which went to wallow desperately in the desert, so that France might at any cost figure among the countries which had fought against the Axis. Thus the five years of the war had been for him one long happy honeymoon. What is more, on those solemn occasions so numerous in this colony, and wherever corruption, hypocrisy, plunder and insensibility reign, his friends liked to render homage to his double vocations of educator and father.

The Juggler had just halted at the foot of the completely blank façade of a building slightly higher than the others, with his ear pressed to the wall, a gesture soon imitated by his followers. They could hear heavy blows, each followed by an agonizing scream, soon buried by growling and yelling voices, which seemed to rebuke or menace the prisoner, as if these men had sworn to put a miserable end to him if he did not keep silent. Then followed more blows, resounding ones these, following each other in a slow rhythm as if applied with skill and deliberation. It seemed that the torturer was taking his time, in the manner of an artist. The victim, who no longer dared to open his mouth, no doubt terrified by the reprisals just promised him, uttered long tearful groans which gave some notion of his pain and pierced the heart of Mor-Zamba, drawing from him a river of tears which flooded his cheeks, whilst pity, anger and despair reduced him to incoherent gestures and rigid tremors, like one who powerlessly watches a child drowning or being carried off by a savage beast.

'That's him,' said Mor-Kinda to his two visitors. 'And it's

been like that for more than an hour. This sort of thing has happened many times since I came here and each time it's exactly the same. They grab someone, they bring him in, hand him over to the Saringalas and the game begins. When the Saringalas have thoroughly worked him over, the others come and take him, to go and release him in the darkness. Nothing seen and nothing known, you get it? But this time, I believe they've decided to finish him off, the bastards.'

'But who are you talking about?' whispered Jean-Louis impatiently. 'Who is beating whom?'

'Who are they beating? Why the followers of Ruben, the trade unionists, of course; but this time it's Ruben himself.'

'And who beats them?'

'The Saringalas, obviously, on the orders of the slave-drivers, the Gaullists, the toubabs, such like.'

'But why?'

'What! You're not going to pretend that you don't understand? The slave-drivers detest his union; they say they'll do anything to wipe it out.'

'And Sandrinelli agrees with them?'

'But of course; he's even their leader, he isn't called the Gaullist for nothing; yes, that's it, one of their leaders. They're all together down there at the moment in his house, at the other end of the compound. I've just come from there, that's why I know quite well what I'm talking about. I saw and heard them; they all arrived just as I was washing up in the kitchen. One of them is an especially dangerous type, ready for anything, a certain Brede, a cousin of Sandrinelli's, apparently. He's the one who got hold of Ruben and brought him here.'

'It's nonsense,' Jean-Louis kept protesting, 'where could they have caught him? Not in Kola-Kola, they'd have been stoned on the spot. So where, then?'

'Perhaps in Fort-Nègre?' suggested Mor-Kinda, also deeply troubled.

'He never goes there! At least, never alone. In any case, the whole town knows him now and the whole of Kola-Kola would be in tumult.'

'Perhaps it is; we don't really know what's going on down there right now.'

150

'We must do something! They're going to kill him,' groaned Mor-Zamba between two sobs.

'Do you know Ruben?' Mor-Kinda asked Jean-Louis.

As the other nodded his head that yes, of course, who didn't know Ruben in Kola-Kola, the Juggler made a back for him and Jean-Louis, perched on his friend's shoulders and leaning his head forward, managed to look down through a big gap in the roof timbers, crudely posed on top of the masonry, instead of being properly attached. It was certainly Ruben whom he saw, by the light of a hurricane-lamp placed a little distance away on the concrete floor, being tortured by three scarfaced Saringalas who took turns to thrash him incessantly with an enormous rattan cane which combined the crushing weight of a cudgel and the stinging flexibility of a whip, in one. They had stretched him out on the floor, so that his back and buttocks were exposed to their blows. If he tried, in his piercing agony, to turn on one side and so escape the blows, or if he set his hands to his wounds, they trampled on his feet or his toe-nails with their boots; sometimes a Saringala would abandon his instrument, jump upon his back and stamp upon it with rage.

Mor-Zamba, who had climbed on the Juggler's shoulders after Jean-Louis, says now that he could read Ruben's agony clearly in the lines of his face; in the bloody and swollen cheeks; in the glazed but dry eyes, which occasionally illumined and seemed then to search the visage of death; in the brow creased with anticipation of the blows; in the spasm which deformed the mouth with a frozen grimace. The vision of this mask of martyrdom still haunts him today, he tells us, and will doubtless never abandon him.

As Mor-Zamba became less and less able to contain himself, the three Koleans left the institute and took the route which wound vaguely over the high ground towards the College of Fraternity.

'Let's go to the college,' Mor-Kinda suggested to Jean-Louis; 'you're quite at home there. We'll tell them what's going on; they're known to be militant Rubenists and some of them even *bandasalos*. We'll see what they decide to do.'

The College of Fraternity, which had just been promoted to

the rank of lycée, the first in the colony, but which everyone was still in the habit of calling 'the college', was in fact scarcely a kilometre from the Institute of 18 June. Opposite the proper classrooms, all closed at that hour and on the other side of the avenue, was the African boarding house, spread out in little brick pavilions, all roofed with tiles, standing low and light like the blocks in the barracks, and arranged at various depths around a sloping courtyard. The youngest pupils occupied the pavilions farthest back from the avenue; the most senior lived right by the street, and many of them were still awake, despite the late hour. There was a curfew, but in two of the rooms a glimmer of light could be seen, shining dimly from hurricane-lamps; young people could be seen going to and fro in a relaxed manner, bare breasted and with loin cloths round their waists. In one of these rooms they were dancing to a beguine rhythm played by a musician in underpants, who sat on the headboard of his iron bed, and who was doubtless displaying his talent on the guitar.

There was no wall enclosing the establishment and the pupils, after wandering through the suburbs, returned at last without any restraint. The three friends entered the room where the dancers were and Jean-Louis, recognized at once, was greeted with a salvo of compliments of which his companions could not guess the occasion. No one seemed surprised to see him at this hour, as if anything could be expected of him.

'Tell them right away,' advised Mor-Kinda.

'What is it?' asked the boarders, intrigued by the pathetic expressions on the faces of their visitors.

'Ruben is in the hands of his enemies.'

'What are you saying?' protested the boarders, who were now all around them.

'Explain yourself, which Ruben? The leader of the unionists?'

Soon they formed into three groups, each of the friends being solicited separately to explain the affair to the young lyceans, for whom, it seemed, none of the accounts was either succinct or substantial enough. Jean-Louis continued his explanations in the room where he had begun them; Mor-Kinda had been led by the hand into the courtyard, in the midst of which, surrounded by a swelling crowd of students, he recounted with plenty of colour and movement the scene of horror he had just witnessed. As for Mor-Zamba, whose more sober but blunter eloquence was more inclined towards action, he contented himself with stammering painfully, and between sobs:

'We must do something ... something right away ... they're going to kill him.'

It was in this group presided over by Mor-Zamba, in the little court separating the two buildings where everyone had been still awake that, stimulated no doubt by the urgent exhortations of the orator, a student cried out all at once the name of a man whose determination had for some years past changed the face of the colony.

'Dessalines!' cried the young man. 'Where is Dessalines? Go and call Dessalines.'

The students, awoken by the tumult which raged in the pavilions of the seniors, now began pouring from all the nearby dormitories, some in pyjamas, most in pants or wrapped in loin cloths. Those furthest off, who were the youngest, were also awake and began rushing towards the seniors' quarters just at the moment when the others, having seized the gravity of the situation, were trying to go away and get dressed in a jiffy, so as not to be surprised by any turn of events. The eddy of young boarders stirred up the same cries:

'Ruben is in their hands. Ah, that Sandrinelli bastard, it's just like him!'

Dessalines finally appeared, rubbing his sleepy eyes and carrying on his arm the clothes he had had no time to put on, as well as his canvas shoes. He was a big boy, very muscular and well-made, with a very black skin, so far as one could judge by the hurricane-lamp, which was now burning at maximum intensity. Dessalines had been led to the room where Jean-Louis was talking, and soon everyone began flocking there also, shoving in vain for entry, so that the greater part had finally to content themselves to remain outside. Dessalines seemed strangely slow to take stock of the situation, as if he had been awoken with great difficulty from a sleep most unwelcomely interrupted; they had sought him for a long time before recalling that he sometimes took refuge in one of the junior dormitories when he had many nights of sleep to make up, and so it had been on this particular night for this tireless militant, said to be the leader of a group of *bandasalos*, composed indiscriminately of lyceans and of Kolean *sapaks*. Fearing to be thrown into a precipitate, if not inopportune action, suspicious of what might after all turn out to be a provocation – although he knew Jean-Louis perfectly well – he wanted to protect himself with every guarantee, and to subject the three friends to a long interrogation, which had the main effect of making all those convinced of Ruben's imminent assassination boil with impatience.

However, even while listening to the three friends, Dessalines was already dressed and booted; but standing there, a prey to confusion, he still fixed a worried eye on Jean-Louis, as if begging him to recant, to admit that, boastful vagabond as he was, he had invented an enormous lie just for a laugh.

'Dessalines! Dessalines!' they all yelled around him, both like idolaters crying up the name of their hero and like partisans giving a word of command.

'Why Dessalines?' Mor-Zamba was asking himself. 'It was undeniably a war name, but what did it mean?' Whenever he was surrounded by educated people Mor-Zamba always secretly deplored his own ignorance, but never so much as at that moment.

'All right!' Dessalines suddenly agreed. 'Let's go.'

Cries of 'ah' went up all around him, even while everyone began to get moving. Marching at the head of this river of lyceans, Dessalines steered first of all towards the College of Agriculture, which was situated close to the African boarding house. This college was surrounded by a wooden fence. The watchman, who was also in charge of the gate, cried out when Dessalines appeared before him that things there did not go as at the African boarding house and that everyone was fast asleep at that hour. Dessalines persisted in raising his voice and, in any case, the cries of 'Dessalines! Dessalines!' kept rocketing up from the crowd of students massed behind their leader. Somewhere a dog, doubtless a huge brute, unleashed a series of barks which rolled like thunder into the night and froze for an

154

instant the exaltation of the young rioters. A man's voice was heard crying: 'Barca! Down, Barca!' trying to pacify the angry beast. In the near-by house of the director of the school a door screeched and opened, as the altercation between Dessalines and the watchman grew more bitter.

The director, M. Rondeau, was an athletic young man; still in pyjamas, he leapt down the steps of the house and, in a few bounds, came up to Dessalines and exchanged with him a few words which were neither gentle nor particularly sharp, so far as Mor-Zamba, who was some way off, could judge. Finally, without it seeming that Dessalines had to beg him, and perhaps simply because he urged the absolute urgency and necessity of an interview with his friends at the school, M. Rondeau agreed to let him pass.

He was, moreover, an enigmatic man, and even after he had been chased from the colony and forced to return immediately to Europe, no one could ever say with certainty which camp he belonged to, which in those days was quite an achievement for a white man. At this point in his story, Mor-Zamba never fails to linger a little on this strange personality. According to him, he was certainly not against us, but neither was he really with us. If he had been our foe, he could easily have doomed Dessalines after this affair; it would have been enough, for instance, that he revealed to the tribunal that on this particular night, Dessalines had demanded with extraordinary insistence to enter the school and meet his friends, all militant Rubenists; and furthermore that, despite the late hour, he had seen waves of lyceans billowing around his establishment and supporting Dessalines' demand of entry with their cries. On this kind of evidence, any judge whatever would have condemned Dessalines and the other militant students of the Schools' Plateau, without remorse. Furthermore, although called before court during the trial, M. Rondeau failed to make use of these circumstances.

But, all the same, he wasn't really one of us, because when the militant Rubenists became public enemies and no persecution was considered too cruel as long as it crushed them, the whole cell within the College of Agriculture, a nursery of brave cadres and martyrs, was decimated,

155

sometimes brutally and sometimes cunningly, without a murmur of protest from M. Rondeau. Nevertheless, M. Rondeau always refrained from denouncing those of his students who were active in Rubenism; this must be why, not content with stripping him of his post, they also branded him with a sort of banishment.

Just as he went into the college, Dessalines ordered two big boys, who had hitherto kept to his side, to avoid the entrance, to follow the outside of the fence and await him further off; in this way he could reach them across the fence, without being seen by either the watchman or by M. Rondeau, who had returned to his house, and pass them pick-axes, shovels, crowbars and other instruments which the bigger boys of the boarding house and the dozen militant Rubenists of the College of Agriculture had the evident intention to use, if the situation called for it.

To go from the lycée area to the Institute of 18 June, there was a choice of two different routes. On that night the invaders were guided above all by the imperative need of surprise, which dictated that they attack the citadel of Sandrinelli by the most devious route, taking it more or less from behind; but also to give Dessalines and his lieutenants time to impose some discipline on troops inclined to anarchy. They therefore set off briskly down the avenue for almost a kilometre, so that the ranks of the assailants became very much strung out; from there, a branch off the avenue led straight and level to the main gate of the institute. Dessalines and his staff disdained this, following the avenue where it turned towards the left, leaving Sandrinelli's domain on their right and, at the same time, began to cut into a steep escarpment, following the bank which enclosed the flat campus of the institute like a Roman camp. The avenue turned again, this time towards the right; they pushed on for another two or three hundred metres, still at a sharp pace, until the point where a lane at right angles to the avenue cut into the bank; this was the little road serving as access to the residential area of the campus and which, four hundred metres further on, passed in front of Sandrinelli's villa. They had no intention of taking this route, to be sure. Dessalines, who still had only the biggest boys around him, the only real militants in the crowd, said to them:

156

'We're going to get into the institute by climbing the bank and the compound wall; in that way, no one'll hear us. If things turn rough, come back this way, and don't forget to bring everyone with you, especially the little ones. Here they come now. We shall give you cover while you cut around Sandrinelli's villa. Don't fear anything unless we give you the alarm. Off you go with the little ones!'

Dessalines had calculated that if the assailants were brutally repulsed, which seemed to him very likely, but which did not for a moment make him recoil, they could shake off pursuit by scaling the low compound wall and jumping from the bank into the roadway, which would be quite deserted at that hour. If, despite the wall and the bank, they had not succeeded in scattering their pursuers, they had only to disappear into the vague hinterland bordering the far side of the avenue; moving under cover, they would soon reach the nearest African village, where they would easily pass themselves off, having numerous friends thereabout and even, for the larger boys, affairs with the local girls. In effect, Fort-Nègre came to an end at the Schools' Plateau, the last quarter in this direction; there followed an area frayed with indigenous villages, which remained such despite colonization. All this region, where schools and African villages lay side by side, and sometimes even interpenetrated, was then a sort of paradise of natural life where the students, fleeing the constraints of discipline, wandered on Sundays in total freedom.

There one never met a white gendarme, or even a black auxiliary. From time to time a gang of drunken Saringalas intruded there and, after various exactions which proved their power over others, they would move off satisfied.

Dessalines and his selected Rubenists spread themselves out like riflemen and took cover at the corners of the buildings, stretching out like a thread from one side to the other of the raised bank which carried the institute halfway between the director's villa lying at the far end of the vast terrace and the hated structure which they knew lay somewhere behind them, without being able to pinpoint it. They expected that Sandrinelli, hearing the uproar and tumult of the attack, would first release his two hunting dogs, but these would be crushed

157

by the militant Rubenists lying in wait, who would overwhelm them with the fearsome weapons with which they were furnished; later, Sandrinelli and his friends would rush out armed with guns and ready to open fire on the attackers. Then, thought Dessalines, there would be nothing for it but to dispatch one or two militants to warn the students to get out quick, and, for their own part, to die. Despite the virtues which should make him the envy of many heroes of whom history is so proud, Dessalines' inexperience had produced a pretty wretched strategy. Sandrinelli and his friends would not show their faces during the skirmish; they would not even unleash the hounds. This was not merely the effect of surprise. Virtuosi of the shady crime committed with impunity, avoiding like the plague the glare of publicity and of public trial, these new paladins feared above anything having to meet their enemies face to face.

Ignoring the advice of various full-grown militants delegated by Dessalines to guide the young students, the assailants, on their own part, were without imagination. To begin with, they gave signs of hesitation when they were assembled – and nothing is more derisory or more foolish than a crowd in the grip of uncertainty. They could not find the building in which Ruben was held; the Saringalas, doubtless hearing the noise of the approaching force, had stopped beating their prisoner, thereby robbing their enemies of a convenient means of orientation. Joe the Juggler was himself confused by the rum, which he had never ceased to imbibe in little gulps, and was no longer able to find the way among the little buildings of the Institute of 18 June which, plunged in darkness, seemed virtually interchangeable. Nevertheless, the vice of the attackers, carried by a more or less automatic élan, began to grip, but around a goal so imprecise that the affair threatened to turn into a fiasco and sink into a gulf of anarchic flight.

Fortunately Mor-Zamba, who was nothing less than an improvised warrior, had remained lucid and had so carefully scrutinized the shadows that he finally pointed out a building which, he affirmed, could be the one where the Saringalas were holding and torturing Ruben. A new problem now arose: what arms did the enemy dispose of and what risk did they run in mounting a frontal assault? They must send a mission to

Dessalines to get his advice; upon its return, the mission whispered:

'Dessalines says we have wasted too much time; there's not a moment to lose now. The Saringalas have muskets, but no ammunition; instead of opening fire, they can use the butts of their guns as cudgels.'

Decisively reassured, the attackers began operations. A terrible barrage of missiles began to rain on the roof of the little structure, shaking it like a banana palm in a tornado. Then came repeated yells of:

'Sandrinelli, the murderer! Maestraci, the murderer! Langelot, the murderer!'

All the cronies of Sandrinelli, nicknamed the Gaullist or the Potentate, were honoured in the citation except the *mameluke*, who was nevertheless the author of Ruben's capture, merely because Joe the Juggler had suddenly forgotten his name.

All at once, the only door of the building opened, the huge silhouette of a Saringala was cut in Chinese style upon the sooty glow of light. Rather than reasoned courage, it was a reflex of fear and self-defence which hurled the first rank of the young combatants forwards, in a kind of flight to the van, into the doorway, where they vanished, jostling, squeezing, beating, breaking, yelling, trampling blindly, sparing only Ruben himself because he was still stretched out on the concrete floor, incapable of sitting up or standing. Then, abruptly, it was a stampede in reverse.

Next day, when the first investigators arrived early on the battlefield, the three muskets had disappeared; one of the scarfaces lay on the floor with his skull shattered; the other two Saringalas, though gravely wounded and fractured, had been able to play upon the inexperience of the attackers; they had remained hidden right in the institute itself, and had only to show themselves to the investigators, who were also policemen.

One version of the affair which was long current on the plateau claimed that the colossus who took Ruben in his arms before putting him on his back and disappearing in the night with his precious load, had first fought a brief but violent battle with a Saringala who, with the prisoner between his legs, was

159

flourishing his musket, which he held by the barrel. A frantic and twisting wrestling match had ended with the scarface being thrown like a chip from a circular saw against the wall, where the man's head had burst like an egg striking a stone.

Mor-Zamba is content nowadays to confide to us, on the subject of the stampede which has so intrigued all those who have pored over the horrible affair, the most tragically strange without doubt in the history of the colony up till then, that it was caused by the first squirts of blood from the nostrils of a Saringala who had killed himself by hurling his head against the wall.

After this there was no further break in hostilities, other than illusory ones, but rather a sustained crescendo, despite the carelessness of the Koleans, sometimes excessively confident of Ruben's protection, sometimes abandoning themselves to Providence. For a long time it was a matter of oblique and underground campaigns, as if they were afraid of stirring up Kola-Kola, of fanning its belligerent instincts. On 14 July, 11 November, 8 May and 18 June, and on other solemn occasions, Fort-Nègre was abundant in declarations of peace and fraternal love, but at the same time its furtive eye searched for signs of relaxation in the quarter, so as to subject it to sudden attacks, broken off as soon as they had thrown the population into turmoil.

Kola-Kola, however, really demanded nothing, except to survive in a small way with the exuberance of its own nature, as in its own imagination it had always done, on the edge of Fort-Nègre, its neighbour, despised and held at arm's length no doubt, but certainly not its satellite, for it rejected the servitude of that status, never having received any of its profits. Kola-Kola was deprived of everything, even of necessities. Every morning the very youngest of children had, as it were, to go into exile, crossing hostile country in order to go and seat themselves on the benches of a school. With the exception of the Seventh Day Adventists, whose clergy were entirely

African and whose churches lay in Kola-Kola itself, the faithful of the Christian denominations, if they wanted to honour their God, formed themselves into devious processions which circled the slavers' capital by winding paths and led them to the various missions, always placed outside the town to have more space. The Kolean wives gradually resigned themselves, on the eve of their deliveries, to put themselves in the hands of the white-robed sorcerers of the Parant hospital, situated in Fort-Nègre, on the edge of the city for African officials. Kola-Kola did not even have a clinic to relieve its most urgent cases.

But despite all this, Fort-Nègre teased its brains to torment Kola-Kola, the incarnation of its remorse, the swelling denial of its mystic fantasies, the cancer clasped to its side which robbed it of sleep, the seething distress which, like the reflected image of a huge rat-run, began to be the theme of the world's concern, like the mirror of an immense ratage. Thanks to God, as always happens to those who possess material force, Fort-Nègre's initiatives were incoherent, impulsive and disgustingly stupid.

Soon after the attempted assassination of Ruben, the slavers' capital, using its habitual channels – missionary sermons, sarcastic articles in the two weekly papers of the city, confidences demanded from secret agents – began to say repeatedly that the maize beer and Holy Joseph, made, sold and consumed in Kola-Kola, where they were the only source of revenue for many families, as well as in country towns of the interior, where they contributed no less providentially to the immediate relief of the miseries of the poorest folk, led straight to alcoholism and all its evils. There followed soon afterwards an order from the governor prohibiting these drinks and exposing to fines and imprisonment whoever was convicted of drinking, selling or, worst of all, making the above-mentioned beverages. A shower of police in uniform or mufti descended on the quarter and harassed the inhabitants, who were disarmed by the absence of Ruben. The latter had gone overseas to be cured of the grave injuries inflicted by his scarfaced torturers, his followers having concluded that the local doctors were incapable of saving him, either because of their incompetence or because they were suspected of complicity with those who plotted his capture, his agony and, without doubt, his death. At first we thought he was confided to the doctors of Western Europe, because the journals of a capital there announced his arrival at the airport; then, we thought he had made no more than a transit stop on his way to the Soviet Union, a socialist country and one which, so it was said, sympathized with the struggles of the oppressed peoples.

Within a few months, imprisonment for being caught in the act, fines, summary convictions and exactions had almost strangled the circulation and doubtless even the manufacture of maize beer and Holy Joseph among the pinched families of Kola-Kola. It was too late when the dearth of these wares precipitated the first riots, however insignificant. A band of *sapaks* would surround a little group of *mamelukes* who were arresting a poor woman, mother of a numerous family abandoned by her husband or a widow encumbered with children, whom they had caught infringing the governor's order, said to be a protection against so many evils. The young men, their faces distorted with anger, would take the *mamelukes* aside and shout at them an insult invented by *Spartacus*, Ruben's newspaper:

'Dogs of slavers! Dogs of slavers!'

Bit by bit they began stoning them, from far away at first, but soon from much nearer. It was all regulated like clockwork. One of the policemen was struck unexpectedly. The force would then retire; some hours later, or even that night if the aggression had been committed towards the end of the afternoon, as it often was, a troop of Saringalas commanded by a white sergeant would burst into the quarter and seize several dozens of men in the huddle of hovels where the incident had occurred, as well as the woman in question. And for many long months, nothing more was seen of the offenders.

Funnily enough, says Mor-Zamba nowadays, for he, having passed the age of these young firebrands, took no part in their actions, the *sapaks* arrested by the Saringalas were usually the ones who had been involved in the affray; for after the brawl, instead of going to ground and moving off for some time, as he had always done when he had been involved in a confrontation, they made it a point of honour to remain masters of the

162

field, a piece of bombast which makes Mor-Zamba smile, as a man to whom pragmatism has taught the science of both the ruse and the combat. Whenever he could, he would watch, though from far enough away, the unrolling of this now familiar rite. Adventuring into Kola-Kola and manifestly looking for trouble, the *mamelukes* would suddenly descend on a cluster of buildings: their flair would guide them to the miserable house where the occupier had just finished feverishly ranging the too familiar pots. A brief search led them to the pot in question; the poor woman burst into sobs, wept to break your heart, begged not to be taken off at once, to be given the chance to hug her children for the last time when they returned from school, crying that there was no one else to look after them. The *mamelukes* argued that they had strict orders and that time was pressing. Already a crowd had formed at the entrance to the yard. The *sapaks* at first followed the scene with the grave air of pitying choir-boys, but when, having come out of the house, the *mamelukes* began handcuffing their prisoner, the stoning would begin amidst sarcasms, cries and shouts of glee. All at once one heard a baton descend on the skull or shoulder blade of a *mameluke*, sounding it like a gong. The shirts or reefers of the policemen were stained with blood. Another blow with a stick on the neck of a *mameluke*, who fell to his knees first, then on his side, the flight of the two others, pursued by hoots, the victory of the *sapaks* who occupied the field, libations at the expense of the woman whom they had saved, frantic dances, shouts of war. Suddenly, the whistles of the white sergeant, the attack of the Saringalas, with their heads lowered, butts raised, brief tussle, defeat of the *sapaks* with whom the ground was soon scattered, fixing of fetters, departure in file, the poor woman, alone amid all these men, marching beside her defeated fellow citizens. Then followed a week of calm, before the outbreak of a new storm.

Nevertheless, the ranks of the toughest *sapaks* were gradually but inexorably thinning; the *mamelukes* in civilian dress, or even in uniform, began to stroll with ostentation and impunity even in the dark alleys of Kola-Kola. Some inhabitants went so far as to drink with them in a tavern, sitting around bottles of factory-brewed beer, the only one allowed to be sold because, according to the governor, it alone was really wholesome. The *mamelukes* were so much in conquered territory that one saw them carrying on and, to tell the truth, not without success, with the prettiest Kolean girls.

The worst defeat for the braves of Kola-Kola was that two of the fifteen or twenty houses built of permanent materials by its merchants, at the very heart of the quarter, were expropriated and turned into police stations, linked by telephone with the central post in Fort-Nègre and with the barracks of the Saringala auxiliaries; the result was better co-ordination between the *mamelukes* operating in Kola-Kola and the nerve centres of the security forces, whose arrivals and counter strokes in the area became almost instantaneous.

In the eyes of Fort-Nègre, it seemed, the liberation of Ruben by the angry students at the Institute of 18 June, far from symbolizing a unique event whose novel features invited careful meditation, was nothing but an incident which must be prevented in future by a firm hand. There was talk of building a prison or a guard house in Kola-Kola; those who had long ears for sharing the secrets of the gods even claimed to know the chosen site.

This was also the time when Baba Toura was elected president of the Consultative Assembly of the colony, in succession to his great friend Langelot, who had seemed till then to have appropriated the post. Mor-Zamba has made a great effort to summon up his recollections, but this is the only certain thing he can remember about Baba Toura, this man who was to have such a surprising destiny: to satirize the illiteracy of the new president and his total dependence on the colonial administration; of which he was already the insignificant but marvellously docile creature, the wags of Kola-Kola recounted that, wishing to acknowledge the honour which his peers had done him in electing him president, he had maundered through a long address prepared by the governor's office; but at the end, unable to contain his joy and exaltation, Baba Toura had forgotten his text and cried out ecstatically:

'Thank you, France, thank you, thank you, thank you, thank you; yet again, thank you! France, think of us poor little Africans! France, think of us!'

164

'France, think of us' soon became the rallying cry of all the critics.

To tell the truth, the advent of Baba Toura passed almost unobserved; the Consultative Assembly, which contained not a single Rubenist, scarcely figuring in the preoccupations of the ordinary Kolean. Furthermore, this Assembly, an administrative and in no sense political mechanism, inspired nothing but distrust in Kola-Kola where, henceforth, only the most drastic upsets could make any impression. Nevertheless, it was with the presidency of the Consultation Assembly that this Baba Toura, also called the Boozer because of his reputed alcoholism, really took off; a man who was considered feeble and rickety even by his friends, of very limited intelligence, condemned to play a part on the political stage. Mor-Zamba has promised to tell us one day the marvellous but also bloody story of Baba Toura; he claims not to know it all himself as yet; that there are areas of darkness he hopes to enlighten one day with the aid of Joe the Juggler, who glides and insinuates himself everywhere incognito, even inside the ministries of Fort-Nègre, where he has managed, like a sorcerer, to draw forth intelligence, without failing to come back to us at the end of every expedition.

All this happened about the middle of the fifties.

Suddenly, everything in Kola-Kola was reversed, because Ruben had come back. No one announced his return, the Fort-Nègre radio rarely taking any account of events in Kola-Kola and never mentioning any of its personalities; for its part, Ruben's paper *Spartacus*, which appeared regularly to begin with, half in secret and constantly harassed by the police, had suspended publication during the absence of the union leader, and for two years Kola-Kola had been left to the discretion either of its own dreams or of the slavers' propaganda. No doubt Ruben himself did not wish to give advance notice of his return; perhaps he preferred to surprise Fort-Nègre and avoid the troops which he, almost alone, foresaw would be extended by his enemies. He knew very well that Kola-Kola, despite its extent and the number and valour of its inhabitants, was a city under siege.

Be that as it may, one morning Kola-Kola, at first sceptical, then fervent, and in a few hours exalted, learned that Ruben was really back, cured, marching straight forward on his two feet, even though the resetting of his legs, broken by torture, had presented many problems, according to his companions, when they issued their rare gobbets of information. Suddenly the place was flooded with leaflets in which Ruben accused the slavers of having prohibited native beer and Holy Joseph only so as to oblige Kola-Kola to drink industrial beer and thereby to enrich, willynilly, the newly installed 'African Brewery', in which it was rumoured that the highest officials of the colony, including the governor himself, had interests. To serve notice that he had no intention, despite the threats heaped upon him, to modify his line of conduct, Ruben invited his fellow citizens to organize themselves into groups for self-defence and neighbourhood self-help, known as GAVEs; he recommended each GAVE not to exceed ten, or at most twelve, members and to remain always independent of the neighbouring GAVEs, never co-ordinating with them, except in an improvised way in cases of urgency, so that the inevitable repression, in seizing a militant from one GAVE, would not at the same stroke penetrate the other self-defence groups.

Now followed days of spontaneous tumult; the revenge of the *sapaks*, whose fighting spirit was fully recovered, began with the capture, imprisonment and punishment of those *mamelukes* who, deprived in their turn of lucid judgement, had attempted, despite the reversal of the situation, to venture outside the police stations; finally, as might have been expected, this culminated in the grand conflagration of both the stations themselves, the red glare of which, visible for hundreds of metres, was for the Koleans a dramatic harbinger of public enlightenment. As if in a dream, Kola-Kola watched the rediscovery of maize beer and Holy Joseph by their former drinkers, like a family whose members had been far too long scattered by a tempest.

Victorious all along the line, the idol of Kola-Kola might have displayed himself; one expected to see Ruben parade through the streets and squares of his fief. In reality, one saw him less and less; most people thought he was shut up at home; even at the Labour Centre, entirely rebuilt by the hands of militants, he was seen no more and it was in vain that, in the morning, the peasant women with their baskets or, in the afternoon, the students coming down from the Schools' Plateau, all burning to see the Messiah, the Redeemer, the invulnerable one, the magician, stood on tiptoe and tried to peer into the office where he always sat before the attempted assassination and which, in the new building, the workers had reproduced exactly as it was.

Perhaps, people said, he now saw snares everywhere, like all those who have been victims of an ambush. When he did go out, he was protected by a whole army of young volunteers. And even when he appeared before the tribunal in Fort-Nègre, to give evidence in the trial concerning his capture, his escort never left his side. It was, as everyone expected, a ridiculous trial anyway.

It's true that all the guilty parties who could be identified had disappeared. Brede, the young police inspector and Sandrinelli's cousin, who had seized Ruben in Kola-Kola with the aid of a commando of *mamelukes* who were natives of the quarter and knew all its habits and resorts, had left suddenly for Europe, it was learnt. This was true; an article published later in *Spartacus* revealed that Brede was normally attached to the police in Morocco and that, ranging out from there over all of North Africa and even parts of Black Africa, he had specialized in missions described as 'special operations', consisting above all of the capture and execution of local personalities, and especially of union leaders carefully pointed out to him and made accessible by the officials of the colonial police concerned. Brede had already made a sinister reputation in Morocco itself, in Tunisia and, recently, in the French Sudan, where he had committed the perfect crime by effecting the disappearance of a black leader whose body was never found, even though his assassination was virtually a certainty.

As for the two surviving Saringalas, it transpired that they had been dismissed soon after the affair, but as a result of misconduct long before the capture of Ruben, one for habitual drunkenness, the other for insubordination; and that they had been sent back to their own tribe, beyond the colony's frontiers. M. Sandrinelli had little difficulty, before judges of such complacency who kept offering him loopholes, in proving his innocence: his cousin had abused his family confidence, and the director of the Institute of 18 June, Gaullist as ever, enjoying a stainless reputation, swore that he was ignorant not only of the unacceptable purpose for which Brede had taken one of the rooms of the institute, but even that he used it at all. Then came apotheosis for Sandrinelli: after the others came Georges Mor-Kinda, called Joe the Juggler by his Kolean friends, to swear in his favour, to the great scandal of the Koleans in the audience, very few in the interior of the narrow courtroom, but in a great crowd around the High Court (in reality by secret accord with Ruben), that the director of the Institute of 18 June was a generous employer, kind and extremely human, without whom, excluded from society by numerous convictions, alas! justified, he would still be wallowing in the gutter. Sandrinelli had a limitless affection for Africans; he considered them as brothers and he, Georges Mor-Kinda, witnessed that he had always heard him condemn all forms of racial discrimination. Despite the African interpreter, who wanted to force him to speak in Bantu or pidgin and who, despite the solemnity of the place, was constantly muttering obscenities during the address of Sandrinelli's protégé, Joe the Juggler made his whole declaration in excellent French. Such was the atmosphere of the trial that the social status of the witness and the academic quality of his speech did not form, in the opinion of the impassive judges, any contrast which might trouble an ordinary slaver. On the other hand, when he heard of the effrontery with which Joe the Juggler had recited his lesson, Mor-Zamba felt he had met all over again a man for whom he felt an affection not only limitless but at the same time owing nothing to rational justification – in a way a second Abena, perhaps more perverse, but certainly as diabolical.

Two days after the verdict which whitewashed Sandrinelli, and before the same court, Ruben had to appear on his own account on the charge of an outrage against the highest representative of the republic in the colony; his accusation rested on the leaflet which Ruben had issued upon his return from Europe in which he had denounced the collusion of the top administration with private interests in the colony, citing particularly the African Brewery, to whom the interested partiality of the highest circles of the administration facilitated the acquisition of monstrous commercial advantages and the winning of a position of monopoly. Ruben had brought a lawyer from Paris, but neither the energetic and thunderous eloquence of the man of law nor the illumination which shot through even these often tumultuous and awfully confused debates was able to preserve Ruben from an infamous verdict.

In reply to all this skulduggery, Ruben, who up to now had confined himself deliberately to the defence of the workers, leaving to a weak lieutenant the direction of the political movement linked to the Workers' Union, the Popular Progressive Party (PPP), decided to take it over immediately; he declared in the course of a meeting organized for this purpose that he had realized that priority must be given to political action, whose success was the necessary condition for the real transformation of the fate of African workers. It seemed to Mor-Zamba that a bitter debate had taken place simultaneously at the heart of the governing organs of the WU and the PPP, on the opportunity to change the name of the political movement in order to give it, symbolically, a new thrust. At first the majority was for those who wanted to call it the Rally and Unity for National Happiness and Amity, so that its initials would cunningly spell the name of Ruben.[1] In effect, the movement henceforward bore that name. Nevertheless, four months later the other faction of progressive leaders carried the day and changed it back to its former title: Popular Progressive Party (PPP). Mor-Zamba does not know the reasons, doubtless very wise ones, for this revision, but he assures us it was a mistake. For the ordinary people of Kola-Kola, and even the surrounding country, attracted to their great man, their magician for whom they were ready to die, to call the party RUBEN was as if one had fused its members and sympathizers into one family with Ruben as its father. PPP, on the contrary, sounded in their ears like the name of a colonial export–import firm.

The first meeting of the series by which Ruben, renouncing

[1] In French, Rassemblement et Unité pour le Bonheur et l'Entente des Nationaux. (*Translator's note*)

his obscurity, reckoned to explain to his countrymen the meaning of the decisions which had been adopted by the union leaders and political radicals, was the setting for an event whose consequence would be incalculable for the whole black continent, says Mor-Zamba, who has been inseparable from his books for several years past. On the platform they read a six point programme, including the fight for the immediate independence of the colony. At first the smaller and humbler militants and sympathizers, either poorly educated or illiterate like Mor-Zamba, absorbed furthermore in the daily struggle for existence, either did not fully understand the purport of these rousing phrases of their great man; or took them as no more than this; it was just as well, they said, that their leaders should raise their voices, so as to stupefy their enemy or wrench from him some concession.

Why was it that after this everything seemed to hang fire for so many months?

More than ten years have since rolled by, but Mor-Zamba still vividly recalls that particular time and when he evokes it for us, his voice swells both with indignation against the masters of the colony and with commiseration for his brothers in distress. Like a swamp bloated with the rains, Kola-Kola swelled visibly with men rushing from all parts of the country; its horrible tentacles stretched out like the scaly and loathsome talons of some nightmarish hawk. Employment in the slavers' city seemed to fill to capacity, and the waves of hungry newcomers broke at the very feet of the colonial citadel. Rationing of space and provisions, critical reductions in the usual diet, sharpened the egotism of all. When anyone had the felicity to be blessed with a job, however modest, he did everything imaginable to keep it: he bent over backwards, and was even tempted to break away from his fellows. Little by little, even the best became subject to egotism and indifference. They relied on Ruben as on a miracle-worker, and leant upon his militants and companions in the heaviest parts of the struggle. People relaxed their vigilance and gave up the battlefield, especially when the enemy made the pretence of yielding ground and, worse still, of abandoning it altogether.

The truth was that, after the reversal caused by the sudden

170

return of Ruben, Fort-Nègre had called in its troops from their advanced positions in Kola-Kola, so that one no longer saw either big parties of Saringalas on patrol or policemen in uniform. It was said that only a few police agents in civilian dress remained in the quarter and continued spying there. The *sapaks* tried to unmask them by confronting everyone rich enough to wear a safari jacket or, above all, leather shoes; now and again they confronted a man who, appalled by their threatening manner and their reputation, took to his heels like a schoolboy caught raiding; the *sapaks* could always be relied on to pursue them with ferocity. But usually, having caught their victim and thoroughly beaten him up, they perceived their error and when they began to question him they began to realize that even in Kola-Kola plenty of people wore leather shoes and safari jackets, without being policemen in disguise. Several officials of fairly junior rank, natives of the quarter or having relatives there, continued to live there after their admission to an administrative post, whilst waiting to be offered a house in the government quarters. Apart from this, among the other inhabitants of Kola-Kola, very modest workers, labourers and even the unemployed tried nowadays to give themselves the outfit of the black élite, and either ruined themselves with tailors' bills or, like Jean-Louis, bled their parents white or, yet again, started an affair with the wife of a trader for the sole purpose of exploiting her as a source of revenue.

We must consider the evidence: whether by ruse or by perplexity, Fort-Nègre had abandoned its attempt to occupy the quarter; it even gave the impression of a man who had exhausted that belligerent daring, that appetite for trouble which had thrown the hard men of Kola-Kola into confusion for more than a year. But it was perhaps from this very defeat that Fort-Nègre drew the lesson which was to plunge the country into darkness for many long years. According to Mor-Zamba, there is no doubt that the authorities deduced from these events that Ruben was like a heart beating within the living body of his followers; that to kill Ruben would be a blow to the heart of this mastodon, not only in Kola-Kola but throughout the colony.

Had Ruben, for his part, decided to wrest the other suburbs of

Fort-Nègre from the grip of the colonial authorities? Mor-Zamba recalls that, even though he was fully occupied with his apprenticeship, as we shall see, he often heard from his companions in the country markets that the political leader was holding meeting after meeting in these suburbs, where his organization had established little footing up till then; and that at every meeting police agents in uniform or in disguise provoked serious incidents and even opened fire; never during the meeting itself, but always at the end, when Ruben and his entourage had quitted the scene and the crowd had begun to disperse in that state of carelessness and disorder which colours the close of popular assemblies. It certainly looked as though Fort-Nègre had sworn not to lose control of these areas, after its pitiful reverse at Kola-Kola.

Mor-Zamba was continually asking himself about the prospects of his apprenticeship and, still more, about the attitude of Fulbert, whose personality seemed highly enigmatic towards him. About this time, he began to despair. He knew that by tradition in Kola-Kola, as everywhere else in the colony, the career of driver was the one which demanded the longest apprenticeship of any. He had heard of motor-boys who had only got their licences after a noviciate of five, or even six years; but it appeared that Fulbert was making his own exceptionally complicated. One day, when they were going together to the port to interview a group of ex-servicemen who, so the elder Lobila said, had come back from Indo-China by way of France, Mor-Zamba spoke of his disquiet to Jean-Louis, who replied:

'Have you yet held the steering-wheel?'

'Never once!' Mor-Zamba vigorously exclaimed.

'I thought as much,' observed Jean-Louis, phlegmatically. 'Listen, old chap: at the stage you've reached, you want to keep your apprenticeship, not so?'

'Of course,' cried Mor-Zamba. 'It's already cost me so much sweat and trouble that there's no question of giving it up.'

After seeming to hesitate a little, Jean-Louis finally asked him:

'Do you get any money?'

'Yes,' confirmed Mor-Zamba, nonplussed but full of hope.

'How much?'

His life alongside Robert had taught Mor-Zamba a good deal; thus he had acquired the reflex of dissimulating whenever the conversation turned to money. Since he drank little and lived sparingly and without avarice, like all those whose burning ambition makes ordinary life insipid, he had saved up, almost without realizing it, the little bit of money he earned. He would declare only a tiny proportion of this to Jean-Louis, to whom he was now accustomed to speak with some reticence. He had plenty with which to reproach this young man who, in his heart of hearts, appeared to him a monster, now that he knew him better. At his age, how could he go on living a double life, playing hide and seek even with his mother, who was just as much in the dark as his father about the dubious activities of her son? And what a boaster! It was for years now that he had constantly claimed to be on the brink of a big deal; and Mor-Zamba, who remained for so long a dupe, had every time awaited the event, only to be disappointed. The truth was, he was a man quite without financial flair, a born sponger. Every morning he left his father's house early, not without getting his mother to give him breakfast or, if she was out at that hour, which was common enough, one of his sisters, big girls, whom he continued to treat imperiously. To keep his parents guessing, since he was now too old to continue going to the lycée, he claimed that he was going with some friends to study privately for the baccalauréate, by correspondence with the Ecole Universelle in Paris. Like a real student, he was given pocket money, his clothes were washed and he was royally fed. He was seldom there at the beginning of a meal, but arrived a bit late in order to be specially served by his mother who kept the best bits for him.

On this last point, Mor-Zamba was the more resentful in that it was now he who really kept the family group, it seemed to him, normally paying his keep by contributions in kind which far exceeded his just share; but when, for one reason or another, the two parents had not been able to make the amount up, they no longer endured a week of famine, as they must have done before, and as the majority of Kolean families would do; for, carrying the family on his back, Mor-Zamba would then make it a duty to bring more provisions every day from the interior, where the crops in season cost only a tenth of the price. He had really been their salvation, especially since Robert and Fulbert had bought the T 55. And even when he was obliged to remain far from Kola-Kola for several days, as was usually the case in the slack season, because the transport owners hated to dispatch an empty lorry and it often took up to a week to fill one, Mor-Zamba never failed to give a sack of provisions to one of his companions, who would smuggle it with his own load and leave it in the corner of a friend's shop. The elder Lobila, having been informed, would go to the shop at the end of the day and pick up the precious cargo. It sometimes seemed to Mor-Zamba that this family had not really begun to live before his entry into Robert's service.

So much the better for those poor people! he would sigh from time to time, thinking of the two old ones. But recently, when he saw Jean-Louis, sitting at table after a day of sordid dealing, served and admired like a tribal chief by the whole household, he said to himself: Can't one help the real people without the bogus ones getting fat on it?

'So,' said Jean-Louis, impatiently, 'how much have you got?'

'Five thousand francs.'

Jean-Louis said nothing at first, fearing to give the game away. Then, when they had finished interviewing one of the last combatants returning from Indo-China, who had not seen Abena – which meant nothing, according to him, since it was impossible to see everybody – and they were returning in the rain, still on foot, to Kola-Kola, Jean-Louis explained to an appalled Mor-Zamba that, according to the custom of the quarter, a pupil driver had to mark each decisive step of his apprenticeship by organizing a feast, in the course of which he arraigned his master before a tribunal of neighbours and common acquaintances; there, he accused him of unduly prolonging his apprenticeship. In his own defence, the master would enumerate all the grievances with which he could reproach his pupil; he concluded by saying that in return for certain material advantages he would forget his resentment. This was a way of forcing the apprentice to double or treble the price

174

originally fixed on his apprenticeship. So, after years of effort, all the motor-boys, if, like Mor-Zamba, they refused to renounce the great enterprise of their lives, were obliged to submit to the conditions imposed by their masters.

'With Fulbert,' Jean-Louis continued, 'I believe there are four main steps. The first is when you take the steering-wheel for the first time. Be careful! It's only the wheel that you may take, because he will continue to operate the pedals. So, if you want to pass that stage, if you want at last to begin holding the wheel, you know now what you have to do. The second important step, which will come say, three or four months later, if you have managed the first, will be when you no longer only hold the wheel, but operate the clutching pedals as well; in effect, you drive. Fulbert, however, will always be at your side, ready to come to your aid if need be. Third step, three or four months later, again only if you've kept your master's goodwill: Fulbert will entrust you properly with the lorry; you are the only captain on board, and make journeys of some dozens of kilometres. Not in the city, naturally; there are too many regulations. He leaves you alone; he's no longer in the cab; he's playing the pasha in some little bar in a village along the route, or else he's quietly ruining himself with a girl at Efoulane or some other dump of that kind, full of cheap women. And you, my fine fellow, you roar along, never minding that you are still playing at it, because you feel that you are approaching your goal, and what a goal!'

'And the fourth step?'

'When your master judges that you are ready to pass the driving test; he decides to present you on an occasion chosen by him and tells you to apply accordingly.'

They discussed it all the afternoon, all the evening and part of the next morning, because Mor-Zamba was not going up-country that week, the T 55 being out of action. Finally, they signed a pact which restored hope to Mor-Zamba and made him think that people like Jean-Louis had their uses after all. On condition that Mor-Zamba entrusted the affair to his hands, Jean-Louis promised to speed his progress through his apprenticeship with Fulbert. Mor-Zamba immediately handed over his five thousand francs of savings – a big sum in those days! –

with which Jean-Louis promised to organize within ten days the first session of Mor-Zamba against Fulbert, in front of neighbours and friends in common, in the course of a feast. After this, Mor-Zamba would not pay another cent; but some six months later, or perhaps seven or eight at the worst, on the eve of passing his test, he would sign the recognition of a debt to Jean-Louis of thirty thousand francs to compensate him for the expenses and trouble which he would certainly incur, not only because of the ensuing feasts, but also in assiduously courting Fulbert, in jogging him constantly so as to win him round and to get favours from him; for he was a close fisted fellow, as Mor-Zamba would be the first to admit.

When he finally had his driving licence and a position with a slaver-employer in Fort-Nègre, then Mor-Zamba would compensate him with monthly payments of a thousand francs; according to Jean-Louis, Mor-Zamba would then enjoy such a good salary that this would be no burden to him. Jean-Louis offered him only this piece of advice; once he had his licence, even if Robert bought a second lorry and offered it to him, he should recall his earlier aversion for African employers. The real money, he claimed, the cash that counted, was still in Fort-Nègre; it was with the toubabs that one had the best chance to find it, not at Kola-Kola, and above all not with a boss like Robert, who was condemned to perpetual mediocrity.

'If all goes well, as it probably will,' declared Jean-Louis joyously, 'and especially if you have confidence in me, you'll have your licence in eight months at the most, old friend; what do you say?'

'Oh, don't talk any more about that,' Mor-Zamba sighed, assuming scepticism, but scarcely able to contain the joy within him.

What is more, if Mor-Zamba wanted to write a real signature, always preferable to a cross on a recognition of debt to Jean-Louis, but especially on the numerous official papers necessary to his test, the Kolean showed how necessary it was to learn to read; the devil himself would be in it if he couldn't do so within eight months.

'Who will teach me the letters?' asked Mor-Zamba, incredulously.

176

'I, of course,' said Jean-Louis, 'my little brothers and sisters. Everyone will help you. And then, while you're about it, you know, you might as well learn a bit of French. One day you'll have a toubab boss; you'll have to reply to him when he talks to you. Have you ever seen a toubab boss who doesn't talk to his drivers?'

'And what about pidgin, then? I understand pidgin now, all right.'

'Ah, because you're thinking of placing yourself with a Greek or Lebanese? Ah well, my congratulations! You, at least, don't lack ambition. No, believe me, chum, between a black boss and a Greek one, there's no difference – or rather an infinitesimal one. It's true that the black immediately spends in a stupid way everything that he's managed to squeeze out of the simpletons. As for the Greek, he hides the banknotes under his pillow. Then when he has a kilo or two of them, he heads for the post office and tells the clerk to give him a money order so he can send all that to his brother, who has a little shop up there in his native village, on the side of a bare hill. But, essentially, these are shabby fellows, with small ambitions and simple minds. No, let me tell you, a real toubab, that's what you want as a boss. It's not so difficult to learn French. You think it's difficult? In any case, everyone in the house will help you. Come on, we'll begin right away, you'll see. What do you call the lamps which light up the roadway at night?'

'Phares, phares, phares. . . .' repeated Mor-Zamba.

'You see! that's terrific. But that's when they light brilliantly, making a long ray in the darkness. When they light a bit less, what does one say? You don't know? . . . code.'

'Kodeu, kodeu. . . .'

'No. Code, code.'

'You think I'll make it all right?' asked Mor-Zamba, with a ravishing smile, secretly wishing that Jean-Louis would soon go away so that he could abandon himself in solitude to the manifestations of the joy within him.

'Will you make it? And how! It's really too easy; I'll even ask my brothers and sisters to speak nothing but French to you.'

'You're mad, it's impossible!' cried Mor-Zamba, with a snort. 'You're absolutely mad!'

Ruben scoured the whole colony and, as *Spartacus* always appeared so irregularly, Kola-Kola was not able to keep abreast with the stages of this tour, nor with its success. Well before Ruben's journey, the little newspaper had stopped giving this sort of information; it confined itself to giving orders for the struggle, to issuing details of the party's doctrine, or of the form of government and society which they wanted to give the country as soon as it became independent.

By losing temporarily the bursting source of life which was its great man, the quarter, one might think, had also renounced the intoxication of big events; for a long time no spasm had contracted its gigantic, debonair countenance. The self-defence groups, having no more enemies to confront, had fallen increasingly into idleness, even when they had not been tacitly disbanded. Lots of people now openly declared their lack of interest in these matters, saying that they would leave all that to the educated ones, especially to Ruben and his lieutenants, because they understood them properly. Certainly, there were elections which did not pass without some stir; like most of the quarter's inhabitants, Mor-Zamba thought that the elected delegate would go to defend the African cause in Paris, and perhaps at the United Nations in New York. Ruben refused to interrupt his journey through the colony, so that only the lieutenants he had left behind in Kola-Kola took charge of the campaign, although rejecting in advance the results of an election which, they affirmed, one could not expect to differ from the well-established tradition of rigging.

In any case, the quarter was only a part of the electoral district, which also embraced the whole conurbation of Fort-Nègre and a great part of the hinterland; nevertheless, the Koleans hoped that, aided by the mass of their votes and their discipline, Ruben, whom popular pressure had finally persuaded to stand, without demanding that he return to the town, would this time triumph over the candidates of the administration. This would have made for internal conflicts with Fort-Nègre, its governor, his Saringalas and his *mamelukes*. The man with the magical tongue would have made his voice sound in the outer world, in countries where the law had some meaning and the principles of justice some application. The civilized world would learn with horrified amazement about the daily practices in the colony, the cruelty of the Saringalas, the racial discrimination operating in every field, and all the excesses which made life a curse in the country. Paris or even the UN would doubtless send a commission of enquiry which, perhaps for several days, would come to Kola-Kola to interview the people. How could the local authorities deny the evidence of the facts? The governor might then be dismissed, being found guilty of covering up so many and such gross abuses. Then free elections would take place, under international supervision; the Rubenists would emerge in triumph, they would take control of the country and set it on the path of socialism and happiness.

The Rubenist leaders tried hard to stem this soothing flood of visions and fantasies, but nothing would do it; then, in resignation, they distributed detailed instructions which the people followed with a discipline and patience which were painful to see for those who doubted the issue of this latest masquerade; they went off to get voting cards in the offices of Fort-Nègre, where one saw even the old conscientiously forming themselves into queues, in sun or in rain; on the voting day they took their papers marked with the crab, the rallying-sign of the Rubenists, put them meticulously into the ballot-boxes and returned to their wretched hovels, illuminated with hope. The counting lasted all week; the results were announced on Saturday by the radio, but Ruben's name was not among those elected. The lamentations of the quarter announced a wound deeper than any inflicted up to then by the electoral chicaneries of Fort-Nègre. On the Sunday morning, to mark their anger, the *sapaks* and even those of mature age formed themselves into a cortège and paraded from eight o'clock till eleven, in defiance of the Fort-Nègre authorities and their hypocritical institutions.

The only consolation was that Langelot, Ruben's sworn

enemy, who, five years before had been an able enough politician to get himself elected by the Africans of Oyolo, was this time biting the dust, beaten by some obscure black man, whose name was forgotten as soon as read. This set-back seemed to presage the decline of a man who had been the personification of hypocritical oppression, that which publicly proclaims its love for the blacks, but secretly prefers them as slaves.

However, the militants on both sides made the same error in their appreciation of the event: in any case, they said to themselves, this won't lead to anything, because it's no more than a ritual, all the elections up till then having rolled along inexorably in conditions of obscurity which lent themselves to fraud; on the other hand, the inhabitants of Kola-Kola, a quarter captured by the Reds, had furiously manifested their disappointment on each occasion. A new feature this time, however, was that Ruben, from wherever he was, made this declaration, which echoed as ominously in Kola-Kola as in Fort-Nègre: from now onwards all elections would be organized jointly by government representatives and those of the PPP, or else they would be declared null by the genuine spokesmen of the African working masses.

Mobilized completely by his apprenticeship, which now went at a brisk pace, as predicted by Jean-Louis, as well as by his French lessons, given mainly by the latter's sisters, Mor-Zamba took no part in the demonstration, but stayed all morning in the Lobila household, listening to Tino Rossi songs on the gramophone, roughly translated for him by the girls. Towards midday, when the Corsican was singing:

> I have two songs: my sunshine
> And the love of my fair one. . . .

the youngest of Lobila's sons, aged fifteen, came up to Mor-Zamba and whispered in his ear that if he didn't come instantly to the rescue, Joe the Juggler would be a dead man in a few minutes. More amused than alarmed, Mor-Zamba nevertheless followed the boy without delay. He had to free Mor-Kinda from a compact group of devotees of Ruben and of maize beer, who held him prisoner in a low, miserable house, waiting, so they said, for the appropriate hour to put paid to this little rat, as a reward for his evidence in favour of Sandrinelli. The exchange of blows did not last long; Mor-Zamba, decisively raised to heroic rank in the quarter by his many feats against the Saring-alas, his favourite prey, was quickly recognized, and they all went to reconcile themselves in a little bar nearby, where the refugee from Gouverneur Leclerc's labour camp was happy to see the old soldier Joseph, who had spoken so comfortingly about Abena.

Joseph had been invisible recently; Jean-Louis knew only that he had set up house with a redoubtable whore and that, at the same stroke and as if by a miracle, his appearance, his urbanity and his sartorial elegance had recovered their lustre. He had not, however, regained all his equilibrium, because at the moment when Mor-Zamba entered with Joe the Juggler and their new friends he was deafening the customers with the discordant jangling of his epic tale. The boozer made the famil-iar sign with his finger at Mor-Zamba and winked his eye:

'Eeeeh! Ooooh! Come here, old boy. You've hit the moment; I've got something for you, something extraordinary, my lad, really amazing! Don't try to guess, you'll never do it. Look, I never see your cousin Jean-Louis anywhere.'

'I scarcely see him myself any more.'

'Doesn't matter!' cut in the old soldier. 'You've only got to pass it on to him. Will you buy a beer first of all?'

'Certainly; but what's happened, then?'

'Listen carefully, my lad. Eeeh! Oooh! This time, it's serious. Your brother, you know? The soldier, the volunteer of 1941, he doesn't look much like you? He's not so tall as you, for instance?'

'So, you've seen him? You've recognized him? I suspected as much.'

His voice broke and he was on the verge of tears.

'No, not me, old chap, don't get worked up. He's a stocky fellow, not so? With very muscled legs, especially on the fat of the calf. Correct?'

'Exactly.'

'Correct! He has teeth which slightly protrude from his lips, so that they're never fully closed. Correct?'

'Quite true.'

'All right, come straight away; there's no time to lose. I'm going to take you to meet someone.'

While the drunkard raised his elbow and tilted his head to drain the litre of beer which Mor-Zamba had just bought him, the latter and Joe the Juggler took leave of their companions, after leaving them something with which to finish the evening pleasantly.

In another bar a few minutes' walk away, Joseph set them face to face with a pale, moustached mulatto, a certain Maisonneuve, a taciturn and rather unpleasing fellow. He had come back from Indo-China by way of France and North Africa; no, he hadn't come by boat; as a French citizen, he was entitled to an air-ticket. He certainly knew Abena and had even fought at his side in the ricefields of the Mekong delta, even though they weren't in the same unit. This Abena was a magnificent soldier, a man whose courage had become legendary in the whole expeditionary force and who might have become an officer; he was one of only two or three blacks thought worthy of that honour. Officer! did his listeners really understand what he was saying?

'Officer, that's really something!' cried the old soldier, raising the bidding. 'Two or three pips on the shoulders, think of that here, my boys. Officer, ah! ah! And why not four or five pips later on? The most difficult thing, you know, is to get started, but once started, why then. . . .'

Unfortunately, continued Maisonneuve, in his soft and almost disdainful voice, unfortunately, he was one of those whom the army calls a headstrong ass, stubborn as a mule, with a profoundly contrary spirit. Once he got an idea in his head, it was useless to try to get it out again. What a pity! Because with all that ability and all that courage, he had it all cooked. But what a pig-headed fellow! It was on that account that he'd not only been excluded from the stage where they knock officer-cadets into shape, but had even been broken from his rank of sergeant-major.

'But can't you tell us where he is at this moment?' asked Mor-Zamba at last.

'In Algeria,' replied Maisonneuve quietly; 'I left him in the Aurès mountains.'

'In Algeria!' cried Mor-Kinda with a jump. 'Why in Algeria? I think I've heard Sandrinelli saying that his brother has also been there a while. His brother is not a soldier, he's a policeman. What's going on in Algeria then?'

Maisonneuve explained to them in a few words the reasons for the war raging in Algeria. Joseph then took them off to his house. His Adele was not yet back and he himself had to poke into the corners to discover some refreshments for his guests. After this, he displayed on the table a little Larousse dictionary in which he showed them a map of Africa and the position of Algeria at the top of the continent.

'Courage, boys!' shouted Joseph, 'he's getting nearer, your brother is!'

'Just as long as he's not dead, at this very moment,' joked Mor-Kinda. ·

'When will you stop speaking such horrors?' Mor-Zamba begged.

'Horrors! Big words all of a sudden. O.K., it's all right, I've said nothing.'

However, when they had left the old soldier, Mor-Kinda was unable to restrain himself from continuing:

'What kind of war-mania is this, that your brother has? He's crazy, that fellow. And then, just think what he's thrust himself into this time? At bottom, he's a kind of Saringala, if you really think about it.'

'Shut up! Shut up, will you. If you knew him, you'd know that he must have a reason. But you don't know him at all, and yet suddenly you presume to judge him. He certainly has his reasons for behaving so.'

'Fine, fine, that's all right, forget it.'

'And what about you, you remember the day when you testified in Sandrinelli's favour? The Kolean mob were still talking about it that evening, when I got back from Efoulane. "What a little shit!" they all said. And yet, it's not true you're a shit.'

'Yes, and what of it? You're not going to compare us, I hope? That's really unjust, you know! Simply because he's your brother, no one can make you see reason. I have a referee, see! And what a referee! And he, what of him? Just tell me who gave him permission to go making war all over the world. Not even you, who are his own brother. If I count correctly, it's fifteen years now, do you hear? Fifteen years that this bloke is running people through all over the world, and without any personal profit!'

'I've told you a thousand times that he wants to get a gun.'

'A gun, a gun! What kind of crazy notion is that? He gets a gun, and then? That's just a pretext. He loves combat above everything, that's all! And for preference, bloody combat. Listen, even among brothers, you know, men can be of many different sorts. If you want my opinion, your brother is not a man one can really approve of. You do just as you wish but, in your place, I would forget him, I'd let him drop. Every time you think of him, you've only to say to yourself: "He's a Saringala, a murderer. He kills, he rapes, he steals, he tortures...." Like that, and you'll forget him, I promise you. Look, my time is up; I'm off. Have courage, old chap.'

Less than five months after his pact with Jean-Louis, Mor-Zamba had reached the stage where, in the course of their expeditions up-country, Fulbert would leave him to manage the lorry entirely, and sometimes even left him alone or with Robert in the cab, at first for half-days, then for whole ones, and finally for many days together. Sometimes, comfortably instal-led in their headquarters at Efoulane, a hundred and fifty kilometres from Fort-Nègre, far from their wives and all the uproar of family life, old campaigners gripped by the demon of noon, the two partners would urge him to push further into the country. Then it would happen that he took passengers into the cab or even, when he was short of money, on to the platform, for the peasants were not fussy; and rather than buy an expensive seat of their choice in one of the one-ton Renaults turned into buses which now brightened the route, they preferred to travel in extreme discomfort, provided it saved them money. Mor-Zamba did not only visit the towns and riverside villages along the tarred road, where travelling was a pleasure, but often had to go still farther, by the little tracks, to reach country villages seldom visited; there he discharged his goods and delivered them to the manager of the local shop; for, in many of these distant centres, Robert had created small trading-posts which he confided to the management of a local.

But Robert's affairs were far from prospering in these remote places, disappointing from every point of view. The managers were incompetent and quite often dishonest as well. It was an inveterate habit of theirs to dip into the stock and distribute gifts right and left, hoping to make up the loss by selling the rest at double or triple the prices fixed by Robert for the whole chain. Then, when they saw that they couldn't sell any more, the higher prices having driven away their needy customers, they ran off or, more often, pretended to be absent when they heard the lorry stop. Mor-Zamba would enter the town, find the door closed at the manager's place, make enquiries in the neighbourhood and receive evasive answers from the people who were nearly always accomplices, having benefited from the largess of the imprudent trader. When he met with this now familiar situation, Mor-Zamba would go off without unloading. Unable to distribute either imported goods, because nearly one manager in every two was in flight and the other had never finished his stock, or the local products, because the T 55, already full, could not carry peasant foodstuffs to the markets in Kola-Kola and the other African suburbs of Fort-Nègre, the lorry ran most frequently at a loss, consuming petrol for nothing and wearing itself out uselessly. During the slack season, if Robert wanted to sustain his activity, these losses accumulated on all sides and finally cancelled out the exorbitant profits of the cocoa season.

Robert had certainly tried to remedy this decline, which he attributed uniquely to the rapid corruption of village souls in contact with urban degeneracy. At first he had tried, with some success, to bring charges against the more harmless cases, had improved his relations with the city police and had brandished the threat of arrest. In reality, Robert now had less and less hold over his agents, the peasants becoming steadily less impressed by urban intimidation, and his soiled merchandise became an irreparable loss.

Mor-Zamba returned to Efoulane and reported to the two partners, who showed concern but none of the inflamed passion he had expected. The two men seemed to him more and more lacking in enterprise, except when it came to pursuing the pleasures of an easy life in Efoulane, a big village somewhat off the main road, but still near enough to it to be considered a roadside settlement by the great majority of Koleans. Efoulane was in fact joined to the tarmac by a short stretch of stony road, buried in dust during the dry season and, in the wet season, riddled with pot-holes full of yellow water, which spouted under the tyres.

It drew from this ambiguous situation a charm to which Mor-Zamba had willingly submitted. In their daily life the people reminded him of the Ekoumdoums, whose gestures and habits they reproduced; but in their aspirations they belonged more to Kola-Kola. What chiefly struck the visitor, and what, by their own confession, held Robert and Fulbert besides, was the unparalleled number of elegant and beautiful women, attractive even when badly-dressed and, according to the connoisseurs, always healthy, in contrast with the frequently poxy women of Kola-Kola. At Efoulane, as at Ekoumdoum, the young pubescent girls sauntered through the streets and squares with their bare breasts erect, the short cloth which covered their hips ending above the knees; readily offered, one might say.

The district chief, the chief of police, the principal of the public school and the supervisor of the Catholic mission were all Africans, and the moral climate there prefigured that blissful relaxation, that laxity of morals, that racial toleration, which Ruben often told the Africans would be the portion of their country once it had ceased to be a colony. There were some twenty firms there, nearly all run by blacks, even those which were branches of the big colonial companies.

So the indifference of Robert and Fulbert towards commerce and transport reached such a point that, whenever it was essential to enter the slavers' city, where the controls were pitiless, they would order Mor-Zamba to go back alone to Kola-Kola. On the tarmac road the controls, very rare in any case, were in the hands of black policemen, with whom Mor-Zamba knew how to deal with all the coolness and nobility of manner of a veteran driver. There was nothing to fear with the Saringalas, notoriously illiterate as they were. They demanded to see the driver's papers; Mor-Zamba thrust Fulbert's at them; they pretended to examine them but, despite the photo, held them upside-down. Above all, one must not laugh; after a long moment, they gave everything back with that frozen expression on their scarred faces which made the people dread them, saying: 'Allez, go!' to show that they too understood pidgin.

With agents in uniform or, more rarely, *mamelukes* in plain clothes it was a different comedy. They could read very well, these ones, even too well. In hailing you, with their wide, mocking smiles, they would call:

'You well, my brother?'

Said in a certain way and supported by a look which pierced straight into that of their object, these words meant: 'We know very well, and so do you, that no one is perfect; least of all a lorry driver.'

The driver would then slide a five-hundred-franc note into the sheaf of papers which he thrust at the *mamelukes*: they, deeply moved by this worldly wisdom, quickly returned his documents, adroitly relieved of the note, and, amid great gusts of laughter, convulsively shook his hand whilst crying:

'Bon voyage, my brother. A kind thought. Thank you, my brother. . . .'

Mor-Zamba had quickly learnt to read well enough in Bantu, but very ill in French. But it was enough to bring Jean-Louis, who had disappeared, to suddenly emerge and demand his signature on the recognition of debt.

'Did everything go as I predicted?' he demanded.

'Exactly,' replied Mor-Zamba, without trying to conceal his joy. 'And you, we don't see you any more?'

'I think I'm big enough now to fly with my own wings. I've found a place in Fort-Nègre. I'll tell you later on.'

In exchange for his recognition of debt, Jean-Louis equipped Mor-Zamba with all the papers necessary for his test and, notably, with an identity card, a learner's licence, which served instead of a professional licence, as well as three sets of forms of various colours which Jean-Louis had already filled in with his own hand and which he made Mor-Zamba sign along with his identity card, on which Jean-Louis had given him the name of Nicholas.

187

'I, Nicholas?' cried Mor-Zamba.

'Nicholas Mor-Zamba, doesn't that suit you? I like it fine. Nicholas Mor-Zamba, Mor-Zamba Nicholas.'

'Nicholas.... Why Nicholas? You find something in me which makes me look like a Nicholas?'

'But, my dear fellow, Nicholas is not a person, it's just a name, it means nothing at all. A name is just like a word; it doesn't contain any reality, supposing that the reality of things exists. A name, it's simply a façade; and you've got to have one. As for that, I've given you the least stupid façade I can: that's the main thing. You must never appear a simpleton. Simpletons are the eternal pawns, always exploited and deceived. When one can get out of the camp of the pawns, believe me, it's not the moment to dilly-dally. You see, Nicholas, you're now a gentleman, and no longer a hick.'

They agreed to meet the next day at a shop in the slavers' centre. Jean-Louis led Mor-Zamba to a studio from which the learner-driver soon emerged, furnished with eight identity photographs. Immediately they went to an office, which Jean-Louis entered without ceremony; when they came out a little later, the photos had been stamped and stuck on to the cards and forms.

'Don't worry about anything,' said Jean-Louis; 'I'll take all these to the right person, as you might say. A few weeks from now, perhaps in a fortnight, I'll bring you your appointment myself. Chin up, old chap.'

Despite his brand-new Christian name, which should have made him into a citizen instead of the hick which he was said to have been up to now, Mor-Zamba nevertheless failed his test for the driving licence, both on the code and the driving. As for the code, he scarcely understood the questions put by the white examiner, only just landed, who spoke in an astounding manner, as if he were dealing with a Parisian rather than a Kolean; what is more, Mor-Zamba could not point out on a black and white sheet the panel announcing an un-manned level crossing.

As for the driving, everything went even more briskly. The examiner spoke to him incessantly, asking him if he were married, how old he was, how long he had been learning to drive. Already put out by not being able to reply with sufficient ease and spontaneity to the young examiner, Mor-Zamba managed to wreck everything when he was asked to make a half-turn, although he had carefully practised this manoeuvre, because it was compulsory. He forgot everything: instead of stopping first over to the right, looking in his mirror, sticking out his left hand before moving off in first gear to the left, he shot off across the road obliquely, as he had seen acrobatic African drivers do, though these were already possessors of licences, then threw the steering-wheel violently back whilst stamping on the brake-pedal, bringing the lorry to a sharp, trembling stop on the edge of the gutter, and the examiner against the windscreen, where he narrowly missed smashing his forehead.

The young white man, pale and mopping his brow, told him to come back in three months, as the regulations prescribed. That time, he was failed again in his driving but passed on the code, because he had worked specially hard on his French and the preservation of his poise. Three months more, and he was again failed on the driving. At the fourth set-back, Mor-Kinda confided to him the rumour which was circulating in all the suburbs of Fort-Nègre, but especially in Kola-Kola: that African applicants were systematically failed unless they had the formal protection of an employer.

'And don't imagine that Robert can be of the least use to you.'

'Yes, I know; neither he nor Fulbert really wants me to pass my test, you are thinking. I'm not so stupid, you know; they would have to pay me if they don't want to lose me. At least eight thousand francs a month, the current salary in Fort-Nègre. And where would they find them, these eight thousand francs, since their affairs are at present in a dreadful state?'

'There's a bit of that in it,' Joe the Juggler acquiesced slowly; 'but there's something else. In the eyes of the authorities, Robert is not a real employer; and that's easy to understand, because Robert's position is not in order, has never been in order, despite all Jean-Louis' efforts.'

The vast majority of Kola-Kola's transport contractors and traders were in fact in an irregular situation, confined to it either by their illiteracy or their negligence, both causes for a swift discouragement in the face of the dizzying colonial bureaucracy, or perhaps by the calculated inertia of the higher administration. For example, the Kolean transporter usually acquired his vehicle through secondhand channels, from a white employer in Fort-Nègre, who for various reasons no longer needed it. He paid the going price for it cash down, but received in exchange that, at the moment of announcing the sale of the vehicle, the seller, on much better terms with an administration which was generally indulgent towards him, had the vehicle licence made out in the name of his Kolean partner. This operation was carried out in front of the slaver and, under his orders, the black clerks, so intractable and suspicious with their own compatriots, followed every flicker of his eye or finger.

Immediately, the Kolean would take to the road, headfirst, burning to recover the sums, enormous for someone like himself, which this investment had just cost him. The new owner was not enrolled on any commercial register; yet every January he had to pay a tax which was punitive and unique, depending on the type and power of the vehicle figuring on his papers. In this way, everything continued as if African ownership did not exist; what is more, only one African appeared among the members of the Chamber of Commerce.

Since they did not belong to any category of the law, conflicts which broke out among black owners would have been resolved by force if they had not long acquired the habit of having them judged by the commissariats; that is to say, arbitrated. Every Kolean owner was thus obliged to have a protector in the police or in the Department of Economic Affairs, as highly placed as possible and preferably a white, because the whites had the reputation of disdaining the petty bribes of the slums and being affable, courteous 'godfathers', in contrast with the minor black officials, who were cunning, greedy and coarse. Robert had tried in vain to get himself taken as a protégé by the Director of Economic Affairs, by bombarding this great figure with almost daily petitions in which Jean-Louis had displayed a positive genius for lavish flattery, without ever getting anything but the driest of replies, wrapped up in official formulae.

Robert had then fallen back on an African official, one of the highest in rank then; he, at least, did not disdain to come and dine with Robert and even, in return for services rendered, to accept a sort of payment in kind much in vogue in Kola-Kola, according to Mor-Zamba, and which consisted of lending his wife to his protector for so many nights. Mor-Zamba tells us that many times Robert lent Dorothy in this way to the official who watched his affairs in the department.

Paradoxically, this arbitrary system, even if it conveniently consigned the small African proprietor to outer darkness, was not without disadvantages to colonial tranquillity; it got away with things with an impunity which was little calculated to inspire the population with a taste for law and order. Thus there could be no question of repeated offences, because the petty black proprietors were not listed in the appropriate services. What a blessing for these ignoramuses, lazy and generally lacking in probity, who, in a country even slightly regulated, could not have existed for long. Fortunately for Robert and his fellows, the colony was riddled from top to bottom with crookery, incompetence and the vilest corruption. Many departments did not even have a record office, and when a driver lost his licence he was obliged to repass the test, because the original from which the new copy could have been taken had been destroyed. Mor-Zamba says he now understands why the colony always lacked the funds to set up a proper administration – for, often enough, what the Africans interpreted as malice towards them was mainly the result of an incapacity to face up to the most essential tasks. He explains that the colony permitted the big import–export houses to repatriate all their profits, and, since its own resources were limited to customs and excise dues, plus the capitation tax on Africans, it could only become impoverished, growing ever more incapable of a budget matching its needs. From then on, it could only resort to cutting its necessities, or denying their existence, instead of trying to satisfy them.

Jean-Louis had now really and truly vanished, and Mor-Zamba, who would have liked to present his new difficulties to him, was put out. He had not clapped eyes on him since the eve of his last examination when, faithful to his promise, he had come for the fourth time to bring all the necessary papers. On the other hand, his friendship for Mor-Kinda grew stronger every day and it was the latter who, whenever they met, brought him up to date with political events and with the activities of Ruben. As a militant in the apprentice drivers' union, Mor-Zamba had soon tired of working every day at one minute panel of a tapestry, without knowing its dimensions or who held its extremities. He would unhesitatingly have given his life to again rescue Ruben or any of his lieutenants from the hands of the *mamelukes* of Fort-Nègre. Without being involved, he needed to imagine the difficulties and results of an enterprise, if not its actual state.

On the instructions of Paris, the Consultative Council had just received new functions. It would now have real legislative powers, at least in all matters concerning neither defence nor foreign affairs. Ruben, who had also disappeared again, published a demand to participate with the colonial authorities in the preparation of fresh elections for a new council, without which, as he had already announced, the PPP would not recognize them as having any value. Once again, all Kola-Kola held its breath; would the new governor, specially sent in order to incarnate the new policy, show wisdom and accept the demands of the former union leader, or would he, like his predecessor, take refuge in disdain and brutality? And in that event, what would be the issue of a fresh test of strength?

That same day, Mor-Zamba took Joe the Juggler to the hideout of Ruben's principal lieutenant, before whom he risked making the following revelation:

'Yesterday, my boss Sandrinelli wrote the same letter to his cousin Brede, in Morocco, and to his own brother at Constantine, in Algeria. To both he said, in effect:

' "The decisive moment has arrived; get ready to embark. We are now into the main business, which is the shaping of the new Legislative Council: the list of candidates is almost complete now. But we still need one or two fellows having the reputation of militants, to hoodwink the metropolitan press, especially those types who certainly won't fail to squeal like polecats. But the big chief doesn't want to know anything, he wants them all strictly on the same footing. That just isn't reasonable. That's where we stand: we must succeed at all costs. Afterwards, everything will run by itself." '

'How do you know this?' someone asked.

'Madame Sandrinelli asked me to go and tidy up her husband's study at about 6 p.m.; she was in a rage and kept shouting that it wasn't a study, but a pigsty. It's true that the floor was all covered with orange peel, cigarette butts and crumpled paper. I swept while Madame Sandrinelli herself opened both the windows to air the place; then, while I was dusting the furniture by flicking it with a cloth, Madame Sandrinelli went out. I had plenty of time to loiter by the boss's desk, and that's how I managed to read everything.'

'Where was Sandrinelli?'

'Somewhere or other in the institute.'

'How come that he has so much confidence in you?'

'He doesn't really have confidence in me. He thinks of me as a poor bugger who doesn't understand a thing. It's true that I do nothing to disillusion him. I'm always careful to talk broken French in front of him, and he loves that. By the way, in my job you must always speak broken French and behave like an idiot. That's the best thing, from every point of view.'

The same day, he introduced Mor-Zamba to Sandrinelli, presenting him as his cousin, and asked him to act as patron for his driving test.

'Hello, cousin!' cried Sandrinelli, with a big pasha's laugh, standing on tiptoe to stroke Mor-Zamba's chin caressingly. 'You never told me you had a cousin, you little miser. Where does he live?'

'In Kola-Kola with me, sure,' replied Joe the Juggler, clowning it up still more.

'Ah yes, in Kola-Kola, of course, Kola-Kola, yes, Kola-Kola. Blessed Koleans, get along with you. Ah la la, these blessed Koleans, all the same. You say he hasn't got a "godfather"; why hasn't he got one?'

'Because he did it all on his own,' replied Joe the Juggler, always in broken French, with an idiotic effrontery which amazed Mor-Zamba. 'He managed to learn to drive all on his own.'

'Hm! Hm!' said Sandrinelli, 'and can he really drive now?'

'Oh yes, yes! Very well.'

'Ah! Ah! and once he's got his licence, what will he do then?'

'Ah then,' said the Juggler, 'he'll become a driver.'

'Where?'

'With an employer.'

'Who's that?'

'We don't know yet; we have to find one.'

'Come and see me again at that point,' said Sandrinelli suddenly, like a man who's just made a discovery. 'Come and see me again then: I'll get your cousin a job with a man who's one of my friends and an excellent employer. The important thing is that he doesn't start managing on his own again, your cousin, once he's got his licence. What an idea! You must have an employer; everything goes sweetly then. Isn't it so, cousin? Isn't it sweet-sweet, a nice little boss? Isn't it sweet-sweet, a little boss, eh? Yes? Then laugh aloud, don't be afraid to show your joy, cousin. Laugh, come on.'

Sandrinelli took them from the lobby, where they had been standing till then, into the main reception room of his villa, a large, square room lapped in a twilight which seemed glacial to Mor-Zamba. He had never advanced so far into the intimacy of a slave-driver; he observed the gleaming neatness of the objects when the light touched them, as well as the decorous arrangement of the furniture. He did not at first notice a woman sitting far away from them at a round table, with her back towards them, apparently absorbed in a delicate task whose nature Mor-Zamba could not guess; dark hair, rich and abundant, fell over her neck before spreading out on her back and shoulders.

Leaving the two men standing near the door of the room, Sandrinelli disappeared into his study and soon returned with an envelope whose edges he was busy licking; then he sealed it carefully, held it out to Mor-Zamba and told him:

'Cousin, you have only to give this to your examiner as soon as he calls you. But above all, once you've got your licence, come and see me again. Promise? What an idea, to struggle along on your own!'

'But what are you telling those two poor boys, Antoine?' the woman interrupted, without turning round. 'Look, it's ridiculous! Does it amuse you to mislead them? You're not going to reproach them for trying to set up for themselves, if they wish to? Frankly, how provoking you can be. There are days when I don't understand a thing. Sometimes the natives are useless good-for-nothings; sometimes, it's especially important that they shouldn't try to manage on their own. If just once we could have one who doesn't expect everything from others! I can assure you if I was in their shoes there are times when I'd snap my fingers in your face. What a land of fools!'

But Sandrinelli had already finished with his two protégés and was ushering them through the door, not without declaring, half-joking and half-serious:

'Ah, my boys, women! women!...'

Mor-Zamba and the Juggler strolled through the grounds of the institute until it was time for the latter to take over from the day-servants at the director's house.

'What's this fellow really up to?' Mor-Zamba suddenly burst out.

'Shsh!' whispered the Juggler, his finger to his lips. 'Speak more quietly.'

'You really think he understands Bantu?'

'I'd be amazed, but you never know with people like that. Stoop down a little and I'll tell you: it seems he's a queer.'

'What?'

'A queer. You don't know what that is? No more do I; he's never tried it on with me; I can't be his type. But you, old chap, watch out! It seems you excite him.'

'I don't understand a word you're saying.'

'It's simple. Sandrinelli is one of those men who want to be treated as women by other men, or treat the others as women. Do you see what I mean? Apparently, that's the reason for his attachment to Baba Toura. No one's ever been able to say which one is the man and which the woman.'

'But between ourselves, do you really believe this thing happens?'

'Yes, it happens! I'll bet my last franc that it does, especially among those people. You don't know them. They have all the vices. When I think they came here to teach us religion and good will! What good has two thousand years of Christianity done?'

The following week, Mor-Zamba received an imperious command from Fulbert and Robert, still installed at Efoulane, to make a tour of the peasant towns in the interior but, when he returned to give an account of his journey and its setbacks, he found the two partners in violent conflict. With their eyes shot with blood, wild, sweeping gestures and foaming lips, they abused each other to admiration. A shocking spectacle that these hitherto honoured, respected and equally courted men should be at each other's throats in front of those to whom they had been models of dignity, sophistication, competence and application. Their breathlessness and dishevelled appearance made one suspect they had already come to blows. As chance would have it, the official of the Department of Forestry, Ginguene, M. Albert to the Africans, found himself in the midst of the crowd of idlers quickly gathered around the two antagonists, his shorts and shirt immaculate as ever, and his eye, as always, slightly ironical.

'What's going on? What's wrong?' he asked Robert as he came up to him.

The Kolean merchant, who was very flattered at being addressed by M. Albert instead of having to make the first approach, calmed down a bit; what is more, instead of carelessly offering him his little finger as usual, the colonial official held out his whole hand to shake. Very much a man of the world, Robert made a superhuman effort to smile and even to exchange a few refined civilities with a man of M. Albert's quality. All this honour, especially when heaped on him like a consecration in front of such a mob of peasants, would have made any Kolean die of joy; everyone thought that Robert was lost to the farcical scene he had been playing.

'This man and I were partners,' he explained to Ginguene, speaking boastfully in his bad French; 'but he has tried to rob me. Well, he won't carry it to Heaven with him!'

But suddenly leaving Ginguene stuck there, he threw himself, eyes aflame and face convulsed with rage, on Mor-Zamba,

196

whom he had just spotted, and with whom he was seen to exchange a few words in a low voice. Mor-Zamba led him briskly to the T 55, stationed a hundred metres off, where Robert threw open the door and took some papers, leaning forward with his feet on the ground. He rushed straight at Fulbert and pushed the papers under his nose, before shouting brutally:

'You filthy wretch, just see if these papers aren't in my name. Just see if this lorry is not my property. We bought it together and the property is indivisible? Get stuffed! Just look if these papers are not in my name. Where do you see your own, you stupid bastard? Can you even read? It's twenty years now you've been in the city and you haven't dared learn to read, with good reason. You wouldn't have enough years of life left to learn to read, blockhead. And when will you ever get your hernia operated on? Just wait till it strangles you....'

Seeing the onlookers laughing with their jaws gaping, M. Albert turned to his neighbour, who happened to be Mor-Zamba at that moment, and asked:

'What did he just say? What did he tell him?'

Unable to translate the subtle rhetoric of his master, Mor-Zamba, who was reluctant to admit defeat, replied:

'He said to him, "old bollocks of the moon!"'

'Bah,' cried M. Albert, thoroughly disappointed; 'and that made them laugh? They're easily amused.'

It was not long before Mor-Zamba learnt that the two men had stupidly chased the same girl; and, despite their age, which should have instilled some reason and moderation, they had flown at one another like two young bumpkins.

Fulbert, whom Robert had forbidden to enter the lorry, was obliged to remain in Efoulane but, beaten all along the line, he had not even the consolation, though in a manner master of the field, of holding and enjoying the object of dispute. For Robert had immediately demanded that the girl's parents hand her over in marriage on the spot; prevailing over their brief perplexity by the manifestations of his power in the five-tonner, the fine appearance of his servant and the love which he soon displayed with no less vigour than usual. Robert himself carried to the lorry the meagre and hastily-assembled bundle of his new wife's effects; he helped her up into the cabin by seizing her hips and heaving her on to the seat. And, to crown this rite of undisputed conquest, it is certain that Robert, if he had been able, would have taken the wheel of the T 55 himself.

The new governor, coming to initiate a policy announced to the sound of trumpets as entirely new, rejected as insolent and offensive to the honour of a new democracy the offer of collaboration from a rebel proposing to help in the organization of elections. As the sole authority of the Republic, legally empowered to preside over the election by the people of their own representatives, save to delegate some part of his authority, though only where the need arose, to those whose task was to assist him, the proconsul, in a solemn proclamation, vowed to discharge his historic mandate with the zeal, impartiality and constancy which, in all times and continents, must mark the presence of a people whom destiny found always ready to measure itself against ever new duties.

No need to report that the elections were a triumph for the new governor, if not for the republic; the following day, in defiance of the slowness of communication habitual in the colony, the proconsul was able to announce a list of delegates on which, in his own opinion, there figured only a few black sheep, who would doubtless not long remain there.

Three weeks passed; then, late and obstinate as only the poor know how, because they are the symbol of justice, *Spartacus*, the pitiful journal of the PPP, enumerated and verified a long series of irregularities and often gross frauds, indicating that the governor had intended to impose a corrupt solution by force. At the end of this indictment, Ruben declared the elections null and void. The same day the governor ordered Ruben's arrest and issued a decree dissolving the Popular Progressive Party and all the organizations which might be termed its sisters, daughters or cousins.

Barely an hour later the Saringalas arrived in front of the

198

Labour Centre at Kola-Kola but, finding no one there, they sacked the place and carried off all the documents they could find. The new governor had just won his first military victory.

The concern caused by the outlawing of Ruben, and the authorities' evident determination to break at all costs the resistance of Kola-Kola to a Baba Toura solution, clearly the result of long planning, imposed several months of calm upon the scene, if not upon the wings, as if, before throwing himself into a storm of confrontation, everyone wanted to draw back and take stock of his forces. In public edifices ringed with armed troops, ringed in turn by empty streets and squares, well away from a people who were far from indifferent, though deliberately kept in ignorance of events so as to strengthen and consolidate the situation, ceremonies so lacking in pomp as to be imperceptible installed the Consultative Council, the Legislative Assembly and Baba Toura, formerly president of the Consultative Council, now prime minister of a state born without aid of drum or trumpet.

At the same time Kola-Kola was subjected once more to efforts, better concerted now, at colonial occupation; the scarfaces reappeared in compact patrols, as well as *mamelukes* in plain clothes or uniform, marching always in threes or fours. Once again, permanent buildings were requisitioned and transformed into police stations, linked by telephone with the nerve-centres of the governor's security forces.

Joe the Juggler was in the vein of making sombre predictions, drawn from the ever-significant behaviour of his patron Sandrinelli and his friends who, as on the eve of Ruben's capture, began once again to gather every evening at the Institute of 18 June. Paradoxically, instead of being a subject of torment to the Juggler, this prospect seemed to him filled with promise and stimulated to the point of exaltation certain instincts then unknown but discernible long since. Mor-Zamba, for his own part, hoped desperately for a peaceful issue, not because he lacked the aggressive spirit, but because he doubted the effect upon the career opening before him of the peril to which Kola-Kola must be condemned, as soon as Ruben issued his words of command.

For several months, there were no such words from Ruben;

his organizations, although banned officially and with their known leaders all in exile, in jail or in hiding, were none the less existent, even palpable; keeping the quarter under pressure by certain signs such as the collection of dues and, from time to time, a striking event like the capture, imprisonment or, more rarely, the murder of a *mameluke* who had rendered himself especially odious. The quarter seemed to have stepped back several years, but the impression was misleading; the *sapaks* had learnt the lesson of the battles over Holy Joseph, fought and lost during Ruben's stay in Europe; they had learnt to strike suddenly and to melt away again in the bewildering maze of the Kolean hovels.

And then, students returning from Europe revealed to their bemused compatriots the truth which had been hidden from them by Fort-Nègre, its officials and its press — Ruben was continuing the struggle, no longer with words, but with arms; no longer in the wretched slums of the cities, but in the forest; no longer ringed with political activists, but with fighting soldiers. In addition to the union and the party, Ruben had prepared a weapon for the heroic phase of the struggle, and Kola-Kola had never guessed it! To convince the unbelieving, the students showed them cuttings from the Western press, where long articles and photos of Ruben dealt with the situation in the colony, bringing to light the obstinate refusal of the colonial authorities, in spite of all evidence, to accept Ruben as the natural spokesman of the native populations. These young people spontaneously became propagators of the Rubenist faith, and their various arrivals now provoked the same enthusiastic sensation as had met, long before, the return of the ex-soldiers.

Mor-Zamba understood that fate held Kola-Kola and Fort-Nègre in the teeth of its machinery on the day when Joe the Juggler revealed, between chuckles, that Brede, Sandrinelli's cousin and the same young policeman whose audacity had formerly captured Ruben in the heart of Kola-Kola, had returned to Fort-Nègre, this time under a false identity. The potentate's brother was also within the walls of the slavers' capital, having disembarked at the airport only a few days after Brede.

'Eh! and at night, get it?'

Mor-Zamba pointed out that most of the planes of the chief French airlines (and Sandrinelli's brother had come by one of these) had always landed at night at Fort-Nègre airport; nevertheless, he didn't fail to mention this detail to the general meeting of the Fourth Secret Committee, in front of a member of the Permanent Commission of the Supreme Secret Committee of the Union (for, in reality, by force of circumstances, the unions and all their federations had been transformed into secret organizations for action and resistance).

The underground leaders of the quarter, whether political or unionist, having met to consider the state of affairs, discussed the evidence furnished to Mor-Zamba by Joe the Juggler. They quickly understood the necessity to know how to take the reappearance of this Brede; he was undoubtedly a sort of boy spy, presumptuous and henceforth inoffensive – a young policeman who, as a child, had read too many comic strips depicting the exploits of Tarzan. He would need too many devices now to be able to approach with impunity the strategic places or personalities. There could be no repetition of the seizure of Ruben; that just was not a serious possibility.

On the other hand, they puzzled in vain over the second person, this Sandrinelli of whom Joe the Juggler knew only that he too was a police agent, without being able to define his rank or his speciality. They tried without success to extract a little light from a whole night full of sharp debate. Since the mystery of this policeman and his mission in the colony remained impenetrable, they questioned two students specially invited to this emergency meeting because they had recently returned from France; they asked them to explain the difficulties of the political situation in which the colony found itself, as they might be seen not only by informed European opinion, but also by the French political authorities. Above all, bearing in mind the experiences of recent years and the demands imposed by the Algerian rebellion, what temptations might the French government feel to finish with this new resistance front, now springing up in the colony?

The somewhat unrealistic views of the two students,

inspired the secret leaders with nothing more than a working hypothesis, which the immediate future would help to confirm or deny: Sandrinelli, the new policeman, was without doubt a specialist in the smashing of secret organizations, to which he had been able to devote himself in Constantine; it was probable that the transfer of police officers from North Africa was made in anticipation of a train of violence, set off by the decision to impose Baba Toura at any price; in other words, to achieve a solution by force. From now onwards, Kola-Kola must expect an invasion of more or less hastily-trained spies; at first, they would be easily unmasked, so long as they were not themselves Koleans (an eventuality which the secret leaders imprudently and unanimously dismissed, so high did they pitch the level of political consciousness in the quarter).

The PPP underground leaders, both those of the unions and those of the reconstituted GAVEs, therefore received orders to notice above all the appearance of any stranger in the quarter, and to announce it if it lasted more than a day.

Full of zeal for this assignment, Mor-Zamba became, in Kola-Kola, a militant tormented, coiled and bunched upon himself, showing to the world a grave and searching visage, like a prowling cat.

But once out of the quarter and rolling over the tarmac or bouncing over the pebbles in his T 55, he became a man without cares; he never stopped whistling and singing; he delighted in the tales of women which flowed ceaselessly from Robert's lips.

Mor-Zamba became one of the first victims of the new phase in the eternal war between Fort-Nègre and Kola-Kola, only a few days before his test, which he was certain to pass, having his craft now well in hand and a recommendation in his pocket from Sandrinelli, whom everyone knew to have become a close adviser to the prime minister of the autonomous colonial government, without ever quite abandoning his mask of director of the institute. Thus he was arrested one morning, a little before noon, just as he entered Kola-Kola on the way from Efoulane, being taken in a routine check carried out by a plain-clothes *mameluke*, a youth hitherto known for laxity, if not favour towards the nationalist and revolutionary militants of Kola-Kola, and even considered by some to be a secret Rubenist.

But that morning he showed a shifty eye and a closed face, like a butcher who has received the strictest of orders, like a man resolved to ignore the rites and liturgy of the happy life. He took readily enough the papers which Mor-Zamba thrust at him, having first slid several banknotes among them; he glanced superficially over them, but did not give them back.

'Just keep still, you hear!' he shouted in French.

He walked round the front of the lorry and climbed into the cab, seating himself beside Mor-Zamba.

'Wetin happen, my brother? What's going on, my dear?' Mor-Zamba kept repeating in pidgin or in Bantu.

The phlegm which the Kolean militant had cultivated for more than a year in the interests of passing his test lent him an irreproachable countenance: even though he felt the wind turning against him, he gave no sign of concern or even of plain nervousness, pushing his insolent coolness to the point of refusing to glance at the *mameluke* seated beside him, who doubtless wished to impress him by, for example, insisting on speaking French. It seemed to Mor-Zamba that, in this atmosphere of terror, that cruel language at last found its ideal employment.

'Fine! fine!' exclaimed the *mameluke*; 'We'll go straight to the Central.'

'Wetin you say?' asked Mor-Zamba in pidgin.

'You understood me very well!' cried the other in French, getting into a rage. 'I said: Let's go to the Central Police Station. And here's a bit of good advice – don't try to play the simpleton.'

The little *mameluke* felt in the pocket of his safari-jacket, a garment popularized by the heroic iconography of General Leclerc and of which the white colonizers of the country, in homage to the man they considered their second patron saint after de Gaulle, had created a civil dress both elegant and imposing, and brought out an object of dull grey metal which he waved clumsily under Mor-Zamba's nose. The latter, who knew nothing of firearms, thought this must be a dummy pistol with which the *mameluke* hoped to intimidate him, but the other quickly disillusioned him by firing a bullet which shattered the windscreen and made the militant Rubenist jump.

'You get it now?' cried the *mameluke*; 'it's no dummy. We are all armed now; now we shall teach you how to live, you bunch of savages. Start your engine and get moving....'

People passed nearby and walked beside the T 55 without a glance, deafened by their own voices, or by the rumble of traffic, which was not dense at that hour, however; others looked on uncomprehendingly from their own doorsteps, gazing placidly and vacantly at a scene whose pathos and violence they did not suspect. So, on a public street and at such an hour, right in the heart of Kola-Kola, a petty *mameluke* could neutralize a Rubenist by jumping into his lorry and forcing him to drive to the Central Police Station, smashing his windscreen in the process, without alerting the *sapaks*!

'Why didn't I cry out? Why didn't I resist? Why didn't I try subterfuge? I was so stupefied that my brain was fuddled and I did nothing but wait for some outside assistance,' thought Mor-Zamba bitterly, while he entered the courtyard of the Central Police Station, got down from the lorry and went to the entrance indicated by the *mameluke*, who still threatened him with the pistol; really, he overdid it, because there was no longer any question of Mor-Zamba running away, given the density of *mamelukes* of every sort per square metre in that fortress.

Until his first interrogation, he thought his arrest had been an accident and had nothing to do with his activities as a militant Rubenist. But that same afternoon, and above all during the sleepless night following, with his eyes blindfolded, he was bombarded with the most startling questions, battered with blows, flogged with a rawhide whip, thrown on the concrete floor, trampled, picked up again, questioned afresh and once more rained upon with fists. This man who had been tempered by so many trials, who never uttered a cry or asked for mercy, who refused to give up his secrets, discouraged his butchers at the very moment when he was suddenly seized with panic, remembering all at once what was rumoured among the militants of Kola-Kola: they said over there that, in order to subdue the most stubborn Rubenists, the *mamelukes* of the Central used to crush their testicles with their boots. Now he was pushed into a dark cell, thrown among the other accused, pressed tightly together and silent as ghosts; he discovered bit by bit that no one took the slightest care of them; they were not worked up because nobody fed them or because their beards remained unshaved for weeks on end. They lived, waited, slept occasionally, despite the cramp of their limbs, alongside the piss and ordure which fell into a gutter winding along the wall, through which they were supposed to flow away. But the truth was that they didn't flow at all and that tight hole was filled with the most revolting odour, to which, to his great amazement, the orphan of Ekoumdoum finally accustomed himself also; as if he had been resolved in advance to endure everything, except the idea, which really terrified him, of losing his testicles.

They did not blindfold him for his second interrogation, presided over by a white police officer whose questions were translated into pidgin. Where was Ruben? Where were his secret lieutenants in Kola-Kola? How did they know that Ruben had been captured that evening when he, Mor-Zamba, went to release him at the Institute of 18 June? For it was he who freed him, was it not? Who was with him that evening? Who was in command? To all these questions, he replied that he had no idea what they were talking about; he could scarcely speak, with his stomach knotted, his mouth dry, waiting every moment for the blows to fall. But they didn't hit him any more; before shoving him back into the stinking cell they gave him a little water to drink and some groundnuts to chew. It seemed to him that they only treated him with a certain care as one would an enemy who must not be prematurely destroyed.

One morning some men who had dragged him from the cell with especial violence pushed him into a corridor, then down the narrow steps of an unlighted staircase which led to the basement. He suddenly found himself in front of a kind of window, pinioned by two athletes who held his arms with both their steely fists. When the panel covering the window was slid back, one of the athletes cried to him in pidgin, while crushing his arm cruelly:

'Filthy Rubenist, take a look at that! That's what's coming to

205

you; and what's more, you'll all be killed. This one also refused to talk.'

Stupefied, terrified and trembling in succession, Mor-Zamba saw in the brightly-lighted room a naked man whose feet were both tied to one end of a horizontal bar, while his two hands were lashed to the other. Thus suspended, with his belly uppermost, the victim, who struggled from time to time as if trying to escape, resembled a big beast which some happy hunters were carrying home. Two servants, in civilian dress with their sleeves rolled up, busied themselves like feverish ghosts with the controls of the apparatus, which they were perhaps trying to get into the best position. For, manipulated by them with many grating sounds, the bar descended slowly towards the ground, so that the victim's back stopped at a height which Mor-Zamba nowadays estimates at thirty or forty centimetres from the concrete floor. Then the two servants straightened up and moved away, mopping their brows with their palms and puffing, like men who have just made an immense effort.

A third man, whom Mor-Zamba had not noticed before and who perhaps came from an adjoining room, spread out some newspapers, crumpled them and piled them up on the floor underneath the wretched man; he then sprinkled them with petrol (or perhaps rather with gas-oil) and set fire to them with a match, as if the victim had been an antelope whose hide he wanted to scorch before roasting it and chopping it up. But the sufferer was a living man, not the body of an animal, as Mor-Zamba was soon reminded. During several moments, which seemed to him an eternity, the man, wrapped in flames, shouted, twisted, convulsed and contorted himself with spasms so furious that Mor-Zamba could not bear the sight and closed his eyes. But he was unable to close his ears and had to listen to the victim's cries of agony.

At first, he said, the poor man, no doubt surprised at the novelty of the treatment inflicted on him, uttered cries of pain mingled with terror; then he emitted a sort of horrible roar, like a pig being stuck, just before the blood spurts and chokes the beast in a thick death-rattle; finally, when the flames were extinguished, the sufferer, torn with pitiful sobs like a boy who has just endured the test of circumcision, wept all the tears in his body, snuffling, shitting noisily on the floor, begging for mercy and praying aloud.

Taken back more dead than alive to his cell; waiting every moment to be dragged to the torture-chamber and roasted in the midst of the flames; already spent by a suffering such as he had never endured; he distracted his mind from that insupportable anguish by ceaselessly questioning himself, striving to understand things, like the dying, of whom it is said that they review their whole lives a few seconds before giving up the ghost.

What could really be at stake in such atrocities? Was it really still a question, for one party, of putting Ruben in the governor's place; and, for the other, of opposing this change by every means? It was on that day that Mor-Zamba realized for the first time that Ruben's struggle was not aimed solely at political emancipation, nor even at the recovery of the nation's resources, but perhaps above all at certain objectives which we would take long to attain. How else could one explain the redoubled anger, ferocity and barbarous inhumanity of the opponent?

Who could have given him away? The question seemed to have no sense; everyone in Kola-Kola knew his double exploit: he had liberated Ruben and killed a Saringala in doing so, two feats which formed the origin of his heroic reputation in the quarter, often renewed subsequently by his brushes with both *mamelukes* and Saringalas. Anyone at all, a girl for example, could have told this to a *mameluke* on the same pillow, or simply by mere inadvertence or boasting. And the policeman, having long kept his heavy secret to himself, could have suddenly decided, out of sheer zeal or to win a bonus, that it was time to unburden himself on the bosom of a superior. But he would deny it to the last, with still more serenity now that he was sure that, not having witnessed the scene, the *mameluke* with whom they would confront him would hesitate sooner or later, even if he began by bluffing to display his confidence; there would be variations in his account, he would break off and get muddled up.

But he was not confronted with anyone; he was held for two

weeks under close watch at the Central Police Station, in that abominable cell which communicated by a squint-hole with the Charge Office, a big low room filled, especially at night, with an endless, shuffling procession of fresh suspects. According to their behaviour they were treated differently by the *mamelukes*, all in uniform, all black. Those who put on a resigned or submissive face, or even that indifferent look often seen on hardened delinquents, were simply registered and quickly pushed into one of the cells. But if a suspect showed a bit of pride, if he was reluctant to answer the *mamelukes'* provocative questions – for example: 'How many fucks can your fifteen-year-old sister take in one night?' – they were mercilessly roughed up, with batons and boots, or even with bare fists. Most of these uniformed men, who were not even Saringalas, but sons of the soil, compatriots of those they thus tormented, were huge athletes, endowed with a herculean strength. Sometimes, when half asleep, choked by the stench of the cell, Mor-Zamba would awake with a jump at the screams of a suspect who was being horribly beaten; he would get up, make his way with difficulty through the tangled legs of those sitting asleep and get to the squint-hole, through which he watched the atrocious scene, illuminated by the harsh glare of a shadeless lamp hanging from the ceiling.

One day, the refugee from the Gouverneur Leclerc Work Camp had a sudden impression that important changes were being made in the administration of the Central Police Station. He was abruptly transferred, without explanation, to the adjoining prison and put into a cell where life seemed to him altogether bearable, no longer in company with political prisoners or ambiguous characters (doubtless the ears of the police, charged to overhear the conversations of the militants), but with common law criminals; credulous and talkative men whose minds were almost exclusively turned to the preoccupations of sex and food.

At last, one morning, he was pulled out of his cell and taken to the law courts, escorted by lofty-looking scarfaces. The courtroom was a vast chamber with bright walls, which resounded when even a single voice was raised, as happens in a church. When Mor-Zamba appeared, the judge read out the charge in a rapid voice, like all white men, accusing him, to his great astonishment, of driving a lorry without a licence for almost a year – which was actually less than the truth. Not a word about his activities as a militant. What was going on?

Translating a question from the white judge, the African interpreter asked him if he admitted the charge.

'Certainly,' replied Mor-Zamba, whose mind was on other matters.

'Good,' cried the judge, when the accused's reply was given to him; 'twenty-four months, that's the fixed sentence!'

Then, leaning towards the clerk, another white, a much younger man, with a shrewd red face, and wearing shorts, he whispered loudly in his ear:

'Here at least is one of them who doesn't try to shroud his guilt in a web of lies, where the good Lord himself couldn't recognize His children.'

And, while the young clerk was convulsed by a choking laugh, without interrupting his writing for a moment, the judge opened another file and called upon another accused; meanwhile the helmeted *mamelukes* seized Mor-Zamba and handed him over to the Saringalas to be taken to the cell-block, and from thence to prison.

The prison of Fort-Nègre was a fortress left by the first colonizers, a little outside the European town, showing to the eye lofty crenelated walls, watch-towers and angle-turrets, machicolations and loopholes; but inside the walls it was full of squalid little hovels like those of the locations, long, low and covered with corrugated iron, containing the dormitories, the dining-hall and the infirmary. The inmates were only allowed one visit each month. But in reality it was very easy for them to communicate with the outside, for every morning they left the prison and went in groups to perform certain tasks in the town, under the lax vigilance of an ungainly and nonchalant Saringala, who carried on his shoulder an obsolescent musket. Anyone could approach them, embrace them, offer them food or even drink at any time; the Saringala shut his eyes; then, as soon as all indiscreet presences had vanished from the horizon, the Cerberus was invited beneath the abundant low branches of the mango trees bordering the road and given his share of the victuals. This was the price of his silence, which he would have been very imprudent to overlook. The scarfaces who were left to care for prisoners or to do other innocuous tasks were believed to be alcoholics; the convicts only had to beware of the ferocity and tenacity of their resentment.

The first time that Joe the Juggler came up to Mor-Zamba, the sight of the prisoner froze him with horror.

'What they've done to you, the bastards!' he muttered.

'And at that, you didn't see me that day,' replied Mor-Zamba; 'nor the next day or the one following. I'm almost cured now. In the end it will be nothing to worry about, or very little. I was pretty lucky. Perhaps I'll tell you about it one day. I was afraid of having a tooth broken; but, you see, not even one!'

There could be no question of discussing politics there, amid all those strangers. Joe the Juggler, deputed by all Mor-Zamba's friends to visit him, would only decide to meet his friend there, outside the prison, if he had in his hand either some food brought by the chances of his profession or, more often, a parcel and a message of sympathy from the Lobila family, and especially from the two young daughters.

The pace of serious events was quickening, and the Juggler would wait for their monthly meeting inside the prison, where conversation was paradoxically more free, to give Mor-Zamba, now suddenly inflamed with political zeal like a neophyte on the morrow of his conversion, the news of some vicissitude or misfortune which would crush the poor man; as if Sandrinelli's steward had determined to assassinate him with successive blows of despair.

During the first month, he told him that rumours were circulating in Kola-Kola that Paris had been the scene of great political upheavals which, according to him, thoroughly briefed by his enforced vicinity to Sandrinelli and the latter's friends, could not augur well; for they had filled the slavers with arrogance and joy. On the Wednesday of the previous week the potentate and his friends, among whom the former Deputy Langelot did not seem the least exalted, as if he hoped soon to take revenge for his electoral defeat, had been unable to restrain the free flow of an almost delirious gaiety; all evening and for most of the night they never stopped bellowing the

210

Marseillaise, gambolling like kids, draining dozens of bottles of champagne, and crying as each cork flew from the bottle: 'De Gaulle in Algiers! Long live free France! Long live Gaullist and French Africa!'

Towards midnight they suddenly jumped into their cars and, with a screeching of their horns in regular rhythm, made their way first to the governor's and then to Baba Toura's. During the following days, the Juggler often heard Sandrinelli proclaim that they had extracted a decisive concession from the two men; they would send away immediately all the French officials who, by their speech or their attitudes, had shown the slightest disapproval of the choice of Biture for the post of prime minister of the first autonomous government of the colony; as well as anyone who had suggested, even in the most indirect way, any *rapprochement* with the rebels and their leaders.

'What do you think about it?' he said to Mor-Zamba, as a kind of conclusion. 'Personally, I think it's all pretty shabby. We could see some sport here very soon. I'm beginning to know these blighters. Let's see what Ruben says about it.'

'You ought to be overjoyed.'

'Yes, I ought. But you are stuck in here, and that changes everything.'

He gave him a tattered cutting from *Spartacus*; a sort of rag which he unfolded with infinite precaution and smoothed out with many careful glances in all directions.

'It's too difficult for me,' begged Mor-Zamba; 'you tell me what it says.'

'Ruben says,' whispered the Juggler, 'that the more new the political leaders in France may seem, the more they resemble their predecessors: they announced the new governor to us like an openminded and understanding negotiator; but, just like those he followed, he proceeded to organize elections whose results were known in advance. Then, they introduced a so-called autonomous government, in which the premier and more than half the other members are tribal chiefs, former officials, or traditionalists devoted to colonialism and opposed in principle to independence, or others who didn't even understand what was at stake. What can we expect of those whom recent events have carried to the head of French affairs? What can we expect of a man who comes to power by a *coup d'état*? What can we hope from a man whose advent has convulsed the slavers of Fort-Nègre with joy? What illusions can we have about the man who organized the Brazzaville Conference, which aimed at bolting the door in the noses of the African people, cutting off all means towards the free disposition of themselves? What can we expect except further masquerades, more bloodshed, ever yet more misery and more humiliation? The only means to the conquest of liberty is battle. . . .'

'If I understand rightly,' asked Mor-Zamba, 'it's Sandrinelli's friends who are now in power?'

'Precisely. One could almost say that he's now the governor. No, rather, the prime minister, that's him.'

'He was already that, old fellow!'

'Yes, but now it's almost official. The Biture is just a joke. Every toubab in Fort-Nègre who wants some favour, such as a permit or something or other, will come to our place now.'

'To your master's place, you mean.'

'Yes, of course. According to Sandrinelli, the authorities here want to stamp out the Reds completely, without fear of any commission of enquiry or other embarrassment of that kind.'

'And who are the Reds?'

'You know quite well! That's what they call the Rubenists, the "Reds". You're a Red yourself. If you can just get out of here! . . .'

Some months later, he revealed that Jean-Louis was without doubt a *mameluke*. He had said one day to Joe the Juggler's sister, with whom he had been living, that he suspected her of infidelity. Quite out of control, he had threatened her in the most senseless way and promised the most horrible reprisals against her lover if she didn't immediately return to him. He had even told her, 'Think of your brother, and above all of your mother's grief, if anything should happen to Joe. And I can certainly assure you that something could well happen to him; you know, one word from me would be enough to get him locked up again, but this time for good!'

'That was going a bit far. If I ever see him again, I'll have something to say to him, I will. What does he take me for, a murderer? Lock me up for good – and then what? One thing's certain, my poor sister has a real case on her hands now. She says he's quite crazy and that he could easily kill someone.'

'And do you believe all that?'

'You bet I believe it. And just listen to this: Alphonsine swears that Jean-Louis is loaded with wads of notes, as thick as that! And do you know where he lives nowadays? At New Caledonia, the town of the *mamelukes*, just behind the hospital, in a smart villa. You should see it!'

'Have you been there?'

'Of course, I had to, since it's my sister's. And listen to this too, just to see if Alphonsine has hallucinations. Imagine, my dear lad, that Jean-Louis has a car now! Not a new one, certainly. But do you know many Africans, either in Fort-Nègre or Kola-Kola, able to buy a car, even a secondhand one? And at his age too! Where did he get the money? No, there's no need to look far for the truth. All this must have begun when they found him a house down there; that's the time when they took him on as a spy. Do you want to know the truth? You won't hold it against me? Swear and spit! Up to now I've just been beating about the bush. Well, it was Jean-Louis who turned you in.'

'My God! My God! My God!' groaned Mor-Zamba. 'Do you know what you're saying?'

'Certainly. I even have proof, you know.'

'Yes, Alphonsine.'

'That's it!'

'She doesn't like Jean-Louis, your sister. But this is what puzzles me: if she doesn't like him, why does she go with him?'

'That's between themselves, and I can't stop them. No, this time it wasn't my sister, you know, but Fulbert. I went to find Fulbert and threatened him; that always works with the old ones, you know! The old are always scared; it's scarcely credible. I said to him in a big voice, "Confess the truth and nothing will happen to you, I swear. If not, Mor-Zamba's friends will avenge him. You know what they're like – no mercy! So, speak up and I promise that no one will touch a hair of your head. What happened to Jean-Louis over this Mor-Zamba affair? Did you want to take revenge on Mor-Zamba by urging Jean-Louis to denounce him?"'

213

'My dear chap, you should have seen him shaking. "Oh, I swear, I swear, he made me do it. I didn't push him into it. He came to me spontaneously, asking how much I'd give him to get Robert's lorry seized. He didn't say anything about trouble for Mor-Zamba. As for me, I like Mor-Zamba very much; I've always been on good terms with him. I've got nothing against him, because I have no reason for it!" And do you know how much Jean-Louis picked up by all that business? Twenty thousand francs! Not at one stroke, twenty thousand, no less.'

'Twenty thousand!' cried Mor-Zamba, understanding all at once and sinking into dejection. 'Twenty thousand francs for getting a lorry seized. And the other chap paid up?'

'Perhaps you're wondering why Fulbert didn't denounce Robert himself; and exploit the fact that his enemy was on an illegal footing in having his lorry driven by an unqualified driver?'

'Oh, I know that Fulbert is really a man incapable of doing evil – unprompted.'

'Yes, but there's more to it,' continued the Juggler; 'the mamelukes might have taken an interest in him too, and he didn't want that. No one wants that in Kola-Kola, except other mamelukes. That's what one has to grasp first of all, and I'm the one who grasped it. Only a mameluke knowing all about the affair could have denounced you. Because what happens when an informer sets out to denounce someone? The mamelukes question him so thoroughly that they finish up knowing all about him too. Suppose, for example, someone says to them that Mor-Zamba was involved in the affray at the Institute of 18 June? The mamelukes will immediately ask him how he knows, and end up by discovering that he was there too. And so he gets cornered as well.'

'Yes, but he could also tell them, "All right, I was there, but I didn't really know what I was doing. And, from now on, I'm on your side."'

'Or else, he's already an informer and so no one is surprised, because he's only doing his job.'

'Let me pursue my idea. So he says to them, "Certainly, I was there, but I didn't understand what was happening. Now I understand and I want to support you." And the others would

214

reply: "Yes, but what about the man you're denouncing, are you sure he knew what he was doing, eh? Perhaps he was pushed along by events, by the atmosphere and his own impulsive temperament?" And then, not wishing to kill me uselessly, or perhaps thinking about the future, they would leave me in peace for a bit, and only prosecute me on the count of driving a vehicle without a licence. I begin to understand why they sort of let me off the hook; I was worried that, if they let me go, like that, nasty-minded people could have made much of it.'

'Yes, but in any case, he's already a *mameluke* and that's what matters.'

'So was that really his big deal? What a poor fool.'

Much later, Joe told him that the authorities were claiming that Ruben had been killed in the bush.

'Don't believe a word of it, my brother; don't believe a word of it,' begged Mor-Zamba, on the verge of weeping.

'I'm only telling you what's being said.'

'Oh, it's not true; it's a rumour they're spreading to dishearten us. Look at the people here, look around you at the other visitors. They are laughing and joking; they wouldn't behave like that if Ruben were dead. It wouldn't pass off just like that. It's not possible, think it over a bit.'

'You mean it? Well, for my part, I'm still wondering if it isn't true, even though I haven't seen your friends since you were taken off. Don't they have confidence in me?'

'What makes you think it's true?'

'What? Ruben's death? You know his village, it's not very far from Fort-Nègre; it's Boumibell, a little town about a hundred, or a hundred and fifty kilometres at most, up-country from Fort-Nègre along the railway to Oyolo. Well; they say that his corpse was displayed there for a whole day, and formally recognized.'

'Don't believe it,' murmured Mor-Zamba, and this time his face was bathed with tears. 'Don't believe it; they start all these false rumours just to demoralize us. It seems that's called psychological warfare. Don't believe a word of it.'

'But I only wish....'

'Don't believe it, brother, I beg you.'

'All right, all right, have it your way. Forget what I said.'

Then, in the course of another monthly visit, the Juggler told him, as soon as he entered the prison, that he was the bearer of amazing news.

'Ruben is alive!' cried Mor-Zamba triumphantly, so radiant he did not notice how loud he had shouted or how many heads were turned towards him with astonishment and hope.

'Wrong!' whispered the Juggler, more cautious than ever. 'It's a question of the arrival soon in Fort-Nègre, or rather in Kola-Kola, of guess who? Well, my dear, of your own brother!'

He had seen Joseph the drunkard again, in company with the mulatto Maisonneuve. The latter had decamped from the slavers' city to come and live with his mother in Kola-Kola, as if choosing decisively the black portion of his inheritance. The two men had asked the Juggler to keep the news secret – at least, not to mention it except in front of Mor-Zamba, Abena having insisted that his brother be informed that the wanderer was no longer so far away from him.

'But what does this mean?' asked Mor-Zamba in confusion. 'Why doesn't he just come and see me if he really isn't so far away?'

'Perhaps it's not so hard to understand,' suggested the Juggler; 'if he makes a mystery of it, it's because your brother is obliged to surround himself with mysteries; in other words, he's a Rubenist leader.'

'Ah, that's exactly what I thought!' exploded Mor-Zamba once again. 'That's something I could have predicted. Ah, that fellow! How else could he have ended up. How happy I am to know it. You see, I told you the other day that he had his reasons for acting as he did! I never doubted him, you know? I always knew he'd return and that he'd be in our ranks. What marvellous news!'

Then, after a pause:

'You know, he isn't really my brother.'

'No?'

'That's right, he isn't really my brother.'

'So, what is he then?'

'I'll tell you one day. And Ruben?'

'In the end, you know, I was convinced that Ruben was truly

dead. The governor read a long address on the radio yesterday. He said especially that, now that the evil prophet had met the end he deserved, all the political problems, "could be discussed and could receive solutions which, whilst giving satisfaction to one party, would protect the honour of the other".'

'What does all that mean?'

'Most people in Kola-Kola think that now Ruben's dead the authorities believe they have elbow-room to dole us out an independence in their own style: first of all, they want to place at the head of affairs a man of their own, a politician whose blackness extends only to his skin. That's already done, really – it's Baba Toura the Biture; with him in office, one step is already taken. As he is invincibly docile, they want to use him as the perfect screen; behind him, they will continue to govern and everything will go on as before. We will have Independence, but nothing will be changed, do you see?'

'Do you really think it's possible?'

'What is?'

'That we shall have Independence and that everything will go on as before?'

'Some very educated people are convinced of it; especially the students, you know, those who are just back from Europe. They say that there are heaps of countries all over the world with presidents of the republic, ministers and even generals, tanks and aeroplanes, and yet they are still colonies of other more powerful countries. They give the example of South America, where the independent republics are, in various degrees, nothing but colonies of the USA. Well, we people, we shall be just like them. Ah, I've just remembered, I've brought you something about that – it's a leaflet which is circulating in Kola-Kola, a proclamation by the external leaders of the PPP. You'll see what they say about it all. But you must promise me first to be careful. Look well all around us, while I bring out the leaflet. Nothing in sight? Can I go ahead? Yes? Right. . . .'

'A PPP leaflet? That's terrific! So they're still active?'

'That's what they keep saying. The struggle continues, they say, even if Ruben is dead, as the authorities claim.'

'Ah, you see, they "claim". And what else are they doing?'

217

'Collecting funds. They're great at that. And then from time to time they organize a *mameluke*-hunt through the jungle of Kola-Kola. That's terrible, I can tell you. Jean-Louis can no longer set foot there; he'd quite simply be executed. He's made such a reputation in the whole quarter that the rest of the family ought really to shut themselves away for pure shame. The rumours about your brother are presenting him as a sort of magician; they say he can disappear and reappear at will, and even that he's invulnerable. Personally, I hate that kind of fable; those are fairy tales only fit for the most fuddled bushman.'

Mor-Zamba, turning towards the wall to hide the leaflet, had begun to spell it out in a sing-song voice, like a child learning to read, breaking off frequently, without turning round, so as to ask Joe the Juggler the meaning of a word.

'"With Baba Toura, that black Gauleiter of de Gaulle, independence will be nothing but the pursuit of colonization by the same means, though perhaps under other forms. This is an independence which corresponds in no way with the objectives pursued by the PPP since its foundation. Our country will enjoy nothing but a nominal independence. Instead of being an instrument indispensable to the full development of the people it will reveal itself, every day more clearly, as the collar by means of which the agents of colonialism and imperialism, hiding behind Baba Toura, a new type of chief, will continue to hold him prisoner in his own land. The people will continue to walk naked and to die of hunger in a country bulging with resources. If the Nazi methods against which our people are fighting should succeed, those who are using them will not hesitate to extend their field of application...."'

'What do you think of it?' asked the Juggler again, when his friend had finished reading.

'I don't quite believe all of it,' sighed Mor-Zamba. 'That another black, a man having our own skin, could change horses and make us suffer in the same way? I can't manage to believe that! But it must be true, because they say it.'

The fact is that what had only been a conjecture for the

218

average Kolean up till then now suddenly began to take shape. A new governor was appointed, who announced on his arrival that Paris had decided to grant independence to the Colony. Wishing to create, according to his own words, a dynamic of reconciliation before that historic event, if it ever took place, the Governor proclaimed a general amnesty for all political offences, but he excluded all those found guilty of having spilled the blood of the innocent. A week later, the amnesty was extended to all first offenders under Common Law.

In any case, when Mor-Zamba returned to Kola-Kola, the climate should have been one of reconciliation; quite the contrary, for the Rubenist organization, which had been suppressed since his arrest, was now putting itself slowly, inexorably back on a war footing. He found himself assigned, being the best placed to accomplish the task, to co-operate with Mor-Kinda to catch Jean-Louis, by hook or by crook, so as to bring him alive before the Supreme Council (or at least before its Permanent Committee); failing that, to extract from him all the revelations possible about the events which had led to the capture of Ruben on the central front (if he had been captured) and about his execution (if he had been executed).

When Robert saw Mor-Zamba again, he displayed a quite unforced and profound joy; the misfortunes of his employee had pained him like a father. The police had accepted his version, which was to swear on his soul and conscience that he had been deceived by his driver, who had assured him that his papers were perfectly in order; that if he had committed an offence, it was only that of negligence. But, although he had got off with a fine, that, coming on top of the decline in his business, had almost ruined him. The T 55 was moving again, but his affairs were in a lamentable state. Rascality had swept through the interior and had choked all business. How could one trade with people who were faithless, deal with brigands, negotiate with savages? The whites were lucky to have on their side the police and the Fort-Nègre tribunals charged with punishing fraud. But the black trader had no such recourse.

'We shall never become big men of business now, in this generation, you see!' he concluded, philosophically.

Mor-Zamba let him talk. Robert proposed to put him in

training with the manager of a bar; once he had a good grasp of that, Robert intended to begin one of his own and put Mor-Zamba in charge of it. It was no good thinking about passing the driving-test for some time yet. In any case, Mor-Zamba was no longer even thinking of it.

The punitive association of Mor-Zamba and Mor-Kinda (more commonly known as Joe the Juggler) underwent a long process of adjustment before it finally satisfied them. To begin with, it was difficult enough to harmonize their normal hours of leisure. Although they were simply a cover for his activities, both in his own opinion and that of the Fourth Committee (the Committee of the Fourth District of Kola-Kola, where he lived), and although they earned him no salary, Mor-Zamba's duties still exercised some constraint on his liberty. So as to be free at the same time as his friend, he had arranged, with great difficulty, that his duties at the bar should not commence before two in the afternoon, when Joe the Juggler, a few hundred metres away, was preparing to go marketing for the institute; this meant a good hour's walking, right through the centre of Fort-Nègre, just to reach the market. As Sandrinelli's employee returned to Kola-Kola each morning by eight o'clock at the latest, the two friends had at least six hours each day in which they had nothing to do but get hold of Jean-Louis.

When discreetly urged by her brother alone, Mor-Zamba having remained out of sight in the street so as not to startle the girl, Alphonsine was not able to offer the decisive aid which they had too quickly assumed. The two young people had just got married, quietly and furtively, without even telling their parents, except that the girl's mother had agreed to go and register her consent at the registry in Fort-Nègre. Everything had gone very smoothly, as it should for a man who enjoyed unusual facilities in all the offices of the administration.

According to Alphonsine, Jean-Louis had no time, except between midnight (when there was a curfew in those days) and about eight-thirty in the morning: this was the interval which he spent at his house, an elegant little villa of a dazzling white, which he and his wife occupied alone. Going out then, he would return several times during the day, always unexpectedly, always demanding some short moments of intimacy with his wife, or occasionally taking a hasty snack.

But where did he go? Although well-educated for a Kolean girl, Alphonsine appeared unable to say where her husband worked; what, even approximately, was his occupation; or what was his rank in the hierarchy. But she wanted to promise her brother that she would tell him everything she could find out in the future, and that she would not alert her husband by informing him of the activities of the two Koleans. It seemed to Joe the Juggler that her sentiments towards Jean-Louis were modified; she, who not long ago had said he deserved worse than hanging, now seemed ready to make common cause with him; as if, entering the skin of a legal wife, she found herself very much at ease there – unless it was just that, more simply, their money had corrupted her. One should never search people's motives too closely, even when it is a question of one's sister.

Their own enquiries revealed to them, however, that Jean-Louis really no longer worked with the police, as he had once revealed to Alphonsine, but for two totally different departments. In the morning he went to the governor's palace, to an office in the basement, whose entrance bore a brand-new inscription: National Press Agency. Printing machines, which worked automatically without human intervention, rattled away there for hours on end.

In the afternoon he went to the General Secretariat of the Legislative Assembly (formerly the Consultative Council); when the councillors were sitting, he followed their debates, sitting beside a white official who seemed to be his boss, and who was teaching him an administrative technique whose principle and utility the two friends could not penetrate.

Having heard their report, the Permanent Commission of the Supreme Secret Committee declared itself unable to take a verdict and called a meeting of the whole committee. In the course of the only meeting of the committee, a mature, fit-looking man, very well fed like all the rare high African officials, and with several grey tufts in his hair, elucidated the mystery. The governor was forcing the pace with lots of young Africans who seemed capable, so as to rapidly transform them into important functionaries in the future pseudo-national government. It was said of him that he was a gambler from more than one viewpoint. And anyway, hadn't the colonial administration already formed an official élite, in more than forty years?

'A minute number,' replied the man, full of confidence, assurance and serenity. 'And you can be sure they won't be forgotten in the big scramble that's coming.'

But, they objected, Independence is only a few months away, and how could they form in that time a boy whose education didn't go beyond School Certificate and who was totally lacking in experience of affairs?

'The truth is, it's not right to speak of forming these very young and inexperienced boys,' declared the man without the least irony or anger in his voice, quite unlike the habitually bitter or vindictive tone of the other orators, who seemed to feel themselves already defeated. 'It's a purely psychological operation,' he continued, 'and with three objectives. On the one hand, a certain number of officials, modestly placed in the hierarchy, but enjoying a certain seniority and the prospect of responsible posts as of right, have proved somewhat reticent; they are unhappy about the manner in which Independence is being handled. Between themselves, they deplore that instead of dealing with Ruben, the Father of the Nation, the authorities hunted him down and put in his place a complete unknown, whom the country possibly doesn't want. The Gaullists, who in colonial matters were worse than the men of the Fourth Republic, wanted officials like that to feel that they could be dispensed with; so they could take it or leave it. The proof? Look at a Jean-Louis; a young man who, today, is intrinsically nothing. But what couldn't two or three months of solicitude do? And there were all the young people coming out of the local lycées; the Fraternity Classical Lycée, the Félix Eboué Technical Lycée; which it was wrong to belittle, as though they didn't exist; not to mention all the young graduates of French universities; and one shouldn't forget either the many professional schools, whose products each year were on a level with School Certificate holders. By the medium of a Jean-Louis, Sandrinelli, Langelot and the other Gaullists seemed to be telling them: "Look at the future ahead of you, so long as you rally to Baba Toura," or, in other words to us, "Only Baba Toura, with our support, can offer you a prospect." Do you remember that phrase from the inaugural speech of the new governor: "I want to assure you and repeat to you that revolt and rebellion can only lead to despair." And finally, comrades, if all our high African officials are incompetent, which is inevitable, bearing in mind the spirit which presided over their choice and their training, what a boon! One only has to back them with an "adviser", chosen from among the colonial personalities. Looked at from far away, this façade, which is undeniably African, makes a certain impression. But the reality will not change; isn't that the essential thing?'

In fact, the governor had succeeded in plunging everyone into confusion. In the other suburbs and in the African districts of Fort-Nègre, whose total population was far inferior to Kola-Kola's, and where the Rubenist organizations were only superficially planted, especially as they were inhabited mainly by the privileged, the inhabitants were urged to prepare hastily for the Independence celebrations. They were told that Ruben, with his last breath, had advised them to welcome with frenzied joy the day when they would be offered that Independence for which he had sacrificed himself. At the same time, the police were trying by every means to break up the secret Rubenist cells in Kola-Kola, though without success, for they met with a resistance which was daily more warlike. It was now a question of ritual exchanges of gunfire every night, followed by wildly excited accounts on the morrow. One night there was a real pitched battle, the first of its kind, which lasted only a few minutes; it was fought around the Avenue Gallieni, an important street in what the slavers' press dubbed 'the black sewer'. Official propaganda exalted the indestructible friendship which must be cemented between the two peoples but, at the same time, they rearrested the political prisoners who had been released from the jails a few months earlier, under the general amnesty. Rumour had it that they had been shipped off to the

223

North, from which not a word could be learnt concerning their fate.

In the Fourth Secret District, everyone was imminently expecting the arrest of Mor-Zamba.

'What did they say when they released you?' Joe the Juggler kept asking him.

'They made me say exactly where I lived,' Mor-Zamba would reply, with unruffled patience.

'And what did you tell them exactly?'

'That I lived between the Avenues Gallieni and General Leclere.'

'And after that?'

'Between Tranformer No. 2 and the bus park for the North.'

'With directions like that, old chap, they'll come and pick you up just when they like; I know what I'm talking about. Your friends are right, don't stick around there, get moving. I'll look after my bof on my own (as he derisively abbreviated the French "beau-frère", brother-in-law). And once I've got my hands on him, I'll send you word.'

So Mor-Zamba was hidden away from the bloodhounds of Fort-Nègre. And soon Joe the Juggler, who never lacked ideas, matured a diabolical scheme in his narrow head and came to broach it to Mor-Zamba in his retreat.

'Tell me,' he said on arrival; 'one thing looks pretty certain to me. If I can get Alphonsine here, it will be easy enough to persuade her to spend a night with her mother.'

'So what?'

'That's clear enough. The other one can't sleep without her, if I know him well. We must take advantage of that right away, while he's still crazy about her, because inevitably he'll cool off eventually.'

'And then?'

'I'll give you the signal, you'll nab him, take him to your friends and make him talk.'

'And what about the reprisals afterwards? Can you picture your poor mother dragged to the charge office and the prison? Unless you are really thinking of his execution. Personally, I prefer to think that they'll let him live all the same. I can't imagine anything else.'

'Well, he won't dare torment Mother, because of Alphonsine.'

'But you've just said that he'll leave her one day! Then, if he's vengeful, he will remember and get his own back.'

'You're right. Do you think a man always tires of a woman in the end?'

'He must.'

'Why?'

'Because it's always the same thing with a woman. There aren't a thousand different ways of going with them.'

Three days later, Joe the Juggler came back triumphant. This time he was certain he had found the solution.

'Look, I'll make him think that it's his own mother who's mortally sick.'

'Yes, but she won't be, and as soon as her son arrives, she'll cry, "Me, sick? What rubbish! I'm as fit as a flea, as usual. Don't bother about me. Just get on quickly with your new job. Be keen; try always to please your superiors, that's the best way to get on...." You know how she is.'

'Don't worry, she won't tell him that. I'll take my own precautions.'

'You great scoundrel!'

'Just wait a bit. You know her well enough, but so do I. Solid as a rock, I agree, but that's because she never drinks. And very quick to take alarm, like all strong people, as soon as her health causes her any trouble. On those occasions, Mother Josephine is unrecognizable. And just tell her that Jesus has visited her during the night, or the Blessed Virgin or her parents. You've been a nurse; what effect does sodium sulphate have? There's always heaps of it at the pasha's place (as he called Sandrinelli). I think Madame must use it as medicine.'

'Sodium sulphate? I don't know, but I don't think it's poisonous. If I remember rightly, it's given to people who are constipated.'

'Incredible! That's exactly what I want. Do you think that if I gave her more than the dose taken by Madame Sandrinelli, which is a teaspoonful, she would have diarrhoea? That's neat! Since it's something that never happens to her, she'll be convinced she's got amoebic dysentery, or something like that. I

225

think that could carry her off all right. It caused one death this year in the mulattoes' pavilion at the Institute of 18 June.'

'I think that could be done,' agreed Mor-Zamba, deeply interested, looking at his companion with mingled admiration and terror.

The fact was that the Juggler, more than ever faithful to his personality, would show himself much more satanic than the good Mor-Zamba could imagine. He began by spreading in the Lobilas' neighbourhood the rumour that Fort-Nègre, in order to crush the Reds, who had been rendered more virulent by the death of their leader, instead of being discouraged, had decided to spread various microbes in all the African suburbs, and especially in Kola-Kola. These microbes could cause many different maladies, all of them severe. He had been warned of this by his boss who, being very fond of him, had warned him to beware above all of the wells dug by the machines of the so-called Hygiene and Prophylaxis Service. It would be safer from now on to drink the bottled water sold in the big Fort-Nègre shops, or else to revert to the wells formerly dug by the people themselves, which the administration had never filled in. At the same time, he strengthened his links with his brother-in-law's family, generously supplying them with bottles of mineral water, so as to spread among them a psychosis about ordinary water, to which the elder Lobila alone refused to succumb.

'Just remember,' he said to his family, 'just remember that the white man's microbes can do nothing against the stomach of a black, and especially not a Kolean stomach. His stomach is already a sewer, that Kolean, so one little microbe more or less.... In a white's stomach, yes, that can cause all sorts of havoc, or in the stomachs of those who live like them – Jean-Louis, for example, who's a real white nowadays. But a genuine Kolean, just think, my dears!'

Mother Josephine Lobila, uncertain about the truth of the matter, did as women often do, young or old, when they encounter white medicine; she took it and she left it. She drank mineral water at the house, persuaded to it by her daughters, who solemnly told her that it was criminal to play with one's life, since you only had one to enjoy; that good health, the illusion of all fit people, did not exempt one from fighting against disease; quite the contrary. But as soon as she got away from home, at her neighbours' for example, she drank the same water as everybody else. Finally, towards the end of the month, the Juggler offered a big blow-out to the Lobila family, adding his own mother, and exhausting his modest salary to do it. He said it was to compensate for the wedding feast of which they had been deprived by the bizarre proceeding of his bof. One did not see one's children married every day, and such children! Such an event could not pass without some celebration.

The repast stretched far into the night and Joe the Juggler, who had obtained three days' leave from Sandrinelli on the pretext of marrying off his sister, was extremely active throughout. He made sure that by ten in the evening all the guests were unrecognizable, whether to themselves or their neighbours, having reached that pitch of benevolence where they offered everything and agreed to everything. Mother Josephine, normally abstemious, went so far on that road that she could not remember accepting many glasses of red wine from Joe the Juggler. They tasted very strange to her, but her son-in-law reassured her by saying in the most imperturbable style:

'That's what they are making nowadays – nothing better to be had. This is what my boss gave me when he heard I was marrying my sister. Go on, don't worry about a thing, grand-mother. Drink up....'

The Juggler's plot succeeded beyond all expectation, and on the following day Sandrinelli's servant, still on holiday, had plenty of leisure to expend in reproaches both bitter and triumphant.

'I said so before,' he proclaimed, 'I've done my bit in warning my black brothers against the criminal machinations of Fort-Nègre. I told you all: don't drink the water of the Hygiene and Prophylactic Service. But what can you do? People never believe you until there's been an accident or, who knows? a still worse catastrophe. I believe Mother Josephine has dysentery.'

Although the neighbours, who, after long hesitation, agreed to examine the stools of the patient, declared their surprise that they were not bloody, the Juggler's learned hypothesis was unanimously adopted, and only the natural repugnance of Koleans for the hospital prevented them from sending the poor woman into Fort-Nègre that very day; instead, to gain time, they decided to consult her son and leave the decision to him. As for Mother Lobila herself, already gripped by the frenzy predicted by Joe the Juggler, she kept insisting as soon as she was laid low that it would be a waste of time to send her to the hospital, because her hour had come; she had only one desire: to see once more her beloved son, her great man, the sole consolation of her last moments, as he had been of her whole life; that she already saw the saints and the angels pressing round her bed and waiting till she consented to ascend with them; she could not keep Jesus and His mother Mary waiting, who were perhaps already impatient for her arrival aloft.

When he was told of all these circumstances, Mor-Zamba, who had witnessed the dying at the forced labour camp of Gouverneur Leclerc, felt some real disquiet.

'Are you certain you didn't exceed the dose?' he asked Joe the Juggler.

'What do you want me to tell you? To begin with, I'd have had to know the right dose, which I didn't. And anyway, as I've told you already, we were all tight by that time and I don't remember a thing – mainly the fault of Holy Joseph. It's true it was a pretty dirty trick, that one. I'm still all mixed up about it.'

Jean-Louis first sent his wife, who announced that her husband, who was on a trip to Europe, would not be able to visit his mother's bed, alas! To all the pressing questions of neighbours assembled to comfort the stricken family, Alphonsine replied with the evasive disdain of a wife whose husband is destined to higher things, according to the secret revelations of the Hindu Professor Krishnarahdja, a specialist of world-wide reputation in horoscopes by correspondence. Someone had seen her husband very recently in Fort-Nègre? And why not, if he left still more recently? He didn't take her along? Well, no, he didn't. It seemed that the wives of high officials didn't benefit, like their husbands, from the waiving of all formalities. Only Joe the Juggler was not deceived by these subterfuges; he went straight away to warn Mor-Zamba.

'You can go out for once,' he told him, 'so as to alert your friends.'

Jean-Louis turned up very late in Kola-Kola, towards two in the morning, when everyone was either sleeping or apparently sleeping in what was in reality the Fourth Secret District of the quarter.

Scared but perfectly lucid, confident in his star but knowing himself detested in his native quarter, stripped of all illusion if the underground militants should get hold of him, he had disguised himself, hoping to escape recognition, as a *sapak* musician, brandishing a guitar, supported by an ostentatious red scarf at his hip, a darker one at his neck, dark glasses and an Australian hat with steeply-turned brim; but he hadn't been able to restrain entirely his lust for display and he wore a splendid checked shirt, doubtless of nylon, floating over a pair of tight-fitting dacron trousers, along with very elegant shoes of old marbled leather, with rounded toes. Whoever looked closely at these might perceive the perforations which seemed to shoot reflections under the light, however faint, of the last street-light in Fort-Nègre, situated at the entrance to Kola-Kola and marking the frontier between the two agglomerations, just like the Shell service station before which it was planted.

For as soon as he stepped out of his secondhand Peugeot 403, which he had just parked at the Shell station, out of the halo of the street-light so as not to be conspicuous, but far enough from the waves of Kola-Kola darkness, so that he could find it again when he returned, Jean-Louis, extravagant vision, carnival clown, was followed by two shadows who, in the distance which still separated Alphonsine's husband from the first hovels of Kola-Kola gained on him rapidly as he went. Joe the Juggler's stroke of genius, or rather of naïve geniality, had been to suppose, opposed as he was to any other hypothesis, that Jean-Louis would only venture into the quarter at night – and he'd be sure to come alone, being ashamed to show the Fort-Nègre people his humble family in Kola-Kola and, even more, to show the shabby hut in which he had grown up, which would have earned him the envy of plenty of young Koleans worse lodged than himself. He had just left Fort-Nègre and had plunged into an oblique alley among the first, so familiar, bundles of sheds. He had perhaps another kilometre to cover before reaching his mother's bedside, when, at the meeting of two lanes, a man called him from some way off in French, at the same moment turning upon him an electric torch which froze him on the spot.

'Musician, have you got a fag? I'm out of them.'

Holding his guitar in his left hand, the *mameluke* felt successively in the two pockets of his shirt, then the two straight pockets of his right trouser, the side one and the hip-pocket; then, with panting breath and mounting frenzy, he took the guitar in his right hand and, with his left, rummaged in the left pockets of his trousers, beginning with the side pocket and moving to the hip, from which he finally managed to extract a packet of crumpled cigarettes, offering them to the man already arrived at his side, and now completely blinding him with the torch.

'Thanks!' cried the man simply, seizing the offered object, but at the same time taking Jean-Louis' arm and leading him off, as one might lead an old friend after a long absence.

But he led him in a direction which wasn't Jean-Louis' and, when the latter showed a certain reluctance, he told him:

'Let yourself be led, musician. Come quietly, there's a *band-asalo* just behind us, who'll seize you like a jackal if you show reluctance or if you attempt to shout. Look, if you have any doubt; go on....'

When the *mameluke* turned round, a third man was in fact walking close behind them, holding in his right hand an object voluminous enough to be perceptible in the darkness, but small enough not to encumber in any way its carrier who, as if caught by surprise, made no attempt to disguise it. Jean-Louis was well qualified to know that the *bandasalos* were not given to joking and inspired fear in even the highest levels of the force.

A striking token of its dissidence was that Kola-Kola continued to live at night, despite the absence of street-lighting. From time to time, Jean-Louis would hear two men, or sometimes several groups, whose voices reached them distinctly through the mass of hovels, greeting or parting from each other with the words: 'Remember Ruben!' 'Remember Ruben!', a

230

pidgin expression which, in homage to the great man of Kola-Kola whose death was no longer really in doubt, had become the daily salutation in the quarter, especially among the young. Occasionally, he heard a new-born babe yell furiously; but soon this cry would be replaced by the deep voice of a man who spoke in a complaining tone, interrupted also from time to time by the crystalline laugh of a girl, doubtless very young; and yet one couldn't say whether the couple, deep in their house, were about to make love or if, happy and relaxed, they were strolling a little in the night to round off their pleasure.

Jean-Louis was reflecting that he was born here and that he could have made it his only happiness to stay here all his life. More crushed than a man who walks towards the execution ground, his legs more and more feeble, he leant upon his companion of the evening, who soon found himself obliged to speak some words of encouragement. His dazed eyes sought in vain to fix a décor which lacked all sharpness, rendered even more viscous by the shadows, seeing in it the last image which destiny had decided to offer him, in the guise of a viaticum. So it was upon this, this nightmare, this cursed scene, that his eyelids were about to close, like the gulp of foul water swallowed by a drowning man before the saturation of his final spasm. Silent sobs shook him piteously, like an old engine no longer capable of idling without stalling.

Once he had been shoved into the narrow room prepared for his reception, his eyes were energetically blindfolded in the darkness; he was made to sit in an old cane armchair; then someone lighted a hurricane-lamp and pushed it close to his face to identify him. No doubt about it; this was certainly the redoubtable mameluke, the man whom the informed militants of Kola-Kola said was without heart, without pity, the most cynical, perhaps, of all the informers in the history of the colony – he who had won a reputation of being capable of denouncing his own mother and, whilst waiting for the Saringalas to come for her, to extort from her, to the tune of his filial declarations, her last savings, so that he might add them to the thirty deniers of his treachery and put all this money into a devilish orgy, that very night.

Gathered all around him, the members of the Permanent

Commission of the Supreme Committee, all mature men well-experienced in their encounters with many *mamelukes*, were suffocated by the notion of such moral ugliness in a man so young, so fresh as it were; as if his turpitude ought really to erupt on his face in purulent boils, if not in great splotches of leprosy. Now Jean-Louis wept abundant, silent tears, which flowed down his cheeks, beneath the mask of his blindfold. Between two sniffles which rose from the depths of his breast, they could hear a deep, quavering groan, at once infantile and revolting, like everything else about such a young scoundrel. In looking at him, Mor-Zamba, who had been admitted exceptionally to this meeting of the Permanent Commission, along with Joe the Juggler, felt all the chagrin of an elder brother; he had for so long misjudged the real character of Jean-Louis, aided by the reticence of those who might have enlightened him about the man with whom he shared the same house, the same meals and, to a certain extent the same family, and who might thus feel some affection for him. At length, a man walked in without knocking and said to the others in a voice both joyful and subdued:

'Remember Ruben.'

'Remember Ruben,' someone replied.

'Comrades,' he continued, 'I couldn't come any sooner, forgive me. Now we can begin.'

'Jean-Louis,' he went on, 'there's already a sentence of death upon you. We shall suspend it, if perchance you deserve to stay alive. We know all your crimes, but we want above all to know the intentions of your masters, since these concern not only the future of our case but the survival of a whole town, I mean Kola-Kola. Kola-Kola, perhaps three hundred thousand souls! Let's talk frankly and loyally – then perhaps we shall be able definitely to revise our verdict.'

Alone in the midst of the faint halo of the hurricane-lamp, ringed by shadows and by judges disguised by the night, so that he could not have seen them even without his mask, Jean-Louis, without ceasing to sniffle, talked all right. From the start, the members of the Permanent Commission were certain of his sincerity, that the truth flowed from him, despite himself, like a spring gushing from the earth, whose waters were choked as soon as they issued, for lack of space. Sometimes in pidgin, sometimes in French, according to the language in which the question was posed, he displayed a zeal for co-operation observed only in the voluntary turncoat.

So far as Jean-Louis was able to judge, the intention of the authorities was not at that moment to take issue openly and without disguise with Kola-Kola. Their earlier reverses had finally taught them the danger of underestimating the Rubenists. They would not mount the next attack until they had sufficient forces to strike a decisive blow. The top leaders were working out a strategy on two levels, military and diplomatic. On the military level, they were awaiting reinforcements of men and arms. The colony had never had real troops or modern weapons, but the whites had skilfully insinuated in the minds of the blacks the conviction that they deployed troops and armaments without number, so that the whole peace and security of the privileged rested on this illusion. The Africans, who overestimated the forces of colonization, had held themselves in a state of silence and fear. But those days were over at last, and the meagre troops of the colony, barely twenty battalions, counting all effectives, were fully occupied in hanging on to the first front of the Rubenist offensive. Until the recent political upheavals in Paris, the dread of the authorities had been the appearance of a second front, to which they could oppose nothing.

'So they no longer fear the opening of this second front?'

'Less; what they need above all now are reinforcements.'

'And Algeria?'

'I heard a military expert declare in the course of a training session that a hundred thousand men more or less up there would not really change anything. On the contrary, a hundred thousand here would change everything. We haven't reached that point yet, of course; but it could happen and we'd better take account of it.'

'Do you know what is meant by "intoxication", comrade?' someone asked him in French.

'Do you mean,' replied Jean-Louis, 'that the expert spoke like that in the secret hope that we would repeat his words round about, so that the rebel leaders would hear of their enemy's plans and get discouraged? Personally, I don't believe it's intoxication. You see, for example, I was believed to have broken off all contact with my own people, until ordered otherwise. And it'd be better for me if no one ever knew I'd been in Kola-Kola tonight, supposing you were to spare my life. I know too much, you see.'

'Comrade, you say that the colonial troops can scarcely contain the first Rubenist front; is Ruben not dead, then?'

'What! You don't know it for certain?'

Jean-Louis stopped weeping; he began to perceive that he had shown some pertinence in his replies, even a certain boldness which had not failed to make a good effect on these warriors who, without knowing it, admired virility. Furthermore, he was rendering an invaluable service to the Kolean leaders; perhaps he had even saved his life. Yes, Ruben was certainly dead; it was his body which had been exposed a whole day at Boumibell, his native village. No, it wasn't a lie invented to unnerve the Rubenist soldiers and militants. A combatant in Ruben's immediate entourage had been suborned by the agents of the colonial government, who had promised mountains and marvels of benefits if he gave away Ruben's hiding-place; the soldier had hesitated at first but they had given him a first instalment of the price for his co-operation, and he had finally succumbed. Ruben had been surprised and captured, judged and condemned on the spot, then executed immediately.

'Did the Biture know all this?'

'The Biture was put in the picture by radio, from the first moment of the affair to the last. But calm has not been restored down there, whatever they do, and the big leaders consider that a very bad sign. For it looks as if Ruben was not the providential man of the rebels, as they thought before. Apparently, he has found a successor, and that's an idea which doesn't please them at all. There are just as many ambushes down there now as in Ruben's lifetime.'

'Comrade, the proclamation of Independence is really fixed for the beginning of the year; that's to say, in three or four months, not so?'

'Correct.'

234

'Will the reinforcements be here by then?'

'It's not likely, if I understand correctly; but I can't guarantee it. They don't tell us everything.'

'So from now till Independence, Kola-Kola is not in danger?'

'Kola-Kola is not in danger before then, for a very simple reason, which is not military, but diplomatic. One has to understand this: it's the national government, not the colonial administration as such, which will attack the problem of Kola-Kola and, for that matter, that of the rebellion.'

'No, comrade; the war of national liberation.'

'The war of national liberation, excuse me. Only in those conditions can such an action, which may take long to accomplish, escape international censure, for it would be the act of a legitimate government operating within its national sovereignty. But, to achieve its aim, the national government may, quite legitimately, appeal for the military aid of a friendly country, with which it will already have signed a treaty of mutual assistance. So, no one can say a word against it. It will be child's play to get this mechanism going, just as long as the Biture becomes president of the republic. That's why, after Independence, Massa Bouza must first of all get himself elected president and get a convenient constitution voted in by universal suffrage. There will be a referendum on it, no doubt. Eighty or eighty-five per cent in favour. After that, he'll appeal to France, which will dispatch an expeditionary force. As soon as they are ready, I believe those troops will go into action on the first front, and doubtless on other fronts. Our strategists say they are convinced that other fronts will open up very soon, beginning, for example, with the one now being formed in the south-west, which they have baptized the Hurricane-Viet front. At the same time, the troops which have been fighting down there will be sent up here, with instructions to sort out Kola-Kola once and for all.'

'And what's the motive for this switch-over?'

'The troops now fighting on the first front are mostly black; they must be of such a nature to pass for our national army in the eyes of observers. They're now trying to Africanize the leadership more rapidly, by accelerated promotion of subalterns and NCOs picked up all over the place, in various garrisons of French Africa; they're going to benefit from lightning advancement. They'll be supplemented by the three or four St Cyr graduates from this colony, who'll finish their studies in France this month; these last will be named right away as battalion commanders or lieutenant-colonels, even if they don't have real command. As for the others, go and look if such and such a black soldier or officer is really a Saringala or a national.'

'Comrade, what plots are the Fascists and imperialists contriving against Kola-Kola?'

'I believe Kola-Kola will be flattened or, more probably, burnt to the ground and, to make sure that not even a charred beam will survive, they will pour petrol on the remains of the first blaze and set fire to them again. You see, Kola-Kola is really a nightmare to them. They're convinced they will have achieved nothing as long as it's still standing. If you let me live, I'll warn you when the menace hanging over Kola-Kola is taking shape by taking away my family, or by some other sign which we can agree right away. I'll let you into all the information to which I get access. I beg you, just let me live, and I'll render you great services.'

'Comrade, what does Baba Toura say to all this? Does he agree to having his brothers exterminated in his name?'

'Baba Toura? But, sir, Baba Toura has no brothers. Baba Toura has nothing, because Baba Toura is nothing. He doesn't exist, because he never grasps what's going on or what he's being asked. There's some question that Massa Bouza will soon return very discreetly to Europe for his fourth alcoholism cure, which will certainly be no more effective than the other three. But this is an urgent necessity; he's got to be more or less presentable, at least during the Independence ceremony. Personally, I've never seen the Biture in a sober state; it's an expression which has no meaning for our chap. The first time I had the chance to see him, you know, was in the morning, at about eight o'clock, perhaps. Well, maybe you won't believe me, but Baba Toura already had his dose aboard. This man is a disgrace to us all, I assure you; the only difference between you and us is that we daren't say so. Oh look, I forgot to give you this important piece of information; only one event could precipitate Fort-Nègre into an immediate murderous attempt against Kola-Kola, before the assembly of the massive resources I've just spoken about; that's if Hurricane-Viet should decide to appear in the quarter. For one thing, it would be a sign that arms are hidden there; for another, the high-ups are convinced that Hurricane-Viet is now the only Rubenist leader who is really dangerous. He's been in Indo-China, where he's said to have made the reputation of a formidable warrior.'

'Comrade, no one knows who Hurricane-Viet is?'

'Hurricane-Viet is the battle-name of Abena, Mor-Zamba's brother. We know where he is at the moment, I was going to tell you, anyway. But we are convinced that he's been charged with opening a second front. But not having the means of attacking him at present, or even of stopping him from entering Kola-Kola when he wants to, all our military men can do is watch him and try to keep tabs on him. He has very few arms and would dearly like more. He thinks there are some in Kola-Kola, or that he'll meet here an emissary from the first front who'll tell him where to get them. Tell him above all not to quit his zone, if he doesn't want to put you all in peril. As soon as our people are told of his absence, they'll assume that he's in Kola-Kola, and then they'll try something on.'

'You no get shame?' someone asked him in pidgin. 'Shame to have betrayed so many men, even your friend Mor-Zamba, your fellow at table every day, almost your brother? Because it was certainly you who turned him in; useless to deny it, because Fulbert has confessed everything. So, don't you really feel shame, from time to time, in the depths of your heart?'

Then, Jean-Louis began to weep again, sniffling more than ever, with tears channelling down his cheeks once more. Then, suddenly a puddle appeared under his chair, spreading out in plain view, as though a tap had been opened somewhere, fascinating the watchers, voyeurs in spite of themselves, and distracting them from the plea which Jean-Louis was uttering, a plea which merited particular attention.

He had not begun to guess at first the gravity of the crisis, nor the ravine of hatred and bloodshed which already separated the two sides. He thought he would be able to play tricks on his superiors, but no one could touch them for cunning and Machiavellism; they could always lure you deeper into betrayal, alternating threats and rewards, caresses and blows, sublimity and vulgarity. If one tried at last to draw back, it was far too late. It was Joselly N'Dongo, the former owner of the dance-hall 'La Belle Africaine', who had corrupted him. Every time Jean-Louis met this man, he saw that he was loaded, and he told Jean-Louis that nothing was easier than filling one's pockets. At first he said it was the Indian, Professor Krishnarahdja, who had worked marvels for him, and that he owed everything to this man. Joselly N'Dongo had persuaded Jean-Louis to send through him to the professor all the details necessary for the drawing of his horoscope. That's what Jean-Louis did. A month or six weeks later, Joselly N'Dongo, that bad penny, told Jean-Louis that he had his horoscope at last; his future would be profoundly altered, in a manner which would delight him, if he entered the service of the state. Jean-Louis had replied:

'All right, I'll start preparing my state exam.'

But Joselly N'Dongo replied: 'Not at all! You, a native of Kola-Kola, preparing for an exam, like a common bushman? Come with me tomorrow, and I'll introduce you to a man who'll get you into government service, just on your good looks.'

That was how he was introduced to Commissioner Maestraci, who recruited the spies by promising them that, if they proved themselves, he would get them promoted to the rank of assistant inspectors, even those who were uneducated, because it was he who organized the recruitment exams, even if he had to falsify the results when he detected a valuable quality and, when he said valuable quality, he meant the qualities of a police officer.

His judges told him some names and Jean-Louis recognized them all as those of *mamelukes* in the espionage branch, except two or perhaps three names, on hearing which he shook his head.

'Why did you do these things?' someone asked. 'Why?'

'I said to myself,' replied Jean-Louis, more voluble than ever, as if he were delirious, 'I said to myself: You weren't born to suffer all your life, like your pitiable father. You were born to

238

enjoy good things, not to squat in that sewer full of water, which steams in the sun like a swamp in a jungle clearing, when Fort-Nègre lies open to you.'

'And do you still think so?'

'I beg you, just spare my life. Don't kill me, and I'll keep you informed of everything. No, it's not possible any longer; I can't stand that old life any more; it would seem too mean to me. Do you know that there's one man, a man like my own father, that poor dupe, who's been trying to get his driving permit for ten years – who still hasn't got it, and doubtless never will? Do you call that a life, yourself? Well, it took me only two months to get my licence. Do you think that's just? How can you force a man who can make his way in Fort-Nègre, to bury himself in this hell of misery and despair?'

'We don't reproach you for your success, but for having purchased it with the coin of others' suffering.'

'Perhaps, but did I really know what I was doing? Do you sentence to death a child who kills his brother in play? Can you kill a man who didn't know what he was about?'

Although the governor still couldn't make up his mind to announce the date for the Proclamation of Independence, it was no secret to anyone in Fort-Nègre and in suburbs like Kola-Kola, that the event was imminent, so that the tension was mounting on all sides, and was visible in the big African quarter in the proliferation of leaflets, or inscriptions on walls and pavements, hasty scribblings of the two words: 'Remember Ruben' or, often enough, just the letters 'RR'. Then, the pavements and walls of the white town were invaded in their turn. Finally, the chauffeurs and lorry-drivers, first of Kola-Kola and later of the other African suburbs of Fort-Nègre, joined in the universal cult of the great martyr, by crying out in their own language: 'Remember Ruben', with three short and two long blasts on their horns. Noon was the ritual hour, but their wrist-watches gave the time with a variation of, perhaps, five minutes – and during all that interval the whole quarter, and once even the whole of Fort-Nègre, resounded with 'Remember Ruben', like so many dogs howling at a death.

Informed by word of mouth, the newcomers from the inland towns, and especially from Oyolo, which lay four hundred kilometres by train from Fort-Nègre, were no less disquieting to the colonial authorities, with whom the prime minister of the young autonomous state had secretly and definitively made common cause, to the great astonishment of the Africans. It was said that planes had been sent to overfly the western provinces, the most populous ones, to intimidate an unprecedented agitation developing there. Tanks, unloaded in the port of an adjoining colony and travelling from the south towards Fort-Nègre, had entered the country, with orders to crush bloodily any attempt to seize power by the Reds and the Rubenists, whose sinister design, claimed the radio, had long been to massacre the peace-loving population.

In Kola-Kola, even the most clear-headed and impassive underground leaders found it hard to separate all the official intoxication and propaganda from the news coming over the 'bush-telegraph', which, though always very distorted, never lacked its core of truth. When night fell, most of the Africans barricaded themselves in their hovels. Rather than have to regain their suburbs in the dark, and expose themselves to a situation where violence, real or virtual, was already raging, the domestic servants ceased going every day to their employers in the centre of Fort-Nègre. Even Joe the Juggler, although he could have reached the Schools' Plateau without difficulty, by his usual detour, preferred to stay at Kola-Kola, for fear of missing the pathetic events which, it seemed to him, could not be long in unfolding themselves.

The rumour did in fact spread, a few days after Jean-Louis' interrogation by the Permanent Commission of the Supreme Committee, that Hurricane-Viet was in the quarter, or was about to arrive there. The Permanent Commission hastily assembled and took all the precautions they judged most effective to resist a raid by the forces of Fort-Nègre. They placed at all strategic points, wherever a police commando was likely to penetrate, a group of armed *sapaks*, chosen from among the best trained, with the potential for sending them a quick reinforcement if they were attacked. The leaders were not disturbed by their first taste of battle, nor by the inexperience of their troops and officers; they thought that, far from gaining the effect of surprise so necessary in this sort of operation, the assailants would get the impression of having fallen into a trap and grow discouraged.

Mor-Zamba had been hidden away, in case the slavers, hearing that Hurricane-Viet had a brother in Kola-Kola who was a known Rubenist, should be tempted either to seize him as a hostage or to organize a trap around his house in the hope of luring Hurricane-Viet to a rendezvous. For, whatever other reasons Hurricane-Viet had for penetrating Kola-Kola, it was known that he longed to see once more a brother whom he deeply loved and from whom he had been separated for at least eighteen years.

The Juggler was shut up with his friend, impatient to set eyes on and, with luck, even to touch Hurricane-Viet. But he was like quicksilver, a man impassioned by the open air, by movement, sensation, spectacle and strong emotion; delights of which he was now cruelly deprived; he took consolation in an irrepressible babbling.

'Anyway,' he said to Mor-Zamba, 'if this Hurricane-Viet is not your brother, who is he exactly? Why is it you won't tell me, however many times I ask the question?'

'Because I feel the moment has not yet come.'

'When will that moment be?'

'I don't know, but I feel it coming.'

'You know, I myself never had any brothers, but since I've known you I no longer regret it. It's true that at first, when I didn't know you well, you seemed rather bizarre to me. Jean-Louis mocked you behind your back; it was he who led me into calling you "bushman" – that little bastard. But the fact is you are good, really a good person. And it's funny, but people only have to find one person like that, good, gentle and obliging, for them to start despising him. It was my mother alone who brought us up, Alphonsine and me, by toiling ceaselessly at her sewing-machine. I never saw her with a man. I often thought, she must have been really young, too, when my father died, way up there in the back-country, very far from here, among

241

real bushmen. Oh, but those people are proper bush! I've been there many times with my mother. Jean-Louis is right on that point, at least — the real life is here. When my father died, it seems that custom dictated she should become the wife of his brother — of my uncle, that is — an old devil who already had three or four wives by the same means, through inheritance.'

'One might suspect he killed his brothers to get hold of their wives.'

'But no! There's no need to kill many of them; it's enough for one to die, provided he's got plenty of women, you see?'

'It's true, I didn't think of that. How stupid I am!'

'Mamma wouldn't have it; she packed up and took us with her; she learnt her trade in a little town down there, at her sister's. And then, we came here, just like that! I wasn't born here, like Jean-Louis.'

They were shut up for three days like that, with the Juggler unreeling the endless skein of his confidences, when suddenly he couldn't stand any more, and wanted to go out.

'Be careful, then, that you don't come back, old chap,' warned Mor-Zamba.

'You think so?'

'You know quite well, someone could follow you and see where you go in.'

'Yes, of course. . . .'

Joe the Juggler was cut off by a terrible detonation, a sort of thunderous roar which seemed to lift Kola-Kola off the ground, shaking the frail timbers which cracked here and there in the darkness, as though struck by the brutal blast of a cyclone. Other explosions followed, shorter and less rumbling, while there soon came the continuous clicketing-clicketing sounds of running wheels, like so many powerful, distant sewing-machines. These seemed to be coming from the direction of the Shell service station, on the Avenue Gallieni, at the point where Kola-Kola met the first fringes of Fort-Nègre. There came shouts, like those of men exchanging improvised orders, then searing screams, which were quickly snuffed out.

Now they heard a sort of all-consuming noise, like the huge breath of an elephant which browses on the march, where the fierce rasping of his teeth mingles with the ripping of branches and the snapping of dead twigs under the pounding of his monstrous legs.

'Things are happening out there,' cried Joe the Juggler, impatient and regretful, when silence fell again.

'Be quiet, listen!'

'Is that all you can say?'

'Be quiet!'

'O.K. I'm not staying here any longer.'

'Idiot! This is no time to go out, you aren't armed and are sure to get killed. Stay here a bit.'

At that moment, the feeble door of the house where the two men were hiding was shaken by four heavy thuds, swiftly followed by four more; then a voice, well known to Mor-Zamba, which seemed to him to come from the beyond, as if all the dead had suddenly resurrected and had articulated distinctly, like a spell, the two words composing his name.

'Mor-Zamba, Mor-Zamba, Mor-Zamba, open up quick! I've only got a few minutes, my brother. Open up. I must tell you something amazing. I've got a few minutes.'

The rectangular wooden door was fastened by a rudimentary sliding bolt. Joe the Juggler, who was not familiar with it, had some difficulty in getting it open. When at last the door was open, instead of rushing in like a whirlwind, as might be expected of a man who had just claimed to be pushed for time, the visitor turned his back on the two friends and leaned forward, as though to observe a scene without, or to assure himself of the issue of a drama; only then did he turn and enter the house, where Mor-Zamba had just relighted the hurricane-lamp, which had been extinguished by the first explosions of the battle. He carefully closed the door, without haste, though still panting a little like a man who had run far but had now almost recovered his breath.

'You can turn up the lamp, you know?'

These were his first words, as he calmly took off a very modest raincoat which up till now had made him resemble an ordinary Kolean.

'That was pretty hot,' he added, 'but it's almost over now.'

'What was it?' demanded Joe the Juggler, boldly planting

himself in front of the newcomer, whilst Mor-Zamba, who had approached with the greatest circumspection, still looked at Hurricane-Viet from some way off, with one hand on a heart which was now beating infernally fast.

'What? Why, the clash wanted by Brede. And lost by him. What luck that I should be in the quarter just at that moment, and in process of inspecting our positions, do you hear, my dears? I don't want to boast, but just imagine what would have happened without that undreamt-of chance; yes, I can well say undreamt-of; I, who have seen chances of every colour.'

He was not really talking to the two friends, but to himself, one might have said, like a man who has lost the habit of dialogue with others. Mor-Zamba finally came up to him, feeling him all over as if he had just fallen:

'At least you're not wounded anywhere?'

'No, not yet,' replied Hurricane-Viet, with a laugh. 'It's not that I want to brag, boys,' he continued, while Mor-Zamba sighed 'ouf!' like a man relieved at last of an insufferable anguish; 'it's not that I want to brag, but do you know your little *sapaks* were well and truly about to swallow the bait? Ah, they certainly don't lack courage; on the contrary, they're real tigers. But that isn't enough to make a proper soldier.'

'What do they lack, then?' asked Joe the Juggler.

'The essential thing, you see! Everything, in short. Cunning. Once there, you might as well send them straight to the slaughterhouse. You haven't changed, dear brother, it's really you,' (putting his hand on Mor-Zamba's shoulder and looking up at him, being perceptibly the shorter), 'do you remember our long stay in the forest, to gather the materials for your house? I've forgotten everything, perhaps, except that! So that was the only thing that counted, during those long years at Ekoumdoum.'

'Hurricane-Viet!' Joe the Juggler kept murmuring, ecstatically.

'It's amazing to see you again,' the newcomer continued to Mor-Zamba. 'Nineteen years, do you realize?'

'So, you were just inspecting our positions?' demanded the Juggler. 'And then?'

'Don't talk to me about it! Just porters, yes, a whole caravan of porters, at a moment like this, in Kola-Kola! You'd have to be

244

crazy not to smell something fishy. But no, not a soul suspected anything. There they were, and they got away with it! All very simple! There were enough of them to occupy Kola-Kola in a single night and take prisoner all the leaders, and even the combatants. Porters in battledress, and in boots, what's more, oh really! Between ourselves, they have money to throw around in the colonial army. Anyway, that's their affair. Oh yes, I understand well enough. Or rather, I try to understand. But our boys should at least have noticed the big sacks under which these supposed porters were bending; in a way, these were just like the sacks carried every day in Kola-Kola; but acceptance ended there. Cartridge belts, huh! A belt, that shouldn't deceive anyone. As soon as my attention was drawn to them, that was it!'

'So, then?' cried Joe the Juggler.

'I ordered the blowing-up of the service station; there was nothing else for it.'

'Why?'

'To throw the enemy off balance, of course. Listen carefully, old chap: the great thing is always to throw the enemy off balance. Our own is like a servant carrying a big faience bowl in his overloaded hands. If, under the effects of surprise, he should drop his precious vessel, how could he gather it up again without long delay? While he is blaming himself for his blunder, assembling the fragments of his bowl, inventing his excuses, or even a whole system of defence – for he must defend himself in front of his master – well, old fellow, during all that time, you've got him at your mercy.'

He was wearing a pair of khaki drill trousers and bush shoes, a kind of tough canvas bootees, together with a striped shirt with rolled-up sleeves, quite unmilitary in appearance. Except for the brave mockery of his smile, the vigour of his glance, the impulsive generosity illuminating his whole face; all traits which made him highly recognizable; his appearance and dress that night did not resemble in the slightest the photograph which had recently been circulated in hundreds of copies, in which a blouse with breast-pockets and epaulettes, a big pith helmet and a broad cartridge-belt gave him an extremely martial air.

245

'So, what happened next?' Joe the Juggler kept asking.

'One party of Brede's commandos was already in Kola-Kola. Hearing the explosion over towards the Shell station, they quite simply threw down their sacks, containing all their arms; then they tried to flee, in pure panic. The *sapaks* ought to have captured them, but instead they were content to taunt them. A proper shambles! This is one feat of arms that Fort-Nègre won't quickly forgive Kola-Kola!'

'And the others?'

'They made off. Brave, perhaps, but not foolhardy, oh no! The *sapaks* should have pursued and tried to capture Brede, whose men were in full flight. Brede is just like his fellows: if they aren't confident that the whole thing's already in the bag, don't worry, they won't even attempt it. I know them. They'll prey upon Kola-Kola so long as it seems wide open to the first bold man who comes along. Kola-Kola is like a patrol which has ventured too far from the main troop, and whose position has been revealed to the enemy. Will its leaders be ready to save it, at the cost of exposing their army to the hazards of a doubtful, perhaps desperate combat? Or will they just let it be massacred, stopping their ears to exclude the fusillade and the screams of the dying?'

'And you too, you haven't changed a bit,' exclaimed Mor-Zamba.

'You see? And now listen to something I've sworn to tell you one day, cost what it will. When I've told you this news, I wonder if my destiny won't be accomplished. Dear brother, I've kept myself alive all these long years for this moment above all others; have you been back to Ekoumdoum since you got out of the labour camp?'

'What would I have to do there? Who do I have in Ekoumdoum? No, the idea never so much as crossed my mind, you know.'

'I thought as much. Well, now listen, just imagine, you are really a son of Ekoumdoum! You couldn't marry Engamba's daughter, because you had the same blood in your veins as her!'

'It's quite possible,' cried Mor-Zamba, with more lassitude than surprise.

'What a welcome you'd have received, though, if you had

returned to Ekoumdoum. You really must go back, you see. After the very mysterious disappearance of the last chief, his family was dispersed and sent away from Ekoumdoum. All his wives (there were three of them) were sent back to their original clans with their children, and it turned out that these were all very far away. They were ordered, under pain of the most frightful threats, not to bring up their male children, who were still very young, under the idea that they were from Ekoumdoum. And, as testimony to the terror and violence of colonialism, nobody in Ekoumdoum ever dared to ask after these children. They, for their part, having now grown into mature men, and perhaps to the threshold of old age, have always abstained from giving any sign of life to the Ekoumdoum clan; they have abdicated everything – the rights of their father, vengeance for an abominable crime, and even the blood of those who brought them into the world – rather than bring a frown to the brow of their master. When you go back to Ekoumdoum, there's a task you can set yourself; make enquiries to discover them, or the families they have founded.

'Only one young girl, whose mother had just died, escaped the colonial manhunt; at her own request, she was confided to the care of Engamba. Despite the complicity of the city, the child was threatened with a terrible fate if her secret should ever be discovered. An early marriage with a man from far away was perhaps her only chance of survival. So Engamba married her, before she even reached puberty, or rather I should say sold her, to a man who often appeared in our country selling various articles, mostly matchets, axes, spades and other tools for working the soil. This man belonged to the Ebonglon clan, inhabiting a country very far from Ekoumdoum, actually beyond the frontier, in the adjoining English colony. That girl there was to become your mother. Ekoumdoum now knows the whole story. When I heard that we were being sent to the front, I couldn't resist the weakness of going to embrace my mother first. Armed with a travel warrant, and joining one lorry after another, I only took four days to get back to our place. But I didn't enter Ekoumdoum till nightfall, so as to avoid meeting anyone except my own family. And that's how my mother came to tell me your identity. One of your brothers had traced step by step the trail you once followed, your mother and you, and had arrived at Ekoumdoum, where he had recounted your history.

'But let's not jump ahead. Although mother of seven children, your brothers and sisters and yourself, your mamma could never accustom herself to the life or the manners of her husband's clan; she had such an intense nostalgia for Ekoumdoum that she lost a good part of her reason. All the treatment she had was in vain; she was trundled from one famous medicine-man to another, but nothing worked.

'She stayed some time with the man charged to cure her, then moved off again, always in the same direction. They went after her and brought her back to her husband, but she wouldn't stay in that country.'

'So you know the whole story?'

'No, only the outlines, but I've never stopped going over it since.'

'Why did you never tell me?'

'It was like a nightmare; one doesn't tell people nightmares. One of her children, yourself, was inseparable from her; you followed her in all her flights and shared her precarious existence. They tried to part you, but they soon saw how terribly she missed you and how you, lacking her presence, fell into a disturbing lassitude. One day, you found each other again and began another escape; no one came after you, and you set off along the roads. They thought that you would probably go in a circle, and that in any case they wouldn't lose sight of you. After a few years, your people decided that you were big enough to be separated from your mother, but they couldn't find you anywhere, although they scoured a great part of the colony. They never dared to reach Ekoumdoum, fearing to be blamed for their negligence in not taking every possible care of you two.'

'When my mother died, of sheer exhaustion, I believe, we were not far from Ekoumdoum, three or four days' march, or a little more – I can't really judge now how far it was; it's all so long ago and my memories of it are all mixed up. She didn't tell me anything before dying; she wasn't capable of explaining things, because her mind was almost gone. Poor mother! Only

248

her instinct made her still follow the trail, like a dog homing in on its lair. When I reached Ekoumdoum, the same instinct, which I must have inherited from her, must have told me that this was undoubtedly the place where my mother wanted to die, despite the strange welcome I received there.'

'Now it's time for us to part, dear brother. You must go back there. You'll chase away the present chief and become the legitimate one in his place; you'll change everything in Ekoumdoum. Agreed?'

'Change everything, but how?'

'In a good way, as you well know, being compassion personified; in such a way that everyone will be not only happy, which is nothing much, but filled with pride in himself. That's something you understand much better than me. All I can do to help you is to get you two guns, oh! pretty harmless ones. Do you know that nothing is ever so difficult as to get oneself a good gun? One day I'll explain that to you, perhaps. Now come on, follow me.'

'I'm coming too!' interposed Joe the Juggler who, for once in his life, had been content to listen, throughout the whole recitation of Mor-Zamba's drama.

'Of course,' Mor-Zamba assured him.

They crossed Kola-Kola, awash with shadows, almost as Jean-Louis and Mor-Zamba had done during the latter's initiation into the night life of the quarter, but with rather more haste. Hurricane-Viet moved with the same ease as Jean-Louis had once done, through a scene flattened and softened by the darkness, still the same after twelve years of experience; a scene where nothing arrested the glance or guided the traveller, even when a flame shot up from the burning service station.

'It's impossible,' Joe the Juggler protested to Hurricane-Viet, 'you guide yourself better through Kola-Kola than I, who have always lived here.'

'Just a matter of habit, old chap. When you've learnt to steer through the jungle at night, you know how to deal with the darkness in Kola-Kola.'

The blaze was still active at the Shell station, and even seemed to be spreading. Every few minutes, a brilliant glare threw zebra stripes over the quarter, without, however, invading all its pockets of shadow. At rare intervals came a loud explosion or a crackling sound.

'They must fire into the shadows,' Hurricane-Viet observed.

'Who's shooting?' asked Joe the Juggler, exalted by the battle.

'Our own people, with small arms and a mortar, poor lads!'

They went into a house full of busy men, who moved ceaselessly from room to room, always carefully shutting the door behind them. In the corner of a large room, a group of young sapaks was gathered around a man who seemed to be their instructor; others took turns near-by in practising the handling of small arms; they suddenly broke off their activities and turned as one towards the rebel chief, murmuring with ecstatic admiration, 'Hurricane-Viet! Hurricane-Viet!' The same scenes were discovered in every house they entered. It seemed that Hurricane-Viet was searching for someone he couldn't find; he was mostly indifferent to the homage of his admirers, though he sometimes rewarded them with a little wave of the hand and a scarcely perceptible smile.

'Are you annoyed about something?' Joe the Juggler asked him, as they emerged from a house which Hurricane-Viet had just searched in vain.

'Of course I'm annoyed, that's the least I could be. For organization, this isn't too hot. There's no one really in charge, no one who makes them feel — I don't say, his fist, because we've no need of that — but his touch, his style, his personality.'

At last, in a house exactly like all the others they had visited, Hurricane-Viet found his man. It was Maisonneuve, pale as ever but now moustacheless, in a very anxious mood, as though overwhelmed and overworked almost to desperation. When he saw Hurricane-Viet, his thin lips tightened again, while a gleam of solitary complicity lighted the depths of his eyes; he ran right up to Hurricane-Viet and they conferred together, leaning upon each other, almost cheek to cheek.

'Don't upset yourself, old comrade,' Hurricane-Viet told him finally. 'Make the best of it, and we'll extricate ourselves with what we have. I know quite well it's no party.'

Maisonneuve disappeared at the end of the room, through a door which he slammed quickly behind him, like a man who

shakes the treasure which he has left for the day in an unfre-
quented house.

'It's impossible! Maisonneuve is one of us?' exclaimed the
Juggler.

'He's always been one of us; if not, how could he have told
you hintingly about me? He's the military commander
appointed by the Supreme Secret Committee of Kola-Kola. But
he's not happy; they don't always follow his advice, and yet
he's the only man who's really competent militarily.... So, to
sum it up, you didn't really know much? In any case, you won't
be able to betray anyone in future under torture, eh, Mor-
Zamba? It will soon be too late for you to do that, not so?'

'For Joe too!' cried Mor-Zamba; 'we shall never leave each
other, he's sworn it. Not true, Joe?'

'You bet,' agreed the Juggler.

'In order to get to Ekoumdoum,' Hurricane-Viet advised, 'go
on foot for preference and keep off the main road in daylight.
Don't submit to any control, whatever it is. Never put yourself
in the position of having to justify anything to any kind of
authority. Can you handle a gun? No? That doesn't matter. I'm
just going to show you how to handle a carbine. I hope to be
able to give you two, but only one will have a telescopic sight. If
you get into trouble, fire first with that one, because that's sure
to hit. Once you get to Ekoumdoum, if you manage to get hold
of Van den Rietter's Winchester 33 Carbine, or his successor's
(they all have the same guns), as I advise you to do, don't make
any attempt to use it, or only in the last extremity; unless
someone has providentially taught you how to do so. It's an
extremely dangerous weapon. It will be enough just to show it;
you've no idea how much one can get just by brandishing a
good gun. Before you set off, I'll send you a little portable
pharmacy; just think, Mor-Zamba, how many sufferers you can
relieve in our country with a simple quinine mixture, you who
have been nurse to so many poor devils! In that way, you'll
conquer so many mothers' hearts!'

Sure enough, a young bare-chested boy in khaki cotton
shorts brought them a gun with telescopic sights. Hurricane-
Viet stooped over him and spoke in his ear in an almost pater-
nal manner before sending him off and turning to his two

companions, in order to explain to them the mechanism of the 22 long rifle. They were surrounded by the clicking of small arms (machine-guns, no doubt, reflected Joe the Juggler) which were being manipulated in the adjoining rooms whose doors, from time to time, would open a little before being briskly slammed again. He showed them patiently how to dismantle the gun in such a way that, slipped into a bundle its presence would never be suspected.

The same young man returned with another carbine, this one without a special sight, which he offered to Hurricane-Viet.

'It's exactly the same gun,' the rebel chief explained to his two companions. 'Just remember that you must never expose yourselves uselessly. Always be very prudent. But, as I've just said, if you ever find yourselves forced to shoot, never do so until you can be sure of hitting, and always open fire with the gun which has the good sight. Now it's time for us to part; I'm just waiting for the storm to calm a little, otherwise we shan't be able to see in front of our noses.'

A storm had in fact been raging over Kola-Kola for a quarter of an hour past, with furious volleys of rain.

'One day, perhaps, I'll come and admire your labours.'

'When? Tell us when you're coming,' begged Joe the Juggler.

'In ten years? In twenty? In thirty? Who knows? Above all, no rush, boys. Take your time, prepare everything carefully, don't worry about delays, time is nothing to us. Africa has been in chains, so to speak, from eternity; whenever we liberate her will be soon enough. Our struggle will be long, very long. Everything you see at this moment in Kola-Kola and throughout the whole colony is nothing but a puerile beginning. Many years from now, or a few months hence, or even after the approaching destruction of Kola-Kola, in the course of which thousands and thousands of our people, women and children among them, will probably die, there will be people to smile at the memory of these preliminary stirrings, as one does in thinking of the innocent games of childhood. Remember Ruben.'